RATS
NIGHT OF TERROR

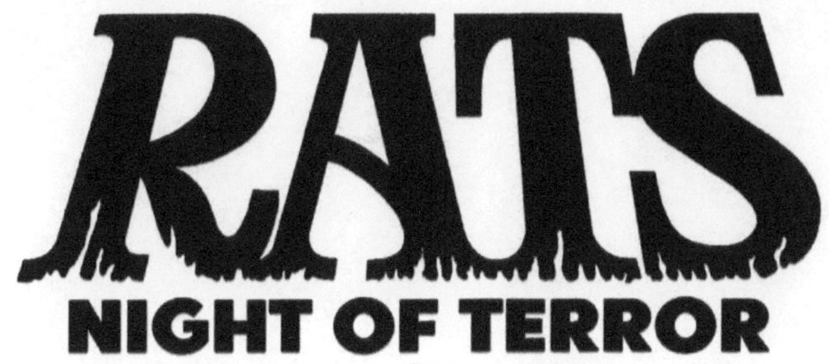

A NOVEL BY
BRAD CARTER

INSPIRED BY
THE ORIGINAL SCREENPLAY & STORY BY
CLAUDIO FRAGASSO AND ROSSELLA DRUDI
THAT BECAME BRUNO MATTEI'S
RATS: NIGHT OF TERROR

Encyclopocalypse Publications
www.encyclopocalypse.com

Remembering Rats
Rossella Drudi and Claudio Fragasso

Rossella Drudi

The story for RATS was conceived and written in 1982. The idea started from imagining the transformation of society centuries after the end of a nuclear war that destroyed the earth.

So my imagination must be contextualized to the historical period I was living in at that moment: the 1980s. It is important to note this detail.

In Italy, we were emerging from an armed struggle that had lasted for more than ten years. It had been a period of attacks and massacres against politicians and representatives of state institutions by the far-right and far-left extra-parliamentary movements. The red brigades (aka the B.R.) and the black brigades (aka the Nar) and other extremely dangerous movements were widespread.

In those days, there was no internet, no social media, and no mobile phones, only the landline at home or the coin-operated phones in booths and bars. Only large industries had computers, which they called the "big brain" and which took up an entire room. These big brains were used to process astronomical calculations.

People were slowly regaining confidence, timidly putting their heads out of their homes again. The only means of information available were newspapers, radio, and television news. There were also free radio stations, most of which were outlawed. These stations were most sincere in reporting the facts, as sometimes happens today on social media.

So, under the influence of the terrible period I experienced, I decided that our post-nuclear story had to be different from the well-known film MAD MAX. On the other hand, the producers didn't care much what the structural concept of the story was, they just needed it to involve warmongering set in the future. It was a genre that sold well in all world markets at the time.

But the writing and therefore the ideas had to be based on the budget available for the film.

We needed the right idea, an original concept that allowed us to overcome budget problems. When there's no money, you need lots of ideas.

I've always been passionate about animals and insects. I like to study how they evolve in their societies. The animal that disgusts me most in the world is the rat. But at the same time, they fascinate me with their intelligence, resilience, and spirit of adaptation to every type of environment and climate on the planet.

In my research, I've read that mice may be the only animals to survive after a nuclear war, along with cockroaches, filthy insects that I really can't stand. The cockroach is perhaps even more indestructible than the rat. Of course, it wasn't nice to imagine a future world inhabited only by rats and cockroaches but that's where I started to develop this story.

So, in agreement with Claudio to whom I had told the

idea, I began to imagine a society dominated by rats, but we only discover this at the end of the film. In the finale, we find that rats have, over the years, perfectly adapted to the external environment, to the point of living on the surface like humans of the past. Rats that, over the centuries, had evolved not only in the development of the brain, but also the physique, which had transformed into a perfect human body. They've become bipeds like us, but with a huge head disproportionate to the rest of the body, the head of a rat. This is revealed only in the final frame, the well-known twist.

This new breed of human-rat had learned to communicate, to use all technological and scientific tools, to read and write until they became self-sufficient in everything. They had widely developed telepathic faculties with which they communicated with each other. In contrast, the surviving humans lived underground in place of rats and were not advanced at all. In reality, it was exactly the opposite. A sort of social reversal. The men who lived underground were the descendants of a community of scientists, who after years of preparation, which took place before the outbreak of the nuclear war, had dug underground, armoring everything to protect it from radiation. But not the anti-atomic bunkers that we know, but real underground cities, equipped with everything to survive. This wasn't shown in the film, but it remained as part of the original script.

Nuclear war explodes in 2015, and after five centuries of underground life, a first group of humans decides to venture to the surface. The film begins like this. With this strange team of young men and women, led by a sort of prophet named Deus, who has a shaved head and a triangle on his forehead. He's a spiritual man, a guide capable of predicting the future and communicating telepathically. A psychic, a chosen one capable of leading people on a righteous path of non-violence and universal love. Deus perceives the new entities that populate the surface psychically, but is unable to contact them despite making many attempts. Entities that do not show themselves and are not seen or that do not want to be seen, but that are present and spy on them by observing them. Deus begins to understand many things about what has happened on the surface, but his companions do not believe him and laugh at him.

Unfortunately, the character of Deus was almost completely eliminated in the film, compared to what I had written. It's a real shame because Deus as he appears in the film is an almost meaningless role, stripped of all his peculiarities.

Deus, once he manages to enter into telepathic contact with the evolved mice, without knowing that they were mice, receives their technology and history through a mental vision. Thus he discovers the secrets of their technologies. But all this, I repeat, is not in the film.

As I have said in other interviews, I very much love epics, Greek and Roman mythology, the Old Testament and the Bible. They're all sources of great inspiration for me. In this case, it was useful for choosing the names of the characters even if not all of them have epic names, like Videogame (the name of the character played by Gianni Franco in the film). His name was chosen to highlight the most used technological game in the eighties. Video games were as popular then as social media is today. But let's return to our group of these new "Argonauts," who fled both from the underground life of their ancestors and from the radiation-soaked surface life. Each of them represents a precise human typology, for better or for worse.

The characters were vividly drawn, with all their defects and strengths accentuated to the point of stereotype. The group, which has two leaders who are constantly fighting each other, must deal with a world invaded and dominated by rats. Rats are everywhere, in every environment and space the group explores. The rats are normal-sized rodents that appear to have a leader who guides them in the fight against the intruder, man. Cannibalistic rats that, like a sort of zombie, attack humans to feed on them. They bite humans until they kill them, or penetrate their bodies through the mouth, rectum, or vagina. Rats capable of communicating with each other, of organizing themselves for a mass military attack like a real army. The group of humans defends itself as best it can.

The humans find a place where, in a large, still functioning greenhouse (it was only large in the script), all types of greens, vegetables, fruits, legumes, and cereals are grown. There is also a laboratory which, through a sophisticated system of pipes and filters, transforms putrid water into drinkable water. There were also chickens and other animals (these also remained only in the script) and everything people needed to feed themselves. The place appears intact, even if dated, and a series of strange tools similar to old and enormous computers keep everything alive. After a while, the group is attacked by the rats.

First, the rats pollute the water. Rats can drink it without getting sick and dying, unlike humans. So the rats' plan to eliminate humans, in addition to attacking them and killing them by eating them, is to prevent them from surviving by infecting the food and destroying the laboratory and greenhouses. Only in the finale is it discovered that those rats who remained small, but had super developed brains, are the "worker people" of another super-evolved race of rats who command and control them. This superior race of rats was born from the mix between the rats and the surviving humans. This hybrid is the result of genetic evolution, which has rewarded the rat for its perfect adaptability to the radioactive environment, mutating the rodent into a form with a human body and a super evolved head, but not a head of a human shape and proportions, but the head of a rat.

Yes, I'm perfectly convinced that rats are smarter than us.

Think of what happens when bait is placed to kill them. After a few months, the rats no longer touch the bait. Mice are able to communicate with each other and pass on the knowledge acquired to their children. The new generations of mice do not approach poisoned bait, because they already know that it is deadly for them and therefore must be avoided. For this reason, those who carry out rodent control always use bait with different flavors and compositions. Today, we still don't know how mice transmit these notions to their offspring, but they do it.

So, returning to the original story of the film, which is very different from what is depicted on screen. There were two "breeds" of rats that had evolved in different ways: one composed giant rats with human bodies and mouse heads, and the other made up of of normal-sized rats with superior intelligence. The second race was dependent on the first, but both are hostile towards humanity. The humans, in turn, perceive the rats as a dangerous error in the evolutionary chain, and one that should be eliminated. This is the meaning of the extermination that the giant rats carry out in the finale, against the group of survivors. The intelligent rats see the extermination of humans as necessary for a world without wars.

While I still think rats are nearly indestructible, I also think cockroaches are almost immortal. They've lived in every era since the dawn of the primordial soup. And that's why they fascinate me. Who knows, maybe one day I'll write a futuristic novel about them.

Rossella Drudi, 2024

Claudio Fragasso

The film RATS was born in a controversial period of my career. After many films co-directed with Bruno Mattei, I wanted to break away to direct a film that was all mine. Now Bruno, who didn't want me to leave, proposed that I would have a larger role in the next film. I had carte blanche for filming and directing the actors. I collaborated with Rossella on writing a screenplay full of twists and original ideas.

In the early 1980s, the Mad Max films were popular, but both Rossella and I didn't want a simple copy of a post-atomic story. Rossella had a more compelling idea, and thus RATS was born. In our screenplay, rats had taken over the world by eliminating the community of scientists, who lived underground, and fought to overturn the established order of society. I dedicated myself body and soul to this project in which I believed very much. I also wanted to experiment with an ensemble film for the first time in my career. I wanted to make a film with many actors and diverse characters always together in each scene. A well-matched group of young actors locked in a claustrophobic environment. Trapped like...well, rats. But, as the saying goes, between saying and doing, there is a sea in the middle. I don't know if the translation of this saying will make sense in English. Anyway, I'll try to explain it. It means that original intentions often cannot be realized as they were written and intended. In cinematic terms, this means having to deal with what you have available.

The film was financed as an Italian-French co-production, and for this reason, some actors are French. It wasn't easy to coordinate the Italian actors with the French ones. It wasn't due to language problems; we all understood each other perfectly. Furthermore, in addition to the French and Italian characters, there were also two American actresses such as Geretta and Cindy. Everyone could make themselves understood. The problem was one of personality. The atavistic rivalry between the "cousins" from beyond the Alps had given rise to a sort of parochial challenge and competition between France and Italy. The French gave themselves airs of superiority and the Italians reacted by being bullies.

Sometimes this type of competition was even fun. And both Bruno and I liked to instigate them to encourage them to give their best efforts on set. We'd play pranks on them to lighten the atmosphere when it got heavy. But this only happened during the first few days. Then I tried to find the right harmony in the group. In the end, with great difficulty, I think I succeeded.

Perhaps the French were a little affected by the fact that the Italian actors were all old friends with whom I had already made many films. Ottaviano Dell'Acqua, who plays Kurt in the film, is an acrobat actor, otherwise known as a stuntman. I'd previously worked Massimo Vanni, who plays Tauros in the film. I had him as a weapons master and actor in other films. Gianni Franco, who portrays Videogame in the film, is a good actor6 and long-time friend. Fausto Lombardi, who plays Deus in the film, who began his acting career in my debut 35mm film, "DEFINDIMI DALLA NOTTE (1981). Not to mention the composer of the soundtrack, Maestro Luigi Ceccarelli, who I've known since we were kids. He composed the music for my first super eight film PASSAGGI (1977). In short, I surrounded myself with professional friends for this film. And in the end, they too blended well with the French, giving rise to new friendships. And I have to say that both Bruno and I had a blast. We shot everything in the De Paolis Studios, which for many years to follow became the home base for many films I directed.

On this subject, I want to tell you a strange and funny fact.

Years later, I was shooting another film there LA BANDA (2001), aka OUT OF BOUNDS and THE SQUAD (titles for the foreign market). During a break, I met Daniele Taddei, the new owner of the former De Paolis Studios, which had been renamed Studios Tiburtina. Since we were friends, Daniele talked about all the vicissitudes he had to face after taking over the studios. But the biggest problem of all was the rodent control that he had to carry out during the restoration work on the rooms and the entire external area of the studios. Daniele attributed the proliferation of mice to Dario Argento's film INFERNO, which was also filmed there, saying they were very strange, different from other mice. I burst out laughing because he didn't know anything about RATS. In fact, the rodents that escaped from my film and those of Dario reproduced with each other, giving rise to a new breed, which was difficult to eliminate. Yes, because the rats in RATS were laboratory specimens, the white ones, they had to be covered in coal dust to make them black like sewer rats. On the other hand, those in Dario's film were real sewer rats. The mouse trainer, the *toparo*, collected them one by one at the end of each scene. Evidently, some managed to escape, settling in the studios. Daniele said that now he finally understood why one of his workers had been so scared after encountering them. This employee said that he was attacked by a group of rats in the basement and one of them jumped on him and tried to bite him. Nobody believed the story at first. But it was true. The ones he encountered were cannibalistic rats like the ones in RATS. The new breed was born from crossing my mice with Dario's. And here we both burst out laughing. Subsequently, however, they managed to eliminate them all by perfectly purifying and sterilizing the studios. No more mice in the former De Paolis.

We mistreated those poor animals so much. Today it would be impossible to do the same things again due to correct animal laws. Honestly, I wouldn't do the same things anymore either. Painting lab rats black wasn't a good for them, but we've done worse. For example, in the scene where Massimo Vanni (Tauros) catches fire when he is attacked by rats, many live rats were glued to his clothes along with the already dead ones. These things cannot and must no longer be done. I love and respect all animals. Those were different times.

Here are some other curiosities about the film.

In the scenes where we see the rats raining en masse from above, I used a very simple yet effective strategy. Not having many rats available, I had them placed in large jute bags, filling them to capacity. Then the bags were overturned on the actors, but one at a time, each time picking up the previous batch of rats and repeating the act. In this way, and thanks to the editing, it seemed like there were thousands of rats. I have to say that the final effect was good.

For the creepy scene of the mouse coming out of the actress's mouth, I had the idea of putting a fake rat head inside a condom. The actress stuck her tongue in the condom, keeping everything hidden in her closed mouth and, when action was called, she slowly opened it by pushing the tip of her tongue out of her. The effect was surprising, so much so that in some old copies of the film it was censored and cut. I remember that Bruno laughed a lot when he saw her. He was beyond satisfied.

My relationship with Bruno went very well in this film. Bruno kept his promise, leaving me free to act as I wanted. The choice of De Paolis to shoot the film was not accidental. In the studios, there were still part of the sets from the film ONCE UPON A TIME IN AMERICA by the legendary Sergio Leone, my favorite director. I had the honor of walking around the bar and what remained of its New York streets. In apocalyptic films, there is always a mix of ancient and modern, and those places worked well for our film.

RATS did very well at the box office and was sold all over the world, a great success of which I'm still proud. Seeing it again today after so many years, despite all the budget limitations and other things, the film still looks good. Bruno was also very satisfied with the final result. Generally, with his typically Roman brand of jocular cynicism, he didn't lend much importance to anything. He was quick to downplay everything, but I knew that he liked the film and he so demonstrated with the care with which he edited it. As I have said many times, he was the king of editing.

What else can I say about RATS, a film which brought me good luck? An American producer who had seen the unfinished film wanted to meet me and proposed that I make a film that involved dogs for him. It all happened so quickly. On the evening of the screening of RATS, now finished and ready for release, I had organized a dinner with the entire cast, crew, and a few friends. It was an important dinner, because many of the wishes made during the toasts came true. In fact, the next morning, I left for Madrid, where a new adventure awaited me. It was MONSTER DOG, a new American film I was going to shoot in Spain with Alice Cooper as the protagonist. But that's a whole other story.

Claudio Fragasso, 2024

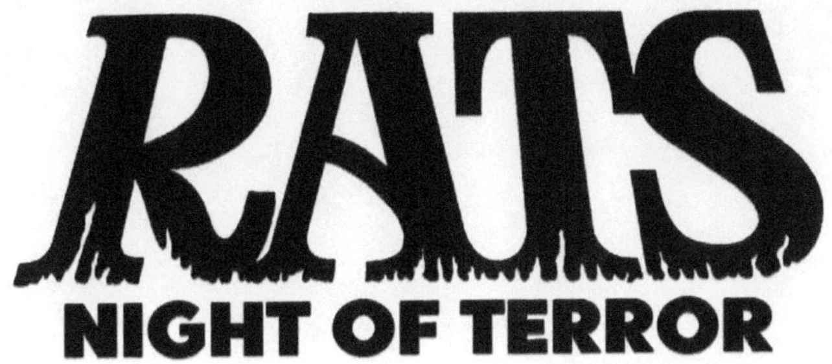
RATS
NIGHT OF TERROR

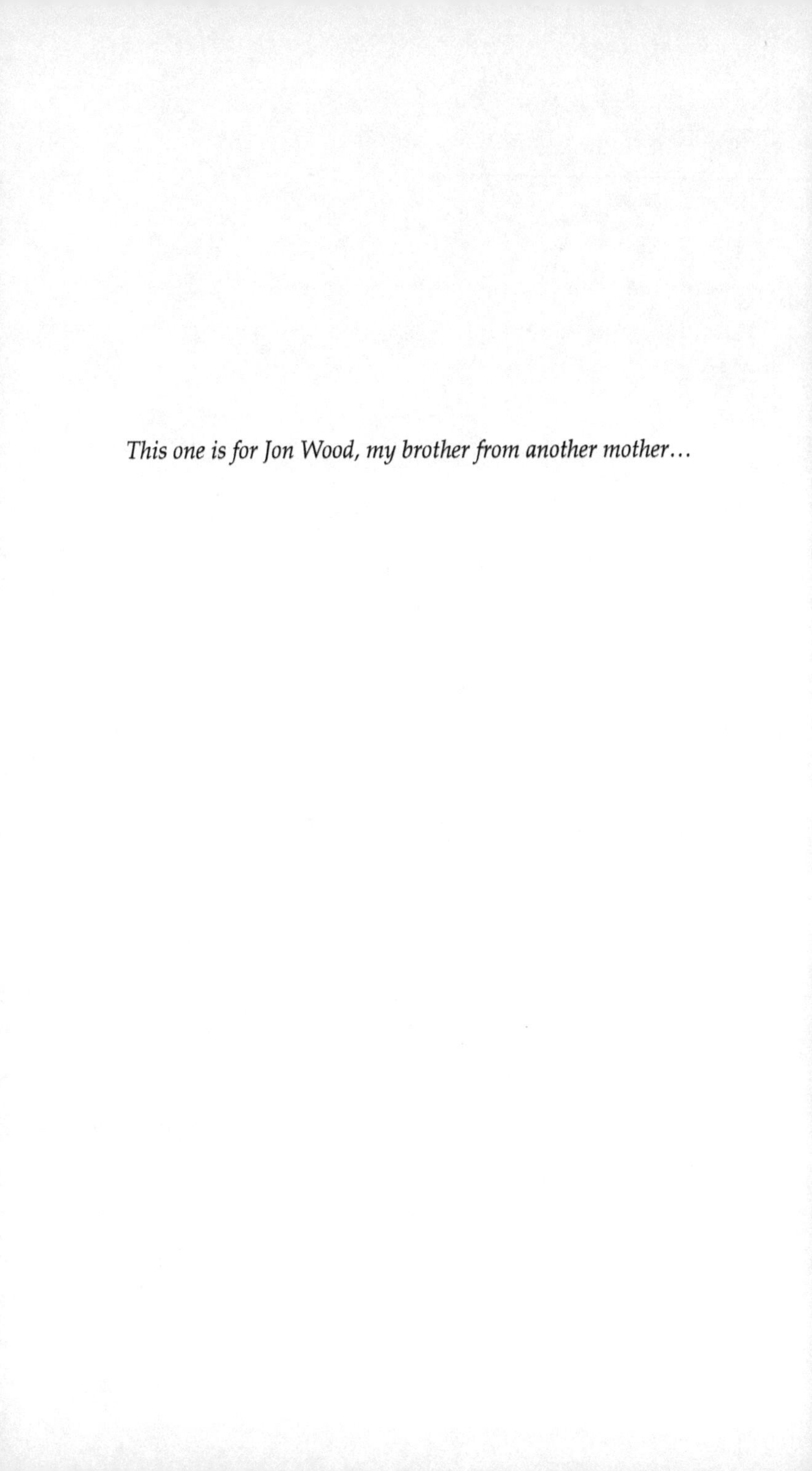

This one is for Jon Wood, my brother from another mother…

The probability of the apocalypse cannot be realistically estimated, but it is surely too high for any sane person to contemplate with equanimity.

— Noam Chomsky

By gnawing through a dike, even a rat may drown a nation.

— Edmund Burke

Part One

The Wasteland and the Colony

Chapter One
Methuselah's Final Descent

The old man trudged through the dead city. He dragged behind him a squeaky-wheeled wagon laden with his meager worldly possessions. The noise generated by the wagon, to say nothing of the old man's labored breathing and near constant hacking cough, would have been more than enough to attract the notice of the city's inhabitants, if indeed there were any. Like so many of the cities and towns he'd visited, this one was as empty and silent as a tomb. Even the roaches had abandoned this maze of crumbling concrete and cracked asphalt. His only companions were the piles of bones that littered the ground. Stripped bare by long-departed scavengers, and bleached white by years of sunlight and wind, these bones were the only indications that life had ever flourished in this place. The aftershocks of the Event[1]* had lingered so long in the city that even the plant life had been choked off.

---

* [1] The name commonly given to the catastrophic environmental disasters at the end of the 21st century CE. Historians disagree on the exact nature of these disasters, putting forth theories that range from simple climate shifts, to the use of technological weapons. Some have even suggested that the origins of the disaster were extraterrestrial or inter-dimensional in nature.

The old man paused at the intersection of two streets, dropping the handle of his wagon and pressing a hand to the small of his back. He groaned as, one by one, his vertebrae crackled and popped. The dead city's atmosphere was so still and silent that the air seemed to swallow these small sounds.

"And yet somewhere in this landscape of desolation lies the gateway to the saviors' realm," the old man croaked, quoting one of his favorite passages of scripture.

His hand moved seemingly of its own accord to pat his hip pocket, where he carried his two most prized possessions: a tattered, dog-eared copy of *The New Scripture of Clementine, Annotated Edition*[2*] and a metal flask of firewater. Although many verses in the former strictly forbade the consumption of the latter, the old man figured that the gods wouldn't begrudge him some small measure of relief. He was, after all, the sole remaining member of his congregation, the others having long ago succumbed to consumption, dysentery, the grippe, or some horrible combination of all three. A pilgrim alone in the wasteland, he'd earned the occasional nip from his flask. It was one of the few things that gave him some small measure of physical comfort.

Glancing down at the pitted surface of the road, he saw a hollow-eyed skull grinning up at him from between his feet. The old man looked around but couldn't find the rest of the skeleton.

"An orphan, I see," the old man sighed.

He drew back his foot and gave the skull a kick. Well, perhaps it was more of an emphatic nudge than a kick, because the skull only rolled a short distance away. At least it wasn't staring at him anymore.

The old man reached into his pocket and withdrew the

---

[*] [2] Named for the prophet Jeremiah Clementine, who rose to prominence in the first generation born AE (After Event). The exact origins of his doctrine are unknown, but the belief system outlined in his scripture became one of the dominant religions until the Great Reformation after his death in 100 AE.

flask. He'd filled it at the last outpost, trading off a rusty pocket knife for eight ounces of extra potent firewater. Perhaps half of that amount remained in the flask. He unscrewed the cap and sipped carefully, bracing himself for the burning sensation of the oily liquid on his tongue. He hadn't asked the moonshiner at the outpost what was in the liquor, and he didn't care. It was enough that the stuff worked as advertised. Once he'd forced himself to swallow the burning mouthful, it hit his gut like a flaming meteor. The old man squeezed his eyes shut, waiting for the fire to cool. Then, a wave of relief broke over him. The pain in his back subsided, although these days, it never truly disappeared. He'd long ago accepted that such aches and pains were now simply a part of his life.

And what a long life it had been.

His mother had named him Bertrand, but that was a dead name. When he'd been baptized into the Church of the Wasteland, he cast the name aside and taken on the moniker of Methuselah. At the time, the name was seemingly chosen at random by the High Magus. It had been a busy day at the baptismal font, and the High Magus had christened dozens of children, giving each of them a new name to go along with their new faith. But if the choice had seemed random at the time, it had proven prophetic. He was old. So old, in fact, that he'd lost track of his age. He was positively ancient. And once the last members of the congregation had passed away, victims of some vicious strain of plague to which he alone was immune, he'd stopped counting the days. It was enough to know that a new day followed the one before.

He squatted next to his wagon, wincing at the stiffness in his knees, and rummaged through his belongings until he found the crowbar. He straightened up, hefting the heavy metal bar in his hands. It was early in the day, but there was still much work to be done. A city this size would have an extensive subterranean network beneath its streets. It would take him days to explore it. Well, that is unless his decades-long search finally paid off and he came face to face with one of the Elders Below. Should that long-awaited and prayed-for event finally come to pass, he could cast off what remained of his worldly possessions and join the Elders in the paradise below the surface. He could leave behind this sin-befouled world and its ruined cities, radioactive deserts, and cruel inhabitants.

"As it was written," he whispered, "so shall it come to pass."

He stepped off the curb and onto the street, heading for the first manhole cover he sighted. He slotted the edge of the crowbar into the notch in the pitted metal lid, and applied all his weight. At first, the lid didn't budge. Years of disuse had allowed it to settle in, and now it was almost as if the lid had become part of the street. But Methuselah knew better. Years of experience told him that a little persistence was all he needed, and eventually, after a few minutes of curses muttered through labored breaths, the manhole cover broke loose. With a cry of determination and one last burst of effort, the old man flipped the metal disc over. There was a brief rush of stale air from the darkness below, then silence. Methuselah paused just long enough to catch his breath and dig out the small chemical torch he kept in his pocket, then he began his descent.

The manhole opened into a shaft that was an access point to the city's sewer system. The ladder attached to the wall was actually just a dozen U-shaped metal rungs mounted directly to the concrete, but these rungs appeared sturdy enough. Perhaps a younger, healthier man might have had trouble, but the old man had shed weight over the years until he was little more than a skeleton covered in knotty bands of muscle and sunburned, wrinkled skin. With the torch clamped between his mostly toothless jaws, he worked his way to the bottom of the ladder.

Once his feet touched the damp concrete of the tunnel, he took the torch from his mouth and held it overhead. The torch was a plastic tube about twice the size of one of the old man's fingers. The alchemists who'd sold it to the old man assured him that the chemicals trapped in the tube would glow for a decade, perhaps longer. He hoped their assurance was truthful, because he'd begun to notice a slight dimming of the torch's light. Then again, maybe it had been a decade since he'd traded a wagon load of salvaged metal for the torch. Time had grown slippery, indistinct. His memories grew hazier with each passing day. He was the last of his congregation, and he was slowing down. If he failed to make contact with the saviors who dwelt below, he would be lost to time, consigned to the same oblivion that had consumed so much of the world since the Event. Preventing that outcome was all that remained of his purpose in life. If only he could make contact with the saviors…

The greenish yellow glow of the torch gave a sickly cast to the old man's surroundings.

The trench in the tunnel's floor may have once carried a rushing torrent of water to the city's treatment plant, but now it had been reduced to little more than a trickle. The old man was tempted to peel the layers of rags away from his feet and dip his toes into the sluggish stream, but he discarded that idea. Calloused as it was, the skin on the soles of his feet might be broken here and there, and that would mean certain infection if the water was contaminated. The post-Event world was awash in plagues. They lay in wait at every turn, ready to claim another victim. As a pilgrim in the wasteland, Methuselah knew very well that maintaining one's hygiene— both the personal and moral varieties—was a difficult task indeed, but he did his best.

The maze of tunnels was seemingly endless. He marked his progress by scratching signs on the walls with a chunk of chalk. He paused at each junction to call out. His hoarse voice echoed in the empty warren of concrete tunnels. Hours slipped by as he trudged through the gloomy passages. And each time he stopped to call out, his pleas for salvation were answered only by echoes and the faint trickling of water.

But then, just as he was starting to despair at the thought of exploring yet another ruined city in vain, something answered him. He stopped in his tracks and called out again, just to be sure he wasn't experiencing some type of auditory hallucination. He poked a finger into each of his ears and scraped out the accumulated wax. He cocked his head to one side and listened. He strained, offering a silent prayer to the Elders Below.

Please answer me, you exalted members of a wise and benevolent race…I am your humble servant and I plead for you to return to the surface and reclaim the earth…

For a moment, the tunnel fell silent again, and Methuselah's heart sank. Perhaps he'd mistaken the sound of the sluggish stream for something else. Perhaps—

Then he heard it again. A chittering, squeaking noise followed the scratch of movement over concrete and a low, raspy sound that might have been voices.

"Hello?" Methuselah called. "I am Bertrand that is called Methuselah. I am a pilgrim who has traveled many miles to beg an audience with the Elders Below. Please, hear my humble prayers…"

This time, there was no mistaking it. The sounds that greeted him were voices. The language they spoke was foreign to Methuselah's ears, and the timbre and tone of the voices was rough and raspy, but the sounds seemed organized. Surely there was meaning behind the syllables. The unintelligible sounds seemed to be an invitation of sorts. The harsh voices were urging him to press onward, to follow them deeper into the maze of tunnels. Something lurking in his mind, some until now disused portion of his brain, processed the seemingly nonsense sounds into something coherent. While his ears couldn't decipher the sounds as words, this newly awakened part of his brain could unravel their meaning with ease. His ears may have been incapable of understanding, but his mind was fluent in the language of the Elders Below.

"Yes, I'm coming…"

Methuselah's knees wobbled as he moved deeper into the subterranean labyrinth. His pulse hammered, straining at the limits of his ancient heart.

"I'm…coming…" he gasped.

No longer concerned about the possibility of disease lurking in the water, he splashed through the stream. The water was cool as it seeped through his makeshift shoes. The bottom of the concrete channel was covered in slimy mud that squelched underfoot. It felt glorious. He tossed aside his chalk, certain that he'd never need it again. The Elders had chosen to reveal themselves, and salvation was at hand.

He slogged through the muddy stream, his breathing labored and his muscles aching. But the voices—alternately squeaky and guttural—grew louder and more distinct with each step.

Onward and onward, he forced his feet to continue their march, although his strength was flagging. His lungs burned with each breath. A stitch throbbed in his side. His head ached and his eyes burned from the chemical haze wafting up from the sludge beneath the water. But to Methuselah, these were minor annoyances. The urge to slow down, to rest and catch his breath, was merely a temptation of the flesh, no better than the times in his distant past when he'd been seduced by the harlots who haunted the trading posts of the wasteland. Age had granted him the ability to ignore those base urges, and it seemed that it had also granted him the ability to ignore these more immediate pains. In fact, he quickened his pace as he drew nearer to the source of the voices.

"I'm almost there," he gasped, pausing for a moment as the tunnel terminated in a T-junction.

Holding his torch aloft, he gasped at the sight his cataract-clouded eyes beheld. He'd thought he was in a sewer, but it seemed that he'd strayed into a charnel house. The tunnel floor was littered with bones. Some were heaped in piles against the walls, others were scattered and strewn haphazardly across the damp floor. It was shocking, but nothing that he hadn't encountered before. He'd explored many dead cities, and had seen the places where the former inhabitants had interred their dead. Most of these improvised tombs had obviously been arranged with some amount of care and reverence, but every so often, he found one such as this, where the bones had been heaped with utter disregard. He'd yet to discern a reason for the different customs, but the ways of the past were strange and inscrutable. The Event had wrought many changes upon the planet, and the people of old had reacted as they saw fit.

He pressed a hand to his chest and offered a prayer for the souls of the departed. His reverie was interrupted by the sounds that filled the tunnel. They seemed to be slowly rising in volume.

He closed his eyes and listened, straining to determine the direction from which the voices were coming.

It seemed to him that the sounds were coming from both directions. He kept his eyes closed, wondering if the acoustics of the empty concrete tunnels were playing tricks on him. But as the sounds drew nearer, there was little room for doubt. They *were* on both sides. He opened his eyes and held the chemical torch aloft. The green glow carved a hazy halo out of the darkness, but it didn't extend much more than a few meters.

His heart began to pound as the sounds grew louder. A giddy sense of elation took hold of him, and he bounced from one aching foot to another, swinging the chemical torch this way and that, eager for his first glimpse of the Elders. His lungs worked like ancient bellows, wheezing and rasping as they pumped air in and out of his chest.

And then, at last, his faith was rewarded. A figure stepped out of the darkness and paused on the edge of the chemical torch's flickering light. It wasn't a luminous being that the High Magus had described during his hours-long pulpit-pounding sermons. The figure wasn't one of the tall, long-limbed angels clad in spotless white robes of Methuselah's dreams. It was of average height and had nothing mystical about it. No glowing aura or wreath of purest light. The only illumination about it came from a shoulder-mounted chemical light.

Nevertheless, the time had arrived. After years of searching, he'd finally found one of the Elders.

"My lord..." Methuselah knelt. Stagnant, chemical-rich water soaked through his pants as his knees sank into the muck covering the rough floor. "At last, you have revealed yourself to me..."

The figure stood there, unmoved by his exaltations. It was clad in a bright yellow body suit made of thick plastic and knee-high boots of black rubber. Atop its head was a helmet which trailed hoses connected to metal cylinders which it wore like backpacks. A black-tinted face plate hid its features. It looked more like a member of the toxic waste disposal crews of the days immediately following the Event rather than a savior of humanity. But Methuselah knew that the ways of the Divine were often mysterious, and he was determined that his faith would not waver, especially when his pilgrimage was at its end.

"Please," he said, raising his shaking hands in supplication. "Guide me to that paradise deep below the surface of this ruined planet, so that I may rest in the flowering gardens of the almighty..."

The Elder looked back at him through its dark plastic faceplates. Then it raised a hand and pointed to something behind Methuselah, where the volume of the chittering noises continued to swell. The old man scooted around on his knees to follow the Elder's gaze. And then, he saw the object of the Elder's interest. The source of the strange noises became apparent. Methuselah's rapturous joy gave way to stomach-churning revulsion, which was in turn replaced by sheer terror. A horde of giant black rats racing toward them. They were close enough that he could see their twitching pink noses and sleek, oily black fur coats. The rodents, like so much of the post-Event fauna, were swollen to grotesque proportions. Their bodies were the size of one of Methuselah's thighs. They dragged thick, leathery tails behind them, and the claws that splashed through the water and scraped against the concrete walls were dagger-like, curving to cruel points. Pink lips twitched aside to expose needle-sharp incisors and blood-red tongues. Their dead black eyes were glassy, reflecting the Elders' flashlight beams.

"No," Methuselah pleaded, scrabbling backwards until he cowered at the Elder's feet. "No, please, save me…"

The figure glanced down at him. Then it drew back one black-gloved hand and dealt him a sharp slap. The blow sent Methuselah sprawling. Stinking water splashed over his face, burning his eyes and singeing his nostrils. He forced his stinging eyes to remain open, too frightened of the oncoming rodent army to look away. There were hundreds, perhaps even thousands of them. They stood there, arrayed in neat rows like soldiers presenting themselves for inspection. Their wet noses twitched as they settled on their haunches.

Methuselah whimpered. "Spare me, oh merciful savior…"

The figure in the yellow suit raised its hand and waggled its fingers in the air. Then it turned on its heels and began to walk away, heavy boots squelching in the muddy water.

"No," Methuselah gasped, struggling to regain his footing. Twin spikes of pain twisted in his hips, and he knew that the bones were broken. Alone in the wasteland, such an injury was a death sentence.

Despair settled on Methuselah's shoulders like a weighted blanket. It wrapped him in a suffocating embrace. As the first tears spilled over his eyelids, he felt a sharp pain in his right foot. He turned his head back to the horde of rats, and watched in horror as one of the rats sank its overgrown incisors into his ankle.

He shrieked in pain and terror, swatting at the rat with hands twisted by decades of untreated arthritis. The blows caught the rat in its meaty flank, but they did nothing to deter it. The rat's fellows broke formation, swarming over Methuselah's body. Their claws tore through his flesh with the slightest pressure. His agonized screams were drowned out by a cacophony of squeaking, chittering rodent voices.

And then, at last, his world faded to black.

Chapter Two
The Job Interview

Kurt stood at the front gate of the compound, his arms raised over his head while a pair of Lord Hannibal's men frisked him for weapons. The guards were giants, their bodies covered in layer upon layer of chemically-enhanced muscle. Their faces were pig-like, with noses broken flat, and beady eyes sunken deep beneath protruding foreheads. Victims of one of the innumerable plagues that crawled over the wasteland, the guards' flesh was scabbed and flaking. Kurt was glad he'd tugged his scarf over his mouth and nose before approaching them. He had no idea if their disease was contagious, and he had no desire to find out.

Once they were satisfied that Kurt was unarmed, they parted wordlessly, returning to their posts on either side of the gate.

"Hey, no problem," Kurt said. "I can let myself in."

He pulled the latch that held the two panels of corrugated metal together, and dragged the gate open just enough to slip through.

The space inside the walls wasn't much different from that of the outside. The dusty ground was covered in patches of scrub vegetation. At the center of the compound was an enormous skeletal tree, reaching its sharp branches through the early morning mist that hovered overhead. Apart from that giant tree, the town looked like most wasteland settlements. A half dozen large buildings were scattered through the enclosed space. They were squat, single story structures, made of dark brown bricks and scraps of metal. The lone exception to this style of architecture was the town's greenhouse, which was situated near the skeletal tree. A pair of armed guards flanked the greenhouse door. To their left, a chain-link enclosure housed a herd of bristly black pigs. They were snuffling through a trough heaped with reeking slop. Dirty children played in the alleys between the buildings, their bare feet raising clouds of dust as they chased one another. A pair of dogs had chosen a spot near the greenhouse for a romantic rendezvous. One had mounted the other and was pumping frantically, its hind legs coming off the ground with each thrust. The guards urged them on, offering advice and critique.

It was a paradise by wasteland[3]* standards.

A man dressed in a brightly patterned caftan emerged from one of the buildings and walked across the open space to meet Kurt. Like the children, the man was barefoot. His head was covered by a bright red turban.

"You must be Kurt." The man raised his hand in greeting as he approached.

"I am indeed," Kurt said. His hand dropped to his hip, instinctively reaching to rest against the holstered butt of his absent pistol. It was a nervous tic born of countless deadly encounters during his time in the wasteland. The pistol was back at the team's campsite with the rest of their gear. No one carrying a weapon could get near Lord Hannibal. There were

---

* [3] A widely accepted term for the interior of the North American continent, the epicenter for the Event in the western hemisphere.

few laws governing life in the wasteland, but that one was ironclad.

"My name is Percival," the man in the caftan said. "If you'll follow me, Lord Hannibal is ready to receive you."

Kurt nodded, falling into step with Percival's shuffling pace. As they passed the tree, the dogs paused long enough to sniff the air, then got back to business. Percival led him to the largest of the buildings. He opened the front door and stood aside so that Kurt could enter.

"After you, sir." Percival smiled, revealing a mouthful of shiny, metallic teeth. "Nice choppers," Kurt said, stepping into the building's dim interior.

By wasteland standards, the large single room was palatial. The floor was covered with moss so thick and soft that it could have been carpet. A small army of naked women lounged on the spongy floor. They reclined on large, overstuffed cushions, smoking pipes of some sharp-smelling drug. An equal number of well-fed cats moved among them, peering into the shadowy corners of the room for any stray vermin. Guards were stationed in each corner of their room.

Unlike those Kurt had seen outside, these strongmen appeared to be plague-free. But like their diseased colleagues, they were armed. Each wore a pistol on one hip and a machete on the other. They stared Kurt down as he picked his way through the maze of reclining, stoned beauties.

They smiled at him and whispered offers and entreaties in voices hoarse with hash smoke. Their bloodshot eyes blinked slowly.

A water filtration unit burbled away in the center of the room, spilling its output into a gleaming metal tank. And on the far end of the space, seated on a pile of cushions was the man himself, the wealthiest man in the wasteland, Lord Hannibal. He was dressed in a caftan similar to the one worn by Percival, but his head was uncovered. He raised a hand in greeting, displaying fingers laden with gold rings.

"I know just what you're thinking," Lord Hannibal said, his voice high-pitched and warbling. "*I thought he'd be taller. Am I right?*"

"Well…" Kurt wasn't sure how to respond.

Lord Hannibal threw back his head and laughed, startling the nearest group of cats, who bolted across the room. Kurt supposed he *had* been thinking something along those lines. Lord Hannibal was so small he was almost childlike in appearance, if not for the hairline that had retreated halfway back across his skull, and the goatee sprouting from his chin. The pair of tall, buxom women flanking him seemed almost comically oversized in comparison. They regarded Kurt with heavy-lidded eyes.

Lord Hannibal snapped his fingers. "Ladies, make room for our guest."

The women rose slowly and slunk away, their movements as languid as those of the cats around them.

Lord Hannibal patted the cushion to his right, and invited Kurt to sit. The arrangement felt awkward, but Kurt had been in plenty of situations far less comfortable. He lowered himself onto the cushion, careful to keep as much space between himself and Lord Hannibal as possible.

Something about the little man made Kurt's skin crawl. His eyes were too big for his face, and too widely spaced. Or maybe it was those long, slender fingers decorated with heavy rings. Or maybe it was the fact that Lord Hannibal had been responsible for thousands of deaths during his reign.

"So, this team or yours has made quite a name for itself over the past couple years," Lord Hannibal began. "Only a couple years working this deep into the interior and you've already got some big jobs under your belt. A man in my position might see that as some sort of threat to the security of his empire."

Kurt swallowed drily. "I don't know what you've heard, but we've always stayed outside your territory. And if we ever did anything this far west, we'd have paid taxes on any salvage."

"Relax. If I'd thought you were poaching in my backyard, I wouldn't have bothered with the invitation. I'd have had you killed in your sleep, and then dragged back to my vacation home in the mountains to be processed into cat food."

The way Lord Hannibal spoke the threat—in his high, quavering voice—was just as unnerving as the words themselves. Kurt shifted around on the cushion, trying to find a comfortable way to sit.

"Now, let's get down to business." Lord Hannibal rubbed his hands together. "I know you run one of the best salvage crews in the game. And I'm a man who appreciates talent. I happen to have a lead on a spot that's ripe for the picking. An abandoned settlement—a city—that's loaded with pre-Event treasure. Tech, agri, weapons…you name it, it's there. Might even be some functioning infrastructure. I'm interested in the tech stuff. Anything that might be functional. You're welcome to the rest. Radiation levels are within the acceptable range for short term occupancy. I can provide all the information you need about where to find it, plus my personal guarantee of safe passage through the wasteland, in exchange for an even split on the takings."

"No offense, but why not just go raid this abandoned city yourself?"

Lord Hannibal smiled. "These days, I choose not to get my hands dirty. I paid my dues out there in the wasteland for twenty years. That's a young man's game."

Kurt wasn't eager to get into business with someone of Lord Hannibal's reputation. The cartels back east were bad enough, but this little fucker had dropped more bodies than the red death. And consequently, that was the exact reason that Kurt knew he couldn't refuse the offer. If his team wanted to operate in the interior—and when it came to wasteland salvage, there really was no richer territory—it meant fostering a good relationship with the various warlords who ran things between the coasts. Otherwise, it was risk attack from all sides.

"So what's the catch?" Kurt asked. "If this place is such easy pickings, what makes you think another team hasn't already ransacked it?"

"No catch," Lord Hannibal replied. "Think of this as an audition. Impress me and there will be plenty of jobs down the line. Good paying gigs too. Take a look around, my friend. You like what you see? Take into consideration that this isn't even one of my nicer settlements. This is just an outpost."

Kurt had to admit the place was impressive. The greenhouse and water filtration unit alone elevated it to a level of luxury that he'd rarely encountered since his team had moved operations to the interior.

"That's not really an answer to my question," Kurt said. "Why, if this place is such a cherry, hasn't it already been picked?"

"I never said it wasn't without danger or risk," Lord Hannibal replied. "Perhaps your team isn't the first to have tried. But you know how it is. Nothing worth doing is easy. But you and your team, you know how to take care of yourselves, right? I've done some asking around, and your reputation says that you don't mind resorting to violence if necessary."

Kurt shrugged. It was true that his team had been in their fair share of scrapes. You didn't last long in the salvage game if you weren't ready to spill a little blood.

"There's something in that place that's managed to scare off plenty of salvage teams," Lord Hannibal explained. "Maybe the local wildlife has been too much for them. But none of those people came as highly recommended as your squad."

Kurt raised an eyebrow. It sounded like Lord Hannibal

was implying that the abandoned city was occupied by mutants, descendants of those people too stubborn or stupid to flee underground in the immediate aftermath of the Event. Supposedly, there were some mutants who had devolved into violent cannibals who were little more than animals. Kurt had never encountered them, but he'd heard plenty of hair-raising firsthand accounts from those who had.

"I know you might not like the idea of working for someone else," Lord Hannibal continued. "Guys like you, I've seen them come and go. You start as a lone wolf, but then, as the years go by, you gather a pack. Suddenly, you're the alpha male and everyone's looking to you for guidance. It's a heavy responsibility, all those mouths to feed. Presses down on your shoulders like you were carrying a load of boulders. I'm offering you a chance to shrug off that load. I'm offering you a shot at stability. Not much of that left in the world, especially in the wasteland. And I don't think I need to mention that this is a job that comes with certain perks. Creature comforts, if you will."

"Oh yeah?"

Lord Hannibal smiled. He raised a hand and snapped his fingers. Across the room, one of the naked women detached herself from the ornate hookah pipe she was sharing with a trio of friends. She stretched, arching her back and rolling her head around on her shoulders. She exhaled a thick cloud of hash smoke from between her full, pink lips. Then she made her way towards Kurt, her slow walk accentuating the movement of her hips.

She lowered herself onto the cushion beside Kurt and draped her arms around him.

"This is Soledad," Lord Hannibal said. "She's eager to show you the sort of perks that come with the job."

Her hand moved to Kurt's lap. Despite her obvious intoxication, she found what she was looking for with practiced ease. Kurt opened his mouth to protest, but he could only manage a weak grunt as Soledad popped open the buttons of his fly and slipped her hand into his pants.

Kurt cleared his throat. "Look, this isn't necessary."

Lord Hannibal reclined on his elbow, an amused expression on his face. "Refusing my hospitality? Come now, that's not something you really want to do, is it?"

Kurt knew better than to protest. Any resolve he might have still possessed melted away as Soledad tugged his pants down just enough to free his erection. And then she lowered herself to the floor, kneeling between his thighs.

Lord Hannibal giggled girlishly, covering his mouth with one hand while he watched.

Soledad took her mouth away from Kurt's manhood just long enough to say, "Don't look at him. Focus on me instead."

Kurt met her bloodshot gaze and relaxed. It wasn't the first time he'd performed this act before an audience. He'd grown up in a subterranean crèche on the east coast. His people had been Acolytes of the Holy Seed, a religious sect that preached repopulation by any means necessary. Privacy had taken a backseat to procreation for the Acolytes. Like many of his fellows, Kurt was eventually determined to be infertile, and therefore a drain on the crèche's resources. Having been bred to multiple women without producing a single offspring, he'd been expelled from the group in the prescribed manner. He was given a weapon and enough supplies to carry him for a week or two, and then shoved topside to fend for himself. Most exiled Acolytes died in short order. But not Kurt. He'd endured every manner of torture and humiliation that the topside world could throw at him and had thrived. Getting sucked off by one of Lord Hannibal's concubines in a crowded room was no problem.

The muscles in Kurt's buttocks tightened as he climaxed. He collapsed back on the cushion, breathing heavily. Soledad detached herself from him and sauntered away wordlessly.

"And since we've arrived at the end of the pleasantries,"

Lord Hannibal said, straightening up from his relaxed pose, "can I assume we have a deal?"

Kurt nodded as he tucked his wet and wilting member back into his pants. "Yeah. We got a deal."

"Splendid." Lord Hannibal rubbed his hands together. "You'll use a transponder to find the location. No paper maps. This is the big time. Transport vehicles are already on the scene, leftovers from the latest failed expedition. I assume you have drivers who can handle something big?"

"Yeah, my guys Taurus and Viz can drive anything with wheels."

Lord Hannibal's smile was that of a predator with a temporarily satiated appetite. "Then I reckon this meeting is adjourned. My man Percival will escort you to the front gate. He'll also fix you up with a transponder and a voucher for another of my outposts, and fill you in on any details you might have questions about. You're dismissed."

* * *

The team was preparing the evening meal on the chemical stove when Kurt made it back to camp. Their motorbikes were parked in a circle to mark the edge of camp. Made of salvaged steel, aluminum, and iron, the vehicles were a stout enough barrier. The members of the team were gathered around the glowing stove, chatting among themselves. One by one, they fell silent as they turned to watch Kurt's approach.

"Welcome home, boss," Max called. "Taurus and Duke clipped a pair of coyotes right after you left this morning, so we're having a feast."

Kurt's stomach rumbled at the smell of the roasting meat. The five mile walk from Lord Hannibal's outpost to camp had been mercifully uneventful, but it still had its share of hills. Not to mention the day's other exertions.

"Welcome back, brother." Deus, the team's resident mystic, detached himself from the group, and met Kurt with a warm embrace. "Your return is timely. Diana was so worried that I was afraid she wouldn't be able to eat, even with meat on offer."

Kurt returned the hug, although with less enthusiasm. Like Kurt, Deus was a former Acolyte who had also survived life topside by a combination of wit and strength. But whereas Kurt had ditched his faith in favor of a more pragmatic philosophy of survival at all costs, Deus had grown stronger in his religious beliefs. Deus—tall and gaunt, his bald head tattooed with religious symbols—had spent years scouring the interior wasteland for religious texts and artifacts the way Kurt searched for resources. Theirs was a friendship born of their shared heritage. Their arguments could be fiery, but like all members of the group, they depended on one another for survival.

Diana waited for the manly embrace to pull apart before grabbing Kurt by the waist and pulling him close to her. She stood on tiptoe to whisper in his ear, "I missed you."

She pulled back just far enough to plant a kiss on his lips. Kurt tried to return the gesture with equal passion, but he couldn't help recalling Soledad's pliant warmth. Diana was unlike the stoned concubine in just about every way. Whereas Soledad was tall and buxom, Diana was short and athletically built. Her limbs were firm and toned from a life of physical toil. But her face was soft enough, almost childlike with large, clear eyes and a small, upturned nose that was covered by a spray of freckles.

"I missed you too, love," Kurt said, delicately extricating himself and facing the rest of the group. With Diana at his side, he cleared his throat and told them about Lord Hannibal's proposal.

There were eleven of them in total. They'd numbered thirteen when they began their westward push across the wasteland two years ago, but a sniper had taken out Quinn during a botched caravan robbery, and Lana had succumbed to the red plague only a few weeks later. Some of them, like Kurt and Deus, had grown up below the surface, in crèches or ancient bunker communities. Others, like Diana and Rosemary, had spent their entire lives topside, growing up in the hardscrabble coastal settlements or as part of caravans. The lone exception was Duke, who'd lived the majority of his life in the interior wasteland. The son of a deposed warlord, he'd spent his childhood on the run. All in all, they were a motley cast of characters, but life in the post-Event world made strange bedfellows of humanity.

"It sounds to me," Deus said, "like you made a deal with the devil."

"You gotta understand," Kurt explained, "I had no choice. If we're going to carve out a life for ourselves, we're going to have to deal with people like Lord Hannibal. I don't like it any more than you do."

Duke took the opportunity to chime in. "Yeah, well, I'm relieved that you feel comfortable making this decision for all of us. You know, he was probably one of the sons of bitches who killed my father, and now I get to be his errand boy. Pretty sure I like it a lot less than you do."

They locked eyes for a moment. This wasn't the first time Duke had voiced opposition to Kurt's leadership. Each time, it ended in a staring contest that Kurt won. The outcome of this particular stare-down was no different, but it seemed to Kurt that each contest was longer and more intense than the last. Maybe it was just the green glow of the chemical stove playing tricks on his mind, but Duke's eyes seemed to sparkle with resentment.

Diana stepped in front of Kurt. She crossed her arms defensively beneath her breasts. She was short enough that Kurt could see over her head, and he kept his eyes fixed on Duke.

"Maybe you should try putting the team's interests ahead of your own," she snapped at Duke.

"Hey, there's no need to get snippy." Duke shrugged. "Didn't realize it was that time of the month."

Diana tensed and took a step forward, but Kurt pulled her back.

"Knock that shit off," Kurt said, careful to keep his voice light. "Yeah, I made a big decision. But we came to the wasteland to raise enough salvage to buy our way past the north border wall. We came out here to secure a free existence and a future, so if anyone has serious objections, they're more than welcome to walk away. But if you're staying, best remember I was the one who put this team together, and when it comes down to it, I call the shots."

For a moment, no one answered. Kurt hoped his fancy talk did the trick and kept the team focused. They glanced around at each other, their eyes asking the unspoken question. Then, Deus spoke up.

"I'm with you, brother," the mystic said.

Viz, the team's handyman, slapped his thigh and laughed. "You know I'm along for the ride, wherever it happens to take us."

One by one, they voiced their support.

Next was Rosemary. "You're the man, Kurt. I'm with you."

Taurus, Lilith, Lucifer, Myrna, and Max all murmured some variation on the theme. Finally, Duke shrugged, admitting defeat.

"Well, I can't exactly go back to walking the wasteland by myself, can I?" He sprang to his feet and extended his hand to Kurt. "No hard feelings, huh?"

Kurt shook Duke's hand, deciding to let the challenge to his leadership slide for the moment. A small, yet very insistent voice in the back of his mind told him that, sooner rather than later, Duke would stage some sort of mutiny, and that Kurt would be wise to act preemptively. But that was a headache for another night. At the moment, he had to clue the group in on Lord Hannibal's big score.

"It's a small piece of one of the old cities, from before the Event," Kurt explained. "And according to Lord Hannibal, it's full of salvage. Tech, agri, weapons…the whole shebang."

Practically untouched, to hear him tell it. He provided a location transponder in return for an even split. If this salvage is only half as rich as he promises, it's still going to be enough to move our timetable forward considerably. I know it's risky working for a maniac like Lord Hannibal…" He paused to look at Duke, then continued, "But if this is the type of job he throws our way, we might be able to make our way north next spring. After that, we can spend the rest of our days sipping cocktails on the shores of the Great Lakes, and doing whatever it is civilized folks do. Maybe I'll take up woodworking or taxidermy. It's endless leisure time up there, I'm told."

That last part did the trick. The murmurs of approval became the excited chatter of overlapping voices. When the clamor died down, Duke spoke up again.

"That's great and all," he said, "but I'd just like to point out one little thing."

Kurt nodded. "Go on."

"The route you described takes us through a big patch of forest. So far, we've worked the foothills east of the mountains, the open ground of the southern deserts, and now this heartland prairie shit. We've never ventured into any of the great forests."

"So what?" Diana asked, slipping her arm around Kurt's waist.

"Unlike the rest of you, I *have* been in the great forests. And I know the sort of shit that's in there, lurking behind every tree and inside every cave. I'm talking about mutants, both human and animal. The woods are crawling with those scary motherfuckers. Zero chance we don't go up against them." Duke paused to let that sink in, looking around at the rest of the team. "It's going to make the canyon job look like a cakewalk."

Mention of the canyon job was a bucket of cold water thrown on the team's enthusiasm.

That job was the one that claimed Quinn's life. What was planned as a simple robbery of a supply caravan had turned into a three day siege during which they'd huddled in a cave, hiding from sniper fire. If not for the cover afforded by a sudden thunderstorm, they might not have made it out alive.

"That's true. Lord Hannibal's job requires two days' journey through one of the forests of the interior," Kurt admitted. "And although the rest of us have never experienced the place for ourselves, we've all heard the stories. But life on a wasteland salvage team is a risky proposition. We all knew that when we signed up."

Duke raised his hands in surrender. "I'm just saying."

* * *

Later, as they lay beneath the starless grey sky, their bellies full of roasted coyote, synthetic carb, and boiled scrub nettles, Kurt and Diana spoke in whispers while the rest of the team slumbered.

"Is this the right thing?" she asked. "Working with Lord Hannibal, I mean?"

Kurt shifted around in their sleeping bag, rolling onto his side to face her. "You been talking to Duke or something?"

She recoiled a bit. "You can't be serious."

"No, it's just..." He sighed, remembering his encounter with Soledad and wishing he'd possessed the resolve to refuse her advances. "I think it's the right move. For one thing, we can't operate out here in the wasteland without his protection. And for another, the sooner we can go north, the better. And that means getting as much salvage as possible as quickly as possible."

"Yeah, but that stuff about mutants..."

"I know," Kurt sighed. "But crossing paths with mutants was always a possibility this deep in the interior. I gotta tell you, it's not the forest that worries me as much as what might be waiting for us in the city. If there's something worse than mutants, I'm not sure I want to find out what it is."

"Well, something's keeping people away from this city, especially if it's the prize that Lord Hannibal claims it is. But you're right. Everything we do is a calculated risk. If this job means getting up north sooner, then it's worth it."

"You sure do know how to talk. No wonder you're the leader of this outfit."

They lay there in silence, watching the sky for those rare moments when the clouds would break and the stars could peek through.

"Do you really believe it?" she asked.

"What do you mean?"

"That there's a place for us up north? A place away from all this..." She sighed, looking skyward, searching for a gap in the ever-present layer of grey clouds.

Now it was Kurt's turn to sigh. Like the other members of the generations who'd grown up in the post-Event world, he'd grown up hearing stories of the Good Old Days. Although a poisoned, decaying world was all they'd ever known, Kurt had heard plenty of tales from the elder members of his crèche about a green planet, a place of abundant vegetation, clean air, clear water, and gleaming cities full of healthy people. They were stories passed down through generations, from the period just after the Event, when humanity had retreated underground, through the present day, when people were venturing topside in greater numbers. Kurt had heard these tales, and like the other children, dreamed of a place where such a world could begin anew. The northern territories, past the blasted expanse of the wasteland, were the stuff of fairy tales.

None who'd ventured into that place had returned to confirm or deny the rumors of a place free from the red plague and radiation-mutated life forms. Still, even fairy tales might contain a kernel of truth.

"I don't know if I believe it or not," Kurt answered honestly. "But I know one thing: if there's a possibility of something other than this hell, it's worth fighting for. If we die along the way, well, I suppose that's still more than most have done with their lives."

Chapter Three
A Nighttime Visitation

Soledad waited until Hannibal finished before turning her head and spitting a mouthful of semen onto the dusty ground. She scrubbed her lips with the back of her hand, then settled herself onto the cushion beside him. They were in a small gazebo near the center of the town. On nights like these, he enjoyed slumbering beneath the stars. There were plenty of armed guards lurking in the shadows, both inside and outside the outpost walls, so he never worried about his safety. And if any of the residents happened to be out for a midnight stroll and got an eyeful? Well, that was just fine with Hannibal. It would be a story they could one day tell their grandkids.

"There you go, my dear," Hannibal said as he shoved his penis back into his pants. "There are those who say romance is dead, but you refute that with your grace and ease."

"Yeah, that's right," she said hesitantly, bracing herself for a slap. "Of course, my lord of the wasteland."

Lord of the Wasteland.

Hannibal nearly laughed out loud every time he heard those words. Ridiculous. He was the runt of the litter. Born of a half-wit whore, he was his father's shame. And yet, he'd clawed his way to the top of the dung heap that was the interior wasteland. What he lacked in brawn, he'd made up for in brains. Decades of careful scheming had elevated him above the rabble.

Perhaps a thousand betrayals had paved his path to the throne of his sordid fiefdom, and petty and squalid though it may have been, it was one he intended to rule until his death.

And yet...*Lord of the Wasteland*?

It was a joke. This was a world of shit, and being its lord was nothing to crow about. Still, one had to make a living, and there were far worse ways of doing it.

"It's a wonderful life, isn't it?" Hannibal said, running his fingers through Soledad's hair.

"Yes, my lord," she purred, nuzzling against his chest. "It's wonderful to be here with you."

Hannibal snorted. He shrugged her away from him. "I supposed you'd say that. Here, you have your fill of hash and food and clean water. All you need to do in return is spread your legs or open your mouth. Those of us with real responsibility don't see it as quite so wonderful."

Soledad's glazed eyes moved slowly from side to side. Clearly unsure of how to best respond, she remained silent.

"Get away from me." Hannibal waved a hand dismissively. "I need to think."

Soledad departed without delay, bounding naked through the warm night air on her way to the residence she shared with the rest of the whores. Hannibal watched her go, wondering how much hash vapor she'd suck down to rinse the taste of his seed from her mouth. Then he dropped back on the pile of cushions and peered through the holes in the gazebo's roof, at a sky whose stars were mostly hidden behind a veil of grey clouds.

His thoughts returned to the business of the day. Kurt had seemed dependable and capable, the sort of man you'd like to have at your side when the going got rough. It was almost a shame to send him into the heart of the wasteland. But that was what the client had paid for, and that was what the client—

No, he chided himself silently. *They aren't your* clients. *They're your bosses. Out here, you may be lord of the wasteland, but in the grand scheme of things, you're just another scavenger. True, you're perhaps the best scavenger, but that's only because they've allowed you to be.*

He shuddered at the thought of those who pulled his strings. His bosses were ruthless and determined to an inhuman degree. And perhaps that shouldn't have been surprising. They were, after all, the best suited to inherit the earth.

The sound of approaching footsteps pulled Hannibal out of his reverie. One of the men from the front gate was standing at the gazebo's entrance. The guard announced himself with a polite cough, then stood at attention, waiting to be acknowledged.

Hannibal snapped his fingers. "Speak."

"Lord Hannibal, you have a visitor at the front gate," the guard answered.

"At this hour?" Hannibal shook his head. "Tell whoever it is to fuck off until morning."

"Sir, it's one of the..." The guard shot a look over his shoulder in the direction of the outpost's front gate. "It's one of the...uh...*you know.*"

Hannibal fought the urge to spring to his feet. He didn't want his men getting the idea that there was something out there that could provoke such a reaction from their ruthless leader. But he couldn't do anything about the quickening of his pulse or the sinking feeling in his stomach. He forced himself to rise slowly, wiping his sweaty palms on his pants.

"One of the *Colonists?*" Hannibal forced himself to speak evenly, despite the sudden onset of nerves. "It's not some boogeyman. You can say the name without whispering and glancing around like you're summoning some devil who's going to steal our women."

"Freaks me out, just being around them," the guard said as Hannibal shouldered past him. "They ain't natural."

"Good thing I didn't hire you for your diplomacy."

"Huh?" The guard's slow shuffle kicked up plenty of dust.

"Never mind. Let's get this over with."

The big musclebound lunk picked up the pace, leading the way to the front gate. When they arrived, he announced their presence and pulled one of the double doors open to admit a figure clad in deep wasteland gear. Hannibal nearly laughed at the sight of the Colonist shuffling through the gate in his cumbersome outfit. The Colonist wore a full helmet respiration unit, complete with dark visor.

"Not really necessary," Hannibal said, gesturing vaguely at their clothing. "None of my outposts are in the danger zone for radiation or particulate matter in the air. We're also negative for the red plague and our water filtration system is top notch. This is the new cradle of civilization, if you ask me."

He regretted the choice of words as soon as they were past his lips. The Colonist could be touchy about talk of civilization or reclamation of the planet's surface. They saw themselves as authorities on those topics, and their devotion to reshaping the future according to their ideas bordered on fanatical. Insults to their dogma were simply not tolerated. Thankfully, his slip of the tongue went unacknowledged.

Hannibal bowed slightly, too nervous to bristle at the deference he was forced to show, then turned to lead his visitor in the direction of the meeting hall. As they made their way across the outpost's central avenue, a pair of cats detached themselves from the shadows, and stalked toward the Colonist. They kept their distance, moving parallel to the group.

"Don't worry," Hannibal said. "The meeting hall is off limits to our feline population."

The translator device on the Colonist's shoulder crackled. A mechanical voice said, "In the future, please secure these animals before welcoming a Colonist into your compound."

"Yes, of course. My apologies," Hannibal said.

But he couldn't help wondering just how the hell he could be expected to do that when a Colonist showed up unannounced. And, more practically, how the hell did one go about rounding up a few dozen cats, most of whom were feral? But he knew better than to say any of this aloud. Hell, he was nervous even *thinking* it. If the Colonists could communicate with each other telepathically, who could say if they might be able to go poking around in his thoughts? He knew that was most likely not the case. If so, what was the purpose of these visits at all? And, more to the point, why bother working with him in the first place? Still, it gave him the shivers just being this close to one of the Colonists. He was one of the few people who'd been in their close proximity and lived to tell the tale.

"Here we are," he said, unlocking the door to the meeting hall. "Please, make yourself at home."

Like most of the buildings in the outpost, the meeting hall was a squat structure made of salvaged materials. The interior was sparsely furnished with mismatched tables and chairs. It was much more utilitarian than Hannibal's personal quarters, but it was much more Colonist-friendly, being free of cats and hash-addicted whores. As the doors swung open, the generators coughed themselves to light, powering up the chemical lanterns that lined the walls of the room. It was a system dreamed up by Hannibal's chief engineer. Hannibal thought it lent a touch of class to what was otherwise one of his rudest and most remote outposts. The Colonist didn't seem impressed. Of course, it was hard to tell with his face hidden.

The Colonist sat at a large circular table in the center of the room. Hannibal never knew whether he should sit or stand during these meetings. He'd done both, and never received any indication that either choice was a breach of protocol. This time, he chose to sit, taking a seat opposite the Colonist, who immediately asked, "Has the next group of candidates been engaged?"

"Yes. I met with their leader this very day." Hannibal found staring into the Colonist's dark visor unnerving, but he didn't want to appear disrespectful by looking away. Perhaps, one day, he'd figure out the protocol for these situations, and open some sort of school. An academy for collaborators. A cotillion for race traitors. Take your fucking pick, and learn to survive in a world that was changing by the day.

"What is the group composition?" the Colonist asked.

"Well, I…" Hannibal stared at his reflection in the glossy surface of the Colonist's visor. "There are both males and females in their number, but I don't know how many of each. Nobody told me I was supposed to keep track of that."

The pause that followed was, for Hannibal, profoundly uncomfortable. He shifted on the hard surface of the chair.

"Was there any evidence of the red plague among them?" The mechanical voice was free of any inflection.

"If there was the least bit of evidence of plague, he wouldn't have made it past the front gate. My guards are trained to spot that."

The Colonist rose, signaling an end to the meeting. The mechanical voice spoke one final time. "I'd like to remind you that although you call yourself the lord of the wasteland, you are far from the only one prospering in the inland region. Many of your brethren would jump at the chance to secure the Colony's protection. Remember that."

Hannibal nodded. "Of course."

The Colonist moved swiftly toward the exit. Hannibal had to hurry to catch up as they crossed the courtyard. Speaking in deferential tones behind closed doors was one thing, but he couldn't afford for any of his men to see him behaving submissively, even in the presence of a Colonist.

As they neared the front gate, one of the outpost's many cats burst from the shadows, advancing at a run directly towards the Colonist.

"No!" Hannibal screamed, trying to jump into the path of the oncoming tabby.

The cat must not have cared one bit for his protest, because it shot past him without breaking stride, and launched itself at the Colonist, yowling and hissing. The Colonist's gloved hands snatched the animal out of the air. Without an ounce of hesitation, he grasped the cat by the neck with one hand and used the other to twist the tabby's head violently, snapping the beast's neck with a sound like a snapping twig. The Colonist tossed the dead animal to the side.

Hannibal gasped an apology as he unlatched the front gate. The Colonist didn't spare him a glance as he stepped through the opening into the pitch darkness of night in the wasteland.

* * *

Hannibal considered retiring to his private rooms for the rest of the night, but he knew sleep would be impossible to come by. So he made his way back to the brothel/hash den, and picked his way through the maze of slumbering prostitutes and cats. He collapsed onto the cushion-covered bench that served as his throne, and listened to the soft sounds of snoring. One of the prone forms stirred, then rose and stretched, silhouetted by faint glow of the water filtration unit. She advanced by clumsy steps across the room then deposited herself next to him. He knew without turning his head that it was Soledad. None of the others treated him with such familiarity.

"You look stressed out," she said, placing a hand on his thigh.

Hannibal grunted.

"It was one of them, wasn't it?" she continued. "One of the rat people."

"It was one of my Colonist contacts, yes," he snapped. "And if one of them ever heard you utter that name—*rat people*—you'd be dead."

"But it's true, isn't it? They got faces like rats is what I hear. And the reason they can't talk is 'cause rat mouths can't make words the way our mouths can."

"Those are just stories invented by small-minded imbeciles. I swear, sometimes you act like a child."

Soledad shook her head. "It's just what I've heard, that's all."

"Nobody who's seen a Colonist's face has lived to tell about it." Hannibal leaned back, sighing as Soledad massaged his thigh. "Rat people? I'd laugh if I wasn't so sick of hearing that same bullshit story over and over again."

Although, sometimes, Hannibal wondered. He'd heard the stories too, and they were so widespread that there had to be some grain of truth buried in the layers of nonsense. The Colonists *weren't* human. Of that, he was utterly convinced. His personal theory was that they'd come to Earth from another planet. After all, plenty of people held to the theory that the Event had been of extraterrestrial origin, so it made a certain kind of crazy sense. All the weird mannerisms, the telepathic communication…it certainly *seemed* alien. And he preferred to think of himself as a pragmatic man bridging the gap between humanity and an enlightened species from another planet, rather than a self-serving collaborator working with a bunch of giant rats.

Warlord or not, he still had to be able to look himself in the mirror.

Chapter Four
Colonial Politics

Brother Grainger's lungs wheezed and crackled as his breath came faster and faster. His joints ached with the effort of movement. The subterranean air was dry—a boon to his ancient lungs—but the exertion was becoming more than he could handle. He supposed that was as it should be. He was old, after all. Ancient by the standards of this cursed world. And his body was slowing under the inexorable weight of passing time. Bit by bit, it was shutting down. As far as Grainger was concerned, that was just fine. No one was meant to live forever. And he'd done his part for the species. For eight decades, he'd labored in the subterranean world, working towards the glorious day when his race would reclaim the surface of the planet and return it to its former glory.

But then, he thought, *was it ever really glorious? All we have to back up that assertion are the tales passed from one generation to the next. The Event wiped most history away.*

He'd come to accept that he wouldn't live to see the culmination of this work, and he'd made his peace with that. Now, he longed only for a quiet retirement. A warm, cozy space he could call his own, and plenty of food to fill his belly, that was enough for him.

But until then, there was still work to be done.

And such is life, he thought, pausing at a bend in the tunnel to catch his breath and scratch a spot behind his ear.

The Colonial Council convened each day at the Delta Colony's central hub. The largest of the subterranean settlements, the Delta Colony occupied much of the middle of the continent. Its population numbered over a million, for now, at least. Birth rates were plummeting and had been doing so for the last few generations. It wasn't for lack of trying. Like their forebears, the Colonists were prolific breeders. Polyamorous and community-oriented, they seemed designed by nature to thrive. And for the first generations born after the Event, that held true.

And then, some unknown defect had crept into the gene pool and poisoned the waters. Viable offspring were becoming increasingly rare. Those who didn't succumb to cradle death were sickly, feeble. Those who appeared physically capable often displayed mental defects and physiological abnormalities. Their hybrid species was still new in the grand scheme of the planet, and already it was dying. Some of the clan's scientists put forth a theory of reverse evolution, predicting that, within an alarmingly small number of generations, the species could return to its pre-Event lowliness.

Grainger paused to lean against the wall of the tunnel. His mouth hung open, his long whiskers twitching as he gulped air. Beneath his robe, his tail trembled. He held his hands up before his black eyes and observed them shaking involuntarily.

Palsy. That's just great.

He resumed his slow march down the tunnel. As he rounded a bend, he was met by Brother Lorne and Sister Ursula. They were something of a power couple in the Delta

Colony. The youngest members of the Council, they wielded enormous influence in not just the Delta Colony but the entire underground world. This influence was largely due to Lorne and Ursula's ability to produce healthy offspring in great numbers. They were as close to monogamous as their species came, not due to some ancient sense of morality, but rather the fact that, for whatever reason, his sperm and her eggs could unite to create a healthy litter every three or four months. And yet, they were the most vocal supporters of a genetic diversity program.

Greetings, Lorne projected the thought loud and clear, as if he had to communicate extra clearly when thinking at his elder.

How are you feeling, Brother Grainger? Ursula chimed in. *As we were walking, we thought we heard something about palsy?*

Oh, it's nothing to worry about. I'm just fine. But Grainger knew that it wasn't fine. Not at all. Palsy and shortness of breath were one thing, but the inability to separate his private thoughts from those he intended to project was cause for concern. If he couldn't segregate his internal and external voices, he'd end up exiled to the surface without a respiration unit.

The trio continued down the tunnel. Ursula's belly was swollen with her third litter of the year, and her progress was just as slow as Grainger's. Lorne stood between them, twiddling his whiskers between his thumb and forefinger. It was easy to see why he was a hero of the people and the de facto leader of the Council. Not only was he quick witted and virile, he was also an impressive physical specimen. Lorne stood a full six feet tall. He was long-limbed and well-muscled. Even his tail had the appearance of great strength. His black eyes sparkled, even in the low lighting of the tunnel. His fur was dark brown streaked with black, the hair sleek and shiny. When he drew back his lips, his exposed incisors were always freshly filed to an appropriate length and bleached white. He dressed in clothing stolen from human settlements rather than the rough, utilitarian robes favored by most of the Colonists.

Truth be told, I'm sick of these endless meetings, Lorne projected. *We need more action and less talk.*

I concur, Grainger replied. *But I'm afraid we three are the only Council members who aren't deeply in love with the sound of our own thoughts.*

Ursula squealed a short burst of laughter, then projected, *Who could possibly love the sound of that rubbish? Endless bickering when we all know that a successful cross-breeding program is our only hope.*

Grainger nodded.

Ursula shuddered. *I'm sorry. I know it's necessary, but I can't help it. The thought of mating with one of them…it makes my skin crawl. All that hairless flesh…and those monkey faces…*

You should keep an open mind. Some of our brothers and sisters find the idea quite erotic, Lorne laughed. *I've heard stories…*

Grainger shook his head. It was irksome to hear the bestiality jokes coming from the likes of Lorne and Ursula. The genetics research involved test tubes and arcane scientific machinery. Those who opposed funding the program reduced it to dirty punchlines about sex with humans.

I'm not sure it's something you should be laughing about, Grainger answered. *Sooner or later, it's a situation that will have to be addressed seriously. Our kind cannot continue without the cooperation of the humans. Taking their sperm or eggs without consent isn't just a moral conundrum, it's also the type of thing that can bring about open conflict.*

We've fought them well in the past, Lorne countered.

Yes, while they were still scattered and bewildered by the Event, Grainger answered. *And there's other dangers to consider as well. Common ancestor or not, our lower brothers and sisters outnumber us a hundred to one. Perhaps they shouldn't be forgotten in all this back and forth.*

Lorne sniffed. *They're animals.*

Yes, Grainger projected, *but then again, what are we?*

We are the meek who shall inherit, Lorne answered.

The trio fell into single file as they ducked through the narrow doorway to the Council chamber. The remaining six members were already seated and talking amongst themselves.

Grainger's skull filled with overlapping voices. Although their meeting wasn't scheduled to start for another five minutes, the Councilors who were present had already gotten down to the business of arguing. Thoughts flew through the air like bullets. A dozen shiny black eyes stared daggers across the round table in the center of the room.

…you'd have us abandon our identities…

…our only salvation lies in genetic diversity…

…you're talking about genocide…

…and return the planet to human control…

…selective breeding…

…our children won't recognize us and we won't recognize them…

…declining population…

Grainger sighed. He cut his eyes sideways to look at Lorne and Ursula. They smiled, their lips pulled back to reveal carefully filed incisors.

Here we go again, Grainger projected as he trudged across the room, his pink tail dragging behind him.

Once he'd sat down, and Lorne and Ursula had taken their seats, the cross talk began to fade. Lorne—appointed by his peers to the role of head parliamentarian—banged his gavel on the table, cutting off the lingering arguments.

Lorne's thoughts rang out loud and clear. *Let this meeting of the Colonial Council come to order. We will begin with the traditional moment of silence to honor the Event, which elevated our kind from the sewers and trash heaps to the enlightened status we enjoy today.*

Like the others, Grainger bowed his head and made a show of meditating on the glorious Event, but his heart wasn't in it. He couldn't remember when it happened, but at some point, he'd lost his absolute faith in his race's dogma.

He'd had his fill of sermons about the Event, when the planet was unbalanced, the food chain thrown into chaos, and the old order irrevocably dissolved. Exactly what had triggered the Event—and indeed, what the Event even entailed—was a truth lost to time. All that remained was conjecture. The mystics said it was the hand of the creator, reaching down from the heavens to change the balance of nature. The scientists said it was the result of war between human tribes. The cynics—and Grainger had begun to count himself among their number—said it didn't matter. The Colonists had inherited, and now it was their turn to rule the planet. When the next Event came—and it would come, eventually—who would pick up the pieces? Maybe the insects. Maybe the fish. One could only hope they'd do a better job. Grainger laughed inwardly. Here they were, still debating the manner in which they'd emerge from their subterranean Colonies and repopulate the surface world, and he'd already planned the species' apocalypse. Perhaps "cynical" was too mild a term for what he'd become.

Finally, the moment of silence concluded, and Brother Lorne launched into his opening remarks. He put forward some ideas about furthering the Colony's interests through genetic alteration, all with the goal of eventually reclaiming the surface of the planet. It was the usual stuff, but Grainger had to admit that the youngster had a way with words. What he was proposing could have been framed as eugenics at best and a quiet genocide at worst, but Lorne steered his proposals in a different direction. Yes, he admitted, the species would be unrecognizable within ten generations, but so would *homo sapiens*. The combination of their races was the only path forward. All others ended in extinction, for human and Colonist alike.

The opposition, in the form of another firebrand named Cornelius, sat with his arms folded across his chest, biding his time until he could offer a rebuttal. Cornelius was unlike Lorne, not just ideologically, but physically as well. Rotund and battle-scarred, Cornelius was missing one eye and most of his tail as a result of a botched topside raid on a human outpost.

When Lorne concluded his remarks, Cornelius stood slowly and glared at each member of the Council. His whiskers twitched as he bared a pair of incisors filed to cruel points.

Look upon me and remember how the humans feel about our kind.

He flipped back his eyepatch to reveal the empty socket beneath. He turned his back on the Council and raised the hem of his robe to display his stump of a tail, which hung limply just above his knees. The members of the Council shifted in their seats, clearly uncomfortable with the show. Grainger was the lone exception. He was the only other member old enough to remember the days of raiding human outposts. These raids were supposedly done in the name of collecting supplies, but more often than not turned into the wholesale slaughter of humans.

They had their chance at supremacy on the surface of the planet, and they only succeeded in bringing about the Event.

Lorne uttered a psychic throat-clearing and asserted, *The exact cause of the Event has never been conclusively established. And at any rate, it was responsible for the upheaval that created our species.*

Cornelius' glare forestalled any murmurs of approval. He plowed on with his remarks. *None of us asked to be born. Next, you'll suggest we worship the humans as gods. After all, this abominable program of yours is nothing but a lot of fancy talk that can't cover up the fact that you want our children to grow up to fuck humans. Disgusting!*

A mental cacophony erupted as the other members of the Council expressed their indignation. They weren't just appalled by the breach of decorum, but also by the gross simplification of Lorne's plan.

Lorne raised a hand to quiet them, then fixed his eyes on Cornelius as he projected, *And I suppose you'd prefer our children devolve to the lowly state of our ancestors. Would you prefer that their hands become claws and that they crawl on their bellies? Would you have them cower in fear from humans rather than mingle with them as equals? No one is suggesting that human and Colonist physically mate. Such a thing is not only a gross perversion, it's also a physical impossibility.*

Grainger sighed inwardly. That was politics for you. It was just two sides with irreconcilable differences pretending they were capable of working towards a compromise. He sat back and let the argument flow across his brain without registering the words. It was enough for him to know where he stood and leave it to the younger generation to fight.

Chapter Five
Mutants On The Trail

They broke camp at dawn, breakfasting on protein cakes and distilled water. They loaded their supplies into their motorbikes' sidecars and raked the dusty ground to erase any sign of their presence. Kurt admired the team's efficiency. The entire process took less than half an hour. They'd survived in the open wasteland by operating with clockwork precision. Everyone had a role, and every role was vital.

Campsite cleared and equipment loaded, they fell into formation. Engines revved, belching smoke as their riders tugged their goggles and masks into place.

Kurt swung his leg over his bike and settled into his seat. He strapped Lord Hannibal's location transponder to his wrist and powered it up. Like most post-Event tech, it was made of salvaged parts that had been slapped together by engineers whose genius outpaced the availability of reliable parts. But the transponder beeped to life without a problem and indicated that the group should follow a course West.

"We're heading West for now," Kurt called over the roar and thrum of engines.

"Remember, it might seem empty in these parts, but

there's plenty of danger hiding out there. If something crawls out of the shadows, we'll meet it with force."

Diana chambered a round on her sidecar-mounted rifle for emphasis.

"Damn straight." Taurus nodded approvingly as he tied a bandana over his bearded face. "Well, what the fuck are we waiting for?" Rosemary asked. "Let's kick it into gear, people!"

Kurt gave the signal, raising his fist over his head. The gesture was greeted with shouts of approval. He dropped his hand to the throttle and put the bike in gear.

Although the morning air was dust-choked and the red sky overhead portended nasty weather, it felt good to have the wind in his hair. They'd spent three days camped while he negotiated with Lord Hannibal. He couldn't remember a time when they'd remained idle for so long. It was nice to see the scenery moving once again. Not that there was much to see this deep in the wasteland.

As the group's leader, Kurt rode point, with Diana occupying his bike's sidecar. Her position wasn't honorary. She was one of their best marksmen, and rode with rifle at the ready. Just behind Kurt, riding his rear flanks, were Deus and Taurus. Like Diana, they were skilled with firearms. They also had a knack for spotting danger early. Duke and Rosemary were the rear guard, making sure that there was no one tracking their movements from behind. Lilith and Lucifer, riding a matched set of jet black speeder bikes, acted as scouts. Their bikes could outrun the others with ease, so they roved and circled the group. The rest of the team rode in a tight formation, towing their supplies of equipment and provisions.

The Wasteland. Badlands of the Interior. The Great Desolation. The scenery was just as bleak as the expanse's various names implied. But it was far from empty. Before the Event—that mysterious, destructive force—had fallen upon the planet, this part of the world had been one of wondrous variety. There had been great swaths of forest and farmland, as well as sprawling cities packed with buildings that reached skyward. The crops may have withered to weeds and scrub brush, but the forests still teemed with life, much of it tainted and mutated by the Event's strange energy. The cities, however, were decaying, haunted graveyards. Microclimates of radioactive clouds and howling tornadoes hovered just above the spires of the tallest buildings. Sinkholes opened and closed, swallowing the rusting skeletons of pre-Event machinery and infrastructure.

But that wasn't all. There were things far stranger lurking in the abandoned cities.

Anyone who'd worked as part of a wasteland salvage crew had stories to tell about the weirdness of the cities. The disembodied voices that whispered through the night. The half-glimpsed figures that emerged from the shadows and seemed to exist only in periphery of one's vision.

The constant scratching, skittering noises of unseen subterranean life. Kurt had experienced all of those things and more. And while Duke scoffed at the notion that there were supernatural forces behind any of the phenomenon, the rest of the team wasn't so sure. Still, they were a roughneck salvage crew, and that meant riding headlong into places where most people feared to tread.

Three hours later, the arid desert environment surrounding Lord Hannibal's outpost gave way to the dense, dark greenery of an ancient forest. Their pace slowed to a crawl. Although there had once been a road carved through the forest, the years following the Event had allowed the plants to reclaim much of what had been taken from it. Some portions of the road remained intact, but most of it was broken by tree roots, and overgrown with tangles of vines and weeds.

Grass grew knee-high through cracks in the asphalt. Kurt

was certain his teeth might rattle right out of his skull as his motorcycle bounced over the bumpy ground.

"This is fucking awful!" Diana shouted from the sidecar. "Are you sure about this route?"

Kurt tapped the transponder. "It says we're right on course. Lord Hannibal told me this was the easiest path to our destination."

"Holy shit, I'd hate to see what the hardest path is like," she said.

Kurt turned his head for a moment to look at Taurus. The big man with the wild beard and broad shoulders was Kurt's second in command. An enforcer at times, and a sounding board for strategy at others, Taurus was Kurt's best barometer for danger.

"Don't like it, boss," Taurus answered the unspoken question. "My gut says we're not alone in these woods."

"Head on a swivel, my friend," Kurt said.

Taurus nodded. He patted the holstered pistol on his hip.

Kurt turned his eyes back to the road. It may have been rough, but at least it was straight and somewhat level. After a while, even the roughness began to subside. It was by no means a smooth ride, but the bone-jarring bumps gave way to those that were merely annoying. He loosened his grip on the handlebars, and let his shoulders relax.

Later, when Kurt had time to replay the events in his mind, he'd blame this relatively comfortable stretch of road for lulling him into a false sense of security. But he knew that wasn't the truth. Even Taurus, whose ability to sniff out such things bordered on preternatural, didn't see the ambush until they were in the thick of it.

The things that burst from the trees lining either side of the road could only loosely be identified as human. They had the same basic build as humans—two arms, two legs, and a head that housed the major sensory organs—but all the components were so twisted and malformed that one could be forgiven for thinking that the attackers belonged to some new, undiscovered species of primate. Some were squat, with short limbs covered by lumpy slabs of muscle. Others were tall and gangly with arms that dangled below their knees. Those that weren't naked wore rough garments made of animal hides. All of them were covered in patchy tufts of coarse hair.

Their rheumy, swollen eyeballs bulged from misshapen skulls. Their mouths—some of them packed full of pointed fangs, others nearly toothless—hung open as they screamed high-pitched war cries. Brandishing spears, clubs, and blades made from salvaged metals, they emerged from the forest on all sides. Despite their oddly formed legs with mismatched joints placed seemingly at random, they were fast.

"Fuck!" Taurus shouted. "Hostiles incoming! Defense formation!"

There was a brief roar of engines as the team swung their bikes into a tight circle. The mechanical noise was abruptly silenced as the riders killed the ignitions and dismounted. Behind the wall of their armored motorcycles, the salvage crew drew their weapons.

"Weapons free!" Kurt gave the order, and a fraction of a second later, the guns began to thunder.

Diana swung the barrel of her sidecar-mounted rifle in a slow arc as she fired. It was the closest thing they had to the firepower of pre-Event weaponry, and it could slam out three rounds per second when its clockwork components were well-oiled. And since Diana disassembled and cleaned the gun every night, it was well-oiled indeed. Duke operated a similar rifle from the other side of the formation. Although his weapon was just as well-maintained as Diana's, his aim wasn't as precise. Many of his shots went wide of their mark, slamming into tree trunks or boulders. Lilith and Lucifer both carried long-range rifles. Their weapons were just as deadly as the sidecar-mounted guns, but the scouts weren't there to use them. Kurt cursed himself for sending his scouts so far afield.

And yet, the team still had plenty of firepower. The other members of the team fired smaller rifles or pistols. Although they were slower than the big guns, they were more accurate if the person firing it could keep a level head during a fight. And although they'd never encountered a gang of wasteland mutants before, the members of Kurt's team had been in their fair share of scrapes, and they weren't quick to panic.

The initial burst of fire ripped through the first wave of mutants. Some of them—mostly the tall, slender ones—were cut down easily enough. The sidecar-mounted guns nearly tore them in half. But the squat, muscly ones didn't go down so easily. Their thick hides—because you couldn't call the cracked leathery material that covered their bodies "skin"—seemed to absorb the impact of the bullets. Thick blood oozed from the wounds, but these short figures, with their piggish jowls and stumpy legs, seemed to care little about the pain, if indeed they registered the sensation at all. Fortunately for Kurt's team, this variety of mutant was slow. Hobbled by their short legs and wide hips, they couldn't manage much more than a waddle. They swung their clubs and jabbed with their spears and blades, but the primitive weapons and ragged onslaught were no match for the guns.

Still, Kurt thought, *there's so damn many of them.*

He began to wonder if they'd eventually be overwhelmed by the mutants' sheer numbers.

An order to conserve ammo would have been redundant. The team lived by the rule of finite resources. They were already doing their best to choose their shots. Even Duke, prone to fighting with reckless abandon, wasn't simply firing wildly. He remained calm, choosing his shots for maximum damage.

"Something's gotta give, boss." Taurus stated the obvious. "We can't just sit here throwing bullets into the crowd."

Kurt dodged a spear thrust, and fired at one of the fat mutants. The bullet punched straight through the mutant's single milky eye. The back of its head erupted in a chunky spray of red and pink. Kurt managed a quick glance around the formation to take stock of the situation. Myrna was on the ground, clutching her left shoulder. Blood leaked from between her fingers.

Rosemary knelt beside her, and pulled Myrna's hand away from the wound, then staunched the flow of blood with a sprinkle of coagulant powder and a bandage. Rosemary was the team's battlefield medic, and she had her work cut out for her at the moment. Viz had taken a club blow to the face and lay unconscious at the center of the formation, his nose a broken, bloody mess.

Max's chest was crisscrossed by slashes from a mutant's blade. Although blood had soaked through his shredded shirt and was dripping down his arms, he continued to take careful aim as he fired his pistol.

"These motherfuckers got zero quit in them!" Duke shouted. "What do you suggest, fearless leader?"

"I suggest you shut the fuck up and keep shooting," Kurt snapped, although he saw the man's point. There were no signs that the onslaught was waning.

All around Kurt, guns roared and belched flashes of fire. The staccato percussion of firearms mixed with the delirious battle cries of the mutants. Many of them frothed at the mouth, while others paused their advance just long enough to hack up mouthfuls of vomit which they spat into the matted hair that sprouted from their heads and faces. Their eyes— some had only one while others had three or even four—were wide open and wild with berserker madness.

"Oh, gods of earth and the void…" Deus paused to fire point blank into a mutant's leering face. "We beseech you to help us destroy these pitiful creatures and grant us victory!"

Then, as if Deus' strange gods had heard his prayer, two

shots rang out from above. Kurt looked up and saw that his scouts had returned just in time. Lilith and Lucifer had climbed high into the trees and braced themselves against the stout branches. With their rifles held against their shoulders, they were picking off the mutants at a steady clip. But even with these newly arrived reinforcements, the mutants showed no signs of retreat.

"Oh, gods…" Deus turned away from the attackers. He holstered his pistol and dropped to his knees. "Grant us thy divine fury! Bestow upon us the power to smite our enemies! Let ours be the glory!"

"Fucking hell, Deus…" Kurt stopped shooting just long enough to slap his friend on the back of his bald head. "Would you knock that shit off?"

Deus paid him no mind. He went on shouting incantations to his oddball gods, his hands raised in supplication to the red sky overhead. Kurt drew back his foot to give the mystic a kick in his holy ass, but was stopped short by what he glimpsed emerging from the tree line. A pair of colossal bears lumbered out of the forest, bellowing as they made their way toward the road.

Bears?! Kurt's mind reeled at the sight of the slowly advancing animals. *Bears are cute and cuddly compared to these monsters.*

Like the army of twisted humanoids, the bears had been mutated by the lingering traces of the Event's awful radiation and emissions. They were as tall as three men and nearly as wide. As they approached, they used their massive paws to swat aside trees the way a human explorer might push away a stubborn patch of weeds. The drops of frothy drool that fell from their lips muddied the soil of the forest floor. When they planted their feet on the road, their claws punched through the ancient asphalt. Each step tore away chunks of the road.

One by one, the mutants turned their heads and shrieked in terrified awe at the sight of the two beasts. Suddenly, the fierce battle cries were replaced by hushed chatter that sounded fearful, perhaps even panicked. More importantly, the mutants' focus shifted away from Kurt's team entirely. They stared at the bears in rapt horror. Their foaming mouths hung open in disbelief.

One of their number, a hairy brute with a third eye that stared unblinking from a cavity in his cheek, broke ranks and charged at one of the bears. In one hand, he brandished a spear with a jagged metal tip. His other hand gripped a roughly hewn club. The two bears stared down at the misshapen man as he charged. Although he was big for a man—Kurt put him around seven feet and well over three hundred pounds—he wasn't even half as tall as the smaller of the two bears. A dozen or more of his fellows followed, perhaps inspired by his show of bravery, or simply coming down on the wrong side of the fight or flight question. They charged with their weapons held high. They screamed and raved, but it was apparent to Kurt's ears that their hearts weren't in this fight. The confidence they'd had while attacking a crew of outsiders had deserted them.

Kurt wondered if their diminished brains had the capacity to understand how foolhardy their charge was. In the end, he decided it mattered little. Whether the mutants understood it or not, they were all going to die in short order.

The mutants converged on the bears. They stabbed with spears, hacked with blades, and pummeled with clubs. Some of them pulled hunks of broken asphalt from the ground and hurled them. If the bears were hurt by the assault, they gave no indication. To Kurt, the hulking creatures seemed mildly inconvenienced, if anything. The larger of the bears—a furry giant whose slavering jaws opened to reveal teeth nearly the size of Kurt's forearm—leaned over to swipe with its paw at the crowd of attackers. Cruel claws raked a bloody path through the crowd. The bear scooped one of the mutants into its mouth and disposed of it in three chomps. The smaller bear—although it was strange to describe such an animal as small—followed its companion's example. Soon, both bears were feasting. Some of the mutants screamed as they were devoured. The lucky ones were dead before the bears chewed them to bloody pulp.

The mutants may have been composed of drooling, inbred idiots, but even they recognized the hopelessness of the situation. Those who weren't dead or halfway down the bears' gullets fled into the forest, screaming in terror as they crashed through the underbrush. The bears finished off what remained of their meal and then followed the shrieking mutants into the trees. They left behind a litter of broken bones and scraps of bloody flesh. Almost immediately the air was swarmed with insects the size of small birds. The buzzed overhead in slow circles before descending on the scraps of the bears' feast.

Kurt shook his head in disbelief. "What the fuck just happened?"

"I'll tell you exactly what happened," Deus said, putting a hand on Kurt's shoulder. "The gods answered my prayer."

* * *

Kurt told Rosemary to patch up the wounded as quickly as possible. Once they were safely (and literally) out of the woods, she'd have time to attend to them more thoroughly.

"You got it," she said, wrapping a roll of fabric bandage around Viz's chest. "Give me two minutes and I'll have them ready to move. I don't want to be here when those bears—or whatever they were—decide to come back for dessert."

Kurt looked at Viz. "You going to make it?"

Viz nodded. "It's just a scratch. Nothing I can't handle."

"Good man," Kurt said.

He left Rosemary to it while he checked on the rest of the team. Amazingly, there was nothing beyond superficial damage to any of the bikes, and it looked like no one had sustained more than some nasty looking flesh wounds. And just as Rosemary had promised, they were ready to move in short order.

Lilith and Lucifer climbed down from their snipers' perches and made their way over to Kurt. Lucifer tipped him a lazy salute.

"We were riding parallel to your position," he explained. "Saw that gang of mutants on the move and put two and two together. Had to keep our distance because we were so outnumbered. Picked off a few on the way. Got here as fast as we could."

"Slow going on account of how we had to hang back," Lilith added.

"Good work," Kurt said.

"Yeah, but I think you should really be thanking those damn bears," Lucifer laughed.

"Speak for yourself." Lilith planted the butt of her rifle on her hip and struck a sexy pose.

"I shot a couple dozen of those ugly motherfuckers. As usual, a woman has to come along and save the day."

Lucifer slapped her on the ass. "I got something saved for you, woman."

Kurt left them to their flirtations and continued his inspection of the team. Everyone appeared to be taking the day's events in stride. This may have been their first encounter with mutants, but it was hardly their first firefight. And although there had been some injuries, none of them were immediately serious. As long as Rosemary could successfully stave off serious infection, everyone would walk away with a few fresh scars and one hell of a story.

"Let's mount up and get the fuck out of here," Kurt announced.

Efficient as always, the team didn't waste time answering him; they climbed onto their bikes and into their sidecars.

"It's a good thing you keep me around," Deus said as he wheeled his bike alongside Kurt. "I prayed for divine intervention and it was given to us."

"Yeah, you said that already," Kurt said.

"I'm simply reminding you that we are surrounded by divine power, even in this wasteland." Deus stirred the air with a complicated hand gesture. "Blessed are we."

Kurt smiled, but he knew there was nothing divine about what had just transpired. Out here in the wasteland, it was just the way of things: every predator was prey for something more ruthless.

Chapter Six
A Secret Army

It took Cornelius three hours to travel from the central hub of the Delta Colony to the western border. From there, it was another hour to the condemned tunnel system beneath the abandoned city. Destabilized by the turn of the century earthquakes, the maze of tunnels which had once connected the Colony to several outposts was now considered off limits under penalty of law. But Cornelius didn't care about that. As far as he was concerned, he was well beyond the reach of the law.

He seethed every step of the way. The straps of the backpack he carried—heavy with tinned provisions—bit into his shoulders. The pain was sharp, magnifying his annoyance until his jaw throbbed with it. He ground his back teeth. His incisors bit into his lower lip.

This deep underground, the tunnels dripped condensation, and it wasn't long before his robe was soaked through. He cursed himself for not dressing for the occasion, but he'd been preoccupied with the arguments of yesterday's Council meeting.

He paused before reaching the border gate, stepping into a shadowy alcove to wait for the guard to pass. These days, nobody had much interest in straying beyond the comforts of the Colony, and the border was a post reserved for the elderly or the well-meaning incompetent. The guard on duty this morning was an obese, doddering specimen, his shuffling gait made all the more awkward by his protruding belly. He looked as pregnant as Sister Ursula. As he limped past, Cornelius caught a few stray thoughts from the old codger's brain.

Just a couple more hours until I can sit down to a plate of sausages and a pitcher of beer. Gods be damned, but don't my feet ache.

Cornelius sneered. He waited for the old fool to pass out of sight, then sprang from the shadows and tossed his backpack over the fence. He checked to make sure the noise hadn't attracted the elderly guard's attention, then climbed over the fence. Once his feet touched the concrete floor on the other side of the fence, he was outside the Colony's protection. The sweet thrill of freedom washed over him like a breaking wave.

Finally…

He took a deep breath, filling his lungs until his chest swelled. Although the air was dank and rotten, for Cornelius, it was pure nectar. He broke into a run, his claws scratching on the rough, damp concrete beneath his feet. He stopped beside a door in the tunnel wall. Using a key he produced from his robe's pocket, he unlocked the door and stepped into the small room behind it. There, hanging on a metal hook, was his yellow body suit. Beside it, on a set of rusty metal shelves, were his boots and respirator unit.

He grabbed the body suit, then shrugged out of his wet robe and hung it on the hook to dry. He zipped himself into the yellow suit, then stomped into the heavy black boots. Next, he checked his respirator unit. This long after the Event, such a precaution was most likely unnecessary, but Cornelius knew that his survival was instrumental to his species' success in the world to come. Whenever possible, he had to avoid risking himself. He fitted the helmet over his head and clamped it into place. A quick systems check told him that his suit—stolen two years ago from the Colony's emergency center—was fully functional.

At last, he was ready to ascend to the higher levels of the underground world. He shouldered his backpack and left the closet, closing and locking the door behind him, then proceeded further down the concrete path. At the end of this hallway, there was a ladder which led to the upper levels. It was nothing more than a series of rusty metal rungs set into the concrete wall, but they were sturdy enough. Cornelius climbed at a steady pace, enjoying the feel of his muscles working. Fifty rungs later, he'd arrived at the entrance to the dead city's sewer.

Abandoning the silence of his pretentious colleagues, he squeaked and chittered like a member of the lowest caste of rodent as his feet splashed in the stagnant water. Once upon a time, he'd made these vocalizations as a protest against what he saw as the total abandonment of the clan's traditions and heritage. Now, he did it because it felt good. Giving into his primal urges always did. Perhaps there was some philosophical lesson to be drawn from this—Brother Lorne and his slut wife would probably debate it for hours—but Cornelius no longer cared for such highfaluting nonsense. They weren't human, and they never would be. And that wasn't the curse that Lorne and Ursula and their toadies on the Council thought it was. In time, they'd come to see that Cornelius was right about that. And if not, well, they would still serve a purpose in the new world to come. Cornelius knew his race was superior to *homo sapiens,* and if he couldn't make that point clear beyond all doubt in the Council chamber, then he'd do so by brute force.

Truth be told, he preferred the latter method anyway. The greatest progress always began with violent upheaval. That was one of many mantras he'd preached to his small but dedicated group of followers. It wasn't just an empty slogan, either. Cornelius believed it with all his heart.

Deeper and deeper he went into the maze of tunnels, far from the glow of the Colony's lights. He knew every twist and turn of this labyrinth by heart, and even in total darkness, his pace was swift. The last hour of the journey always passed by quickest. It seemed to take mere minutes to arrive at the tunnel junction in the sewer system of the dead city.

Cornelius paused for a moment to catch his breath, then pulled a chemical torch from his robe's inner pocket. He pressed a button, gave the torch a quick shake as the fluids within mingled, then blinked as his eyes adjusted to the device's greenish-yellow glow. The light shone on the bones scattered over the floor. He kicked aside a skull and a mismatched pair of femurs, took a deep breath, and projected the thoughts that called his army to his side.

Come to me, my children!

Come to me, my children!

His ears perked up at the first tentative squeak.

Come to me, my children!

Your leader has arrived!

A chorus of squeaks and squeals joined the first voice. And soon, Cornelius could hear their mental voices. These projected thoughts brought a smile to Cornelius' lips. Childish, perhaps even primitive, these voices were still a revelation. According to all the accepted wisdom of Cornelius' peers, the members of the lower caste were incapable of telepathic communication. The Colonial establishment viewed their lower caste brethren—a living, breathing piece of their evolutionary line—as lowly animals, an embarrassing reminder of their past. They were not allowed within the confines of the Delta Colony, and the penalty for trespass was death. How utterly barbaric, and from a class of beings who thought themselves enlightened. Cornelius spat on the floor in disgust.

The chorus of his army's mental projections came to him in a rush of overlapping thoughts: *yes yes we come to our leader our father yes we come to our father we hunger father we hunger for flesh we hunger...*

Their thoughts swelled to a chorus in his brain, filling him with the exhilaration of pure animal instinct. It felt good to return, even vicariously, to the primal. Cornelius closed his eyes and enjoyed the noise, even when he could no longer pick a single coherent thought from the chaotic whirl of mental voices. He sucked air through his respirator and sighed. This was where he belonged.

In short order, his army appeared, racing out of the darkness of the sewer tunnel to assemble in a ragged formation at his feet. Their thoughts quieted, as did their vocalizations. They squatted on their muscular haunches and looked up at him with their glossy black eyes. Their whiskers twitched in anticipation.

Only tinned provisions this week, Cornelius projected. *I'm sorry, my children.*

A ripple of disappointment spread through the collective. But there was no resentment in them. His army's loyalty was unwavering.

But our time is at hand, he continued. *And soon, your days of starvation and scavenging will be but a memory.*

This time, the thought ripple that spread through the crowd was one of happiness.

Cornelius, spread his arms wide in a benevolent gesture as he took stock of his army. Scavengers or not, they were beautiful specimens. Their fur was sleek and brown-black. Their eyes shone with pure animal instinct. The Event had done little to alter their appearance from the rats that Cornelius had studied in the history books in the Colony's library. They'd survived the Event unscathed, most likely due to their subterranean habitats. And somewhere along the recent evolutionary line, which was accelerated by the after-effects of the Event, genetic material from these humble creatures had mingled with that of humans. Thus, the species to which Cornelius belonged. Publicly, he decried this sort of science as blasphemy, but he did so for political reasons. The bleeding hearts on the Council may have been wrong about many things, but they were right about the origins of the species[4*]. It was the conclusions they drew from such knowledge that were wrong.

Soon, you will once again feast on human flesh, he projected. *The first battle of the coming war is drawing nearer by the day. And though it will be a relatively small affair, it will offer a glimpse of our triumph to come. A deal has been made. Soon you will match your strength against human scavengers from the wasteland. And when you have proved your worth, we'll turn our attention to the Colony. But for now, you must try to be content with this cold, dead food.*

Cornelius unzipped his backpack and withdrew some of the canned foodstuffs. Protein-carbohydrate mush. Vegetable slurry. Vitamin enriched pellets. It was the sort of thing that stocked the shelves of the Colony's emergency shelters. Items that wouldn't be missed. Taking supplies from the pantries of the communal dining halls was the sort of thing that would eventually arouse suspicion. There was a committee devoted entirely to tracking the Colony's inventory of supplies, and they were zealous in their duties. Of course they were. The Colony was quickly becoming nothing more than a collection of bureaucratic eggheads, seemingly intent on transforming themselves into a facsimile of pre-Event humans. They'd long

---

[*] [4] Although the views written in Brother Darius' *On the Origin of Our Species* were considered by the Colonial Board of Education to be settled science, there was still opposition to their teachings, mostly from a vocal minority of religious fundamentalists. They made up a large portion of the political base responsible for Brother Cornelius' election to the Colonial Council.

ago given up exploring the full potential of their young species. They'd traded visions of a glorious future for lives of bean-counting and parliamentary procedure. And that's why Cornelius was careful to cover his tracks. To take only the bare minimum of food. To keep his absences as short as possible. A successful evolution, Cornelius had discovered, didn't just rely on passion. It relied on foresight and careful planning.

He opened the cans and spread the contents on a relatively dry patch of concrete, then stepped aside to watch his troops dine.

Soon, my children. Soon.

When his army had finished their meager feast, Cornelius dismissed all of them except for a squad of three rats. They were young males, not much more than pups, but they were bright-eyed, sleek-coated, and strong. He opened a can of protein mash that he'd reserved, but he didn't set it down before them.

The trap has been baited and set. But that is not enough. The enemy that will soon arrive at the gates of our city is traveling across a dangerous stretch of the wasteland.

The trio of young soldiers were disciplined. They kept their eyes fixed on him rather than the can of food in his hand.

It is essential to my plan that they arrive unharmed, he continued. *Essential for the strength of our army, both as a food source and a demonstration of our power. Before we make our way into the Colony, we must be at full strength.*

Disciplined or not, the soldiers were growing restless.

yes, great leader, yes, they answered.

I'm dispatching you as a scout party. You will be my eyes and ears. Observe and listen, Cornelius ordered. *Keep your distance. Intervene only if absolutely necessary.*

yes, yes, great leader…

Cornelius emptied the contents of the can onto the damp concrete. *You may eat. You'll follow this path to an outpost…*

While the troops devoured the brown glop, Cornelius projected a map of the route to Bruno's Last Rest into their consciousness. Their eager minds—enhanced by the slowly evolving brains in their skulls—absorbed the information. It burrowed deep into their brains, settling into the same folds of tissue where instinct resided. They would know and follow the path without conscious effort. Like migratory birds, they would simply feel that they were moving in the right direction.

The prevailing wisdom of the scientific community held that such a projection into the brains of their lower cousins was impossible. The Colony's deep thinkers dismissed such notions outright. Their bigoted ignorance was the greatest weapon in Cornelius' arsenal. It assured him that when his revolutionary army crashed through the Colonial gates, they would have the element of surprise on their side. The Colonists—grown flaccid and weak beneath the blanket of worldly comfort—would recoil in shock and awe. Devastated and defeated, they'd have no choice but to look to him for leadership. And he would oblige them with an iron fist.

Chapter Seven
Breakfast Of Champions

Duke was already awake when Taurus shook his shoulder and told him it was his turn for guard duty. Even though Taurus wore soft-soled boots and was as stealthy as any member of the team, Duke had heard him coming. No, that wasn't quite it. Duke had *felt* him coming. He'd *sensed* Taurus' approach. A lifetime of surviving topside had given Duke a sort of psychic radar. He didn't think much of it, really. That was just how it went in this world. You either developed a survival mechanism or you died.

"Last shift has arrived. Looks like it's your turn, my friend," Taurus said, gripping Duke's shoulder.

"Thanks," Duke said, unzipping himself from his sleeper bag.

"All quiet out there." Taurus pulled the night vision goggles off his head and passed them to Duke. "Should be an easy job."

"Sounds good to me. I got no problem with easy jobs. Sleep well," Duke said.

He stood and stretched, yawning away the last vestiges of sleep. His aching body protested. The battle with the mutants had left him bruised and sore, but he'd escaped any serious injury. They'd been lucky. Kurt had managed to steer them directly into an ambush, and it was a miracle that Viz, Max, and Myrna had escaped with mere flesh wounds. Had it not been for the arrival of those bears…

Duke collected his rifle, tugged on the night vision goggles, then picked his way through the camp. He stepped outside the circle of sleeping bodies and began his slow march around the perimeter of the campsite. He paused halfway through his first lap to piss. He sighed with satisfaction as the stream of urine spattered and splashed on the dirt. Just a few yards away, Rosemary was sleeping. The thought of being close to her while his member was out in the open thrilled him. Ever since Kurt had assigned her to his sidecar, Duke had been struggling to find a way to get into her pants. In his experience, women were never easy, but this one was a particular challenge. Still, Duke was sure he'd find the chink in her armor. He was nothing if not confident. And that was why he was certain that not only would he soon climb atop Rosemary, but he'd also find himself leading the team. Kurt had given it his best shot, but he'd proven time and again that he didn't have what it took to survive in the wasteland. Duke didn't understand why the others hadn't arrived at the same conclusion yet, but the time was coming when he'd be able to offer them undeniable proof.

And if they don't like it, Duke thought as he shook off the last drops, *they're always free to go their own way. Rosemary and I won't shed any tears for them.*

He continued his perimeter stroll, gazing through his goggles at the flat expanse of grassland. After the day's battle, Kurt had led them off course so they could be safely out of the forest by nightfall. Lord Hannibal's transponder beacon had beeped insistently, but Kurt decided to ignore it. He trusted Lilith and Lucifer to scout a route to safety. And, as luck would have it, the scouts delivered. They'd spotted a break in the woods, a large grassland in a shallow valley.

Duke had protested, asserting that the low-lying position made them sitting ducks for another ambush, but he'd been overruled. Kurt, typically overconfident, waved off Duke's input.

Duke had gone to sleep half-hoping that they might be attacked during the night. Maybe then the rest of the team would see how unfit for leadership Kurt was. But so far, the night had passed without incident. It was quiet, almost eerily so, compared to the constant shriek and chatter of wildlife in the forest. That would change in a few hours, when they broke camp and got back on route to their destination. Back into the forest they'd go, following Kurt on this latest adventure.

Duke sneered and hawked up a wad of phlegm. He spat on the ground as he put one foot in front of the other. He envisioned a series of scenarios in which he could seize leadership of the group. He'd send Kurt and his bitch Diana packing, then take Rosemary as his own, whether she liked it or not. And then? Well, the world may have gone to hell but there was still glory to be had. Lord Hannibal was getting too comfortable atop the food chain. Someone was bound to come along and topple him from the throne. Duke saw no reason that he himself shouldn't be the one to do it.

He was so wrapped up in his fantasies, each more elaborate and violent than the last, that he didn't see the creature emerge from the tall grass at the edge of the valley. By the time he noticed it, the animal had drawn close enough that Duke could have seen it even without the aid of the night vision goggles. It was a wild boar, all bristly fur and curved, razor-sharp tusks. Like the bears the team encountered during the day, the creature had grown to grotesque proportions. Its sides, crisscrossed with heavy scars, worked like a bellows as it breathed in the damp night air. Its glowing red eyes stared back at Duke with unblinking intensity.

"You're a big ugly motherfucker," Duke whispered, raising his rifle to his shoulder.

The boar took a step forward, seemingly as a challenge. Duke smiled at the animal's stupid bravery. His finger tightened on the trigger. He drew in a slow, deep breath, and then—

DEVOUR YOU

The three syllables roared inside Duke's skull. He dropped his rifle and clapped his hands over his ears. But the gesture did nothing to quiet the guttural vocalizations in his brain.

KILL EAT DEVOUR

The boar began to plod forward, clearly in no hurry. Duke dropped to his knees and grabbed blindly for his rifle as tears ran from his eyes. His vision blurred. He tore the goggles from his head and tossed them aside. At last, his fingers closed around the rifle's grip. He brought the weapon to his shoulder. His hands shook as he struggled to draw a bead on the boar.

KILL EAT KILL EAT KILL EAT

The boar charged, its hooves thumping on the packed dirt ground. Duke screamed as he fired. The first shot went lower than Duke had intended, but it was a lucky accident. The bullet splintered the boar's foreleg, and the animal went down face first. Its tusks carved trenches in the ground. By the time it had recovered and began trying to resume its charge on three legs, Duke was ready to fire again. This shot hit the boar's massive right flank, and it toppled the beast again.

HURT FIRE PAIN HURT

The alien thoughts filling Duke's head were just as loud, perhaps even louder now that the boar was wounded, but Duke was able to handle the noise. The adrenaline from the encounter made him giddy, and his own thoughts cut through the mental cacophony.

Gods above, he thought, *it's like that fucking pig is broadcasting its thoughts into my brain.*

The response was immediate. *YES IN YOUR HEAD KILL YOU KILLED ME PAIN*

Duke heard the sounds of panicked movement in the camp behind him.

You're in my head? Pig, are you in my fucking brain? Duke's thoughts were a mental scream.

PIG DYING PIG DYING

Now, the other members of the salvage team were swarming him, peppering him with questions. Duke shrugged them off and staggered across the short stretch of open ground between himself and the dying boar.

I killed you, Duke thought, gazing down at the wounded animal.

YES KILLED PIG DYING YOU KILLED

This is too fucking weird to even contemplate. Duke stifled a laugh.

DEAD...

And then, just as suddenly as the alien voice had intruded into his thoughts, it was quiet. The voices of his teammates swam into the silence.

"Hey, man, you okay?" Taurus asked, standing at his side.

Duke wiped the tears from his cheeks. "Yeah, I'm fine. Big ugly fucker came out of nowhere."

"Good thing you know how to handle that rifle." This time it was Rosemary who spoke. She slapped Duke on the shoulder. "Not bad, partner. Not bad at all."

He smiled. Maybe this was the opportunity he'd been waiting for. "Well, you know, I do what I can to provide for the team. Sometimes, one of us has to step up and do what's necessary."

"Like I said partner, you done good." Rosemary's hand lingered on his shoulder a moment longer this time.

Duke turned and looked over his shoulder to make sure

Kurt was within earshot. Then he turned back to the others gathered around him. He pointed to the freshly killed boar. "Looks like breakfast is served."

* * *

Although it meant delaying their departure by an entire day, Kurt agreed that it was in everyone's best interest to recuperate from the prior day's excitement. He cautioned them that it meant the following day would start early and would entail some hard riding, but no one protested. Taurus and Duke set to work butchering the boar, while Lilith and Lucifer prepared a cook fire. Deus broke out his private stash of sacramental liquor. He went from one person to the next, offering prayers and blessings along with generous portions of the fiery liquid.

Kurt sat on his sleeping bag at the edge of camp, watching the festivities from a distance. Diana detached herself from the group and made her way over to him, a tiny cup of Deus' liquor in each hand. She sat beside him, easing herself down carefully to avoid spilling any of the precious liquid.

"Hey there, hot stuff," she said, offering him one of the cups. "Fancy a shot of the holy liquor?"

He waved it away. "Better not. At least one of us needs to remain sober. You never know what other monstrosity might decide to come out of the forest and try to eat us. But you go right ahead."

"Sure?"

He nodded. "Drink up."

Diana tossed back both shots in quick succession. She winced. Tears sprang to the corners of her eyes.

"Holy shit," she wheezed. "Fuck me, what the hell is in this stuff?"

Kurt chuckled. "Probably better that you didn't know."

He leaned back, propping himself up on one elbow. Once

Diana had sufficiently recovered, she settled against him, sighing contentedly. They were silent for a moment as they watched the activities of the camp. Taurus and Duke were engaged in a good natured argument about how to carve up the boar. Lilith and Lucifer had ducked behind the freshly ignited fire to kiss and grope each other. The others were gathered in a circle around Deus, who was spinning stories from some obscure holy book. His sermons ran from ponderous and boring to ribald and hilarious, in accordance with how much sacramental liquor had been passed out. Judging by the bursts of laughter from his small congregation, the liquor was flowing freely. Beams of sunlight poked through the red haze overhead. Kurt almost smiled as he turned his gaze upward. If you were patient enough, you could glimpse patches of blue sky behind the drifting red and grey clouds.

"A day like this, you can almost imagine what it was like before the Event," Diana said. "Do you ever wonder about that? Do you think it was paradise and that the Event was a punishment sent from the gods? That's what Deus says."

Kurt draped his arm around her and kissed the back of her neck. "Deus is my friend, but he's full of shit. Nobody can say for sure what the world was like before the Event. All we know is that it was different. There's evidence of that. But paradise? I doubt it. If people were around before the Event, there's really zero chance of that."

"What do you mean?"

"I mean that people create great things just to turn around and fuck it all up. That's the history of mankind, right there. As it was, as it is, as it shall be again. That's some of Deus' scripture, I think."

Diana turned over on her side. She pushed Kurt playfully, and he obliged, flopping onto his back. She swung her leg over him, straddling his waist.

"Listen to the grumpy man," she said, leaning over to kiss him.

Kurt kissed her, but he stopped things from going any further. It was one thing for Lucifer and Lilith to go at it in plain view of the rest of the team, but they weren't leaders. Kurt preferred to keep his couplings with Diana more discreet. Diana's face registered some disappointment, but this was a discussion they'd had more than once. She accepted defeat and climbed off him. They lay side by side, watching the slow passage of the clouds overhead.

"We could have lost three of us yesterday," Kurt said. "Viz, Max, Myrna…"

"They were just flesh wounds." Diana waved a hand dismissively. "You heard Rosemary.

After she got them stitched up, she said they were going to be fine."

"It could have just as easily gone the other way. And don't bother arguing the point. You're a beautiful woman, Diana. Probably too beautiful to be out here in the wasteland, but all the same, here you are. And that means you know that the difference between life and death in that kind of battle is a matter of inches."

"They knew the risks when they signed up. You said it yourself."

Kurt turned his head to look at her. She really was beautiful, although not in the same way as the women who lounged around in Lord Hannibal's hash den. Diana had grown up hard, working alongside her brothers at a riverside fishing operation on the west coast. Her childhood had been relatively safe, but she was expected to work from an early age. Working the river was hard indeed, and it had given her an athlete's body. Her arms and legs were lean and toned. Her hands were calloused. She was short and slender, but she was strong. That strength had served her well when a rival fishing company had launched a midnight raid on Diana's village and killed her family, forcing her to flee into the world on her own.

"I heard a story once," Kurt said. "Back when I was still just a child living in the crèche. One of the elders said something about how there were other worlds up there. Past the sky, I mean. He said the stars were the lights of these worlds which were so far away that the mind couldn't even imagine the distance. I used to think about that. I used to wonder if there was someone on one of those distant worlds looking up at the night sky and spotting our little planet."

"That's a nice thought."

"Yeah, but that's all it is," Kurt sighed. "If there are other planets drifting around past where our sky ends, I'll never see them. But if there's a better place up north, well, that's something I might actually see."

* * *

Deus preached and sermonized through the first two rounds of liquor, but by the time the team was tossing back their third shots, he knew it was a lost cause. There was a brief window between sobriety and intoxication when the mind was suited to divine persuasion, and that window slammed shut suddenly. Minds opened by liquor were clouded by the same, and theological discussion gave way to dirty jokes and tall tales.

There was a time when such a shift in mood would have annoyed, even angered, Deus. But that time had long since passed. He'd left the confines of the monastery of The Church of the Aftermath when he discovered that the clergy was a group of perverted hypocrites. The High Magus himself was a child-buggering degenerate who used his divine office as a shield to hide his deviancy. Deus was only a novice monk of seventeen years when this crisis of faith sent him out into the world, armed with nothing but a battered copy of *The New*

Scripture of Clementine and a clockwork pistol he'd swiped from a monastery guard. Two decades among the nonbelievers and heathens had dulled his idealism. These days, he didn't even bother with his daily devotions.

So when his retelling of the Parable of the Whore and the Hat Maker was met with snickers and jeers rather than silent introspection, Deus felt only minor annoyance.

"Very well," he said, tucking his book of scripture into the hip pocket of his trousers. "I see that you prefer inebriation to salvation. Just know that the fires of damnation will make yonder cook fire look like a small spark."

Max blew out a raspberry then followed it up with a rude gesture.

"Funny you should make that gesture," Deus said. "I had considered preaching about the pitfalls of chronic self-abuse by recounting the parable of the blind man and the shepherd's daughter, but I didn't want you to feel singled out."

Max laughed, pressing a hand to his wounded side. "Oh, man, come on…I can't even…"

"I'm surprised your right arm wasn't strong enough to fight off every single one of those mutants," Myrna chimed in, mimicking the rude gesture. "I guess all those workouts haven't been intense enough."

"Yeah, well, anytime you feel like helping out, just holler," Max said.

Myrna rolled her eyes. "You wish."

Deus turned his back and left them to their trash talk. He happened to know that, despite her protests, Myrna had spent some private time with both Max during the team's last sabbatical at the Blue Oasis outpost. Unbelievers or not, these people were his flock, and he made his business to know everything about them. It wasn't always easy. Kurt and Diana were open about their relationship, and you'd have to be blind and deaf not to recognize Lucifer and Lilith's devotion to one another. But aside from those two couples, the team kept their dalliances discreet. While Deus found their discretion admirable, he wondered why they bothered. There was no judgment among the team members. In that regard, many of the unbelievers outshone the members of the church.

He walked to the edge of the clearing and gazed up at the wooded slope leading out of the valley. Although it was almost certainly filled with dangers like those they'd encountered yesterday, the green expanse was beautiful. From a distance, one could almost imagine that the tales of a garden paradise, as told in *The New Scripture of Clementine*, could be true. And it was even easier to imagine that this valley could be a safe haven from the perils of the sinful world.

With some hard work, it could be a homestead to equal those of the east coast or west of the mountains. Not some ramshackle wasteland outpost, but an actual *homestead*. They were surrounded by a forest that could provide both lumber and food. At this low elevation, it wouldn't be hard to dig a well.

He turned in a slow circle, watching the activity around him. Duke and Taurus had improvised a grill to cook the boar. They stood beside the fire, admiring their work. A short distance away, Kurt and Diana were lying side by side, cloud-gazing. Behind him, the rest of the group continued their raucous laughter. For the moment, it was even possible to forget that the world they'd inherited was one of violence and degradation.

Alas, Deus knew their respite would be brief. In the morning, they'd break camp and continue their journey through the forest. They'd face new dangers on the way to their destination, where even greater dangers might wait. That was their destiny, passed down to them from the gods.

* * *

"Blessed be the clarity of thought you receive from this elixir," Deus said. "Brother Duke and Brother Taurus, drink deeply of the gods' blessings."

The bald mystic gave Duke and Taurus each a small cup of clear liquid.

"Yeah, sure," Taurus said, raising one massive calloused hand to accept the offering.

"Why not?" Duke figured he could use a drink.

Deus handed him a cup, then made some complicated hand gestures. "Blessed be, brothers."

Duke tossed back his shot of Deus' holy firewater as he watched the slabs of pork sizzle and drip as they roasted over the slow-burning fire. It was his third drink of the day, but it wasn't doing the trick. His mind was still a confused jumble. During the encounter with the boar, his endocrine system had pumped so much adrenaline into his bloodstream that he hadn't been able to think about anything but direct, immediate action. And in the aftermath, he'd been surrounded by the other members of the team. Unwilling to discuss the experience with anyone until he had time to analyze it for himself, Duke had pushed his confusion to the back of his brain. He was grateful when Taurus and Deus told him they were headed back to the main campsite. Some time alone, that's what Duke needed.

"You got this?" Taurus asked, pointing to their improvised grill.

"I grew up eating wasteland game," Duke said. "This ain't my first barbecue."

The strong man and the mystic laughed as they turned and headed back across the clearing.

And then, finally, Duke had a chance to think about what had happened.

He considered the idea that the voice in his head was merely a product of his own subconscious rather than a telepathic communication from a wild animal. This certainly seemed like the most plausible explanation from an objective point of view.

But the problem with that theory was, Duke couldn't force himself into any objectivity. After all, he'd been there. He'd experienced the whole thing. He'd felt that voice pounding away at the backs of his eyeballs from inside his skull. He'd felt the primal thoughts pushing into his brain. He knew that there was no way that voice and those thoughts were his. They weren't side effects of blind panic either. Duke had grown up in the wasteland. He'd faced down his share of rampaging wild animals. When he'd told Taurus that he'd grown up eating wasteland game, Duke had been telling the truth. Alongside his father and brother, he'd stalked and killed countless strange creatures. Many of those creatures hadn't been passive quarry. When cornered, some of them had turned around and launched a counterattack. Although the boar's size and speed had been shocking, it wasn't outside the extremes of his experience.

When he eliminated the possibility that the voice had originated within himself, what did that leave? Could a member of his own team be fucking with him? Did one of them—someone loyal to Kurt, who suspected Duke of harboring mutinous ideas—try to distract him long enough for the boar to kill him? Again, this theory didn't track. For one thing, Duke was wasteland born and raised, so his senses were highly attuned. If someone in the camp had been awake and following him on his perimeter walk, he'd have noticed. And if one of them suspected that he was gunning for Kurt's spot, there were easier ways of bringing it to the team's attention.

"What the fuck, then?" Duke whispered, using his machete to turn some of the meat.

He faced the only other possibility he could think of. The intrusive thoughts had been actual telepathic communication from the boar.

"Is that it?" He poked one of the larger chunks of meat. "Were you a smart motherfucker? Did you have some superpowers? Hope they don't make your meat taste weird."

He laughed. Maybe the liquor was doing the trick, after all.

But the idea wasn't so strange, really. Out here in the wasteland, you heard plenty of weird stories. Animals with the gift of telepathy wouldn't even be among the weirdest. And what about the Colonists? It was pretty close to accepted fact that they communicated via telepathy, although they weren't animals. Well, they probably weren't animals. Nobody knew exactly what they were.

During his years wandering the wasteland, Duke had never actually seen a Colonist, but he'd heard plenty of stories. His father claimed to have survived a Colonist raid on his childhood village. To hear Duke's father tell it, the Colonists came out of the night as silent, deadly, and invulnerable as armor-plated ghosts. They'd abducted the women and children, tossing them into the back of a transport vehicle like prisoners of war. Any of the male villagers who opposed them were dispatched with cruel efficiency.

Once Duke had struck out on his own after one too many arguments with his family, he'd heard many more accounts of encounters with the Colonists. Some were just as terrifying and violent as the one his father told, but the majority were simply weird. At trading outposts, there were wasteland travelers who told of peaceful encounters with the strange, silent Colonists. None of these tales—even those that were so tall they beggared belief—contained a physical description of what the Colonists looked like beneath their protective suits and helmets.

But there were some aspects of the stories that were consistent across all their various retellings. One strangely specific detail was that cats and Colonists shared a mutual distaste for one another. It was also said that some of these odd beings traveled with human interpreters, people who were somehow blessed (or maybe cursed) with the ability to receive and decode the Colonists' psychic babble. This last bit was the one that stuck out in Duke's mind as he watched the pieces of freshly cut pork sizzle over the fire.

If there were humans who could understand the silent language of the Colonists, could there also be humans who could communicate with the strange animals that roamed the wasteland forests? Was some congenital psychic ability finally rousing itself from decades-long slumber and manifesting in his brain? If that was the case, what did it mean?

Duke thought it over as he sprinkled salt over the meat. After careful consideration, he chose to view this new ability as yet another sign that he was more qualified than Kurt to lead their salvage team. Something—perhaps fate, perhaps the gods Deus worshipped—was showing Duke that it was his destiny to lead. Really, the more he thought of it, the clearer it became.

Chapter Eight
The Black Drug

Deus waited until the camp's attention was fully engaged with their own revelry, then he slipped away, walking towards the edge of the valley. Behind him, the braying laughter and drunken boasting faded from a raucous din to a dull roar, and, as Deus moved even farther away, eventually to silence.

He paused at the edge of the clearing to make sure that his departure had gone unnoticed. Duke was still tending the meat as it roasted and smoked over the fire. Kurt and Diana were lost in their own private world, staring so fixedly at the clouds overhead that they might as well have been drifting through the sky themselves. The rest of the team was still engaged in boisterous fellowship. Deus was quite alone as he disappeared into the tree line at the border between the clearing and the valley walls. Although the weather was as cloudy as any other wasteland midday, the campsite had been pleasantly warm. But beneath the tree canopy, the temperature dropped. It was dim and cool here, which Deus believed to be the optimum conditions for communing with the gods.

He walked until he found a boulder with a reasonably flat

surface and a covering of thick moss. He climbed atop the rock and made himself comfortable. The moss was damp, but it was also as soft as any cushion.

"Better a wet ass than a sore one," he said.

He reached beneath his tunic and searched its various pockets until his fingers felt the smooth surface of the waxed leather bag.

"Yes, there you are." He smiled as he brought the bag out and untied the braided cords that cinched it shut. "The cosmic keys to insight."

The bag contained a coarsely ground powder with an aroma so pungent that it filled the air as soon as the bag was opened. At a short distance, the smell was simply sour and a bit unpleasant. Up close, it brought tears to one's eyes and tickled the hairs in one's nose. Even Deus, who had been familiar with the powder from an early age, had to wipe the tears from his cheeks.

The powder was a formula known only to the High Magus of the Church of the Aftermath and his assistant clerics. And, of course, to Deus. He'd copied the recipe from a book stolen from the High Magus' personal library before his expulsion from the church. Back then, he'd carried the formula scrawled on a scrap of paper. Now, he carried it in his head, having long since committed the recipe to memory. It contained the pollen of certain flowers, the black spores of several varieties of mushroom, the scent glands from a female tree frog, and the egg sac from a river carp. Fermented in a jar, then dried and ground to powder, these ingredients combined to make a substance known only as the Black Drug. It wasn't suitable for novices or nonbelievers. Deus had heard that it was deadly if administered to a virgin, although he'd never witnessed such a thing take place. Of course, it wasn't an easy proposition, finding an adult virgin in this sin-besotted world.

"Gods above and gods below," he said, softly, "I open the doorways of my mind and humbly beseech you to enter."

He pinched a small amount of powder between his thumb and forefinger, then brought it to his nose. The scent was so overpowering that he was forced to close his eyes. He took a deep breath and let it out, then sniffed sharply. A fierce burning filled his sinuses as he blindly fumbled with the bag, careful not to spill any of the precious contents as he placed it back into his pocket. Bitter mucus filled the back of his throat. He swallowed convulsively in a desperate effort to avoid gagging. Although he was an experienced user of the Black Drug, he still found this first part of the process painful. His chest tingled then burned. His heart raced, beating with such force that he was sure that, were it not for his ribcage, it might jump out of his chest and hop away across the forest floor like a toad. His stomach heaved and contracted. His skin seemed to be on fire one second, and bathed in ice the next. He shook with convulsions so strong that he was sure they'd separate every joint in his body.

And then, as suddenly as they'd come on, the side effects stopped. It was as if some switch had been flipped between agony and serenity. A sense of well-being—as warm and inviting as a hot spring—washed over him. His body felt loose and relaxed. He opened his mouth to offer up a prayer, but all he could manage was a string of garbled syllables. The intoxication was pleasant. It was worth the few short minutes of agony he'd just endured.

He slipped off the boulder, throwing his arms out for balance, when his feet hit the ground. His sense of equilibrium struggled to catch up with the sudden movement, and for a moment, the world wobbled and spun around him. His vision blurred and swam, turning the forest foliage into a sea of mingled colors. Gradually, his surroundings resolved into soft-edged focus.

"As it was, as it is, and as it shall be again." The words felt thick and syrupy as he spoke. He couldn't tell if he was shouting or whispering. Then again, he might not have spoken aloud at all. When the Black Drug took hold, perception became too slippery to be certain of anything.

He gathered his tunic and tugged it over head. The cool air felt electric against his exposed flesh. He kicked off his shoes and sighed as the soles of his feet touched the earth. It was such a thrilling sensation that he dropped his pants and stepped out of them. A gentle breeze stirred through the trees and caressed him, seeming to linger on his most sensitive parts. The Black Drug had awakened his physical senses, and soon it would awaken those of the psychic variety. His thoughts had been reduced to a fragmented jumble by the Black Drug in order to clear the pathways of perception. This was what it meant to be the team's spiritual leader.

Whether or not the rest of the team believed in his visions was of little importance. It only mattered that Deus believed them. His faith was strong enough for the other ten members.

He walked deeper into the woods, following the gentle slope of the valley walls upward until he came to a narrow creek. He sat on the bank and dipped his feet into the water. He wiggled his toes and stared at the ripples spreading over the surface of the slowly moving water. Tiny fish swam in the shallow stream. The light that filtered through the leafy canopy overhead was just enough to highlight the fish's iridescent colors. These weren't the toothy, two-headed monstrosities that populated the wasteland rivers, nor were they the beasts with strange tentacles and pulpy bodies that washed up on the beaches of the western coast. They were just fish, the sort that Deus had seen in the ancient books secreted away in the monastery. They swam around his feet, nibbling at his toes.

He was too lost in the sensation to see the two creatures

eyeing him from the other side of the stream. It was only when their sleek, plump bodies launched from the bank and into the water that Deus took notice. He shuddered with revulsion when he saw them, a trio of overgrown rats swimming straight towards him. The frantic movements of their paws churned the calm water to a froth. The tiny fish scattered. Deus tried to pull his feet out of the water, but the Black Drug had slowed his reflexes to a crawl. The urgent messages his brain sent to his extremities misfired off their synapses, leaving him stranded.

And then, the rats were upon him, one on each of his feet. They climbed his legs, their claws sinking into his skin with each step. Although his pain receptors were dulled by the holy drug that coursed through his system, he wanted to scream. Perhaps if his voice was loud enough, it would carry back to camp and someone would come to his aid. But the Black Drug had stolen his voice, and the best he could manage was a groan.

The rats scrambled over his knees and sat on his thighs. Deus whimpered as he bent to inspect his penis. A panicked inner voice cut through the fog shrouding his brain, screaming at him to move for gods' sake. But his limbs might as well have been bolted in place. He was frozen with fear. Just as he was preparing himself for castration via rodent incisors, the two beasts turned to look behind them. Deus followed their line of sight and saw a dark figure standing on the other side of the creek. The two rats chittered and squealed, then sprang off his legs and made a mad dash deeper into the woods.

Deus sighed with relief as he watched their speedy retreat. His relief was short-lived as he turned to look at the figure standing on the opposite bank. It was unlike any he'd seen before, and the mere sight of it conjured up a mad swirl of emotions in his drug-altered mind. Confusion, fear, revulsion —all those negative feelings were present. But so was a sense of intrigue, accompanied by something that could charitably be called arousal.

The dark figure was humanoid and apparently female. She was wearing a hooded cloak and nothing else. She was curvy and tall, with large breasts. His first impression was that she was perfectly formed except for some minor defect. But as he squinted to get a better look, the Black Drug eased its grip on his sense of sight, and the figure resolved into focus. Then, Deus recognized that the defects were far from minor. While the woman had the arms, legs, and torso of a human female, they were covered in fine, dark hair. Beneath the hair, her skin appeared perfectly pink. And that was just the beginning. The more Deus looked at the woman—if indeed she could even be called that—the more intense his horror became.

Her hands appeared to be normal size, with four fingers and a thumb on each. But these digits terminated in sharp, slightly hooked claws. Her feet were similarly made. She shrugged off her single garment, fully revealing her face. The woman had the face of a rat. Widely spaced black eyes above an elongated snout bristling with long whiskers and a twitching pink nose. She did a slow turn, displaying her muscular buttocks. The dark hair was thicker on her back, completely obscuring her skin. A fleshy pink tail sprouted from her lower back and hung to her ankles. She glanced over her shoulder at him and smiled, revealing a pair of oversized incisors.

She continued her slow turn, running her clawed hands over herself. She dipped one foot in the water, then another. Deus was unable to move as he watched her cross the knee-deep water. Her tail splashed behind her as she moved, stirring the slow current into eddies. As she neared him, Deus finally found the strength to stand, but he still was unable to turn away and flee. The Black Drug was speaking to him in its silent language. It told him to stay, that the events unfolding before him were important. Although he was afraid, Deus knew that he was powerless against the Black Drug's influence.

The rat woman paused at the edge of the bank. She stood there, her head level with his waist, gazing up at him with her shiny black eyes. He stared back at her, wondering what would happen to break this bizarre tableau.

"What are you?" His voice came out as a hoarse whisper.

The rat woman cocked her head to one side as if confused by his words.

"Please," Deus said, "I am but a simple wanderer…"

His words died in his throat as he felt a gentle pressure on his scrotum. Although he was too paralyzed to move, his nerve endings were still functional. If anything, they were even more alive. He could feel the slight scratch of the rat woman's claws against his thighs as she took hold of his penis. His body betrayed him. Despite his revulsion, he stiffened in her hand.

"No," he gasped.

She took her hand away from his erection, and shoved him backwards. He fell into a soft, damp patch of weeds and river moss. Then, she was upon him, straddling his hips and easing herself down onto his cock. His body's betrayal of his inner-self continued. He wanted to scream, to push the strange creature away, to run screaming through the forest. But instead, he pushed his hips upward, thrusting in rhythm with the rat woman. She leaned forward, bracing herself by putting her hands on his chest. Her claws drew blood as she moved her hips with increasing speed.

Deus closed his eyes. He wanted this to be over. And this time, his body and mind agreed. The orgasm seemed to build from the base of his skull and travel down his spine to his pelvis. He thrust once more, then the explosion came. He cried out as his body shook. Still moving atop him, the rat woman shrieked. And then, she shuddered into silence. His eyes still closed, Deus felt the rat woman's sex loosen and release him. There was a wet squelching sound as she climbed off him.

The full gravity of the situation slammed into his gut. He turned his head and vomited into the tangled weeds. He opened his eyes and looked around, but the rat woman was gone. She'd disappeared without even leaving footprints on the muddy creek bank.

His paralysis broken, Deus stood up shakily. He waded into the creek and eased himself down into the water, wincing at the coldness, but eager to wash away the wet stickiness on his crotch and thighs. He shook his head to clear the nightmare images of the rat woman's body as he washed himself.

Wet and trembling, he stumbled through the forest. The Black Drug was still having its way with his senses, and his vision was dark and blurry at the edges. The sounds of the forest were amplified to such levels that he clapped his hands over his ears to block out the noise. The rich scent of dirt and decay and animal life assaulted his nostrils. His lungs burned in his chest, working like bellows as he made his way back to the boulder where he'd left his clothes. It couldn't have been more than a mile, but it felt like a day's march. Finally, the large, flat rock was in sight. His relief was so sudden and intense that he wept.

Once he'd dressed and tugged his shoes back onto his dirty feet, he felt somewhat restored. The awful noises and smells had faded. Even the memory of his encounter with the rat woman seemed a distant, though still terrible, memory.

He checked his surroundings, desperate to regain his bearings, then headed off in the direction of the camp. Each step he took made him feel better. Soon, he'd be back among his friends, and he could banish the day's events to the darkest recesses of his mind. He offered a silent prayer in the hopes that it would lessen the possibility that he contracted some strange disease from the rat woman. Although it would be a fitting punishment for having engaged in such strange fornication, Deus didn't care for that possibility at all, whether or not it was theologically a fitting outcome. He told himself over and over that it hadn't been real, that the entire episode had been a dream conjured by the Black Drug.

"Gods preserve my manhood, so that it might not shrivel or become covered in lesions," he prayed aloud. Despite the gravity of his situation, his own words made him giggle. "Gods grant that such a dream never visits me again."

At last, he emerged from the woods and into the clearing at the bottom of the valley. It took every bit of his restraint not to break into a run. He smiled as he walked, quickening his pace. When he got to the campsite, he'd distribute more of the sacramental liquor, and deliver his best sermon yet. He'd begin with the parable of the six-fingered prostitute and the learned professor, emphasizing the professor's moral redemption, then he'd segue into the gospel—

He stopped in his tracks, halfway across the clearing. What he saw wasn't the joyous assembly that he'd left. What he saw was a nightmare of depravity.

A horde of rat people had descended on the camp. He recognized the female creatures immediately, as they might have been twin sisters of the one who'd defiled him by the creek. The males were of similar design, only taller and more broad shouldered. Their genitalia appeared more or less human, which was a small mercy, since the male rat people were engaged in vigorous intercourse with the women of the salvage team. The female creatures were likewise involved with the men. Since the rat creatures outnumbered the members of the team, some of them stood alongside the couplings, idly stroking themselves as they waited their turn. It was an orgy torn from hell, and worst of all, none of the participants seemed disturbed by their circumstances.

"No..." Deus shook his head in disgust and disbelief. "Gods above, no..."

It was too terrible to look at. It was too otherworldly and bizarre to look away. Myrna, Rosemary, Lilith, and Diana lay side by side, their legs spread for the hulking male rats. The women moaned beneath the rat men. A short distance away, the men of the team—Kurt, Viz, Lucifer, Taurus, Duke, and Max—were fully engaged with a group of rat women. As the men thrust and pumped, the female rat creatures squealed with obvious delight.

Deus started to back away, but his progress was stopped by the pressure of long, hairy arms wrapping around him. He looked down and recognized the clawed hands running themselves over his abdomen, slowly circling down to his crotch.

He screamed—

—and awoke on the muddy ground of the creek bed. His naked body was sweat drenched and sore. His stomach and thighs were sticky from his dreamtime emission, evidence that his drug-induced vision wasn't entirely without pleasure.

He slipped into the creek to wash himself, glancing about nervously as he splashed water over his sweaty torso. But there were no strange humanoid rats lurking in the shadows, waiting for their chance to defile his flesh. The forest was full of strange creatures. Of that, there was no doubt. But there was nothing as terrible as the rat people of his vision. Even the mutant clans weren't so terrifying.

He finished bathing, and set off through the forest, reaching the moss-covered boulder in a few short minutes. He dressed hurriedly, eager to be back in the company of his friends.

* * *

Taurus met him at the edge of the clearing. The big, bearded man was a welcome sight.

Taurus was a solid, earthly presence that comforted Deus. Though the man had no spiritual inclinations, and possessed an intellect not unlike that of a child, Taurus was a true friend. Standing there beside Taurus, Deus could almost believe that his experience in the woods was nothing more than a nightmare. But experience told him that no vision induced by the Black Drug was ever just a simple dream. Sometimes such a vision was a clear prophecy, while other times it was full of symbols and enigmas that could never be unraveled. Deus fervently hoped this newest vision was the latter, because if the vision was prophetic, then the future was grim indeed.

"Just about to go looking for you, my friend," Taurus boomed, clapping him on the shoulder. "Duke just said that the barbecue is almost ready. What kind of feast would it be if our holy man wasn't there to bless the food?"

Deus cleared his throat. "Of course. I didn't realize I'd been gone so long."

"Yeah, you were gone all afternoon." Taurus glanced at the sky. "Be getting dark pretty soon. Wouldn't want to be alone in the woods after sundown. Who knows what sort of nasty shit is out there."

"There are untold horrors in every dark corner of this world," Deus agreed.

Taurus raised an eyebrow. "That more of your scripture?"

"No, brother, it's not scripture. It's merely a statement of fact. There are things beyond our worst imaginings in this world, and some of them could very well lay on the road we travel. When we begin to believe that we understand the limits of horror, the universe often contrives a way to show us we have seen but a small portion."

The big man's brow wrinkled as he tried to puzzle out the meaning of Deus' words. Finally, he admitted defeat by shrugging and saying, "Yeah, I reckon so. You're usually right about philosophy and whatnot."

Deus forced a smile onto his face. "But let's not dwell on such things. There is food, fellowship, and plenty of sacramental liquor."

Taurus' smile was broader. It was also genuine. "Now you're speaking my language, brother. Let's go get us a taste of that pig Duke has been cooking all day."

Chapter Nine
The Last Of His Kind

Gar only survived because he was a coward. When his clan attacked the interlopers who rode machines through the clan's territory, Gar had taken a place near the rear of the formation, where the fighting would be less intense. And when the great bears attacked the clan, Gar had been one of the first to flee. He even turned and ran before the surviving elder signaled for retreat. He'd hidden in a cave and clapped his hands over his ears to block out the screams of his kin, who were torn apart by the claws and teeth of the great bears. He'd remained in the cave until the forest grew dark. Then, once he was all but certain the violence had ended, he ventured out of the cave and made his way back to the village to survey the damage.

What he saw there made him sick.

The great bears had left the village in ruins. The clan's houses—small one-room structures made of mud and straw bricks—had been stomped into rubble. The people who'd once occupied them had also been destroyed. Men, women, children…none had been spared the wrath of the giant beasts. The few pieces that the bears hadn't devoured were strewn throughout the rubble.

A few mangy scavengers—dogs, foxes, and rodents—scattered at Gar's approach. One sickly dog, desperate from hunger, stood its ground and growled. It stood protectively over its meal and bared its yellow teeth. For a moment, Gar stood frozen. He'd never liked dogs. When he was a child, a mad dog had come out of the woods and menaced the village children.

Although one of the elders had quickly dispatched the rabid animal, the sight of the slavering, growling dog had haunted Gar's dreams ever since.

But now, he found that his fear was gone. After seeing the great bears up close, this dog was just a pitiful excuse for a beast. The sight of the dog's meal—the hollowed-out shell of a child—stirred a feeling in Gar that he'd seen in other young men, but had never experienced himself: rage. Pure, undiluted anger.

At last, he understood the expression he'd seen on the faces of his father and brothers when they went to war with the other clans. In that moment, Gar finally knew what it meant to be filled with hatred so intense that it overruled everything else. He felt no fear.

Gar stooped to pick up a shard of brick. He hurled it at the dog. Although Gar had never been skilled at rock throwing, this time he actually hit his target. The brick caught the dog just behind its ragged ear. Stunned, the dog walked in a circle, its tail tucked between its legs. Gar scooped up another, heavier piece of brick and stepped closer to the bewildered dog. He drew back his arm and let the brick fly. Once again, his shot found its mark. It smashed into the dog's rear flank, sending it sprawling on the blood-soaked dirt. The dog yelped in pain as it scrambled to its feet. It managed a few steps on its crippled leg, then fell again.

The Gar of old—the cowardly, feeble village idiot—would have let the wounded animal slink back into the trees. But the newly awakened Gar, filled with rage that sought the nearest outlet, had no intention of letting this scavenger live. This time when he stooped, it wasn't to pick up a rock or fragment of brick. This time, he found an axe. He didn't know whether it was a weapon lost by a fallen warrior, or just a tool that had been scattered when the great bears broke the village's storage shed. Gar supposed it could have been both. Its provenance didn't matter to him. What mattered was that it was well-balanced and deadly. He liked the weight in his hand.

"Fucking dog," he spat, advancing on the wounded animal with slow, steady steps. "Bash your fucking brains in. Promise you I will."

Gar may have spent his life until that moment as a coward, but he'd never been a liar. He made good on his promise, smashing the dog's skull with the blunt side of the axe before flipping the weapon around and using the sharp edge to sever the dog's head from its body.

He stood over the carcass, breathing heavily. He felt good.

So this is what it means to kill, he thought.

* * *

Gar gathered as many supplies as he could salvage from the ruins of his village, then set off into the forest. He walked until he was exhausted, then made his camp beside the trunk of a fallen tree. It was good to find a place to rest, but his work wasn't over.

He gathered some dry sticks and arranged them in a pile. A handful of dead weeds and brittle leaves went on top to serve as kindling. It took persistence with the flint to produce the necessary sparks, but soon enough, Gar had a small fire blazing. While the fire crackled, he used a knife to whittle two sticks to sharp points. Then, he unwrapped the cloth bundle in which he'd carried the meat he'd cut from the dog. He impaled the chunks of meat on the sticks, then held them over the fire to cook. His stomach growled as he watched the meat sizzle.

His thoughts turned to his future. He was the last of his clan. His family, his few friends, his whole world had been torn away. Rather than loneliness and despair, he found himself filled with a sense of purpose. Killing the dog had been an epiphany. It was a small measure of retribution, mostly symbolic but enlightening nonetheless. Someone had to be held accountable for the destruction of his people. Someone had to settle a debt with blood. The interlopers had summoned the bears with the noise and stink of their machines. And for that, they would pay. As the last of his clan, it was Gar's responsibility to see that they went howling to their graves.

Their tracks would be easy enough to follow, although their machines gave them the advantage of speed. But their machines also dictated the path they'd have to take, whereas Gar could travel over any terrain he chose. Besides, they were outsiders, no doubt weak from leading lives of ease. Easy pickings for a member of the forest clans, even one who'd spent his life as a coward.

Gar pulled the meat out of the fire. He blew on it until it was cooled enough to eat. It wasn't quite cooked through, but Gar found that he liked it that way. The taste of blood was satisfying.

When he'd devoured the last scraps of dog meat, he licked his fingers clean. Gazing into the flames, he swore an oath to destroy the outsiders who'd brought calamity to his village. He pressed the blade of his knife against his chest and cut himself from nipple to nipple. The blood that ran down his belly sealed his vow. He would kill the outsiders or die trying. And since Gar had never been a liar, he slept soundly that night, free from uncertainty.

Chapter Ten
Better Living Through Science

Grainger took a deep breath as he stepped off the elevator. He fished his credentials out of his pocket and showed them to the guard on duty at the front desk.

Burning the midnight oil, Councilor? the guard asked, passing the ID card back.

Just a routine visit, Grainger explained. *Keeping an eye on progress for my constituents, you understand.*

The guard nodded, but his attention had already wandered back to the book he was reading. The book's cover was plain black, but from the guard's forward-leaning posture and twitching whiskers, Grainger could deduce the content. Violence, pornography, or, more likely, a combination of the two.

A rape followed by murder, Grainger mused, forgetting to hide his thoughts.

The guard's eyes flicked up from the page. *I'm sorry, Councilor, I didn't catch that.*

Oh, nothing. Grainger waved his hand.

The guard gave him a strange look, then went back to reading, his lips moving as his eyes moved over the page.

Grainger walked past the desk and through a set of

double doors. The air on the other side of the doors was cool and dry. The soundproofed walls seemed to suck in every bit of ambient sound until Grainger could hear his own pulse pounding in his ears. He hated this place. And that was why he forced himself to visit it once a week.

The Delta Colony Center for Scientific Research was located on the lowest level of the central hub. Outside of the researchers who staffed the center, few Colonists ever made the descent to visit the facility. As a rule, the Colonists conflated one's social status with how close one lived to the surface. The best lodgings and dining halls were located on the upper levels. The Council offices were located on the upper levels. But the facilities devoted to the continued existence of their species was buried at the very bottom of the Delta Colony. Even the Colonial Penitentiary could be found on a higher level.

Grainger supposed the Colony's scientists had situated their headquarters in such a way out of some unconscious sense of guilt, even shame. Because even for such a young species, whose sense of cultural identity was still in flux, the procedures taking place in the facility appeared to cross every ethical line known to science. It was, even for an ardent supporter of the genetic research program, an ugly thing. The very concept was distasteful. Detractors referred to it as a form of eugenics. The less charitable among them call it bestiality. But all evidence pointed to the program as the best path for ensuring the survival of their species. Grainger believed that evidence, and had hung his political hat on it. Still, he was compelled to face the consequences of his vote, however uncomfortable they made him.

He walked down the hallway and through a door on the left. The door opened into the laboratories devoted to the genetics project. The main lab wasn't a large space. Nothing about the cluttered arrangement of desks and file cabinets suggested that it was the work space of a team of scientists who labored around the clock to solve the most important problem facing their species. Two technicians in white lab coats were standing in front of a pane of one-way glass that looked into one of the smaller labs. They watched with rapt attention, taking notes on clipboards.

Hello, Councilor, one of the scientists—an older Colonist named Dr. Spencer—projected without turning away from the window. *A little late in the night for your weekly visit, isn't it?*

The second scientist—a young technician named Sister Sorella—touched a button on the wall, and a set of metal blinds dropped with a sharp *clack,* obscuring the window. Then, she turned her back on Grainger, and drew Dr. Spencer aside. They shared a bit of private conversation. Grainger couldn't pick up their shielded thoughts, but he got the gist of them. His late night arrival made them nervous.

What are you working on? Grainger tried to keep any note of suspicion out of his thought projection as he moved alongside the two scientists.

Nothing of interest to someone outside the scientific community, Sorella replied.

Oh, you'd be surprised at my interests. Grainger put a hand on the scientist's shoulder. *Suppose you raise those blinds and let me have a look at what's got you so nervous.*

The scientists exchanged another look. Another brief private conversation ensued, with each of them punctuating their thoughts with emphatic hand gestures. Sorella tossed her clipboard on a nearby desk and threw her hands in the air. She shouldered past Grainger on her way out of the room, slamming the door for good measure.

Now what was all that about? Grainger asked.

Dr. Spencer's shoulders sagged. *You must understand, we're under enormous pressure to produce results. You're the only one on the Council who even cares about the progress we've made. Brother Cornelius keeps threatening to terminate the project. If word of this experiment were to get out…*

The sense of dread settling in Grainger's belly was ice cold and heavy. *Dr. Spencer, please open the blinds.*

*You must understand…*Dr. Spencer's thoughts took on a pleading, desperate tone. *All our attempts at incubation have failed. We are at a loss to explain it. The material is compatible with only a few minor modifications. Sperm and egg have met and joined without any trouble. But development seems to halt when the zygote-*

Grainger raised a hand. *Yes, I understand that the project has encountered some troubles. But that is no reason to abandon it, despite what Brother Cornelius might have threatened. However, none of that answers my question about what you're hiding behind those blinds.*

It started as a joke, Dr. Spencer explained. *Something one of our interns suggested over some after-work cocktails. She said that we've tried so many things without success and that perhaps it was time to explore a direct approach-*

Enough! Grainger's patience was at low ebb. *Show me what you're hiding!*

Dr. Spencer seemed to deflate. His whiskers hung limply. *Try to think about this logically. Please, reserve your judgment. After so many failures, the only logical choice was to return to first principles, to bypass the complications of technology and look to nature.*

The scientist pushed a button, and the blinds rattled as they drew upwards. He turned sideways to slip past Grainger, leaving him alone to examine the latest genetic experiment taking place ten levels below the offices of the Colonial government. At first, the sight was too grotesque for Grainger to fully register what was taking place in the room behind the one-way glass. His eyes relayed the images to his brain, but they were so strange that his mind could scarcely digest them.

What was taking place in the laboratory was an orgy. But it was unlike any orgy Grainger had ever seen or imagined.

He was no prude. In his time, Grainger had dabbled in polyamory and bisexuality, just like many of his generation. It was part of their culture, after all, a relic from centuries past, when their species was desperate to populate their newly constructed subterranean world. Sure, Grainger was familiar with orgies and the variety of couplings they entailed. But this was an orgy torn from a drug-addled dream, even a nightmare. There, in the cold, clinical laboratory, a group of humans and Colonists were mingling their genetic material in the most primal fashion: through frenzied mating.

It took Grainger a moment to overcome his disbelief and revulsion. Then his mind began to catalogue the perversions taking place on the other side of the window. A male Colonist mounted a human female from behind. His tail twitched as he thrust against her. Another male stood next to them, either waiting his turn or simply watching. To the trio's left, a female Colonist was astride a human male, rocking her hips back and forth. Her partner gripped handfuls of her fur as he matched her rhythm. Against the back wall of the room, two more couplings were in full swing. Female Colonists lay prone on a large mattress while a pair of human males knelt between their legs.

A trio of lab coat-clad Colonists stood in the corner of the room. In front of them was a small metal table covered with vials of amber liquid, and a dozen or more syringes. One Colonist was scribbling notes on a clipboard, while the others filled the syringes.

Grainger gagged, but he found that himself unable to look away.

The male Colonist who was taking the human female from behind began to shake. He turned his head to stare at the ceiling as his body shuddered. After a moment, he withdrew and stood up. His member glistened in the harsh lighting. Hands on his hips, he breathed deeply. His wilted erection was wet and dripping as he walked across the room and presented himself to the trio of scientists. One of them jabbed a syringe into the naked Colonist's buttock and depressed the plunger.

The Colonist's tail twitched as the drug hit his bloodstream. His penis stiffened until it jutted straight out from his body. He strolled to the center of the room, gazing around at the scene as he waited his turn to rejoin the fray. A door on the back wall opened just long enough for a glassy-eyed human female to enter the room. She presented her naked body to the newly reinvigorated Colonist. He guided her gently to the floor and spread her legs.

Grainger could take no more. He turned away from the grotesque display, and left the room.

* * *

As I said, it started as a joke, Dr. Spencer explained. *The sort of thing you say when having a few drinks after a long day of frustrating failures. But then, someone suggested it might actually work. I can't even remember who it was. Once it was out there in the open, the idea gathered momentum. A return to first principles. Perhaps the direct approach could yield results that our technology could not. It was an idea born of desperation, but whether or not the average citizen is aware of it, these are desperate times. The birth rate is falling just as sharply as the rate of genetic abnormalities and mutations is rising. There is a crisis point on the horizon, and we're getting nearer and nearer to it every day.*

Gods above. Grainger closed his eyes and drank his double shot of grain alcohol in one go. He winced as the liquor burned a line from this throat to the pit of his stomach.

Dr. Spencer drank his own measure of liquor then refilled their glasses.

It made a certain kind of sense, he continued. *From a scientific perspective I mean. A cold, clinical perspective that's disconnected from morals and ethics.*

They were seated at a table in the corner of the research center's mess hall, a bottle of 100-proof grain alcohol between them. Even though they were the room's sole occupants, they made sure to guard their thought projections.

Where did you find them? Grainger asked. *I can't imagine they volunteered.*

The Colonists actually did volunteer. They were prisoners, promised a reduction in their sentences in exchange for their participation in a medical trial of a new drug, Dr. Spencer answered, contemplating the glass of liquor in front of him. *The human specimens, well, I suppose you couldn't call them volunteers. They were…how shall I put this…collected during an expedition to the surface. But their circumstances were such that they would have certainly died if they weren't brought to our clinic for medical intervention.*

You drugged them. Grainger drank more liquor, forcing himself to only sip this time. *You drugged them and forced them to…dear gods…*

A combination of drugs did the trick. Dr. Spencer continued to stare at his glass. *One was a sexual stimulant that put their libidos into overdrive, another was a mild hallucinogen to ease the awkwardness, and finally, a little something to increase fertility. Combined with the genetic treatments that we hope will make breeding between our species possible, of course.*

Grainger shook his head, trying to clear the memory of the horrors he'd witnessed. It didn't work. He was beginning to suspect that the images had staked out a portion of his brain for permanent residency.

Did you think this would remain secret forever? Grainger asked.

Of course not! But we needed to keep it hidden until we knew whether or not the process produced results. If the trials don't produce any viable offspring, then we can consign the experiment to the heap of all the other unsuccessful attempts. But if the program proves successful, it's our belief that our people will overcome their natural revulsion, and see the procedure for what it is: a distasteful yet necessary step to ensure the survival of the species. A mere bump in the road leading us to supremacy on the planet's surface.

Grainger had to admit that it made sense if viewed from a purely logical perspective. If one could manage the highest level of clinical detachment, if one could get past the instinctive disgust, if one could disregard the perverse, unnatural, disgusting process…

He forced himself back to more practical matters. *Brother Cornelius doesn't have much support on the Council, but his ideas are gaining traction among the populace. Before I saw that… abomination…in your laboratory, I'd been concerned about the next election. But that's the least of my concerns now. If word of this were to get out, we might not have to worry about elections at all, because our entire civilization would be consumed by civil war. And I don't need to tell you that such a thing could mean the end of the species.*

Dr. Spencer nodded. *You speak the truth.*

Grainger already knew that. This wasn't the first time he'd discussed their species' future with one of the Colonial scientists. He knew what the prevalence of birth defects in new offspring meant. He knew what declining birth rates meant. And he understood mutation theory. If there wasn't successful scientific intervention within the next twelve generations, extinction was a real possibility. No, that wasn't true. It was a near certainty. And since the Colonists retained the rapid reproductive cycles of their lower animal cousins, that meant action needed to take place within the next four years. These were desperate times. Unfortunately, only a select few members of the Colony had any clue how as to how deep that desperation ran.

Even if the program is successful, I have my doubts that our fellow Colonists will accept… Grainger glanced over his shoulder in the direction of the lab. *I'm able to overcome my revulsion, and understand the logic behind this experiment. Others might not be so understanding.*

Dr. Spencer pulled at his whiskers thoughtfully. *And that is why only a select few of the scientists on staff are even aware of the program. Why do you think we're conducting the experiments at such a late hour?*

Just understand that word of this filters out of the basement, it could mean the end of everyone involved. Grainger stood. *And when I say "the end," I don't just mean our careers. I'm speaking of expulsion from the Colony. Exile to the surface.*

Chapter Eleven

Despite their obvious hangovers, the team broke camp and saddled up with the same practiced ease of any other morning. Aside from Kurt and Diana, the only person who appeared to have escaped the effects of Deus' sacramental liquor was Taurus. Even the mystic himself looked a little worse for wear when the team gathered for breakfast. Deus' eyes were bleary as he knelt to whisper his morning prayers. His hands shook as he raised them skyward in supplication. But he ate as heartily as usual and went about his duties without complaint.

Kurt chuckled as he checked the saddlebags on his motorcycle. He checked the fuel. Although their detour off Lord Hannibal's route had cut into their fuel supply, there was still enough to make it to the next outpost.

"Looks like we were the only ones who didn't overindulge," Diana said as she settled into the sidecar. "Well, I guess Taurus looks like he escaped without too much damage."

Kurt shook his head. "No, he just has an inhuman tolerance for alcohol. There's not a man or woman in the wasteland he couldn't drink under the table."

"A true superpower if you ask me."

"Indeed." Kurt bent down to kiss her, then said, "I'm going to check the rest of the team. We'll roll out soon."

"Good. The sooner we can put this forest behind us, the better," Diana said. "This valley is peaceful enough, but I can't help thinking of all the things surrounding us. Those mutants…" She shuddered. "I'm not sure what's waiting for us in that abandoned city, but it can't be much worse than those damned mutants."

Kurt nodded, although he wasn't sure that she was right. In his experience, there was always the possibility of something worse on the road ahead. But he kept that to himself. He could settle for a bit of dishonesty if it meant keeping up team spirit. Because the more dangerous the job became, the more important morale was. And that was why he hated what he was about to do. Still, he didn't intend to spend the rest of this job looking over his shoulder.

He walked through the camp, pausing here and there to check in with his team. Hangovers notwithstanding, everyone appeared just as eager as Diana to get out of the forest. Rosemary was giving her sidecar one last inspection when Kurt made it to the rear of the formation. Duke was already astride is bike, his helmet and goggles in place, his gloved hands on the handlebars.

"Rosemary, can you help me with something?" He asked, putting a hand on her shoulder. "Diana cut her hand while she was packing up. It's not too serious, but I thought you might give it a quick look. Don't want to risk infection so far from the nearest outpost."

She looked over a Duke. "You all squared away, partner?"

"Ready to roll," he answered.

"Yeah, we'll be on the road in just a few minutes," Kurt said, leading Rosemary towards the front of the formation. He kept his voice low as he confessed that Diana wasn't really injured. "I just needed an excuse to talk to you alone for a minute."

"What's up?" she asked.

Kurt led her to his motorcycle, where he asked Diana to present an uninjured hand to keep up the ruse.

"You've been riding alongside Duke ever since Quinn took a bullet. Almost a year now."

Rosemary nodded. "Yeah, that sounds about right. So?"

"How's it going? You like riding with him?"

"Well, I ride with the whole team. I just happen to ride in close proximity to Duke." She continued her inspection of Diana's hand. "You thinking about getting to the point anytime soon? Because me standing here holding your girl's hand, that's how rumors get started. Now, everyone knows my door swings both ways, but maybe Diana don't want that kind of talk circulating about her."

"How do you feel about Duke?" he asked.

"Not my type," Rosemary answered.

Kurt smiled. "Not really what I was asking."

She dropped Diana's hand and shrugged. "He's solid, I guess. Handles himself well in a tight spot, but I guess you already knew that. Now, you want me to answer the question you're too polite to ask? I'll say this: if there was anyone on the team you had to worry about when it comes to loyalty, I'd say Duke fits that bill. Motherfucker is looking out for number one, you know? But if you're asking, I guess you already know that."

"I've had my suspicions," Kurt admitted.

"Should we be worried?" Diana asked, looking over her shoulder like she wanted to make sure no one was eavesdropping.

"I wouldn't worry, girl." Rosemary patted Diana's head, running her long fingers through a lock of hair. "If he decides to make a move, Kurt here will see it coming from a mile away. See, your man actually is a smart guy, while Duke just thinks he is. And for another thing, Duke's about as subtle as a gut punch. Like, the motherfucker keeps trying to drop hints about how he wants to give me the business, and his hints are just one step shy of dropping his pants and asking me to hit my knees."

Diana wrinkled her nose. "Ugh."

"Yeah, *ugh* is right, girl," Rosemary said.

"Thanks for the heads-up. You better get back there before he starts getting suspicious," Kurt said. "But do me a favor, okay? Keep your ears open for any loose talk about mutiny. We can't afford to have any of that bullshit, especially not when we're doing this sort of job."

"I read you loud and clear." Rosemary glanced over her shoulder for a moment, then said, "Now it's my turn to ask you something. You noticed anything off about Deus? I know the two of you were otherwise occupied with romantic shit yesterday, but he's been acting strange."

"Disappearing into the woods for a while isn't strange for him," Kurt said. "Sometimes he likes to pray or meditate, whatever, by himself. You know how it is with the mystical type."

"Yeah, but since he got back, he's been..." Rosemary looked over her shoulder again. "I don't know...even stranger than usual."

Kurt looked at the group, searching for Deus. The holy man was standing at the edge of the road, his arms folded over his chest as he stared at the forest. As much as Kurt didn't need any added complications, he saw that Rosemary's observations were correct. There was something different about Deus' posture. The holy man's tattooed forehead was creased as if he was lost in deep thought or perhaps worried. The former wasn't unusual for Deus, but the latter certainly was. Of all the people Kurt had rode alongside, Deus was the least prone to worry. When Kurt asked him how he could travel the wasteland without being in a constant state of dread, Deus would simply smile and offer some platitude about the will of the gods or destiny or faith, all of which were his favorite topics of conversation.

But whatever it was bothering Deus, it would have to wait. Kurt already had too many balls in the air to juggle anything else. Duke's growing disloyalty was a more pressing concern, to say nothing of the mission at hand.

"Don't worry about Deus," Kurt said. "He's a little weird, just like any holy man worth his tattoos, but he's rock steady when push comes to shove. I'll keep an eye on him, if that makes you feel better, but I need you to keep yours on Duke. We make it through this job, we can evaluate our membership. For now, I need to keep this team together."

"You got it, boss." Rosemary tipped him a lazy salute and headed back to her position at the rear of the loose formation.

Kurt swung his leg over the motorcycle and sat down. The bike's shocks bounced under his weight.

"You worried about that situation?" Diana asked. "Think Duke's going to be a problem?"

"If it comes down to it, I'll deal with him. But right now, I need to keep the team together."

"That's not really an answer."

"I'm always worried." Kurt sighed. "Sometimes, I think that's really what it means to be a leader. You do all the worrying for everyone else."

He kicked the bike into gear. The engine roared to life, vibrating between his thighs like it might speed away of its own accord. The engines of the other bikes added their voices to the internal combustion chorus. Kurt raised his fist in the air, giving the signal that it was time to move out. Then he pulled back on the throttle and let off the brake.

* * *

Duke decided to ride without his helmet. He liked the feeling of the wind in his hair. It felt like freedom. And he felt especially free as his bike rumbled across the valley and back into the forest. He felt free because he knew his true feelings about Kurt's leadership were out in the open. That little scene with Rosemary pretending to examine Diana's injured hand was awfully cute, but it wasn't at all convincing. The way Diana kept glancing back at him through the whole thing made it clear as to the subject of the conversation. And that was just fine with Duke. He didn't need to engage in cat and mouse bullshit. When he came for Kurt's crown, everyone would see it coming. Duke wanted them to.

He let go of the handlebar just long enough to slap Rosemary on the shoulder. "Head on a swivel, right, partner?" he shouted.

She flashed him a thumbs-up, then slapped her sidecar-mounted rifle for emphasis. Duke wondered exactly what she'd told Kurt. Not that it mattered. All that stuff Rosemary might have thought was loose talk was anything but. If he made disparaging comments about the team's leader, it wasn't a slip-up. He knew what he was doing. He cut his eyes sideways to get a better look at her while the morning sun was still overhead. Soon enough, they'd be back under the shade of the forest canopy, where even a bright afternoon seemed like twilight. That familiar feeling surged through him. It was just as intense as it had been the first time he'd laid eyes on her. Even back then, he'd known that it was his destiny to lead a salvage team through the wasteland. Once he met Rosemary, he had no doubt about who would be at his side when he finally ascended to his throne. Whether or not she knew it, Rosemary would be both his queen and his enforcer. Everyone else was expendable.

He risked one more look at her as his bike hit the bumpy road leading out of the valley. Rosemary's sidecar had been customized to accommodate her long legs. Deus was the only member of the team taller than her, and only by small margin. She was long-limbed and muscular, crowned with a mane of thick curls. She wore her hair in a loose braid while the team was riding, but at the end of each day, she set it free, letting it hang down to the middle of her back. Each morning, she braided it anew, her fingers working with practiced ease. Her dark brown skin looked so smooth and supple, especially the tops of her breasts, which peeked over the collars of the V-necked shirts she favored. Duke longed to press his face into that valley, to feel the softness pressing against his face.

He'd seen her naked, of course. Traveling as the team did, it was impossible not to catch glimpses here and there of one another in the nude. He'd seen her dark nipples and the small thatch of hair at the junction of her legs. He kept those images at the forefront of his brain, readily accessible for the long nights in his sleeper bag. She was perfect.

He put the bike in low gear as they made the last climb out of the clearing. And then, the semi-darkness of the forest swallowed them. The ancient asphalt road was pitted and scarred, but compared to the dirt-and-rock trail, it was a smooth expanse. He could finally unclench his jaw,

at least. Lilith and Lucifer detached from the formation, speeding away from the team on their off-road bikes to scout the surrounding area. Lucifer waved as Duke passed.

"Stay sharp, brother!" Duke shouted.

Beside him, Rosemary put up her rearview mirrors, checking the road behind them for any possible threats. Duke smiled. His partner was beautiful, but she was also deadly. Once, when the team was spending some downtime at an outpost in the southwest, a saloon patron had made the mistake of calling her "Sexy Chocolate." Rosemary had smiled and let the man get just close enough for her to draw a knife and press the point against his crotch while she tightened her free hand around his throat. The team had to cut their vacation short when they discovered that the man who narrowly escaped an impromptu surgical procedure was the mayor's nephew.

The road through the forest was full of curves, but the broken asphalt surface forced them to go so slowly that they navigated the serpentine path without difficulty. It would have been easy enough to relax and let his mind wander if not for the soundtrack of distant voices in his head. They weren't loud or obtrusive, but they were steady and constant. If Duke concentrated, he could pick out individual voices. Some of them were harsh and guttural like the voice of the enraged boar. Others were soft and sibilant. But they were so far away that he couldn't pick individual words from the chorus. It was like the static of a communications radio tuned to a frequency between two signals.

At first, the voices caused his guts to go cold with dread. Now that some psychic switch had been thrown in his brain, would it be impossible to turn it off? Would he have to endure these intrusive voices forever? But he found that he could push them aside. If he ignored them, they faded into the background and were nearly drowned out by the noise of the engines. And once he realized that he had some measure of control over his newfound ability, he began to plot the ways he could use it to his advantage.

* * *

Deus' motorcycle had no sidecar. Like Taurus and Viz, he rode alone. He liked it that way. As a man of holy disposition, he preferred to spend his travel time lost in his own thoughts. And this morning, as the forest seemed to swallow them up, his thoughts were dark indeed. Something was amiss. A curse was hanging over this job. It would not end well.

He knew better than to try to banish the memories of the

prior day's vision. Even if it wasn't his sacred duty to unravel the meaning of the horrible images, he wouldn't have been able to forget them. He knew he'd never forget the feeling of the rat woman's claws as she raked them gently over his scrotum. He knew he'd never forget the sharp, musky scent of her sex as he buried himself in her. And no matter how fervently he wished, he would never forget the explosive orgasm that followed.

There was nothing in the gospels to illuminate the things he'd seen and experienced on the muddy creek bank. If indeed they were images from a dream—or a nightmare—they were as inscrutable as any that he'd ever seen. But with enough contemplation, he'd unravel their meaning. Because the other possibility—that any part of the experience was actually real—was too horrible to entertain.

* * *

Gar picked his way down the steep hill. His weapons and supplies slowed him down, but he was growing used to their weight. The axe in particular was a reassuring presence. While the rest of his supplies were stored in the bundle he wore on his back, he held onto the axe with a grip so tight it made his knuckles ache. Every time he shifted it from one hand to the other, he imagined it smashing open the heads of the outsiders. When he paused to rest, he would speak softly to the axe. It was, after all, his only friend.

His feet slid in a patch of loose gravel, but he managed to keep his balance. A few more unsteady steps and he emerged from the woods into the open space at bottom of the valley. He paused for a moment to look around. Being a member of the forest clan often meant living one's entire span beneath the canopy of trees, only seeing the sunlight filtered through the dense tangle of leaves and branches overhead. The last time a member of the clan had walked across open ground was during the Great Migration, since which many generations had come and gone.

Gar gazed at the sky. The red and grey clouds parted here and there to reveal patches of blue. The sunlight that shone through those gaps was bright and warm upon his face. He could still see it when he closed his eyes.

During his childhood, he'd heard stories of the horrors that befell those who ventured out of the forest. He'd expected to encounter any number of them as soon as he passed the tree line. But now that he was out in the open, he saw nothing that inspired fear. The forest was thick with things lurking in every shadow, behind every rock, ready to pounce and tear apart anything that might be weaker or slower. Out here in the open, there was no place to hide. Any predator wishing to charge would have to face Gar on equal terms. Not only did this make him feel brave, it made him feel strong. If these people he was tracking were a product of this pleasant environment, they were bound to be weak. Sure, they had their machines and their thundering weapons, but stripped of those advantages, they'd be easy prey.

Gar moved across the valley floor, pausing to examine the carcass of a giant boar that had been left as a feast for maggots and insects. The remains of a cook fire still smoldered nearby.

The smell of charred fat and burnt wood wafted on the breeze. Gar shook his head in disgust. These outsiders weren't just weak, they were wasteful. They'd left behind so many useful parts of the slain animal. Not only was there more meat than Gar could carry, there were hundreds of uses for the other parts. The hide could be tanned and made into clothing or blankets. The bones could be bleached and sharpened into weapons or tools. A giant boar would have sustained Gar's entire village for days, and these outsiders had left it to rot. It made Gar sad to walk away from such abundance, but he needed to move swiftly if he was going to close the distance between himself and his quarry.

He paused just long enough to cut some meat from the boar's carcass, then set off across the valley. It saddened him to leave the open space behind and venture back into the forest, but that was where the outsiders' trail led him. And he'd sworn a blood oath to hunt them down or die trying.

Chapter Twelve
The District Of Whispers

Like most of the Colonists of his generation, Grainger had been raised as a member of the First United Colonial Church. As a pup, he'd attended evening services with his pack twice a week. But as he grew older and decided to pursue a life outside the nest, he lapsed in his religious devotion. While he could still remember passages from the catechism and could mumble his way through a handful of hymns, he hadn't given much thought to religion over the years. Someone more devoted to the traditional faith would probably accuse Grainger of making politics his religion. That was fair enough, Grainger decided. The duties of a career Councilman had just as much pomp and ceremony as those of a clergyman. The two professions also shared an equal amount of backbiting and internal squabbles.

As he grew older, and his departure time drew nearer, Grainger found that there were voids that politics couldn't fill, questions that politics couldn't answer. So far, none of these voids or lingering questions had been enough to draw him back to church. But after witnessing the abominations taking place at the research center, Grainger knew he could delay his return no longer.

He finished his duties for the day—signing off on some budget allocations for municipal projects—then locked his office. He walked down the brightly lit hallways until he was out of the central hub. A few other civil servants had also decided to call it a day. They lingered near the elevators and motorized staircases, waiting to make their way home or off to their evening entertainments.

The ten levels of the Delta Colony were octagonal, and housed a population of over a million. And while this sounded like a staggering number to an outsider freshly arrived from the coastal settlements, it was worrisome to those who could remember the days when that population was more than twice its current size. The Colony's political headquarters occupied most of the third level. Above it were two levels devoted to Colonial security. Below, were levels devoted to the commercial and residential districts. Sandwiched between the residential levels and the basement research levels was the religious quarter. Grainger thought the architects who designed the Colony centuries ago must have had a sense of humor when they placed science and religion in such close proximity.

He took one of the mechanical staircases. After a day of being cooped up in his office, the last thing he wanted was to stand shoulder-to-shoulder with other Colonists in a cramped elevator car. The staircases were slower, but they afforded one more personal space. Grainger leaned on the handrail and watched the world go by. A few giggling youngsters dashed past him, too excited about their evening activities to simply ride the staircase. Grainger smiled at them.

He wondered if it was really possible that he'd once been so young and carefree. He was certain there had been a period in his life when he was just as high-spirited as the pups and kittens sprinting down the staircase to an evening in the entertainment district. But that time seemed so distant and foggy that he could only think of it as ancient.

It took Grainger a full ten minutes to descend to the ninth level, known variously among the Colonists as the Holy Quarter, the Churches, or, most poetically, the District of Whispers. All those names struck Grainger as apt, but he favored the most poetic. It was, after all, a quiet place during most hours. This near-silence was oppressive as Grainger made his way from the staircase to the district's main thoroughfare. The high ceilings and stone floors amplified his footfalls.

Even his breathing seemed to echo through the pathways between each house of worship. It wasn't hard to imagine that this is how it felt in the immediate aftermath of the Event, when the first Colonists emerged.

The Colony had no official religion, and as a rule, most residents of Delta Colony weren't overly devout. The largest religious sect was the one Grainger had been born into, the First United Church. It was a moderate institution in its approach to both theology and politics, so it cast the widest net when it came to attracting a congregation. Of all the religious centers in the hushed hallways of the ninth level, the First United Church had the grandest accommodations.

Located at the end of the main path, its towering gold doors shone like a beacon, even in the soft glow of the chemical lamps.

Grainger's heart rate jumped a few notches as he neared the golden doorway. His nervousness wasn't rational. He was a respected member of the Colony, even if it had been decades since he last sat in a church pew.

Calm down, old boy, he chided himself. *There's no stern vicar waiting to ask you if you've had impure thoughts.*

The door swung open before he could knock. And while it seemed that there was indeed a vicar waiting for him, this one wasn't stern in the least. He was young, not much more than a pup, and his smile was warm.

I just happened to look out the window and saw you coming up the front stairs, the vicar projected. *Imagine my surprise when I saw the Colony's most senior member of the Council coming for an evening visit!*

I didn't know if I should schedule something or not, Grainger explained.

Oh, you needn't bother with that. The vicar stood aside and motioned for Grainger to follow him inside. *Our door is always open to any Colonist who wishes to enter. Now, were you looking for anyone in particular? I only ask because we're a bit of a skeleton crew once the evening meal has ended.*

The question brought Grainger up short. This trip was a spur of the moment excursion. He hadn't given any thought to anything beyond showing up at the church. He was certain that the clergymen he'd known as a pup had all made their departure years ago. Some of the vicars and matrons who'd watched over his school might still be alive, but they'd be among the Colony's oldest residents.

I'm not really sure who I need to talk to, Grainger admitted. *But I know I need answers to some very troubling questions.*

The vicar's motions for Grainer to enter became more emphatic. He touched the Councilman's shoulder with his other hand. *Then please, sir, step inside. We can talk over a pot of tea.*

* * *

Cornelius spotted the old fool as soon as he stepped off the staircase.

Why, Brother Grainger, what brings you to the Churches? Cornelius wondered, ducking into the shadows between the Hall of Ancestors and the Delta Congregational Assembly.

Once Grainger had passed by without noticing his presence, Cornelius watched the doddering fool's progress toward the end of the path. He shook his head and snickered when Grainger ascended the stairs to the doorway of the First

United Church. How fitting that a liberal race traitor would choose such an inoffensive, boring house of worship. Officially, the First United Church took no political stance. Hell, they hardly took a stance on anything. But, the way Cornelius saw it, failure to take a side was as good as capitulation to the anti-Colonist agenda that Brother Lorne and Sister Ursula promoted. When the reckoning came—and it would be sooner than anyone suspected—that traitorous couple would be the first up against the wall, right alongside their brainwashed followers.

Cornelius waited until Grainger was safely inside the church before stepping out of the alleyway and continuing toward his destination. As he walked, he wondered again what Grainger was doing there on a weekday evening. That church no longer held night services, and besides, Grainger had never shown any religious inclinations before. Cornelius made it his business to know the habits and allegiances of his fellow Council members. He had a small, yet loyal network of spies whose sole task it was to keep tabs on the likes of Lorne, Ursula, and Grainger. But that was a mystery for another night. At the moment, he had more pressing concerns.

He turned left in the alley beside a small, ramshackle house of worship whose sign read "Ministry of the New Age." But that wasn't what Cornelius called it. The name he used was the same one that members of other, less strictly conservative sects used: Temple of the Rat.

Cornelius didn't use the front entrance. He made his way to the rear of the building, and entered through a discreetly-placed trapdoor. It led to the temple's basement, a dark, musty room crammed with boxes of sacramental wine, bags of moth-eaten vestments, and collections of rusty tools. He picked his way through the maze of clutter until he came to another door. This one required a key for entry. It was a key that he didn't carry on his regular key ring, but rather kept in the breast pocket of his shirt, near his heart. He glanced over his shoulder to reassure himself that he hadn't been followed, then unlocked the door and stepped inside.

The room behind the door was cramped and dim, illuminated by a single chemical lantern. This part of the church wasn't hooked into the municipal power grid. It was another layer of protection against unwanted intruders.

There were no furnishings apart from six mismatched chairs and an upturned bucket that served as a table for the lantern. Three of the chairs were currently in use, occupied by young Colonists dressed in plain black robes. Each wore an expression so serious that it bordered on grim. During their day-to-day lives, they were students at the Colony's single college. But once classes ended for the day, they shed their school uniforms and donned the black robes of their hardline, conservative religious sect. But even among the most faithful congregants of the Ministry of the New Age, these youngsters were thought of as puritans. Some even viewed them as dangerous extremists, although the students were careful to never advocate any political action beyond voting. At least not publicly.

Upon Cornelius' entrance, each of the students stood and saluted.

Hail, wise leader, they projected in unison. *We are assembled here in service of our race.*

Cornelius returned their salute, although, in truth, he cared little for all the formalities.

But his soldiers—and that is what the students were, whether they knew it or not—clearly enjoyed all the military trappings. Cornelius supposed it wasn't too much to give them in return for their blind loyalty. These were his spies, his eyes and ears that could slip unnoticed into places he could not. And in the coming revolution, they would be the strong arm of his regime.

He motioned for the students to sit, then got down to business. *The revolution is drawing near, my good soldiers. I know you've heard those words spoken time and again, but we stand mere days away from firing the first shots. I have prepared a weapon that will give our cause the greatest advantage ever imagined. Our triumph is all but assured.*

What is this weapon, sir? The youngest student, Dorian, asked.

His fellow revolutionaries gave him withering looks for his impertinence, but Cornelius calmed them with a small hand gesture. *All in good time, Dorian. All in good time. But first, tell me what you've learned since our last meeting.*

They each took a turn giving a report. Most of it was the usual fluff, little more than gossip about the powerful members of Colonial society. Wealthy businessmen and liberal educators with deviant sexual proclivities. Minor government officials with addictions to illicit substances. Members of the police force accepting bribes. All the usual graft and corruption that kept a functioning society afloat. To this small cadre of young religious zealots, such things were unforgivable transgressions that the gods would punish in the afterlife. But they were idealistic.

For Cornelius, these scraps of knowledge were more practical. They gave him political leverage that he would need in the coming months. No revolution could be successful without a healthy supply of blackmail. Cornelius listened to each report, making mental notes of the sins his peers would prefer stay hidden. He would pay each of these upstanding citizens a visit soon.

Very good, he projected. *Your work pleases me. I'm proud of everything you've done in the service of our cause.*

Their eager thoughts came to him in an overlapping jumble.

He raised a hand to still their clamor, then continued, *This week, I have only one assignment for all of you. Brother Grainger. As we speak, he is inside the First United Church. I want to know why. The sooner, the better. You're dismissed.*

His spies stood and saluted, then filed out of the room. He waited until he heard the back door slam behind them, then sat down heavily on one of the recently vacated chairs. He closed his eyes and sighed. His head ached. It was a dull pain that throbbed slowly, pushing against the backs of his eyeballs so insistently that he was sure they were going to pop out of their sockets. He'd swallowed a handful of analgesic pills an hour ago, washing them down with caffeinated sugar water. Combined, the two substances should have not only cleared his head but also boosted his mood and energy. But his mood was as dark as ever, his energy was at a low ebb, and the headache had only lost a fraction of its grip on his skull. It felt like his brain was being squeezed in a slowly tightening vise.

The cause of his headache and fatigue was no mystery. The strain of forming a connection with his trio of lower caste spies was taking a toll. Forming a psychic connection with the rats was no easy feat under the best circumstances, and these conditions were far from ideal. The distance was too great to establish anything other than tenuous connection. The visions he glimpsed through their eyes were a blurry, disjointed mess. Their thoughts came to him through fuzzy layers of psychic static interference. He wasn't sure that his responses even cut through.

He reminded himself that any amount of pain was worth the reward that awaited him when his plans finally came to fruition. His resolve did little to soothe the pain.

* * *

Vicar Abraham poured himself a second cup of tea and gazed through the steam at Grainger, who sat across the table, feeling profoundly uncomfortable. They were in the vicar's office, a cozy room located behind the chapel. The chairs were oversized and overstuffed, the herbal tea was sweet and soothing, but still, Grainger couldn't seem to relax.

The vicar blew on his tea and projected, *I'm not sure how you'd like me to answer your questions.*

Grainger shrugged. *Honestly would be just fine.*

Well, of course. The vicar's smile exposed a pair of neatly filed and sparkly white incisors. *What I mean is, from what perspective should I answer? The gospels acknowledge that there was a time when the social status of human and Colonist was quite unbalanced. They speak quite plainly about a time long ago, when our ancestors lived below ground and in the shadows, feeding on the scraps left behind by humans. And these humans were far from the primitive savages we know today. They had technology to rival and even exceed our own. And from historical texts, we know that their society bore some resemblance to ours. But that's not really what you're asking, is it?*

Not really, Grainger agreed. *I'm not asking if there's a theological basis for coexistence among human and Colonist. I'm asking if there's anything in the holy book, perhaps buried in some obscure prophecy, about a time when human and Colonist would unite.*

Vicar Abraham looked confused. *You mean a time when our societies might blend peacefully?*

No. Grainger shook his head. *I mean* unite *in the most literal sense. Biologically. Do you understand?*

The vicar set his teacup on his desk. He fixed Grainger with a serious look. *Genetically?*

Grainger nodded. *Yes. In the name of both species being able to flourish and reclaim the planet. Would church doctrine allow for mingling the races if they produced viable offspring?*

You realize the very notion is considered blasphemy?

I was raised in this church, Grainger reminded him. *I understand all too well the implications of what I'm saying. And believe me when I say that the idea is as disgusting to me as it is morally repugnant to you. But times will soon be desperate, and sooner than you think. Even disgusting and morally repugnant solutions must be considered if they can ensure our people's survival. Surely you can agree with that?*

No, I'm afraid I cannot. The vicar sighed, pinching his snout. *As a member of the clergy, I am compelled to reject the idea out of hand. And yet...*

Grainger leaned forward. *What?*

The vicar sighed. *As someone who studied the rationalist philosophy before entering seminary, I understand — not agree with, but* understand — *your position. The church isn't prepared to go to war with the scientific community over genetics research. After all, we're talking about chemical compounds, test tubes, and computers. It's not the same as bestiality. Because even a scientist with a profound sense of clinical detachment would never suggest...*

Grainger held up a hand. *Certainly not.*

He sat back in his chair and sipped his tea, which had gone lukewarm. The conversation moved to less controversial topics, and Grainger could sense the vicar's relief. After what he felt was a respectful interval, Grainger stood up and apologized for keeping the vicar from his regular duties.

Nonsense. The vicar moved from behind his desk and led Grainger out of the office. *You are always welcome in this house of the gods. You and all your fellow Council members. Brother Garlan and Sister Morraine are active in the church, but I supposed you already knew that.*

Grainger feigned some enthusiasm about the idea of renewing his faith, but he suspected the young vicar knew it was purely for show. Still, the young fellow spewed a steady stream of upbeat thoughts at Grainger as they made their way through the chapel. The First United Church may not have taken many hard political stances, but they weren't shy about currying favor with the government and getting members of the church elected to any available position.

Please don't be a stranger. Vicar Abraham shook hands with Grainger, then opened the front door.

Grainger thanked him again for his time and set off down the main path of the District of Whispers.

* * *

Jane was a full three years older and two semesters ahead at the university, but Dorian was the one who came up with the idea. He'd pulled Jane aside when the meeting broke and laid out the details of the plan in the shadows behind the Temple of the Rat.

Our great leader wants to know about Councilman Grainger, right? Although Dorian projected his thoughts at the level of a psychic whisper, he still paused to scan the dark alley for eavesdroppers. *He also said that the time of revolution is drawing near. Don't you understand? This is what he* wants *us to do.*

He said to follow Councilman Grainger, just like we've been doing, Sully argued. *He didn't say anything about intimidating some vicar.*

Of course, he can't come right out and say it. Dorian smiled and put a hand on the older Colonist's shoulder. *Brother Cornelius may be the leader of the revolution, but he's still a member of the Council. He can't afford to speak so directly. He has to have some sort of...what is it called...oh yeah, plausible deniability.*

The young Colonist's ambition was matched by his persuasiveness, and before he knew it, Jane found herself at the front door of the First United Church. She and Dorian had donned black helmets and black gloves, like they were preparing for an excursion to the surface. They'd taken a circuitous, back alley route to the church, and along the way, Jane had glimpsed his refection is a puddle of water. She looked tough, intimidating. It was thrilling to see herself looking like something other than a university student with few prospects beyond a career in academia. As the group's only female member, she often wondered if the others took her seriously. The Colonist reflected on the surface of the puddle certainly looked the part of a true revolutionary soldier, not some meek bookworm. But that thrilling boost of bravery withered as Dorian pounded his gloved fist on the church's front door.

One of the church matrons answered Dorian's insistent knocking. She opened the door just enough to poke her head through the gap. She gasped when she saw the two disguised youths standing there. Dorian stuck his foot in the doorway before the matron could slam it shut.

We need a word with the vicar in residence, he projected.

We have no vicar in residence, the matron responded frantically.

The gospel is very clear about the sin of dishonesty. Dorian shoved the matron inside the church foyer. She squealed as she fell to the floor.

Dorian stepped inside the building, but Sully hesitated on the threshold. Her bravado crumbled in that moment. A sudden realization about who she was and what she was doing slammed her like a fist to the gut. Standing on the doorstep of the church, an epiphany dawned with brutal clarity, like staring into a floodlight after emerging from a darkened room. Deep down, Jane knew she was no revolutionary soldier. She was a shy, weak, awkward adolescent who had spent her teenage years playing that role, but it wasn't who she really was. Looking down into the terrified face of the matron, who might well have been her grandmother, Jane felt a seasick mingling of fear, regret, and pity for the matron as well as for herself.

Panic took hold of Jane. She felt like she couldn't breathe inside the confines of her helmet. She fumbled with the switch on the faceplate, checking to make sure that the vent was open.

Dorian loomed over the matron. *Pay attention, you old bitch, because I'm only going to ask one more time. Where is the vicar?*

She shook her head. *There's no one else here at this hour.*

I guess we'll do it the hard way, then. Dorian drew back his foot and kicked the matron in the head. The current fashion among university students was mismatched, baggy clothing and heavy work-boots. Dorian was always dressed according to the latest trends, and his foot was shod in a black metalworker's boot. The kick he delivered was enough to shatter the matron's skull. Blood pooled around her as she tried in vain to crawl away from her attacker. Her hands couldn't find a grip on the slippery floor. Her claws snapped off one by one as she sought to pull herself forward.

Her thoughts spilled out in garbled panic. *No not this way hurts gods above forgive don't hurt me my children please no not like this not prepared help me someone please help me…*

Dorian raised his foot again, and this time, he stomped rather than kicked. The thick, hard sole of his boot splattered the matron's head on the polished stone floor. Jane's stomach heaved at the sight. She fumbled at her chinstrap as she struggled to draw breath. She tugged the helmet off her head and dropped it.

You see that? Dorian asked, taking off his own helmet. *Looked like a fucking melon getting dropped off a rooftop. Gonna have to wash these boots, I guess. Look here, there's little bits of skull stuck in the tread.*

Jane swallowed frantically, offering a silent prayer that she wouldn't vomit in a house of the gods. It was a silly thought. She'd just abetted a murder in a house of the gods. A line had been crossed, and there was no going back.

You could have warned me, Jane projected.

Hey, I didn't know the old bitch was going to play dumb like that. Dorian shrugged. *If she'd just answered the fucking question, I could have made it quick and painless.* He reached into his pocket and produced a knife with a serrated edge. *Just tickle her throat with this, and she'd have gone to sleep.*

You never said anything about killing anyone. Jane wiped her mouth with the back of her hand. Her stomach had quit flip-flopping like a landed fish, but she still felt sick.

Come on, friend. Don't play innocent, Dorian laughed. *You didn't think we were just going to come here and conduct a quiet interview, did you? We can't leave witnesses.*

But the helmets...

Dorian rolled his eyes. *Those were just in case someone outside was watching. Try to keep up, friend. Now, let's go find this fucking vicar and see what he can tell us about that race traitor Grainger.*

They found the vicar's rooms easily enough. As a child, Dorian's family had attended the First United Church, but after his mother's departure, the family lapsed. Although it had been ten years since he'd set foot in the building, Dorian remembered the way with only a couple false turns. With each step, Jane offered the gods fervent, silent prayers that Dorian's memory would fail him and they'd be forced to turn back and leave the church. But the nameless gods of the Colony weren't in a listening mood. In a matter of minutes, she found herself standing shoulder to shoulder with Dorian outside the vicar's apartment in the church attic.

Are you ready? Dorian asked.

Yeah, sure. Jane's thought projection didn't match her feelings. She wasn't ready, not for this kind of work. And she knew she never would be.

Dorian knocked on the door. The knock was answered by squeaking bedsprings and soft footfalls from within the apartment. Then a sleep-slowed thought projection: *One moment, Melinda. Let me make myself decent.*

Dorian's lips pulled back in an incisor-baring grin. His eyes sparkled with cruel bloodlust. Jane did her best to match her comrade's expression. She tried to force herself to accept his role in this tragedy. She managed to smile, but inwardly, all she could do was wish that she'd never even heard of Brother Cornelius.

The bleary-eyed Colonist who opened the door wasn't much older than Jane. He was wearing a bathrobe over a simple nightshirt. A pair of wire-rimmed spectacles sat atop his snout.

You're not Melinda. The vicar's thoughts were still slowed by lingering traces of sleep.

Was that the old bitch's name? Dorian shoved the door open, staggering the vicar. He brandished his knife. *She played dumb with us, so she is sadly departed.*

No. The vicar was wide awake now. *What have you done?*

Sit down, Dorian commanded. *We ask the questions, and you answer them. Pretty simple, even for a superstitious asshole, right?*

The gods will judge you for your actions. It's not too late to turn away from this sinful course. The vicar, having apparently decided that Dorian was a lost cause, looked pleadingly at Jane. *Please, we can pray about this. I'll help you…*

Dorian drew back his hand cuffed the vicar across the face. The blow sent his glasses flying. *There are no gods, vicar. It's all bullshit invented to scare us into blind obedience. But there are some of us who have the courage to see this world for what it is, and it's our turn now. We're going to lead our race back to the surface of this planet.*

I see that you're already lost. The vicar sighed.

Right. Let's get down to business. Dorian's smile widened.

Chapter Thirteen
Life At The Outpost

Bruno's Last Chance was the last outpost between the wasteland forest and the abandoned city. It was aptly named, sitting at the edge of dusty expanse of nothingness. It made the roughest settlements of the western coast look like the lap of luxury. Even Lord Hannibal's brothel was palatial by comparison. Bruno's Last Chance was little more than a flophouse and brothel, a saloon, a garage, and general store surrounded by a corrugated metal fence topped with razor wire.

A gang of mutants guarded the front gate. A pair of them —the least deformed of the bunch—carried rifles, while the rest were armed with an assortment of clubs, axes, pitchforks, and knives. None of them looked particularly alert as Kurt made his approach. They continued to converse among themselves as they slouched against the fence, scratching their scabby faces and picking their bulbous noses. Nevertheless, Kurt raised his hands in the timeless and universal gesture of peaceful intentions.

"Hello there," he called. "My team and I are looking to rest and resupply."

One of the rifle-carriers stepped forward. "Got gold or scrap to trade? Salvage team, right?"

The mutant pointed into the distance, where the rest of the team were waiting. They were far enough away that they wouldn't seem a threat, not to these slow-witted guards, at least. But they were well within range of Lilith and Lucifer's sniper rifles. At the moment, both scouts were crouched behind their bikes, watching the scene through their scopes. The rest of the team was locked and loaded as well. If things went south, the mutants would be cut down before they got close enough for Kurt to smell their rotten breath. This wasn't the team's first wasteland excursion.

Kurt shook his head. "We're on our way to a score. Nothing to trade at the moment."

"No credit here. Go away." The mutant's voice was gravelly and phlegm-choked. The bald spots on his head were red raw and oozing pus. Flies buzzed around him.

A trio of rats scampered among his fellow guards, weaving their way through a maze of oversized boots. One of the mutants kicked at them, but the rats dodged the foot. They retreated from the group and disappeared one by one through a small gap in the fence.

"Damn rats," the lead guard spat. "I hope the cats eat them for supper."

The rest of the mutants grunted in agreement, chattering among themselves about how much they hated rats. Some of them opined that there was good eating on a rat, while others said they were only good for feeding to dogs or cats.

"I have a voucher from your boss," Kurt said, steering the subject back to the business at hand. Rats may have been an interesting topic of conversation for this gang of mutants, but he didn't really give a shit about them. Rats were just harmless vermin. On the spectrum of threats lurking in the wasteland, they didn't even register.

The mutant shook his head, scattering the flies. "Bruno say no vouchers. Cash only."

"Not that boss. I have a voucher from Lord Hannibal."

At the mention of that name, all the guttural chatter stopped. The entire gang of mutants straightened up. This deep in the wasteland, Lord Hannibal's name drew attention. More than that, Lord Hannibal's voucher—complete with its ornate gold seal hologram—opened doors.

And that's just what happened when Kurt showed the mutant the screen of the transponder beacon. The device crackled, then displayed a flickering hologram projection.

"Looks legit," the mutant said. The fly-bedeviled brute unlocked the gate and motioned for Kurt to enter. Kurt paused just long enough to give his team the "all clear" signal, then stepped inside. The mutants remained on the other side of the fence. Apparently, this outpost followed the usual rule of keeping any mutants, even those on the payroll, outside and well away from the paying customers.

Kurt paused a few paces past the threshold and gave the place a quick once-over. It was a small, ramshackle version of the outpost where Kurt had met with Lord Hannibal. There were dozens just like it scattered throughout the wasteland. And like all the others, Bruno's Last Chance wasn't a place for letting down one's guard. It may have looked like quaint and peaceful, but a wasteland outpost was always full of bad elements. Kurt's team had learned that the hard way over the years. There were no safe havens in the wasteland.

Kurt made his way across the center courtyard, his boots crunching on gravel and broken glass. He headed straight for the brothel, not because he wanted any excitement, but because that's inevitably where an outpost's boss was found. The brothel was a two-story building clad in mismatched panels of corrugated metal, probably taken from the same salvaged supply as the materials used in the perimeter fence.

Although it looked remarkably free of rust, no effort had been made to paint the exterior.

A pair of guards flanked the front entrance. They were conspicuously armed with rifles and a pistol on each hip. Their weathered faces and impassive expressions were half-hidden beneath the shade of their wide-brimmed hats. They gave Kurt a quick, silent appraisal as he passed.

A sign hanging over the front door designated the place as a hotel, but the lobby was full of scantily clad women lounging on couches. Their makeup-caked faces radiated an aura of boredom and intoxication. Another pair of armed guards were stationed in the room. They stood in a corner, as still and grim as gargoyles. There was a platform in the center of the room, atop which stood a circular desk. The man behind the desk stood as Kurt made his approach.

"Welcome, traveler," the man said. He was an impressive specimen, built like a wrestler.

His meaty arms were covered in a colorful assortment of tattoos. His head was perfectly bald, and a grey beard hung to the middle of his chest. When he smiled, he revealed a mouthful of teeth filed to sharp points.

"You the man in charge?" Kurt asked, pausing to smile and wink at a pair of conjoined twins occupying one of the room's many couches. They were joined at the side and shared a third leg between them. Three legs, two arms, four breasts, and two faces, both of which stared at him with something like amusement.

"You like Trixie and Sherry? I gotta tell you up front that it's twice the rate to take them upstairs. They got two sets of functioning parts though, so you look at it that way, it's not a bad deal," the bearded man said.

"Not that it doesn't sound intriguing, but that's not what I'm here for." Kurt stepped onto the platform and gave the man a good look at Lord Hannibal's voucher. "Am I correct in assuming this is enough to get all the hospitality this place has to offer?"

The man's demeanor changed upon seeing the voucher. He nodded enthusiastically. "You bet your ass it does. Name's Deacon. I'm the boss 'round here. Anything you and your crew needs, we'll make it happen. Anyone gives you any shit, you just let me know and I'll get it straightened out. Just remember your job is finished and Lord Hannibal asks you how it went; a good word in his ear can go a long way for us out here in the wilderness."

Kurt smiled. *Now that's more like it.*

If there was ever any doubt about how much pull Lord Hannibal had throughout the wasteland, this removed it.

"So, what will it be?" Deacon asked.

"Dinner and a place to sleep tonight. In the morning, we'll take some provisions and fuel up our bikes. We'll be out of your hair bright and early."

"It's no trouble. Stay as long as you like."

"I appreciate that, but like I said, we'll be out of here at first light." Kurt could hear the rumble of engines as his team rode through the front gates. The whores lounging in the lobby perked up a bit at the prospect of new business.

"My bum knee has been screaming bloody murder at me all day," Deacon said, reaching down to rub the joint in question.

Kurt shrugged sympathetically. "I'm sorry to hear that."

"Means there's rain coming. Probably tonight. Your crew might want to rethink that early departure. Gets muddy in these parts after a good rain. Makes travel mighty difficult."

"Didn't look too cloudy out there," Kurt replied.

"Yeah, but I'm telling you that my knee is as good as any science equipment when it comes to predicting rain."

"I guess we'll just have to see how it goes. Right now, I'd like to get our accommodations squared away. We've been riding hard for a while," Kurt said.

"Understood." Deacon turned his head and barked out orders. A pair of burly men dressed in overalls emerged from a back room. "Boys, there's a crew of salvage hounds out there in the courtyard," Deacon told them. "Go see that their vehicles get fueled up, lubed, and washed. Then put them in the garage for the next."

The two men grunted and hustled off to follow Deacon's orders.

"Where would a man go if he wanted a plate of food and a stiff drink?" Kurt asked.

Deacon pointed in the direction of the front door. "Yonder saloon can fix you up with a bowl of pork and beans, plus a shot of whiskey or three. Ain't nothing gourmet about it, but it's good, honest food and strong liquor."

"That'll do just fine." Kurt went outside to give the team an update on their situation.

* * *

Gar caught up to the murderous bastards just as they were within sight of the outpost. The elders had always said that outsiders were weak compared to the forest clans, and Gar had seen nothing to challenge that belief. The group he was following stopped to eat and rest, whereas he barely even stopped to piss. They left clear tracks for him to follow, too. It was as if they didn't think they could be attacked from behind.

He lay with his belly on the hot sand and watched the outsiders ride their noisy machines through the outpost gates. A lifetime spent in the shade of the forest canopy had left him unaccustomed to direct sunlight, and his pale skin burned and blistered. He squinted his eyes against the glare. Sweat ran in rivulets down his forehead and into his eyes. He ignored the physical discomfort. Any amount of pain was eased by the prospect of revenge.

One by one, they will die by my hands, he promised. *Their pleas will be like music to my ears.*

Gar himself had never seen an outpost—he'd never wandered more than a few miles from his clan's territory—but he'd heard stories from the men who ventured out of the woods and raided such places. According to these stories, outposts were rich in supplies, but sometimes fortified and well-defended. The raiding parties who attacked them always suffered heavy losses.

But as Gar lay there and studied the outpost, he was convinced that one man might succeed where a party of fifty often failed. Stealth and surprise were on his side, after all.

Once night fell, he'd find out if his newfound confidence was justified.

* * *

The team had gathered around one of the big round tables in the saloon and wolfed down bowls of beans flavored with salt pork, hot peppers, vinegar, and honey. Some of them tossed back shots of liquor, while others stuck to beer, their hangovers still too fresh in their memory for them to indulge in any of the hard stuff. Duke was no shrinking violet. If the booze was free, then he was drinking, hangovers be damned. The waitresses—a pair of doe-eyed and pudgy women—made sure that their glasses and bowls were filled. They weren't much to look at, but they worked with a silent efficiency that Duke appreciated.

"This is a nice place," he said, looking around the room. "Probably not as nice as Lord Hannibal's digs, but then again, none of us even got to see the inside of that little oasis."

He shot a look down the table at Kurt to see if their fearless leader would take the bait. But it didn't look like Kurt even heard him. Duke sighed and went back to shoveling his dinner into his mouth. The truth was, he didn't give a shit if he ever got to set foot in one of Lord Hannibal's outposts. He doubted they were any different than this dump. The saloon that he'd just praised was really just another nondescript building cobbled together from cinderblock, salvaged metal, and petrified wood. The floor was covered in sawdust and sand, and the bar was stocked with one type of liquor and barrels of flat, bitter beer. There was a stoop-shouldered old man in the back corner of the room plucking a mournful tune on a banjo while a couple of the outpost guards tapped their toes, but that was the extent of the entertainment. Well, that was all the entertainment the saloon had to offer anyway. The boarding house was a different story. The cursory glance Duke had given the lobby had revealed plenty of entertainment options there. Of course, none of them were half as appealing as the woman sitting next to him. But she was much more than cheap entertainment.

"I was just thinking," Duke said between mouthfuls, "I don't see any pigs around here. I wonder just what the hell we're eating."

Rosemary, seated to his right, shot an elbow into his ribs. "Come on, partner. I'm trying to enjoy this meal."

He dropped his spoon into his bowl and raised his hands defensively. "Hey, I'm just saying that at least we know where my barbecue came from."

Laughter and murmurs of approval went around the table. Truth be told, the food from the saloon was just fine, but Duke didn't intend to let anyone forget that he was capable of filling their bellies with hot food, even when they were riding hard. Sure as hell Kurt never dropped a boar with a rifle shot then almost singlehandedly barbecued the beast.

Yeah, and he also probably never formed a goddamn psychic link with it either.

Duke chased the thought away with a mouthful of whiskey. He shoved his half-emptied bowl away and leaned back slightly in his chair. He stretched his arms over his head, then lowered them. He draped his left over his full belly and slipped the right around the back of Rosemary's chair.

He glanced around the table. The group was quiet this evening. Kurt and his bitch Diana had their head together in hushed conversation. Same story for Lilith and Lucifer. Seemed like the two couples were excited about the prospect of some privacy at night. The people seated around them might as well have been on the moon. Deus, who could usually be counted on for some decent mealtime conversation, was uncharacteristically silent. Ever since he'd returned from his solitary meditation in the forest, he'd looked distracted. Probably some theological knot he was trying to unravel. Holy men were always wrestling with some internal debate. Duke thought it was a waste of time to worry about such nonsense. He had more immediate concerns.

"I hear desert nights are cold," he said. "Good thing there's plenty of beans on the menu."

"Suddenly, I'm glad that we aren't sharing a room," Taurus said from across the table.

Duke turned to his right. "How about you, partner? You happy to be sleeping alone tonight or would you like some company?"

The scattered bits of hushed conversation around the table went abruptly silent. Duke suspected he might have overplayed his hand. This suspicion was confirmed when Rosemary shrugged his arm away.

"We may ride together," she said, shooting him a withering look, "but we ain't sleeping together. Get that shit straight right now."

"Hey, just kidding." He forced a laugh. "You know how it is. A couple of drinks go right to my head. That's the price of maintaining my girlish figure."

The joke was dead on arrival. Eleven pairs of eyes were on him, and none of them sparkled with amusement. No laughter, just the sounds of chewing. Duke scraped his chair back from the table and stood up.

"Bunch of grim-faced fucks in this crew," he announced. "Like a fucking funeral party. Anyone needs me, I'll be back at the boarding house. Maybe the folks there are in a better mood."

He didn't wait for a response. He beat a hasty retreat out of the saloon and headed across the dusty courtyard. The urge to silently curse Rosemary for being a frigid, humorless bitch was strong within him, but he fought it down. She was still his future queen, whether she knew it or not. It was a dumb move on his part, making that comment in front of everyone, but it was done and that was that.

A couple of cats scampered out of the alley between the general store and the boarding house. They paused in the open space, regarding him with eyes that shone in the flickering light that hung above the building's entrance. Duke stopped a short distance from the cats. He crouched down and looked back at them. One of the cats, a grey tabby cocked its head to one side, interested. The other, a scrawny orange thing, looked away, dismissing him with a sniff.

The tabby took a couple tentative steps forward.

Food? Got food?

The voice came to Duke from within his own head, just as it had during his encounter with the boar. But the voice was softer, the tone gentler.

Hungry. Got food?

"Sorry, little guy," Duke said. "I got nothing. My crew is back there in the saloon, polishing off their dinner. You might try there instead."

Duke reached out and gave the cat a scratch behind the ears. It leaned into the touch and purred for a moment, then stepped away.

Feels good, thanks. Gotta go. Need food.

The tabby set off at a leisurely pace. The bedraggled

orange cat finished giving its paw a tongue bath and headed in the same direction. On its way past him, the cat shot a thought into Duke's head.

Humans are shit. You're shit.

Duke nearly laughed. "Hey, fuck you, buddy."

The cat looked over its shoulder and hissed, then continued on its way toward the saloon. As far as conversations went, it wasn't the worst Duke had shared. He stood up, wiped his hands on his knees, and walked on.

The lobby of the boarding house was bright and lively compared to the saloon. The platform in the center of the room had to be repurposed as a stage on which a trio of women were plucking stringed instruments and singing in a language Duke didn't recognize. He supposed the lyrics didn't matter much when the harmonies were this sweet. It was a shame that their talent was wasted out here in the backside of nowhere. West of the mountains, these three women could have played to a crowded theater. Out here, they were relegated to a fleabag brothel. Duke blinked his eyes. The air in the room was so thick with devil weed smoke that tears ran down Duke's cheeks.

Deacon, the outpost's mayor, detached himself from a couch, where he'd been enjoying the music with a whore on each side. He had a bottle of liquor in one hand and a smoking pipe in the other.

"Hey there, traveler," his voice boomed over the sweet strains of music. "Come sit with me. This liquor tastes like piss, but it gets the job done, and this devil weed makes the world look much better. We can enjoy some good music. They don't know any songs with words from the common tongue, but they sure as hell can sing, ain't that right?"

Duke shook his head. "No, thanks, old-timer. I had some other entertainment in mind."

Deacon may have been drunk and high, but he took the hint straight away. He swept his arm around expansively, slopping liquor out of the bottle. "Well, son, you just take your pick. Lord Hannibal's voucher is good enough for as much *entertainment* as your pecker can handle."

Duke looked around the room. There were at least a dozen whores lounging on the chairs and sofas. Some of them were swaying to the music, while others just clutched pipes stuffed with devil weed and stared at the ceiling.

"Decisions, decisions," he said.

"I won't pretend to know your tastes, but allow me to make a suggestion." Deacon put his arm around Duke's shoulder. "Men will travel a hundred miles out of their way for a night with Trixie and Sherry."

"Which ones are they?" Duke asked.

Deacon slapped him on the back. "Why, they're my twins, of course. They may share one heart, got two working sets of plumbing, if you know what I mean."

Duke followed the proprietor's gaze to a sofa on the far side of the smoky room. The twins weren't just identical, they were joined at the shoulder and hip.

"I know what you're thinking," Deacon said. "But you're wrong. They ain't mutants, just a good old fashioned genetic anomaly. Came here from out west, where they were part of a traveling sideshow. They got tired of their owner beating them and having his way with them, so one night, while the son of a bitch was sleeping, they cut his throat. But you know how it is back in civilization. Some judge would have had them strung up in short order, so they fled into the wasteland. Ended up here, oh, I guess going on ten years ago. They're my prize kittens."

On cue, the twins turned their heads to smile at him. Two tongues licked two sets of lips in perfect synchronicity. Two sets of fingers ran over the exposed tops of four breasts. Three legs crossed and uncrossed, then crossed again in such a complex arrangement that it had to be the result of hours of practice. Duke's first instinct had been to reject the offer outright. He wasn't into exotics. But the experience at the dinner table had left him with a heavy load of pent-up frustration. Maybe the twins would be the perfect outlet. And hell, it wasn't like it would cost him anything to find out. Probably the only chance he'd have to experience something like this, too.

"Yeah, I think they'll do just fine," Duke said.

"Good choice, son." Deacon snapped his fingers. "Sherry, Trixie! This gentleman would like your services for the evening."

Duke marveled at the way the twins moved from the couch to the staircase on the other side of the room. They made their way through the crowded maze of furniture as nimbly as any other person. He wondered if they had over time developed some psychic connection between their brains that allowed them to coordinate their movements.

Maybe you should ask them if they can also communicate psychically with certain animals?

He shoved the thought aside. Now wasn't the time for contemplating life's mysteries. He followed the twins up the stairs, hanging back a couple steps so he could enjoy the view of two asses moving beneath a form-fitting layer of thin fabric. He wondered if it was expensive to have a wardrobe custom made. He had so many questions. He supposed most of them would go unanswered, and that was a shame. However, his most important curiosities were going to be satisfied in short order, if the looks the twins gave him as they paused at the top of the staircase were any indication.

"Come on, handsome, we ain't got all night," one set of red painted lips said while the other giggled girlishly. "Sherry's only laughing on account of she does that when she gets horny."

Well, Duke thought, *I guess that solves one mystery. Sherry operates their right arm. Wonder if they're ambidextrous? Probably a few creative ways to figure that one out…*

They turned, pivoting on their center foot with a dancer's easy grace, and led him down the hall to an open room. He followed them inside, closing the door behind him.

Duke had been in his share of brothels. Growing up in the wasteland, you learned early that certain urges had to be satisfied regularly to keep your wits about you. The easiest way to take care of that, assuming you weren't keen on taking it by force, was to hire a professional. Duke had never enjoyed forcing himself on a woman, at least not the way his brothers had. He preferred a willing partner. And since he wasn't the romantic type, nearly all his sexual experience had been with whores. He wasn't at all ashamed of that. He liked whores. They were willing to do whatever it took to survive in the wasteland. That was something they had in common with him.

Since his experience with brothels and whorehouses was so wide-ranging, Duke knew that this one was on the nicer end of the spectrum. The lights in the room were dim, but he could tell that the bed, if not exactly clean, was at least not damp from the last customer. There was a basin of water on a bedside table, and in one corner, a privy behind a curtain. The floor wasn't spotless, but he felt confident enough to kick off his boots without fear of splinters or bits of broken glass or rusty nails.

The twins disrobed in a matter of seconds. They wore nothing beneath their dress, so there wasn't much clothing to remove. Trixie's hand dropped the garment onto the bedside table, careful to keep it away from the basin. And then, they were in bed, completely naked.

"Come on, big boy," Trixie commanded.

"Yeah, let's see what you got," Sherry giggled.

When Deacon had first suggested the twins, a flicker of doubt had crossed Duke's mind. In theory, the prospect was fascinating, and, from a certain perspective, challenging. But it was the erotic aspect that gave him the moment's pause.

When the time came, would he be able to perform? Or would he actually be repulsed?

It turned out that he wasn't going to have any trouble. As he looked at the twins' naked form lying atop the wrinkled sheets, he couldn't get his clothes off fast enough. He was so erect that he had difficulty removing his pants.

The twins were beautiful. Their matched sets of breasts were perfect handfuls. Their legs—all three of them—were smooth and muscular. Two heads worth of auburn hair cascaded over their shoulders. Both had emerald green eyes encircled in dark blue circles of makeup. Even in the room's dim light, their faces sparkled with glitter. The last time Duke had been on the coast—nearly six years ago—the fashion for women was dark eye makeup and glitter. The trends of the day took a while to percolate into the wasteland, it seemed. But Duke didn't give a shit about fashion.

"Me first," Trixie said, spreading her legs.

Duke didn't argue. In an instant, he was between those legs, sighing as he worked himself inside her. Once he got a slow rhythm going, he leaned down and kissed Sherry while her sister moaned. He pulled back and ran his hands over the pebbled flesh of three dark red nipples. The sisters moaned. Sherry touched herself as she watched, offering encouragement.

"Don't worry," Duke gasped, looking over at Sherry. "I've got enough for you too."

Sherry moaned, her hand darting between her thighs to touch herself while she waited for her turn. Duke offered words of encouragement, but he soon found himself closing his eyes and imagining that the wet tightness gripping his dick belonged to Rosemary rather than Deacon's astounding genetic anomaly.

* * *

The saloon had a back porch that was crowded with mismatched rocking chairs and stools. After they finished eating, the team—minus Duke—gathered there to look at the cloudy sky and circulate bottles of liquor among themselves. The weather was an obvious choice for the topic of conversation. The sun was setting behind a bank of angry red clouds. Gusts of winds kicked up every few minutes, whipping the sandy terrain outside the outpost walls into brief tornados. Thunder rumbled in the distance. It seemed that Deacon's knee was right after all.

There was a storm blowing in.

One by one, the team dispersed, heading back to the boarding house to get some sleep or to stretch their legs with a stroll down the outpost's central avenue. Soon, only four of them remained: Kurt, Diana, Taurus, and Deus. Kurt sat on a creaky rocking chair with Diana perched on his lap. Taurus was on a similar chair, rocking slowly as he sipped from a bottle of the saloon's eye-wateringly strong liquor. The holy man remained standing. He couldn't stay still for more than a moment, pacing random paths back and forth across the petrified wooden boards.

"Damn it, man. Would you sit down?" Kurt said as Deus passed. "It's fucking exhausting to watch you wear a rut in the floorboards. You've been acting weird all day long, ever since you went off by yourself in the woods. Suppose you just spit out whatever's on your mind instead of pacing back and forth like some nervous virgin."

"They're petrified," Taurus said.

Kurt shot him a look. "What?"

"I'm just saying it's not like he's actually going to wear a rut in the porch," Taurus explained.

Diana put a hand to her mouth to stifle a laugh.

"Tell you what, Taurus," said Kurt, "just stick to getting to the bottom of that bottle.

You're in way over your head."

Taurus smiled and raised his bottle. "Cheers, boss."

Diana continued her losing battle with laughter while Kurt turned his attention back to Deus. "I'm saying this as both your friend and the captain of this team. Put your ass in a chair and explain yourself."

Taurus emptied his bottle of liquor and heaved himself out of his rocking chair. "Pardon me, but I think I'll leave y'all to it. Sounds like the boarding house is lively. Maybe I can scare up a game of cards."

"Yeah, I'm sure that's what you'll scare up." Diana rolled her eyes. "Cards, my ass. That place is full to the rafters with whores, and we're here on Lord Hannibal's ticket."

The big man's face flush. He started to stammer out a reply, then thought better of it and headed back into the saloon to refill his bottle.

Deus looked around at his seating options and chose a straight-backed armchair. He sat down slowly, smoothing his robe across his lap.

"Now, spit it out," Kurt told him.

Deus looked at Diana with eyes full of uncertainty.

"No secrets between us," Kurt assured him. "Anything you want to say to me, you can say in front of her."

He felt a brief twinge of guilt as Diana put her arm around his shoulders. He told himself that his encounter with Soledad wasn't his fault. It had been part of a business transaction, nothing more. But would Diana see it that way? The odds of that were grim. But it had no bearing on the matter at hand, so he shook off the notion and focused on Deus.

Finally, the mystic gathered himself and spoke. "We should turn back. Tell Lord Hannibal that you've changed your mind and this job isn't for us."

Now, it was Kurt's turn to laugh. "Stop fucking around and tell me what's really on your mind. Because I know it's not that. We turn tail and run back to Lord Hannibal, we won't get another job worth the pay. And that's if we're lucky enough that he doesn't have some of his henchmen shoot us on the spot."

"And even if we make it out alive, we'll never be able to put together enough money to go north after he blacklists us," Diana added.

"We fought too hard for our reputation to flush it away," Kurt continued. "So if that's what's on your mind, you can rest easy, because there's no fucking way we're walking away from this job. Besides, we're past the point of no return. We're committed."

Deus stared at the darkening sky. There were flashes of lightning on the horizon. He took a deep breath and let it out slowly. "There's something wrong. Can't you feel it? This journey we've undertaken, it's cursed. I've had visions. Terrible omens. Malevolent forces are gathering around us. Damnation lies ahead."

Kurt raised a hand. "Okay, enough with the holy clichés. You got a bad feeling about this job. I get it. This one is a high risk-high reward type deal. It was always going to feel like going against our better judgment. But I was upfront about that from the beginning."

"Terrible visions…" Deus dropped his gaze to the porch, as if contemplating the patterns in the petrified wood planks. "Something inhuman awaits us."

"Yeah, Lord Hannibal said the city had wildlife problems. But we got Taurus and Duke, both of them experienced hunters. Lilith and Lucifer are as good a pair of snipers as you can find. The rest of us aren't exactly shrinking violets. We can take care of business when we have to."

"This mission is cursed," Deus insisted.

Then, it dawned on Kurt what this was really about. "You've been sniffing that goofy dust again, haven't you? That's why you were gone for so long yesterday. You snorted a bunch of that stinking shit and had a bad trip, so now you've got it in your head that the gods have cursed the team."

"The Black Drug is a sacred tool…"

Kurt shook his head. "It's fucking goofy dust, Deus. You can buy the same thing from a thousand pimps and hustlers in the western cities. You see people so strung out on that shit that they can't do anything except stand on street corners and rave about how the Event is going to repeat itself and transform all of us into monsters or whatever crazy idea pops into their heads. You keep sniffing that shit, and you'll end up the same as those idiots."

"You don't understand," Deus said flatly. "You're an unbeliever."

Kurt sighed. "I'm not going down this road with you again. I respect your beliefs. I value your input. More than that, I value your friendship, and that's why I'm going to demand that you hand over your supply of that black shit right now."

Deus continued to stare at the porch for a moment, then stood and produced a pouch from the depths of his robe. He tossed the pouch onto Kurt's lap. "Here you are, my dear leader. I suppose I no longer need it anyway. I bow to your wisdom."

"Cut the shit, Deus." Kurt picked up the holy man's drug supply. He wondered what the hell he could do with it. "I already got Duke acting like an insubordinate fuckwad. I don't need you going all screwy on me. You know I respect your religious beliefs, even if I don't share them. And you know I respect your input. Hell, sometimes I rely on it. But make no mistake, we're committed to this job. There will be no walking away for this team. But if you want to split, I won't stop you."

Deus shook his head slowly. "Abandon my flock? No. Even though I am afraid that we journey into the heart of darkness itself."

He gathered the hem of his robe, holding it above his ankles. Then he jumped the porch's railing and disappeared around the corner of the building.

"Well, you going to explain what the fuck that was about or keep me in suspense?" Diana asked, snuggling closer to Kurt as thunder rumbled in the distance.

"Just typical holy man bullshit," he replied. "But don't worry about Deus. When it comes down to it, he's rock solid. He's been my friend almost from the moment I escaped the crèche."

It was true. Kurt had met Deus when fate threw them together in the sleeper car of a steam train traveling south along the coast. Both of them were fleeing cloistered religious communities and making their first tentative steps into the wider world. Although the faiths they left behind were very different, the two men found enough common ground to continue traveling together as they made their way to the mountains. They found work at the same sheep and cattle ranches as they learned the skills necessary to survive in the outside world. When they left the hard labor of ranch life behind to rob supply caravans with notorious outlaw Julius Rickenbacker, they understood that they shared a bond deeper than simple friendship.

"I hope this job is worth it," Diana said.

"If it helps us get into the northern territories, it's worth it," Kurt replied. "But either way, we got no choice at this point. Come on, let's get back to our room before the storm gets here."

Chapter Fourteen
Red Rain

Gar knew the storm would begin soon. He could smell it. Even though it was the first time that clean, metallic scent tickled his nose without first being filtered through the forest canopy, he recognized it all the same. But that didn't change his plans. If anything, the storm was an unexpected boon. Now, he wouldn't just have the cover of darkness to aid him, he'd also have rain, thunder, and lightning.

"The gods of the forest are watching over me," he whispered.

He was sheltering in a deep hollow between two sand dunes. Sloping walls of red sand towered over him. The color of the sand matched that of the angry sky above him. He lay there, watching the clouds swirl. They hung so low that he thought he might climb to the top of the dunes and touch them with his fingertips. If his mind wasn't so consumed with the prospect of vengeance, he might have been amazed at the terrible beauty of the scene. But all he could do was lay there as the sky gradually darkened from red to black, and the clouds swirled faster and faster.

A faint squeaking sound drew his attention. He turned his head in the direction of the noise, scanning the gently sloping top edge of the dunes that surrounded him. Three rats stood there, peering down at him. They stood shoulder-to-shoulder. Their beady black eyes regarded him with keen interest. The squeaked and chittered as if having a conversation.

Gar briefly considered scrabbling up the dune and killing the rats. He may have been a coward compared to the clan's stout-hearted warriors, but he had always been a skilled hunter. Many times, he'd crept silently upon woodland creatures and killed them before they had a chance to realize what was happening. But he didn't dare risk being seen by the guards at the outpost's front gate, especially not when he still had enough boar meat to quiet his growling belly. He sneered at the rats and opened his bundle of supplies. The meat wasn't rancid yet, but it was edging closer to that state. Gar devoured the little bit that remained. Once he'd slaughtered the inhabitants of the outpost, he could eat his fill of the rich food they were no doubt hoarding behind those walls.

As he chewed, he made a rude gesture at the rats. They bared their oversized incisors in reply, then turned away. Their loathsome pink tails swung over the edge of the dune's rim as they scuttled away.

The gusts of winds became wilder and more frequent, whipping from the top of the dunes to the bottom of the hollow. Grains of sand stung his skin. He drew his animal skin blankets around himself as the lashings of sand drew droplets of blood from his exposed flesh.

Still, he waited. Soon, his time would be at hand.

* * *

Duke was spent. He'd pumped a load into Trixie and had done his best to give her twin sister the same treatment, but his encore performance left something to be desired. The thrill of fucking the exotic twins disappeared as soon as he finished with Trixie. Something like buyer's remorse crept in, and he was ready to be done with the whole thing. But Duke couldn't stand the thought of these women thinking of him as less than capable. Even though he knew he'd likely never see them after he left Bruno's Last Rest, he hated the idea that they might think back on him and sigh with disappointment, or worse, giggle about the encounter. It didn't matter to him that they were whores. They needed to experience his full power.

But the fuck he threw into Sherry was less than full power. It wasn't even fully hard. Still, he thrust away until his hips and lower back ached. Finally, a few half-hearted spurts escaped him and he rolled off.

The twins washed themselves with a rag and some water from the basin. They dressed with the same speed as they'd disrobed, then cooed a few obligatory sweet words before departing.

Duke lay on sheets damp with sweat and semen, staring at the ceiling. There was nothing like an orgasm for clearing his mind. *Two* left him feeling nearly brainwashed. He pulled a blanket up to his waist and listened to the howling wind. Drops of rain slapped against the window and pinged off the building's metal roof. He tried in vain to form some coherent thoughts before he slipped into the slowly eddying current of uneasy sleep. The transition out of the waking world was so seamless that his dreams felt especially vivid and real.

He dreamed that he was fucking Rosemary. There was nothing unusual about that. His dreams of various scenarios involving his riding partner were a common occurrence. Sometimes they even culminated in a nocturnal emission, like he was some teenage boy with a cracking voice rather than a man with years of experience under his belt. But this dream was different.

He was between Rosemary's muscular brown thighs, giving it to her with all he had. But as he gazed down at her, he noticed she was different. This Rosemary had two heads. They were perfectly identical. Their expressions synchronized as they moaned and panted with each thrust. Then, her body began to change. It was like watching the metamorphosis of a strange new breed of insect. Her right hip sprouted a lump of flesh which grew into a third leg. Her ribcage cracked and widened as her chest spread. A second pair of breasts sprouted from her expanding body.

"Don't let me down," the Rosemary on the right said, her hand moving frantically at the newly formed cleft between her legs. "Or I'll go to Kurt and Diana. They can take turns with us. And afterward, we'll make jokes about your limp dick."

"No!" he shouted, trying to keep his rhythm.

The left Rosemary put her hand on his face. "It's okay. Some men just aren't meant to wear the crown."

"No!" he shouted again. "I can do it, I swear!"

But even as he thrust with all his strength into Rosemary, he could feel his erection wilting inside her. The twin on the right laughed as Duke grunted in frustration. His penis, now almost completely flaccid, slipped out. Now, both twins were laughing.

"Get off me," the left twin snorted through her laughter.

"Yeah, you've had your chance," the right twin agreed. "We're going to find your boss, Kurt. He can take care of both of us, I bet. And Diana can watch. She can join in if she wants. She's probably better than you anyway."

"Please, no…" he begged, frantically stroking himself in a vain attempt to coax his erection back to life.

The twins shoved him aside and wriggled out from underneath him. The movement knocked him off the bed. He crashed to the floor…

…and awoke, gasping for breath and tangled in the sheets. They were even more sweat-soaked than they'd been when he'd fallen asleep, and they clung to his skin. He peeled them away, clawing the wet fabric frantically as he struggled to free himself. Once he'd untangled his legs from the sheets' clammy embrace, he heaved himself off the floor. Lightheaded and breathing heavily, his sense of balance failed him. He wobbled for a moment, then sat down on the edge of the bed. The squeaking springs were just loud enough to be heard over the noise of the storm raging outside. The wind howled and shrieked. Thunder rumbled and boomed. There was a sound like rocks hammering against the roof. Duke supposed some hail had joined the party.

I'll have to remind Deus to offer a prayer of thanks to his gods that we weren't caught out in the open during this shit, he thought.

* * *

Gar walked through the storm with grim determination, gripping his axe in one hand and his knife in the other. Each step plunged his feet ankle deep into the wet sand, slowing his progress. He ground his teeth together as he squinted into the darkness. He held his weapons so tightly that his knuckles ached.

When he first emerged from the hollow between the two massive sand dunes, he'd advanced across the open distance in a low, stealthy posture, dodging this way and that to keep himself hidden among the dunes and cacti. Then, he watched the guards retreat into a hastily assembled tent to shelter themselves against the storm. He quit sneaking around and began to make straight for the front gate.

He'd only gone a few steps before his animal skin garments were heavy and sodden. Hail stones—most of them no bigger than pebbles—stung his flesh. The wind whipped up clumps of wet sand and slung them into his face. His hair in hung in sandy, wet ropes. He growled through the discomfort.

The guards' tent was no more than a heavy canvas tarp stretched over a pyramid shaped frame of poles jammed into packed sand. Gar smashed through one of the poles with a single swipe of his axe. It was enough to bring the hastily assembled structure crashing down. The guards howled in surprise. They struggled beneath the weight of the soaking canvas, but not with an urgency that suggested they knew what was coming. Perhaps they thought a heavy hail stone had broken the tent's support, but they didn't respond like a group of trained fighters under surprise attack.

Gar capitalized on their confusion and lack of urgency. He shrugged out of his garments, and wearing only his knee-length pants and his boots, he fell upon the guards, who were still struggling to free themselves from the wet canvas. He stabbed and hacked with blind fury. His knife punched into flesh. His axe broke bones. The muffled screams of his victims were lost in the howling wind and booming thunder.

One of the guards finally managed to free himself, crawling from under the edge of the blood-and-rain-soaked tarp. He was big, his entire body clad in lumpy muscles and bristly black hair. One of his eyes was bulging and oversized, while its fellow was small, sunken, and hidden behind milky white cataracts. He could have been a member of Gar's clan. Maybe he'd once been a proud warrior of one of the forest clans, but an easy life guarding a rich outpost had tempted him away from his people. His massive shoulders and his sloping forehead showed the results of Gar's frenzied attack. Thick, red blood streamed down his face.

"Kill you!" the guard roared, then charged.

Gar sidestepped and swung the axe. The sharpened edge bit deep into the guard's belly.

Gar twisted the handle as he tugged the axe free. Guts spilled from the gaping wound and slopped in a pile at the guard's feet. He staggered then fell to his knees. Gar danced behind him and drew his knife across the guard's throat. He stepped back and let the big man fall.

Another wounded guard crawled out of the collapsed tent just in time to have his skull split open by Gar's axe. A third emerged and managed to make it to his feet before the axe smashed into his neck, nearly separating his head from his shoulders. Before the man's body hit the ground, Gar attacked the writhing pile of canvas with renewed fury, chopping bloody chunks from the disoriented men beneath. Soon, there was no more movement beneath the canvas. Gar stood back and admired his work. His pulse raced. His chest heaved and his lungs burned as he caught his breath. But he wasn't tired. Long hours of chopping wood with heavy axes had built his strength and endurance.

The slaughter had given him a boost of adrenaline as well. For the first time, he understood the berserker fury that the warriors of his clan described. He felt indestructible even though his head swam with the orgasmic intoxication. He breathed deeply. The rich smell of blood mingled with the ozone tang of lightning strikes. In that moment, he felt as if he could hack and slash his way through the planet's population without stopping to rest.

The gate was unlocked. Gar supposed the storm had given the guards a false sense of security. Or perhaps it was laziness, forgetfulness, or some combination of both that caused them to leave it unlocked. Gar shook his head in disbelief. To think that these men could have once been proud warriors of one of the forest clans. He'd killed them without facing even a hint of danger. He wished all those in his clan who'd mocked his cowardice could see him now. But they were dead, every single one of them. Only he remained.

He shoved the gate open and stepped into the outpost's courtyard.

* * *

Duke pulled on his pants and left the room. The hallway was lit only by flashes of lightning outside the windows. That was enough for him to make his way to the staircase. Hand gripping the banister, he stepped down the dark stairs. The first floor of the boarding house was empty. Deacon and his small army of prostitutes had closed up shop for the night. But Duke found what he was looking for easily enough. There was a supply of alcohol behind the desk, no doubt for use as a social lubricant for potential customers and as a recovery elixir for the working girls.

Duke selected a bottle and took it to one of the sofas facing the front window. He eased himself down onto the lumpy cushions and settled in to watch the storm. The prospect of going back to sleep and potentially slipping into the same nightmare was more terrifying than any amount of thunder and lightning and hail.

He took a pull on the bottle and winced. The outpost's liquor was potent, but it tasted like it was distilled from stagnant pools of goat piss. Back when he was a kid, one of Duke's brothers had dared him to taste the luminescent juice from a chemical lantern. The stuff had burned his tongue and left him nauseous and vomiting for the rest of the day, but it had still tasted better than the liquor stocked at Bruno's Last Rest. He wondered if it was distilled in the saloon across the courtyard or if the whores did it during their downtime. Thinking about whores was normally one of Duke's favorite methods for dealing with boredom, but now, it only brought back the memory of his nightmare. He downed another mouthful of the awful liquor to chase those mental images away. Nasty as it was, the liquor was infinitely more palatable than the nightmare.

Outside, the storm was intensifying. Hail came down like shrapnel, splashing in the puddles and beating out a steady din on the roof. Thunder shook the building. Flashes of lightning were so bright that they lit up the entire outpost.

Duke was so enthralled with the lights and noise that it took him a moment to realize that the loud *crack* wasn't due to thunder, but rather a nearly naked man kicking the front door off its hinges.

Duke glimpsed the man in a flash of lightning, and his guts went cold with fear.

The unexpected visitor was a mutant. He was covered in patches of bristly dark hair. His forehead sloped sharply, ending in a brow ridge so pronounced that it hid his eyes in shadow. His only clothing was a pair of ragged leather pants and a pair of moccasins. He growled, his cracked lips peeling back to expose an under-bite so extreme that the teeth of his lower jaw nearly touched the tip of his nose. In his hands, he held a stone axe and dagger. They were crude weapons, and that quality made them all the more terrifying.

Duke's pistol was upstairs, still hanging on his belt. He was shirtless and barefoot, wearing only his pants. The hulking mutant growled something unintelligible. Although Duke didn't understand a single word—or indeed even recognize the language—he got the meaning loud and clear. This ugly son of a bitch belonged to the mutant army that had attacked Duke and his team in the forest. Now, he wanted revenge.

"Take it easy there, big ugly," Duke said, standing up slowly, his hands outstretched in what he hoped was a placating gesture. "Remember, it was those fucking bears that ate your family, not us."

The mutant growled another bunch of garbled nonsense and raised his axe.

"Well, shit," Duke said.

The mutant swung the axe. Duke ducked at the last possible instant. The margin was so narrow that Duke felt his hair blown back by the force of the swing. The momentum carried the mutant forward, and he staggered a couple steps. Duke took advantage of the mutant's clumsiness. He grabbed the mutant's leg and wrenched it sideways, hoping like hell it was enough to bring the big bastard down.

It almost worked. The mutant cried out in surprise and fell forward. Before he came crashing down, he opened his hand, dropping his knife and grabbing the arm of the couch for support. Duke wriggled through the gap between the mutant and the furniture. He grabbed the knife from the floor. His aim was to quickly turn and stab. If luck was on his side, he figured he could sever a major artery and get the hell out of the way while the mutant bled out. But the gods of good fortune didn't favor him, and the best he could manage was a wild swipe across the mutant's ribcage.

Although the stone dagger had been honed to a keen edge and opened a deep gash in the mutant's side, it didn't seem to do much more than push him even further into berserker fury. He sprang forward, looming over Duke with the axe raised. Duke lashed out with the dagger, aiming to bury the blade in the mutant's leg, but his prone position robbed him of the necessary leverage. The blade carved a chunk out of the mutant's calf muscle, but it wasn't enough to do more than elicit an enraged roar.

Looks like it's lights out, Duke thought. He tried to crawl away, but his heels slipped on the blood-slicked floor.

no no no our leader said they can't die not yet must save now kill now kill must survive…

Duke's head was full of a sudden influx of frantic animal thoughts. It was the same primitive language he'd heard from the boar, only this time it was a thin, squeaky rasp rather than a guttural rumble. The stream of consciousness babble was joined by another, similar voice, and then a third. The overlapping thoughts became a jumble of sounds, so panicked and insistent that Duke could no longer pick out individual words.

And then, before he could swing his axe, the mutant's eyes went wide with pain. He stumbled forward, reeling from the impact of three heavy blows to his back. He screamed, desperately clawing at his back. The axe fell to the floor with a heavy thump. The mutant spun, slapping at his back with both hands. He moved across the room in a jerky, erratic dance. His body was wracked with spasms, like he'd been hooked up to an electrical current.

A flash of lightning lit up the room, and as the mutant turned in frantic circles, Duke was finally able to see the cause of the mutant's frantic dance. He was also able to determine the source of the growing chorus of animal voices screeching in his skull. A trio of overgrown black rats had attached themselves to the savage's back. They clawed and scratched with ravenous aggression, tearing the mutant's back to shreds. Their black fur was slick with blood, but their claws were dug in deeply. In another lightning flash, Duke could see exposed vertebrae peeking through the mutant's shredded muscle.

One of the rats climbed onto the mutant's head, its claws stripping away clumps of hair and scalp. The mutant seized the creature with his thick-fingered hands and flung it across the room. The rat thumped against the side of Deacon's desk. It rolled to the floor. Duke was certain that the impact had been enough to kill the creature, but amazingly, it scrabbled to its feet. It wobbled for a brief moment, seemingly stunned. Then, after a quick shake of the head, the rat charged the mutant. It sprang off its muscular haunches, launching itself at the mutant's legs.

Then, squealing with rage and determination, it climbed the mutant's pants, ripping through the tough animal skin fabric and sinking its claws into the flesh of the mutant's thigh.

Duke recognized the rat's strategy instantly. It was going for the softest, most vulnerable parts. The mutant reached the same conclusion, only he was too slow getting there. As he pounded at his shoulders in a desperate attempt to knock the rats off his back, they bit into his hands, attaching themselves with their oversized teeth. When the mutant turned his attention to the rat climbing closer and closer to his crotch, both of his hands were crippled. The rats had stripped the flesh from his fingers as neatly as a starving man cleaning meat from a chicken bone. The scout rat continued to claw its way through the mutant's pants. Its efforts were finally rewarded as it opened a hole in the rough fabric. It thrust its snout through the hole, wiggling its hindquarters to burrow in deeper.

The mutant crashed to the floor. Blood gurgled out of his mouth. He hacked and coughed, but lay still as the rats continued to devour him. They clawed their way into his abdomen, feasting on the organs within.

Numb with shock, Duke heaved himself off the floor. He turned away from the grisly sight and saw the rest of his team standing at the bottom of the staircase. Their mouths hung open. Their eyes were wide with shock.

Kurt broke from the group and dragged Duke away from the mutant's body.

"You okay?" Kurt asked.

Duke nodded, but found himself unable to form a response. His head was still full of the rats' voices. Only now, they were no longer a squealing cacophony of rage and panic. They were a languorous chorus of near-orgasmic pleasure as they feasted on warm flesh and blood.

yes yes so good eat yes full so soft good yes eat...

Kurt drew his pistol and fired a shot at the mutant's body. The rats squealed and retreated through the front door and into the stormy night.

The voices in Duke's head faded to silence, leaving in their wake a sudden rush of vertigo so intense that the room seemed to spin around him. His stomach lurched as his vision blurred and then darkened. He slumped to the floor as consciousness left him.

Chapter Fifteen
Omens And Portents

Deacon and a crew of his armed guards arrived just after the salvage team's appearance. The proprietor barked some orders at his security crew, sending some of them to check the rest of the buildings and the others to find out how an intruder had made it past the front gates.

"Watch your ass out there," Deacon cautioned them. "This dead asshole might have friends lurking about. You come across any mutants, don't bother with warnings, just shoot them."

There were a dozen guards, and all of them had the lean, grizzled look of seasoned killers. They donned raincoats and hats, drew their pistols, and headed out into the storm without protest.

Deacon turned to Kurt's team and said, "Don't worry. There's any hostile elements out there, my boys will cut them down in short order. They're all veterans of Lord Hannibal's outer range troop. It'd take a hell of a lot worse than a gang of mutants to ruffle their feathers."

Next, the bedraggled harem made their way into the room. None of them seemed too shocked or disturbed by the bloody scene. The rest of the boarding house's guests—a crew of mineral prospectors and a small collection of religious pilgrims—joined the crowd of onlookers. Like the prostitutes, none of them seemed upset by the carnage. Kurt chalked up their reaction—or rather their lack thereof—to the fact that they lived this deep in the wasteland. An outpost as remote as Bruno's Last Rest no doubt had a history rich in violence and bloodshed. As for the guests, well, they had no doubt seen worse during their travels. While a dead mutant in the boarding house lobby was an occasion for some excitement, it wasn't enough to rattle anyone too badly.

After a few minutes of chatter, the crowd began to disperse. They made their way back to their rooms, leaving Deacon and the salvage team to survey the damage.

They'd moved Duke to one of the sofas, and he was sleeping peacefully enough. Rosemary gave him a cursory examination and found that he was free of any injury aside from a few minor bruises.

"Doesn't look like any of the blood is his," she said, drawing a blanket over him. "Good news," Kurt said. He turned to Deacon. "Sorry about the mess. Looks like some furniture didn't survive the fight. Hell of a mess, too."

Deacon waved his concerns away. "Don't worry. That voucher you're carrying will settle the tab, no problem. I'm just glad your man made it out alive. I'd sure hate to answer to Lord Hannibal about one of his employees dying on my watch. And that mess? I'll have one of my boys haul the body over to the swine barn in the morning. Once the pigs get done with it, might not even be bones left. As for this place? Hell, just scatter some fresh sawdust around and you'll never know anything happened. Not the first dead body we've had, you know."

Kurt nodded. "I figured as much. All the same, I hate to cause you any trouble."

"Like I said, it ain't no trouble. Now, I'm going to head over to the saloon and get old Barnett out of bed. Make sure he's got some breakfast ready for your team before you have to leave. Storm ought to break before first light. Out here, these damn gulley washers blow in quick, but they never last long."

The front door slammed shut behind him as he ventured out into the rain.

Kurt turned to face the members of his team. "I know it's exciting shit, but it doesn't change anything about the job. The storm is already starting to slack off. Another couple hours, it'll probably be gone altogether. We're still rolling out bright and early, so you better grab some sleep. I'll stay here and keep an eye on Duke."

Many people would have scoffed at the idea that they could sleep after seeing such a scene, but Kurt's crew wasn't made up of most people. They'd seen more than their share of hair-raising shit. The scene in the boarding house lobby was a grisly sight to be sure, but the only casualty was the mutant intruder. Other than being knocked out cold, Duke appeared unharmed. As far as violent encounters went, this barely registered. The members of the team murmured their assent and trooped back upstairs to their rooms. Only Deus and Diana lingered.

The holy man knelt by the sofa and whispered a prayer over Duke. When he'd finished, he touched the tattoo on his forehead in an act of genuflection, then rose and made his way back across the room to where Diana and Kurt stood.

"Don't say it." Kurt raised a hand. "I don't need to hear anything else about how this job is cursed. Shit happens, especially out here in the ass-end of nowhere. This big ugly fucker lying dead here probably tracked us all the way from the forest. Must have been a tough son of a bitch. Duke is lucky he's just sleeping one off. This could have been a lot worse."

Although, he thought, *it would have made things easier regarding the issue of loyalty…*

Kurt shoved the thought away as soon as it crept into his brain. He wasn't ready to write Duke off entirely. And besides, the man had experience in this part of the continent. That alone made him a valuable part of the team.

"It would have been worse if he hadn't been saved by those rats," Deus said. "I believe that's what you really mean."

Diana shrugged. "What's the difference?"

"When one has studied the holy scriptures, one recognizes the signs and portents given by the gods." Deus explained himself in a voice more suited to addressing a slow child rather than an equal. "And they have shown me plenty during the past two days. More than enough to know that those rats didn't appear by happenstance. The curse is becoming more and more apparent. Soon, even the most ardent nonbeliever in this gang will no longer dare deny it."

Diana sniffed, rolled her eyes, and looked away. Kurt could tell that she was reaching the end of her tether when it came to Deus' mystical talk. It had never been a long tether anyway.

She had even less use for religion than Kurt, and she didn't share the same history with Deus. Kurt put his arm around her shoulders and drew her close to his side. Normally, he took all the mystical bullshit in stride. But ever since Deus had started up with this curse nonsense, he found that he lacked his usual patience.

"Man, I'm going to need you to kindly shut the fuck up about all that," Kurt snapped, poking a finger into Deus' chest.

Deus looked down at the finger, then back up at Kurt. He stared into his eyes, but said nothing.

Kurt sighed. "Look, we're all friends here, but I'm still the leader of this team. I put it together and got everyone's vote of confidence. Now I'm telling you that, in the interest of morale, you need to keep your signs and portents to yourself.

Yes, Duke was saved by some rats. Big fucking deal. There's all sorts of weird wildlife out here, and a lot of it is hungry. Lord Hannibal warned me that the closer we got to the city, the more of that wildlife we'd encounter. Maybe this is a blessing. Lets us know that we'd better keep our wits about us."

"Now who's talking about signs and portents?" Deus got as close as he ever got to cracking a smile. He slipped past Kurt and made his way upstairs.

Diana looked over her shoulder to make sure the team's holy man was out of earshot, then said, "All that bullshit is starting to get on my nerves. I don't know how you've put up with it for most of your life."

"Ah, Deus is all right. He's just stressed out by this job. When it comes down to it, he's solid. Sometimes you just have to tell him to put a cork in it." Kurt stepped away from her and sat down on one of the room's tattered sofas. He patted the seat beside him. "Come on, don't stand there with your arms crossed looking all pouty."

"You like my pouty look," she said, dropping onto the cushion beside him.

They sat in silence for a moment, gazing out the front window at the slackening rain. The storm had mostly passed. Thunder still rumbled, but it was distant. The flashes of lightning were merely blips on the horizon rather than explosions of floodlight intensity. Across from them, just a few feet away, Duke began to snore. His mouth hung open, and a thin line of drool ran from the corner of his mouth.

"Well, at least *he's* getting some sleep," Kurt said. "Son of a bitch is out cold. Wonder what he's dreaming about?"

"Probably rats," Diana said, wrinkling her nose. "He saw those nasty things up close. They were probably tearing that mutant apart long before we came downstairs. We only saw them for a few seconds, but that was more than enough for me."

"They're just rats. I didn't know you had such strong feelings about them."

"You know I grew up in Steelhead, right? It wasn't much more than a collection of fishing cabins on the banks of the Brough." She stared at the rain, as if the drops contained tiny pieces of her memory. "There used to be rats living under the sheds where we scaled and gutted our catch. You could hear them scratching in the dirt, waiting for their chance to come out and snatch a meal from the bits we left behind. Sometimes, one of them, usually one of the big ones, would get bold and dig its way into our cabin. My brothers used to make a game out of it, firing rocks at it with their slingshots."

"Boys will be boys," Kurt laughed softly.

Diana didn't find it quite as funny. "One time, Junior got off a lucky shot, and it hit the rat in the tail. I don't know if the rock he fired was sharp or he hit the rat in just the right spot, but it cut right through the rat's tail. Cut it in half. The rat squealed. No, that's not right. It *shrieked.* Then it started tearing around the cabin in a frenzy. Blood was spurting out of its stump of a tail. It got all over the floor. My brothers knew that our father would be angry when he saw the mess, so they started chasing it, trying to catch it with the nets the used to scoop oysters. But that rat was fast. It was like its tail had been slowing it down, and now that it had been cut off, the rat could really move. And the more it ran, the more blood came out. That little cabin of ours started to fill up with the smell of blood."

"Look, sweetheart, I'm not sure..." Kurt grabbed her hand. "Maybe now isn't the time for this story, huh?"

Either Diana didn't hear him or she was too wrapped up the telling to end the story prematurely. Her hand was limp in his as she continued her tale. "They couldn't catch it. Laydon got close. He had it in his hands, but the rat bit him. Chomped right into the skin between his thumb and pointer finger. He dropped it and started yowling fit to raise the dead.

Then, he was bleeding all over the floor too. And wouldn't you know it, that happened to be one of those rare days our father got home early. Most afternoons, he drank at the town saloon until dinnertime, but for some reason, he called it an early night. When he opened the front door, the rat shot out like it had been fired out of a rifle. Ran right between father's legs, the bloody stump of its tail still leaking blood. It left a trail across the porch."

"Bet your father loved that," Kurt said.

"He damn near lost his mind." Diana laughed, but there was no sign of humor on her face. "Even though he was home early, he'd still had plenty to drink. He gave each of my brothers a few licks with the belt, then made them scrub the floor. I felt sorry for them, so I helped out, even though none of it was my fault."

Kurt gave her hand a squeeze. "That's some story."

"Except that's not the end of it," she said. "Once the house was cleaned up and father had his supper, things got back to normal. Like all the fishing families, we went to bed early. My brothers slept in the same room as my father, but I had my own bedroom. I guess that was the benefit of being the only girl. I lay awake for a while. I couldn't get the image of that bleeding rat out of my head. Eventually, I drifted off to sleep. Then…I don't know if it was really late that night or early the next morning…something woke me up. First, there was a movement under the blankets, like something was in bed with me. I guess at first I thought I was still half-asleep and dreaming. But then, I felt a weight on my chest…"

Kurt had a sinking feeling in his stomach that told him he knew where this story was going.

"I opened my eyes and found myself staring at this little hairy face," she continued. "The rat had climbed on top of me and was so close to my face that we were almost nose-to-nose. I screamed and screamed until I tasted blood. My brothers and father came rushing into the room. This time, they didn't mess around with slingshots and nets. Father snatched the rat off my chest and threw it against the wall. It fell down on the floor, stunned. He scooped it up and took it into the next room. I didn't see what happened next, because I was still too scared to move. But I could hear the sound of a hammer pounding on the butcher's block in the kitchen."

"By the gods…" Kurt shook his head.

"It was the same rat," she said. "When father threw it against the wall, I saw that little stump of a tail. It had come back for me. Now, I'm not like Deus. I don't see every little thing as some omen of impending doom. You know that. But I can't help feeling that some of what he says might be right."

Deus maintained his outwardly cool demeanor until he made it to his room. Then, once he was sure the door was locked behind him, he dropped to his knees and clasped his hands in prayer. He begged the gods for guidance. He pleaded for the wisdom to navigate this nightmare. But the gods were silent. Their reticence mocked him.

He rose from his knees and paced the room like a caged animal. He dug into his pocket for his emergency supply of the Black Drug. While he'd surrendered the lion's share of his stash to Kurt, Deus always kept a small amount of the powder secreted away for emergencies. This time, he sniffed just enough to take the edge off his anxiety. The floorboards creaked beneath his feet as he paced. The sound reminded him of the noise rats made.

Chapter Sixteen
Tangled Threads

Brother Grainger was working late again.

Well, that wasn't entirely accurate. True, he was still in his office at the Colonial Government Headquarters hours after nearly everyone else had left for the day, but he wasn't working. He sat behind a desk heaped with papers, lost in thought as he sipped tea from a chipped mug. It wasn't an unusual situation for him. Since his wife, Portia, had died two years ago, he'd become an expert at finding ways to delay his arrival at an empty apartment. For the first few months after her departure, Grainger felt as if his wife's spirit still haunted the apartment. Her presence was a palpable thing, as if she'd imprinted herself on the walls and furniture. But as time wore on, her presence faded until it was gone altogether, leaving Grainger quite alone. It was only then that he became acutely aware of the void left by her passing. Home was no longer a comfort.

He shuffled some papers aimlessly, before giving up the pretense. There was no one around to see that he was simply staring at the walls of his office. His sipped his lukewarm tea and settled back in his chair.

The previous night's meeting with the vicar would have

weighed heavily on his mind anyway, but since the early morning discovery of the two bodies—the matron and the vicar—at the church, Grainger could think of little else. He looked at his rumpled copy of the morning's news-sheet. The editors had made sure to print the headline in oversized type, to wring every bit of interest out of the lurid story.

Murder In The District Of Whispers

PROMISING VICAR AND ELDERLY MATRON SLAIN AT FIRST UNITED CHURCH "NO APPARENT MOTIVE," SAYS COLONIAL POLICE CHIEF

Grainger sighed and flipped the paper over so he wouldn't have to look at the grisly crime scene photos any longer. When he'd first gotten the news, he'd steeled himself for the inevitable visit from the Colonial Police. While the District of Whispers had been quiet during his visit, it hadn't been empty. The Delta Colony wasn't big enough to have empty spaces. There were always eyes watching. Theirs wasn't a culture that traditionally valued privacy. Many Colonists still lived in apartments without doors or curtains. Surely, someone had seen him paying the church a late night visit. But so far, no detectives had knocked on his door.

While it was a relief not to have to defend himself against any accusations, he was still troubled by the turn of events. According to the news-sheet article, the murders had occurred soon after he'd left the religious quarter. He probably hadn't even made it to his apartment by the time the vicar and matron had drawn their last breaths. The timing was too close for him to dismiss it as sheer coincidence. In Grainger's experience, few things were ever that simple. And if he'd reached that conclusion, he had no doubt that the police had done the same.

Murder was a rare occurrence in the Colony. And of the

few that happened, most were crimes of passion with obvious motives. Neither of these could be reasonably applied to the slaying of a vicar and a matron, which meant the ensuing investigation would be wide-ranging and thorough. And it would eventually lead back to Grainger. Where it went from there was anyone's guess. Grainger himself had no idea. Just trying to puzzle it out had given him a headache.

It soon became apparent that his old brain wasn't going to light up with any sudden flashes of insight, so he finished his tea and left his office for the night.

He encountered some of the cleaning crew on his way out of the building. They murmured farewells as they pushed brooms and mops over the floor. Grainger wished each of them a good night and wondered if he might have been happier as a janitor than a member of the Council. Didn't he initially campaign on the concept of the dignity of all labor? Didn't he preach about the satisfaction of finding one's place in the giant subterranean social experiment that was the Delta Colony? But then, he supposed his place was in the Colonial government. If there was such a thing as destiny, a seat on the Council was his.

If he hadn't been so deep in contemplation—in self-pity, if he was being honest—he might have noticed the young Colonist waiting in the shadows just outside the building's front doors. He might have had enough awareness to know that he was being followed all the way from the government building to the central hub staircase. But by the time he noticed anything out of the ordinary, he was already being dragged into the alley between a bar and soup restaurant.

Don't scream, grandfather.

His assailant's thoughts were bullet-quick and serious. Just to be sure, a hand was clamped over Grainger's mouth as he was pulled to the very back wall of the blind alley. Then, giving a quick glance around to make sure no one was lurking in the corners, the attacker released him.

It took a moment for Grainger's old eyes to adjust to the darkness, but after a few blinks, he saw that the Colonist who'd yanked him off the street was a young female. She was dressed in baggy trousers, a tweed tunic, and a bright floral scarf, the style currently favored by the more radical members of the university. She was a big lass, but her oiled whiskers and bright pink tail made her look more like an overgrown philosophy student rather than a strong-arm robber.

What do you want with me, youngster? Grainger tried to make his thoughts seem indignant rather than scared.

You were at the church last night, weren't you? The one where those people got killed.

Grainger nodded. He saw no point in denying it.

Then I need to tell you something. The youth backed away just far enough to give herself room to pace nervously as she projected her rapid fire thoughts. *But you need to understand that it wasn't supposed to happen. I never intended for...things have just gotten so far out of hand. It all made so much sense when it was just talk at the student center. Revolution and all that. A clean break with the past. Cornelius made it all sound so appealing.*

Grainger perked up at the mention of his old nemesis. *Brother Cornelius, the Councilman?*

The youngster nodded. *That's right. He recruited us right off the campus. He's always hanging around the library or the student center...*

Yes, of course. Grainger tried to keep his thought flow gentle and even, despite his growing unease. *Brother Cornelius is a high-ranking member in the education subcommittee. It's perfectly reasonable for him to visit the university.*

That's why it's a great cover, yeah? He gets to skulk around, whispering his ideas into our ears, and nobody gives it a second thought.

Grainger put out a hand to stop the lad's frantic pacing. *Here, girl. Slow down. What's your name?*

She hesitated for a moment, then projected, *Jane. My name's Jane.*

There's a tea house right around the corner, Jane. Let me buy you something to eat, and you can tell me the whole story. There's a private room in back where we won't be disturbed.

Jane hesitated again, but then nodded and followed the elderly Councilman out of the alley. Grainger didn't look back to see if she was following him. Years as a statesman had taught him that if you were confident enough, you didn't need to look back.

He led her into the Rattonero Tea Shop. It was a quiet, dim space frequented by politicians looking to make clandestine deals and lovers keeping secret trysts. As he paused at the front counter to order two strong blackberry teas, Grainger mused that both groups—crooked politicians and illicit lovers —came to the Rattonero in hopes of fucking or getting fucked.

Grainger let the young male Colonist working the counter know that they'd be using the back room. The Colonist nodded. He placed a key on the counter between the two steaming teacups.

Grainger slid some money for the tea, along with a generous gratuity, across the counter.

He passed one of the cups to Jane, then started walking. Once again, he didn't look back as he led the way to the rear of the shop.

The door to the room wasn't exactly hidden, but against the shop's black walls and in the shop's dim lighting, the doorframe appeared almost seamless. Even the doorknob was painted black. The lock and hinges were well oiled. Both were little more than whispers as Grainger opened the door and stepped inside.

The room was furnished with a quartet of cushioned armchairs surrounding a low table. Grainger placed his cup on the table and sat. He waited for Jane to cast a few nervous glances around the room, as if reassuring herself that they were indeed alone. Finally, she sat down.

Okay, Grainger projected, *tell me what's on your mind.*

Jane perched on the edge on the opposite side of the table. She took a sip of tea, then launched into her story.

And what a story it was.

* * *

Brother Cornelius found himself in the basement of the Temple of the Rat for the second time in less than twenty-four hours. Normally, he had a strict rule of no contact with his revolutionary army outside of their scheduled meetings. But this was a momentous occasion.

One of his star cadets—his protégé, even—had summoned him via pneumatic mail to an emergency meeting. The message was coded using the group's latest cypher, and it promised big developments. If it had been anyone other than Dorian, he would have dismissed this promise as a lot of hot air. But Dorian had all the makings of a revolutionary superstar, and after that story in that morning's news-sheet, Cornelius had a suspicion that his protégé had finally lived up to his potential.

When Cornelius let himself into the meeting room, he found Dorian waiting. The potential superstar was pacing excitedly about the small space, puffing hash vapor from a ceramic pipe. Normally, Cornelius frowned illicit drug use. It was a human affectation co-opted by the bourgeois, but he was willing to let it slide in this case. Clearly, Dorian had something heavy on his mind.

Speak your mind, cadet, Cornelius projected, easing himself onto one of the creaking chairs. *But first, sit down. That fucking pacing is wearing me out.*

Dorian sat, then launched into his story without preamble. And that story exceeded Cornelius' highest hopes. If what

Dorian said was true—and Cornelius had no reason to doubt it—then the young cadet had just served up the revolution on a silver platter.

If Dorian's tale was the basis for a novel, Cornelius had no doubt it would have been a controversial hit among the readership of the Delta Colony. It had all the elements of a regular potboiler: murder, sex, and political conspiracies. Some of it even bordered on science fiction. If Cornelius didn't know better, he might have considered that most of Dorian's tale originated in the pungent vapors billowing out of the ceramic pipe.

That fucking vicar came on like he was a regular hard boy, but after a little persuasion, he gave up the goods. Dorian smiled at the memory. *He told me how that old bastard Grainger was asking about bestiality. Can you imagine? That dusty old rat talking about fucking humans! But it got me thinking about how he'd been seen going down to the basement to visit his scientist friends. Everyone knows they've been looking into DNA splicing with humans. Ever since that report about common ancestry came out a couple years ago...*

Now, it was Cornelius' turn to smile. He'd had suspicions about what sort of shit they were getting up to in those basement laboratories. But even his darkest suspicions—his darkest fantasies, really—never went as far as those revealed by Dorian's source.

He's just a lab tech, but he has full access. They think he's a soft fucking liberal like the rest of them, so he has their trust, Dorian explained. *And he's been fucking my sister for the past few months. So he knows if he lies to me, his access to her gets cut off.*

Colonists and humans fucking each other. You see where these progressive ideals inevitably end up. Cornelius was too pleased with the opportunity he'd just been handed to register his full disgust. Even the moderates would reject it outright. It was fringe lunacy masquerading as science. And once the populace was made aware, they'd rally to Cornelius' cause.

Of course, by then, they wouldn't have a choice. The hour of his army's first battle test was drawing near. Once they'd proven themselves worthy, the revolution would arrive at the doorstep of the Delta Colony.

I'm proud of you, Dorian. Cornelius patted the cadet on the shoulder. *The time is coming soon when I'll need a capable lieutenant. Are you up to the task?*

Yes, sir. Dorian saluted.

Our time is at hand, Cornelius projected. *Very soon, we will witness the transformation of civilization itself.*

* * *

Brother Lorne was bleary-eyed and yawning when he answered the door. It was jarring to see the young Councilor with his whiskers and fur in disarray. Grainger was used to seeing him and his wife immaculately groomed and dressed in the latest fashions. It seemed that even a glamorous power couple—Colonial celebrities if such a thing existed—didn't roll out of bed looking beautiful.

Brother Grainger, this is a surprise. Lorne opened the door and motioned for him to enter. He smiled as he noticed for the first time that Grainger wasn't alone. *Two early morning visitors! This isn't some holiday I've forgotten, is it?*

Grainger shook his head and sighed. *I wish that was the case. I'm afraid the occasion is far from happy.*

Hello, young lady. Cornelius bowed slightly, taking Jane's hand in his. *My name is Lorne.*

I'm Jane. The young Colonist glanced around nervously.

Lorne and Ursula lived in an apartment complex on the highest of the residential levels. It was the sort of district favored by successful artists and doctors, with a sprinkling of high-ranking government officials thrown in for good measure. The space was well-appointed and, by Delta Colony standards, enormous. Of course, at any given time, there were as many as a dozen younglings in the apartment. Somewhere in the warren of rooms, a group of nannies was probably beginning to stir. Sister Ursula was famously fertile, but she wasn't overly maternal.

The children she and Lorne produced were shipped off to the academy as soon as possible.

Lorne led them into the kitchen. *Have a seat at the table. I'll put on a pot of tea and get the toaster warmed up. I'm not sure if we can properly call this morning yet or if it's still very late at night, but a pot of tea and some toast is just as good at either time.*

Grainger shrugged off his satchel and hung it by its strap from the back of one of the chairs. He sat down and gestured for Jane to follow suit.

It's okay, he projected. *You're safe here.*

While Lorne busied himself getting breakfast ready, Jane continued to stare wide-eyed at her surroundings. Grainger knew there were plenty of students who'd never been to a level this close to the surface, much less stepped foot in a luxury apartment. The Delta Colony professed to be a classless society, but like much of the patriotic curriculum taught at the academy and the university, that was a myth. Grainger knew that, even in a meritocracy, some Colonists were born with a leg up on their fellows. And radicals like Brother Cornelius knew it too. That knowledge, combined with a fiery sense of species supremacy, formed the basis of his revolutionary rhetoric. Moderates like Grainger had warned of the dangers of the Colony slipping into a caste system, but no one had much cared to listen. Of course not, when the only Colonists welcome in that debate only stood to gain from the growth of such a system. Lorne and Ursula were textbook examples of upper class citizens who were all too happy to argue that the concept of class didn't actually exist. Grainger wondered when they last paid a visit to any of the lower levels.

Lorne plunked three steaming mugs on the table, along

with a plate of toast covered in nut butter and honey. *Ursula makes a much better breakfast, but she's still asleep. She's due to give birth soon, and this last part of the pregnancy always takes a lot out of her.*

Jane took a piece of toast and, after a few cursory nibbles, set about devouring it.

Look at that appetite! Lorne laughed. *I remember the days of my youth, when I could put it away just like that. Now, as much as I love unexpected visits from friends both old and new, I must say that my curiosity is kicking into overdrive.*

Then I'll get right to it, Grainger projected. *As you've probably gathered, Jane here is a student at the university. She's studying history and has a keen interest in Colonial politics. She's become active in one of the campus' political groups...*

Well, that's great. Lorne slung his arm over the back of his chair, sitting casually. *The Council and the lower house could both use an injection of youth.*

You didn't let me finish. The group she's involved with is not the sort looking to gradually bring about change through incremental steps over a generation's worth of elections. Grainger cut his eyes sideways and watched Jane plow through a second slice of toast.

Suddenly, Lorne's posture stiffened. He stared at Jane. *You're a revolutionary, aren't you?*

Jane nodded. *And until yesterday, I was quite proud of it. You see, I know who you are, Councilor. And I know what you are, more importantly. Left unchecked, your power and wealth will grow, but it will do so at the expense of those who live beneath you, both metaphorically and literally. That last part is a quote from the leader of our group. He said it so often that most of us could recite it in our sleep. I guess some of what he drilled into us was bullshit—he was no different than any elder in some respects—but that was one thing that I still believe to be true.*

And who, might I ask, is this leader? Lorne leaned forward, propping his elbows on the table.

Jane finished chewing and washed down her food with a mouthful of tea. *Your friend, Brother Cornelius.*

Lorne looked at Grainger. *Gods of the forefathers...I knew that bastard was up to no good, but he's leading a revolutionary group.*

More like he's leading a terrorist cell, Grainger replied. *Young Jane here has been involved in some direct action lately. Perhaps you haven't had a chance to read the latest news-sheet, so I brought along a copy.*

Grainger pulled the folded sheet from his satchel and tossed it onto the table. As Lorne read the headline, his brow furrowed. Those furrows deepened as he scanned the article. When he'd made it to the end, he shoved the paper away back across the table.

You brought a fugitive to my apartment? He pointed a finger at Grainger. *You brought a* murderer *to my home?*

Hey, I didn't kill anybody, Jane protested. *That was all Dorian's doing.*

What the hell is going on here? Lorne demanded. *Somebody better start explaining straight away or I might wake up my neighbor, who just happens to be a commander in the Colonial Watch.*

Figures that a rich politician has a cop for a neighbor, Jane snickered. *But I'll admit that this tea and toast is much better than what we get from the university cafeteria. And it's so far removed from what they serve at the trade service academy that it might as well be food from a different world.*

Terrorist rhetoric is just that, no matter how eloquently phrased. Lorne sniffed, blowing hot breath through his bed-crimped whiskers.

And living in obscene wealth while others make do with whatever they can scratch together is disgusting, no matter how many liberal platitudes you spout, Jane snapped.

Grainger raised his hands in a calming gesture. He felt like he was in the middle of a subcommittee debate over some minor bit of legislation. *I think we're all just a bit sleep-deprived and our tempers are getting the better of us. Now, suppose I start from the very beginning. I think once you've heard my story about how Jane and I came to be here this morning, you might realize there's something afoot that goes beyond petty politics.*

Sure, I'll listen. Lorne shrugged. *But I'm not making any promises about not waking my neighbor once you get through with it.*

Typical, Jane huffed. She elbowed Grainger in the ribs. *And you said this guy would protect me?*

I'll do what? Lorne's mental voice was indignant.

Grainger knew he'd better get into it quickly, before the revolutionary student and the wealthy politician came to blows.

Lorne, when is the last time you paid a visit to the basement science labs? he asked. *I know you're on the Science and Technology subcommittee, but I'm not talking about rubber stamping requests for funding or having your secretary draft statements about the latest advances in food production or preventative medicine. I'm asking when was the last time you physically took the staircase to the basement and actually spoke to the research staff.*

Lorne shrugged. *I don't know. It's been a few years, I suppose. I've been busy.*

You mean your wife has been busy, Jane projected. *Or have I missed some new advancement where male Colonists can pump out litter after litter of special academy brats? You know something? I'm starting to think this was a mistake.*

Grainger got back to it before the discussion could heat up again. He explained to his fellow Council member just what was taking place in the basement. He laid it out in brutal, direct terms, leaving out none of the gruesome details. In a way, it felt good to get it all out in the open. It was therapeutic to share the atrocities he'd witnessed.

It actually makes sense, Jane interrupted. *Dear Leader*

Cornelius wanted us to press the vicar about the topic of your conversation. He told us you were asking about humans and Colonists mating. Dorian said you were just an old pervert and that Cornelius wanted us to dig up dirt for blackmail. We didn't think you were serious...

Not that I need to justify myself to you, Grainger projected, *but the only reason...the* only *reason, you understand...is that all the science points toward it being the only way for our species to continue.*

This can't be made public. Lorne pinched the bridge of his snout. *It will be the end of our careers.*

I think we're quite beyond that now, Grainger countered. *Cornelius is well on his way to kicking off a bloody coup. Jane here tells me that he has some secret weapon.*

What secret weapon? Lorne asked.

Jane shrugged. *He hasn't told us details. Just that he has something up his sleeve that no one will ever see coming.*

He must be stopped! Lorne slapped the table. *I'll get dressed and we'll confront him right away.*

Grainger shook his head. *Confront him with what? We have no evidence against him. We have her.* Lorne jerked a thumb in Jane's direction.

And it will be the word of a radical student against that of a fourth-term Councilor. Grainger could hardly believe he had to spell this out for him, but then again, Lorne had never been particularly brilliant when it came to political machinations. *Right now, her testimony will be uncorroborated. Worse, it will bring the genetics project out in the open. Then, Cornelius might not even need this secret weapon, whatever it may be. Public sentiment will swing to his side, and it will swing fast and hard. Right now, he's still seen as part of the political lunatic fringe. We need to preserve that perception until the time is right.*

So, what are you proposing? That we just sit on our tails while his minions get away with murder? Lorne's thoughts dripped incredulity.

I'm going to pay Cornelius a visit, Grainger projected. *We go back. He was a student of mine back when I was just a professor of political science at the university.*

Watch your tail, Jane cautioned. *He's always intense during our meetings at the Temple of the Rat, but last time, he was…* She shrugged. *I don't know, just different. Like he always says how our time is at hand and all that, but this time, it was like he really meant it. Like our time might be tomorrow.*

Grainger didn't like the sound of that at all. He turned to Lorne. *I need your help with this. Is there some place you can stash her, at least until I've had a chance to speak to Cornelius?*

Lorne stared at the table for a moment, running his tongue over the polished surface of his incisors. Finally, he nodded slightly, as if coming to a long-awaited decision. *We have an extra bedroom for one of our nannies. Ursula still isn't due for a few weeks, so it's vacant at the moment. She can stay there. But you have to promise me that you'll handle this with discretion. I can't let it be known that I harbored an accessory to the murder a beloved member of our religious community.*

Oh, for fuck's sake. Jane rolled her eyes. *Like you even give a shit about religion.*

Grainger shot her a look. He was aiming for withering, but he knew he probably fell just shy of grandfatherly disapproval. Among the many indignities of growing old was the loss of the ability to properly intimidate someone.

Jane raised her hands in apologetic surrender. *Sorry. I've spent five semesters learning to hate politicians and now I'm sitting down to breakfast with two members of the Colonial Council. Guess I just don't know how else to act.*

Grainger stood up. *Well, try to act decent. Whether you like him or not, this man is putting his neck on the line for you.* He touched Lorne on the shoulder. *Thank you, my friend. I didn't know where else to go. Hopefully, I can head this thing off before it goes beyond the point of no return.*

Lorne nodded. *I may disagree with Cornelius on many things, but I still believe he's a decent fellow. This murder was just the result of some loose talk that got out of hand. It can still be swept under the rug if cooler heads prevail.*

Grainger made his exit. He wished he shared Lorne's optimism.

* * *

Cornelius could have moved upstairs and bought a place in one of the new apartment districts. His Councilor salary, plus the various kickbacks and bribes he took would more than cover the rent. But he chose to stay one level above the District of Whispers, in the same small apartment he'd owned since his days as a teacher at the trade academy. His former students, who went on to become plumbers, technicians, or hydroponic farmers, were his neighbors. They were also his constituency. He'd be damned if he was going to abandon them for a luxury dwelling like his liberal colleagues.

Living in the trades district reminded him of why he took part in the daily struggle. It kept him grounded. Revolutionary leader or not, he was still salt of the earth. And as such, he was still an early riser. That's why he was already dressed and ready to face the day when he heard the knock at his door.

On his way to the front door, he ducked into his bedroom and retrieved his pistol from its place atop his dresser. He tucked the gun into the waistband of his pants and checked to make sure that the hem of his tunic covered the weapon. Normally, he wasn't so paranoid about an early morning visitor, even in one of the Colony's rougher districts. But there had been a murder only one level below, and that meant there was a general sense of unease spreading through the neighborhood. The Colonial Watch was out in force, making their presence known. The knock at the door was most likely just a Watch officer soliciting possible information about the crime. If so, that was no problem for Cornelius. He was known as being a staunch political supporter of the Colonial Watch, having authored legislation that was seen as pro-law enforcement. But then again, maybe it wasn't a Watch officer paying him a visit. One could never be too careful, especially when the revolution was so close to kicking off.

He opened the door, keeping the security chain latched. Peering out through the crack that the chain's short length allowed, he was surprised to see his old colleague Brother Grainger standing on the doorstep.

Good morning, Cornelius. I was wondering if I might have a word. We can go somewhere if you like. I know of a tea shop not far from here…

Cornelius unlatched the chain and opened the door wide. *My door is always open to a fellow Colonist, especially one of my fellow Councilors. Please, come in and have a seat. My abode is humble, but there's plenty of room for two old political rivals.*

Grainger didn't care much for Cornelius' upbeat tone. It was out of character. But he stepped into the apartment and followed Cornelius into the kitchen. It was considerably smaller than the one he'd left a few minutes ago, and much more sparsely furnished. The kitchen table was a wobbly circle of polished scrap metal. The two chairs were mismatched and even less stable. But the tea Cornelius served was high quality. It smelled as tasty as anything served in the upper level tea houses. The cups Cornelius set on the table were delicate things, snow white ceramic with gold filigree rims.

I know what you're thinking, Cornelius projected as he sat down. *Why does a staunch equalist set such a fancy tea service, right? I suppose it's my one indulgence. Now, pray tell, my brother, to what do I owe the pleasure of this visit?*

I think you know, Grainger replied. *Or at least you have some suspicion.*

Cornelius narrowed his eyes and shrugged, his expression impassive.

I know about the vicar, Cornelius. I know it was done at your behest.

Cornelius shook his head. *Not exactly at my behest. My students can be over-enthusiastic sometimes. The lad just got carried away. But since you know about the poor vicar, allow me to tell you about the things I know. Dreadful things. Sexually depraved things. Bestiality masquerading as science. Does any of that sound familiar?*

It sounds like a gross oversimplification, Grainger said, sipping his tea. *I don't understand you, brother. You're smart. You know what the latest science says about the declining population. You know that the only way forward, distasteful as it seems, is cooperation with the humans. We must learn to coexist with them or our species will disappear before we can return to the surface.*

Cornelius laughed. *Please, spare me the sermon. This isn't a Council meeting. You're not speaking to the junior parliament. And this sure as hell isn't one of your political science classes back at the university. Your naïve theories of human/Colonist coexistence don't sway me in the least. You know how humans will regard us when they see our true faces? They'll think of us as nothing more than vermin, just as they thought of our ancestors. Intelligent vermin, perhaps, but vermin all the same. And they will exterminate us without mercy. They've already beaten us in the race back to the surface. How long before they come looking for us?*

Paranoia, Grainger replied. *They can be made to see reason.*

How? By ingesting high doses of sex hormones, stimulants, and hallucinogens? Cornelius sat back, crossing his arms over his chest. *Oh, yes, I know all the sordid details of the perversions of science taking place in the basement.*

Cornelius' mouth was dry. He sipped more tea. *If you know so much, why didn't I read it in the news-sheet headlines? The murder of a vicar is scandalous, but nothing compared to government sanctioned bestiality, as you would no doubt call it.*

This is more than enough ammunition to destroy your political opposition, so why sit on it?

Because I have bigger things in mind, Cornelius projected. *I simply can't afford any extra attention at the moment. But don't worry. Every resident of Delta Colony will soon know all the disgusting details. Of course, by then, the Temple of the Rat will be firmly in control of the entire Colony.*

That's sedition. You're admitting that you are plotting a coup. Cornelius scraped his chair back from the table. *Coming here was a mistake. I thought I could reason with you, but I see that you're quite beyond that. You're insane.*

I agree with part of that statement, Cornelius agreed. *Coming here certainly was a mistake on your part.*

Grainger sniffed indignantly and stood. As soon as he was upright, his equilibrium faltered. He felt as wobbly as the kitchen table. The room spun slowly. His vision blurred at the edges. His joints felt loose and weak. Arms flailing for balance, he collapsed back into his chair. He stared at the teacup in front of him. It had been poisoned.

Finally. Cornelius smiled. *I was beginning to think that elixir would never take effect and I'd have to listen to your bleeding heart babble for hours.*

My friends... Grainger struggled to project a coherent thought as his heart rate increased. *They know where I am. They'll come looking for me.*

Let them come. Cornelius reached across the table to touch Grainger's hand. *By then, I'll already be gone and the revolution will have begun. You see, brother, you were right about the need for our species to cooperate in order to survive. But you were wrong about who we should cooperate with. Our lower cousins were all too happy to join my cause.*

Grainger scratched at the surface of the table as his throat swelled. His breath wheezed and whistled as he struggled to fill his lungs. His heart fluttered in his chest. A wave of panic broke over him. His head filled with Cornelius' mental laughter. It was shrill and cruel, the laughter of a triumphant lunatic.

Finally, mercifully, the laughter faded, along with the rest of the world. Grainger closed his eyes and quit struggling. It was just like going to sleep.

* * *

Cornelius continued to hold Grainger's hand until the old Colonist's pulse stopped. Then he cleared away the dishes, making sure to wash the poisoned teacup carefully. He stood there, looking at the dead Councilor and wondering how he should proceed. The death of the vicar was bad enough, but the murder of a Councilor was a line he hadn't planned on crossing so early in the revolution. If there was ever any doubt in Cornelius' mind that he had the resolve to actually go through with his plans, this act removed it completely. He was committed.

By this time tomorrow, his army would be finishing its feast and preparing to march on Delta Colony. Cornelius would return as a triumphant general. He hoped his revolution would be as bloodless as possible. A few dead politicians and perhaps some members of their security forces. But hopefully few civilians. Cornelius didn't like the idea of beginning his reign with a butcher's reputation. In the end, he supposed that wasn't up to him. His sincere wish was that the populace would be sufficiently awed by the footage of his army attacking and devouring a squad of wasteland-hardened humans, not to mention outraged and disgusted by the experiments taking place in the basement. Those two factors should sway public opinion to his side, if not rally it to his cause.

But those were problems for the future. At the moment, he had more immediate concerns. Namely, the dead Colonist sitting at his kitchen table.

Grainger, even in death, you're a fucking headache. Well, at least there's no blood to clean up…yet.

Cornelius tipped the chair over, dumping the corpse onto the floor. He didn't care for the way Grainger's dead black eyes stared back at him, so he rolled the body over. Then, seizing Grainger's tail in both hands, he dragged the body out of the kitchen, down the short hallway, and into the bathroom.

He stripped the clothes from Grainger's body and tossed them over his shoulder. The sight of the elderly Colonist's naked form made Cornelius wince. Beneath his greying, patchy fur, the old bastard was skin and bones. It was shocking to behold, even though Cornelius had been surprised at how easy it was to drag the body. In the Council chamber or on the floor of parliament, Grainger had cut a stately, dignified figure. His projected thoughts were full of quiet authority, and his words commanded respect. It was hard to believe that the shriveled shell lying naked on the bathroom floor was the same being.

For a moment, Cornelius allowed himself to feel sad. But only for a moment. More than that was an indulgence he couldn't afford.

He wiped his snout with the back of his hand, then lifted the corpse into the bathtub. Again, he found Grainger's dead eyes staring back at him, but this time, Cornelius wasn't bothered by their sightless gaze.

Let him stare. He'll be a witness to the resolve of a revolutionary.

Leaving his dead colleague in the bathtub, Cornelius went through his small apartment, gathering supplies for the arduous task ahead. A large rucksack made of waxed fiber. A set of butcher knives. A jug of chemical solvent. A face mask with goggles. He supposed it didn't much matter whether he cleaned up his mess or not. The next time he set foot in this apartment, if indeed he ever did so, he would be quite beyond the reach of the Colony's laws. But he hadn't gotten to this point in his life by doing things halfway. If something was worth starting, it was worth seeing through. He took his supplies to the bathroom and set to work.

It wasn't difficult. Cornelius kept his knives sharp, and their blades sliced through Grainger's withered muscles and tendons with ease. In a matter of minutes, and without breaking a sweat, he'd separated the dead Colonist into seven pieces: two arms, two legs, a head, a torso, and a tail. He washed the excess blood from the segments and packed them into the rucksack.

Although the work had been easy, it left the bathtub looking like a scene from a pre-Event abattoir. Cornelius took a deep breath and fitted his mask over his snout and his goggles over his eyes. He unscrewed the lid from the bottle of solvent and poured the contents over the tub, rinsing the blood, along with bits of bone and viscera, down the drain.

Goodbye, old friend. You were a worthy adversary.

He turned to the mirror hanging over the sink and gazed at his reflection. For the first time, he saw himself as the soldiers of his army saw him, his features hidden behind the air filtration mask, his eyes obscured by goggles. He looked like an alien warlord rather than a politician mired in a world of dense bureaucracy and incremental change. And even when he stripped off the mask and goggles, he still saw something different in his face. Something had changed. There was a new gleam in his black eyes, something strange and vicious.

Cornelius smiled. The countdown had begun.

Part Two
The Night of Terror

Chapter Seventeen
The Arrival

The city was as silent as a tomb. For a place supposedly teeming with hostile wildlife, it looked empty. But Kurt knew how appearances could deceive. He signaled for his team to keep the formation tight as they rode down the city's central thoroughfare. The motorcycle engines echoed in the concrete, steel, and glass corridors of empty streets and abandoned buildings.

The location transponder mounted on the handlebars of Kurt's bike buzzed insistently, letting him know they were nearing their ultimate destination. The PEE[5*] monitor in his jacket pocket buzzed just as insistently.

Well, we're in the shit now, he thought. *The clock is ticking…*

He glanced over his shoulder at the rest of the team. A few of them were patting their pockets, no doubt surprised by the buzzing of their long dormant PEE monitors. Their grave expressions told him that they'd come to a similar conclusion, that the time for fucking around was well and truly in the

---

* [5] Although its origins are lost to history, the Post Event Emissions monitor was invented to alert its wearer to areas where the lingering effects of the Event were still strong enough to cause physical distress.

rearview mirror. They had seventy-two hours tops before the emissions began to take their toll[6*]. By then, they'd either have the salvaged materials Lord Hannibal had requested, or they'd be leaving the city empty-handed.

He checked the location transponder again. It was doing its job, locking in on any location with functioning pre-Event tech. Kurt had no idea how it worked. For all he knew, it was magic. He wasn't concerned with those details. It was enough for him to know that the transponder had picked up a strong signal and was now pointing the way toward their destination.

He eased off the throttle, slowing their pace to a crawl in order to allow the transponder time to get a fix on the location. The city was a labyrinth, and they were getting closer to its center. Kurt grew increasingly nervous as they pushed slowly onward. He wasn't used to a space so enclosed, so artificial. Although he'd begun his life in a subterranean crèche, his memories of those days seemed so distant that they almost felt false. He'd grown accustomed to wide open spaces. Though he could look straight up and see the same red and grey wasteland sky above, there were walls surrounding him. It was his first time in one of the abandoned cities of the interior, and even though he'd only spent an hour within its confines, he already understood why so many stories about such places felt like tales of horror. A creeping sense of dread seemed to radiate from the streets and buildings like heat waves shimmering above hot asphalt.

Diana reached up from her sidecar to touch his forearm. She flipped up the visor of her helmet to give him a reassuring smile, although Kurt was sure he could see in her eyes the same uneasiness he felt in the pit of his stomach. He

---

* [6] Symptoms of prolonged exposure to Post Event Emissions vary widely among those affected, but most involve a radically accelerated form of cancer that causes sever mutations of internal organs as well as the skin and eyes.

wondered how much of his uneasiness was due to PEE exposure and how much was down to the strangeness of his surroundings.

Duke, Myrna, and Viz all had experience with exploring an abandoned city. Kurt had heard plenty of campfire stories about these experiences. At the time, he'd chalked up some of the strangeness of their descriptions down to simple exaggeration. After all, every good campfire story was, at least in part, a tall tale. But as he led the team deeper into the maze of empty buildings, he began to feel that, if anything, the eeriness had been undersold by the storytellers.

The aftereffects of the Event had lingered for centuries, and there was no indication to suggest they would ever dissipate entirely. But the phenomenon was at its highest concentration in the decaying cityscapes of the wasteland. They were monuments to a dead age, preserved by the same force that had at one time nearly destroyed them.

There was a common belief that nothing could live for long in the cities. Kurt knew this wasn't true. Humans couldn't live there for extended periods. PEE levels reached some critical mass in the body and caused an agonizing death. But Kurt had heard plenty of tales about the lifeforms that could survive and even live in the cities. None of those stories gave him much comfort. According to reliable sources, the plants that managed to survive were thorny, poisonous weeds. And any animal life that could survive was the end result of generations of mutant inbreeding. After all, Lord Hannibal had alluded to this particular city's reputation for dangerous wildlife.

Kurt paused at an intersection, calling a halt to the team's progress. Despite their measured pace, the transponder was having trouble keeping up. He'd heard that, once upon a time, there were man-made satellites circling the earth and beaming communications the world over. He wondered if the transponder worked like that. The thought gave him the creeps.

"This goddamn thing better work," he said, tapping the device's tiny screen. "It would take us weeks to search this place on our own."

Beside him, Diana shook her head. "I'm not hanging around here that long, waiting for emissions to cook my internal organs."

Right on cue, the little metal box resumed its chirping. The screen flickered, then slowly came to life, displaying a rough approximation of the city's layout. Kurt gave the signal to get moving.

The throaty growl of engines in low gear filled the empty city, amplified by the emptiness of their surroundings. The route suggested by the transponder was full of twists and turns. Kurt wondered if the chirping gadget might be malfunctioning and leading them astray. It was easy to imagine that the city was a never-ending labyrinth from which they might not emerge. If that was the case, at least the Duke problem would be settled. It would prove his doubts about Kurt's leadership correct. Behind the visor of his helmet, Kurt smiled bitterly. He knew he had no choice but to kick that particular can down the road, but he also knew he'd better watch his back.

He followed the transponder's directions, leading the team to a hard left turn. As his bike rounded the corner, a trio of animals burst out of an alleyway. They were dark and low to the ground, scampering on four legs ahead of the team's formation. Although they appeared to be much larger than the rats he'd previously encountered, he wasn't alarmed. If anything, he'd expected horrifically mutated vermin. He'd assumed as much when Lord Hannibal warned him of hostile wildlife. After all, the ancient cities were the epicenters of the Event.

Scientists, theologians, and historians may have put

forward a hundred or more competing theories about the exact cause and nature of the Event, but they were in near universal agreement about the idea that the urban population centers—as they were known long ago—were the areas most affected by the cataclysm. The evidence was impossible to deny. And for that reason, people avoided the abandoned cities. Even Kurt, who'd crisscrossed the continent during his years of wandering, had never been this deep into the heart of a city. Now that he was actually there, surrounded by the bleached bones of skyscrapers, he was awestruck.

This was a place where pre-Event people went about their lives. They'd thronged the streets and moved in and out of the massive structures whose purpose Kurt could only guess. Lights had beat back the darkness of night and the endless drone of mechanical devices and electronics had filled the air. Now, the place was only suitable for ghosts and vermin. The former were well represented by the bones littering the asphalt and concrete, and the latter scurried ahead of the procession of motorcycles, as if they were leading the way to the team's destination. And when the transponder began to blat an insistent alarm, Kurt was hardly surprised to see that the rats and the wasteland salvage crew were indeed headed for the same building.

Kurt raised a fist to signal a halt. He pulled his motorcycle to the curb, killed the ignition, and checked the transponder one last time. Unless the device was malfunctioning, this was the spot.

It was a bit different from the towering, angular buildings surrounding it. If Kurt had to guess, this structure was older than most of the others. Or at least it was designed to look that way. A gently sloping flight of wide stairs led from the street to a front door flanked by a pair of giant cats sculpted from a grayish stone veined with thin lines of darker grey and black. The building itself was three-stories-tall and constructed from the same grayish stone as the big cats guarding the door. Skeletal trees stood on both sides of the massive staircase, their naked limbs grey and petrified. The ground spreading out in front of the building might have once been a green space for rest and relaxation, but now it was overgrown with tangles of thorny weeds and carnivorous plants whose gaping mouths dripped acrid-smelling nectar. Strange birds wheeled silently overhead, their wings jet black against the grey-and-red swirls of clouds.

Kurt watched the birds uneasily for a moment, then looked back at the building. He was no expert on architecture, but the place was impressive. No doubt Deus could explain at length the differences between the various buildings. During his time at the monastery, he'd studied all manner of historical subjects. Perhaps when they'd finished the job and were enjoying some downtime, Kurt would ask his friend to explain. But now, it was time to get down to business.

Kurt tugged off his helmet and hung it by the chinstrap from his bike's handlebars. He glanced over at Diana. She flashed him a brief smile.

"Okay, let's do this." Kurt dismounted and turned to face his team. Although he spoke at a normal volume, his voice seemed to boom and echo in the eerily silent concrete corridors of the city. "Once we get inside, let's get down to work. No fucking around. Lord Hannibal wants as much tech equipment as we can salvage. That's top priority. Then we see what we can find for ourselves. First things first. There's a pair of transport vehicles somewhere in the vicinity. Let's find and secure those. Lilith, Lucifer, get on that. Everyone else, you're with me. We're going between those stone lions, right in the front door. Lanterns and torches, people. It might be the heart of darkness in there, so let's shed some light on the matter. And I shouldn't even need to remind you that the order of the day is weapons ready. Stay frosty and keep your eyes on the prize. Sound good?"

Nobody verbalized approval or protest. They just got

down to business. It may have been their first trip this deep into one of the big cities, but they knew how a tight operation was supposed to run. They secured their bikes, checked their weapons, and strapped on their chemical torches and lanterns. In a matter of moments, they were armed, ready, and on the move.

* * *

Duke tried to focus on the task at hand and ignore the strange feeling of unease building in the back of his skull and the pit of his stomach. Ever since their bikes had crossed the threshold of the city, his brain had felt like a few ants were slowly crawling over its surface. It wasn't a painful sensation necessarily, but it was impossible to ignore. More disturbing was the distant babble of psychic voices. They were no more than an incoherent whisper, but they droned incessantly, just out of the reach of his comprehension.

Duke knew what this unease meant. Despite all indications to the contrary, there was something alive in this city. The presence of the three rats proved it. As they'd scurried ahead of the team, they'd paused at an intersection of streets to glance back at the motorcycle procession. Six beady black eyes had fixed on Duke, and he knew in an instant that they belonged to the same rats who'd saved his life at Bruno's Last Rest. There was a time when he'd have laughed off such a notion, dismissing it as the sort of fairy tale bullshit that Deus liked to spout when he was handing out shots of his sacramental moonshine. But that line of thinking had come to an abrupt halt when Duke's head had filled with the giant wild boar's guttural language.

Something was coming. He was certain of that much. Now, he just had to be ready to turn whatever it was to his advantage.

"You good, partner?" Rosemary asked, as the team finished gearing up for their approach to the building.

"Yeah, I'm okay," he replied, pretending to check the pistol he knew was ready for action.

"Because you looked a little preoccupied for a minute," Rosemary continued. "We get in there, I need to know you're watching my back."

He smiled. "I always love watching your back."

"Dream on, lover boy."

Duke thought, *Yeah, laugh me off now, but pretty soon, you'll see me differently. And you'll beg to stand by my side at the head of this team.*

Kurt, looking every bit as pompous as his speech sounded, gave the signal, and the team moved out. Lilith and Lucifer spit off from the team, circling around the building's grounds to search for the transport vehicles. The rest of the team moved up the staircase in their usual spread-and-cover formation. Pistols held at the ready, shoulder-mounted chemical lanterns glowing, the crew made their way up the steps with practiced efficiency. It gave Duke that old familiar thrill that came with being part of well-oiled killing machine. He could only imagine how good it would feel to sit in the driver's seat of that machine.

Soon. Your time will come soon. The voice in Duke's head was gentle, reassuring. He couldn't tell if it was his own or if some member of the whispered background chorus had stepped to the fore and voiced its support.

He remembered his promise to keep his head in the game and watch Rosemary's back. True to his word, he sneaked a glance at her ass as she climbed the steps. It looked just as round and firm as ever, and despite the circumstances, he felt the urge to holster his gun, and grab it both hands. He sighed inwardly, promising himself that his reward would come sooner rather than later.

Duke and Rosemary were the team's rear guard, a role

they'd filled ever since they'd come out of the western mountains and into the wasteland. It was their job to have eyes in the backs of their heads. Duke forced himself to shove aside his own ambitious thoughts along with the constant drone of animal voices. If something attacked them from behind and wiped them out, all his patient plotting would be for nothing. He went up the stairs backwards, sliding each foot backwards until his heels contacted the next step, then climbing carefully. Rosemary matched his movements, negotiating the ascent without taking her eyes off the streets and alleyways surrounding them. So far, everything was as silent and uneventful as a mausoleum, which he supposed was an apt comparison, since the city was the final resting place of millions of people.

Duke counted each stair. Before they'd begun their careful climb, he'd noted that there were twenty of them leading from the sidewalk to the front door of the building. The team's progress was slow, but that was only because they were experienced. A wild charge into the unknown was the sort of thing you could expect from rank amateurs, but a professional squad of salvage mercenaries knew it was better to minimize risk. The group fanned out to the edges of the staircase as they neared the building. Their eyes peered into every shadow, around every corner.

After a methodical approach, they finally arrived at a tall set of double doors. There was a chain wound through the door handles. Taurus tugged a set of bolt cutters from his backpack and snapped their jaws onto one of the links. But he quickly discovered that there was no lock and simply unwound the chain. It rattled and clanked as it fell to the concrete doorstep, coiling like a metallic snake.

"Okay, people," Kurt announced. "This is the moment we've all been waiting for."

He pulled open the doors, and the team marched into the dim and dusty interior.

Chapter Eighteen
The Taste Of Blood

Cornelius surveyed the assembled ranks of his army. It was an impressive sight.

Thousands upon thousands of sleek-furred assassins, arrayed in rows that stretched the length of the sewer tunnel.

No army should march to victory on empty stomachs, he projected. *And since we attack when darkness falls, now we should feast.*

He stepped back and upended the first of the three rucksacks he'd dragged through the maze of tunnels. His arms ached from the effort of carrying the load, but it was the satisfying soreness that was the price of honest hard work. The contents of the bag came out in a wet, stinking pile. The mixture was the same in all three bags: cans of protein mash, vegetable paste, and chopped up pieces of Brother Grainger, bones and all. He repeated the process two more times, backing up a few paces between each dump.

His army's thoughts came at him in a ravenous, eager chorus, but they held their ranks, waiting for his signal. And when he stepped aside and gave the order to feed, they descended on the three piles of reeking slop in waves, clambering over one another to claim their part of the feast.

Cornelius stood back and observed his troops as they devoured their pre-battle meal. He noticed that the rats who happened upon a scrap of Grainger's flesh devoured that morsel with particular zeal. Those lucky enough to find a larger piece of Grainger dragged it away from the crowd, snapping at those who tried to snatch a mouthful for themselves. Their appetite for Colonist flesh seemed to match that of their appetite for human flesh. It was fascinating, really. He viewed it with the same morbid fascination with which he'd listened to the tales of the scientific perversions being wrought on the basement level of Delta Colony.

They were efficient feeders, these lower cousins. In a matter of minutes, they'd greedily consumed every speck of food. They sat back on their muscular haunches, cleaning grease from their whiskers with quick swipes of their pink tongues. Although their bellies were full, their appetites weren't sated, and Cornelius relished their enthusiastic thought projections about the buffet of humans that were even now making their way into the city's scientific research facility.

Cornelius unzipped his hip pack and carefully withdrew the small remote monitor. The device buzzed as the screen flickered to life. He thumbed the buttons, checking the video feeds from each room of the research facility. Although they were grainy and shot through with ribbons of static, the images would serve their purpose. And once the humans illuminated the rooms with their primitive chemical torches and lanterns, the images relayed to the monitor by the hidden surveillance cameras would be clearer. Cornelius only hoped that the monitor's recording function was operational. This sort of device—extrapolated from salvaged scraps of old human tech—was still in its relative infancy in the Colony. In many areas, the Colonists had drawn near the level of knowledge attained by pre-Event humans. Their expertise in medical science and agriculture, for instance, was almost the equal of civilized humans. But seemingly simpler technologies, such as communications, had lingered far behind[7]*. There was nothing he could do but place his trust in the gadgets he'd managed to smuggle out of the Colony.

He squared his shoulders and gazed out over the assembly of soldiers.

And now, my children, the time has come, he projected. *Advance scouts, move out. First squadron prepare for deployment.*

A group of rats detached itself from the crowd and scampered down the tunnel in a ragged, double time march. A second group, much larger than the first, formed into lines at the head of the crowd. They scratched at the damp concrete, eager to follow the advance scouts into action. They were close to the battleground, close enough to smell the blood once it was spilled. Less than a kilometer of tunnels and ductwork separated their base from the research center. The advance scouts would reach their destination in minutes.

Cornelius felt sweaty and confined in his full body suit. After a moment's hesitation, he unzipped it to his waist and let in some air. Although the humid atmosphere of the sewer wasn't much of a relief, he felt less trapped with his bare chest exposed to the elements. He felt closer to his troops. After all, they went about perfectly naked on the surface, seemingly with no ill effects. Perhaps the dangers of the lingering traces of the Event had been overstated by Colonial scientists.

---

* [7] Colonial philosophers speculated about the causes of this phenomenon. The majority of them attributed this discrepancy to cultural differences, specifically, the tendency of humans toward tribal divisions rather than communal living encouraged them to focus scientific research on areas like weaponry and surveillance. Support for this position was drawn from historical evidence that, even at the height of human civilization, a substantial portion of their population lived in abject poverty and died of starvation or easily preventable disease, while their capacity for large-scale warfare was nearly boundless. Many of these philosophers used this same historical evidence to support the theory that the Event was a result of a late period human weapon malfunction.

Cornelius was standing at a spot that was only a few meters below ground level. The air down here was nearly identical to that circulating above. So far, his exposed skin hadn't broken out in a stinging rash or blistered. He might as well have been standing on one of the promenades at the Colony's public baths.

He slipped his arms out of the suit, then tied the loose sleeves around his waist like a belt. The troops chittered and squeaked their approval. He unlatched his helmet and tugged it off his head.

Come unto me, my children. He spread his arms wide, dropping his helmet.

As soon as the invitation was projected into the psychic ether, his loving children began to swarm him. They threaded their way in and out of his legs, stropping their sleek hides against the slick material of his boots. Others clambered over the backs of their fellows to press their cheeks against his legs. Soon, they were piled atop one another in a squealing, undulating mass that rose to Cornelius' waist. He sighed at the gentle pressure against his groin. His eyes leaked tears of joy.

Chapter Nineteen
No Such Thing As A Free Lunch?

Kurt was always first through the door. He didn't know how other leaders did things, but he preferred to lead the charge. Gun held at the ready, he stepped over the threshold and into a high-ceilinged room. The stone floor was littered with bits of broken furniture and shattered glass. The debris crunched under the soles of his boots as he walked.

A circular desk stood in the middle of the room, its surface strewn with strange contraptions, the purpose of which Kurt could only speculate about. Behind the desk was a high-backed chair, and in it sat a human skeleton dressed in tattered rags.

Kurt gestured to Viz. "Go check that out."

"You got it." Viz practically skipped across the room on his way to the desk. The team's handyman and tech expert, he was always eager to get his hands on interesting gadgets. He wrinkled his nose in distaste as he upended the chair, dropping the skeleton to the floor. Then he sat down and went to work checking the desk for anything worthy of salvage.

The tension seemed to ease out of the group as they realized that nothing was going to burst out of the shadows and attack them. There were few hiding places in the room, and aside from the three rats picking their way through the debris, the team was alone, at least in this portion of the building.

The front doors swung open. Lilith and Lucifer announced themselves before entering, then stepped into the room.

"Keep those itchy fingers off the triggers, eh?" Lucifer said, his typically sly grin widening. "It's just me and my old lady."

"Vehicles?" Kurt asked, turning around.

Lilith nodded. "Two trucks. Found them parked behind the building. Completely empty, so unless this building is packed to the rafters with Grade-A salvage, space isn't going to be an issue."

"Both trucks are fueled up and look like they're in tip-top shape," Lucifer added.

"Viz, you got anything over there?" Kurt called across the room.

"Nothing much. Looks like some communications stuff. Non-functioning but seems mostly intact," Viz replied.

Kurt gave him a thumbs-up. "Bag it. We'll sort it out later. I want to take the grand tour and make sure the building is secure before we strip it."

Viz stuffed the few items into his backpack then clambered back over the desk. He pointed to a corner of the room, where some boxy device was anchored to the wall. "See that little doohickey? I think that's an old surveillance camera."

Kurt shrugged. "I doubt anyone's keeping tabs on this place remotely. If you think it's worth it, we can rip that sucker down and take it with us. Have to find a ladder or something. It's pretty high up there."

"Might be worth it, but I don't know," Viz replied.

"Low priority then," Kurt said.

The group fell back into a loose formation, and Kurt led the way across the room towards another set of double doors. They silenced the chatter and held weapons at the ready. Years of wasteland roving had taught them that you never knew what waited on the other side of a closed door.

Kurt pushed through one side of the doorway, holding it open with his foot while he scanned the area on the other side. It was a short hallway lined with doors on either side. The space was dark, but the green light of his chemical lantern was enough to assure him that there were no mutants, animal or otherwise, lying in wait. He motioned for the group to follow him.

He hesitated for a moment, unsure of which room to explore first. One of the doors on the left had a sign beside it that indicated a staircase lay on the other side. The others were unmarked. He raised his chemical lantern, narrowing the aperture to focus the light into a beam which he played over each door.

"I vote for the door on the right," Diana said as she drew alongside him. "Just feels like that's where we should go."

"Then I won't go against female intuition," Kurt agreed. He turned to his right and opened the door. He stood on the threshold as he swept the beam of green light around the room, checking for immediate threats. When the light revealed none, he stepped into the room, motioning for the others to join him.

The combined light from their torches and lanterns was enough to illuminate the room. It was a large kitchen. Two of the walls were lined with pantries and refrigeration units. A sink, stove, and oven were situated on the other side of the room. On the far side of the room, a doorway led into yet another room.

"I wonder what's back there?" Duke piped up from the back of the group. "We should check that other room out too. Maybe split up and cover more ground that way."

Kurt's shoulder muscles stiffened with annoyance. Although he actually agreed with Duke's suggestion, he'd be damned if he was going to let Duke start to chip away at his authority.

"I think we stick together for the time being," Kurt said, turning to make sure Duke saw the disapproval on his face. "Let's get an inventory of this room first, then *I'll* decide our next course of action."

Duke was silent for a beat, then shrugged. "You're the boss, right?"

Once more, the group spread out and began searching the room for supplies. While it didn't appear that any of the items on Lord Hannibal's wish list had been stored in the room, the team was always on the lookout to replenish their own supplies.

The hushed space was soon filled with the sound of cabinets and drawers slamming open and shut.

Viz yelped as he peered into one of the pantries. "Gods above, those are some big fucking rats!"

Kurt trotted across the room to get a closer look. He peered over Viz's shoulder into a storage space packed full of squeaking rodents. There were dozens of them, crammed into every available nook and cranny. They scratched their way through the rotting remains of foodstuffs, clambering over one another in their search for food. Kurt recoiled in disgust, but quickly recovered. The rats were bigger than any he'd ever before seen. They were nearly the size of the overfed cats roaming the courtyard of Lord Hannibal's outpost. Their fur was jet black and glossy under the glare of the chemical lights. Their paws were like strange hands, each finger tipped with a claw that tapered to a cruel point.

"And here I was hoping to get a decent meal out of this," Viz said, shaking his head.

Kurt clapped him on the shoulder. "I grew up in a crèche. During some of our lean years, we ate these things."

Viz's eyes widened. "I can't tell whether you're serious or just fucking with me."

"Oh, I'm serious as a heart attack," Kurt said. "My mothers each had their own special recipe for preparing rat. The key is to cook them with some vinegar. It gets rid of that gamey taste, you know."

Viz made a gagging sound and slammed the door on the rats. He moved away and began rifling through the contents of the cabinet beneath the sink.

Deus was the only one of the team who hadn't joined the search. He stood in the middle of the room, his fist tucked beneath his chin, his tattooed forehead wrinkled. His lips moved in silent prayer as he glanced around the room. Kurt made his way over to the holy man and put a hand on his elbow.

"Look, I know some of this manual labor is beneath a man of your station," Kurt said, "but maybe you could lend a hand just for appearance sake."

Deus didn't find the remark amusing. He looked at Kurt with eyes full of worry. "I don't like this. Not one bit."

"What? Those rats? Come on, man. They're just rodents. Big, ugly motherfuckers, sure, but they're still just rodents."

"Perhaps," Deus said. "But first, a group of rats intervened when Duke was attacked at the outpost. And they practically led our procession through the city. Even you unbelievers cannot deny that. I believe they are a sign from the gods."

"Yeah? And what is this sign telling you?" Kurt asked.

"To leave while we still can," Deus answered. "To march out of here and not look back until we are safely away from this cursed place."

Kurt sighed. "Is that all? And here I was afraid you might overreact."

He moved away from Deus before the holy man could respond. Deus had been in full doom-and-gloom mode ever since he'd come back from his solo hike in the forest. Even for a man given to bouts of melancholic introspection, it was a bit much. Kurt had enough to worry about without adding Deus' omens and portents to the mix.

Kurt decided to give the team another few minutes to ransack the kitchen before he gave the order to move into the next room. Their efforts hadn't yielded a single useful item. What food remained had been either chewed up or shit on by the rats. But he wanted to be thorough. Despite the ominous feeling that came with being so deep in one of the dead cities, he was determined not to alter the team's usual approach. Still, he couldn't deny that there was a strange feeling in the pit of his stomach, a creeping sense of dread that sat there like an ice cold lump.

"All right, let's keep moving," he announced. "We'll check that back room before we head across the hallway."

He led the way past the pantry full of squeaking rats and opened the door to the next room. The stiff, unoiled hinges shrieked in protest as he tugged on the doorknob. Beside him, Diana drew in a deep breath as she raised her gun. Kurt glanced over his shoulder to make sure his team was ready, then he sprang into the room with his pistol and lantern held in front of him.

His heart hammered away in his chest as he swept the beam of chemical light around the room. Behind him, his team made their way into the room, playing the beams of their own torches and lanterns over the walls and into the corners. Again, nothing sprang out of the shadows to attack them. Aside from a few insects and rats scurrying back to their hiding places, the room was unoccupied. It was also less gloomy than the other parts of the building they'd explored so far. Like the lobby, this room was high-ceilinged and spacious. But there was a skylight in the middle of the ceiling that let in some of the late afternoon light. The glass panes were cloudy with grime, but the red and orange light of the slowly sinking sun found clear spots to trickle through.

"This is some crazy fucking architecture," Viz announced.

"You were just waiting to drop some of your vocabulary on us, weren't you?" Max snickered.

Deus stood in the middle of the room, staring up at the skylight. "This place is built like a temple. And indeed it is one. A temple of death."

"Really?" Max glanced around, feigning confusion. "I thought it looked more like someone's bedroom."

Rows of metal cots lined the north and east walls. There were ten beds in total. Their thin mattresses were piled with blankets made of rough, moth-eaten fabric.

"Kind of an odd place for a dormitory, don't you think?" Diana asked. "Behind the kitchen, I mean. This place sure is weird."

"Yeah, and it fucking stinks," said Myrna, standing at Kurt's other shoulder. "I mean that both ways. Like it would be terrible to live here and the situation stinks. But also like it smells really bad in here."

Kurt sniffed. She was right. The whole building had a distinctively unpleasant odor about it. Musty, rotten, and sour, the stink seemed to hang in the air like a yellow fog.

"Hey, boss!" Lucifer shouted from across the room. "What do you think about these cases, huh? Should we break into them?"

The lanky scout, his hair slicked back into a ponytail, was standing in the southwest corner of the room alongside a neat pile of metallic boxes. They were stacked three deep, pushed flat against the wall. Lilith was seated atop the stack, swinging her legs idly, her boot heels thumping against the boxes. With her regal bearing and youthful face, she looked like a junkyard princess.

She gave her hair a toss, whipping it out of her eyes and over her shoulder. "I hope it's food in these things. I think I could go be happy to go the rest of my life without eating another strip of wild boar jerky."

"Hey, that was my father's secret recipe!" Duke cackled. "You just don't know what good eating is!"

Kurt waited for the group's laughter to subside. He knew they were making far too much noise in a building that they hadn't completely secured. Moreover, the members of the team knew it as well. This wasn't their first job, after all. But there were a few extra degrees of tension in the day's atmosphere, and they needed a release valve. Duke's comeback wasn't even that funny, but it gave them an excuse to let off a small bit of steam.

Once they'd quieted down, Kurt gave the order to pull the boxes into the middle of the room. Lilith climbed down from her perch and helped her partner move the first box. Taurus, Max, and Viz joined the effort, and soon the boxes were spread out in a semi-circle in the center of the room. There were a dozen of them, and from the effort they required to move, it seemed like they were packed full.

"Taurus, crack one of those bastards open," Kurt said.

The burly handyman pulled a crowbar from his tool kit and got to work on the box closest to him. Muscles bulging, he got to work. It wasn't easy to get the tapered end of the bar into the seam between the lid and the rest of the box, but once he'd accomplished that part, the rest was easy. The lid came loose with a metallic screech, then clattered to the floor. Taurus peered into the box with exaggerated caution, as if he half-expected a bomb to be ticking away inside. Then his shoulders relaxed, and he announced, "It's food, boss. Cans, freeze-dry pouches, sealed bags…it's all food."

"Try another box," Kurt suggested.

The big man got to work, this time with less obvious caution. When the lid clattered against the concrete floor, he looked into the box and said, "More food. Gods, there's so much of it…"

Kurt gave the order for the team to get busy with opening the boxes. Using whatever tools they had at hand, they got all twelve of the boxes open. Each time one of the lids announced its opening with a metallic shriek, the team members answered with excited yelps. All the boxes—a dozen large crates, really—were packed to the brim with non-perishable foodstuffs. It was enough to keep the team eating double rations for weeks. Kurt let out a sigh of relief. They were only getting started with their search of the building and already it was paying off.

"Gods above, this is actual sugar..." Duke held up a freshly opened vacuum pack. "Not the chemical substitute, but actual fucking sugar!"

"Is this flour?" Rosemary dipped a finger into a similar plastic bag. "It's so white."

She filled the palm of her hand with the white powder, then tossed it into air. It came down in a dusty flurry, settling into her dark curls and over her face.

"Look at me!" she laughed. "I'm white! I'm as white as you motherfuckers!"

Kurt knew it was a wasteful display, but he let it go. Sometimes the best thing for morale was just getting to cut loose. He let the horseplay continue for a minute or two, then called a halt.

"Okay, guys, that's enough grab-ass for one day," he said, raising a hand. "Let's get these boxes sealed back up. We know this dump has a rat problem, and I don't feel like sharing our goodies with a bunch of dirty vermin. Viz and Max, you take an inventory, then Taurus can seal the crates. The rest of you, check out the rest of the room. Some of these beds have some footlockers. Let's see if there's anything useful in them."

The team got back to work. They made a thorough sweep of the room, checking every possible hiding place for useful salvage. Kurt joined in, dragging footlockers away from the beds and breaking into them. There were some useful items within, but nothing out of the ordinary. Mostly, they contained clothing and the personal effects of the people who'd occupied the dormitory.

So far, everything seemed rather routine, despite the warnings Kurt had received from Lord Hannibal. If the wildlife mentioned by the warlord was nothing more than a bunch of overgrown rats, the team had little to worry about. Despite Deus' constant sermonizing, they were just rodents, nothing the team couldn't handle. In Kurt's experience, however, it was only a matter of time before things took a turn. Just when you thought you'd found an oasis of calm or normalcy in the wasteland, circumstances changed, sometimes violently, and you got a clear reminder about the hell you'd ventured into. So Kurt was hardly shocked when Myrna started screaming.

He was on the floor, rifling through the contents of one of the footlockers when Myrna's shrieks erupted. By the time he'd made his way across the room, hurdling footlockers and cases of food, she'd really cranked the volume. He found her sprawled on the floor beside one of the cots. Kneeling beside her, he put an arm around her shoulder to quiet her.

"I just wanted to sit for a minute," she explained, her lower lip trembling. "My gods, I laid on top of that…"

Kurt patted her back and stood back up. The cot was a rumpled mess, the blankets and pillows a lumpy, tangled arrangement. For a moment, Kurt couldn't understand why Myrna was so upset. Then, he saw something peeking out from under the edge of the blanket. Something red and crusty. And then he noticed the movement. Something under the pile of blankets was squirming. He reached out hesitantly, then twitched back the edge of the blanket.

The rest of the team, who had gathered around him to watch, let out a chorus of shocked inhalations at the sight of what was lurking beneath the blanket: a human cadaver in the advanced stages of decay. The flesh was gone, exposing layers of shredded viscera and desiccated internal organs.

Squirming over the cadaver, their jaws working feverishly, were more of the overgrown black rats. They squealed at the sudden interruption of their snack, but they weren't intimidated. They didn't flee at the sight of the humans.

"Goddamn." Duke turned his head and spat. "That is fucking *nasty*."

"It's just rats. Bold motherfuckers, but still, just rats." Kurt turned to look at the team. "And it's not the first dead body you've ever seen. We can deal with this. Taurus, Max, haul this cot out of here. Put it on the front doorstep and burn it."

The two men got to work. They covered the remains, tucking the blankets tightly beneath the mattress to trap the rats. Then Taurus grabbed the foot of the bed, while Max lifted the other end.

"Okay, let's do it," Taurus said.

"Yeah, man, let's have us a barbecue," Max agreed.

The team stood by quietly as they watched the two men carry the bed out of the room. Deus broke the silence to mutter more dire predictions. Kurt told him to knock the bullshit off, then used his best leader voice when he spoke to the others.

"We all knew this wasn't going to be a walk in the park," he said. "We knew there was at least one expedition that had come here and never returned. And from the looks of things, it seems this place had some more permanent residents at one time."

"It's pretty interesting, really," Viz said. "Ask anyone who's ever been in a place like this and they'll tell you no one could live in these cities. Something is going on here. Something way beyond anything we've ever dealt with before."

"Yes, something evil," Deus added. "And once again, the rats…"

Kurt shot him a look. "I told you to stow that bullshit. Myrna, I'm sorry you had a bit of a shock, but this doesn't change anything. Our plan of action is the same. We're going to search this place top to bottom. We'll go hard and fast, but we'll be thorough. We'll strip it down to the bones and fill up those trucks. And in the morning, we'll get the fuck out of here. Sound good?"

The answer was murmurs of agreement all around.

"As soon as Taurus and Max get back, we're going to split up," he continued.

"Hey, that sounds like a great plan," Duke said, his lips twisting into a smug grin.

Kurt ignored him. But he reminded himself that he'd have to deal with Duke's insubordination in the harshest possible terms once this job wrapped up.

Chapter Twenty
Computers And Corpses

Taurus and Max stayed outside the building until their impromptu rat barbecue had ended in a smoldering pile of ashes and blackened metal. Once the fat stopped sizzling and the embers died to a soft red glow, they headed back to the dormitory. By the time they arrived, Kurt was already sending the team out to explore the rest of the building.

"I saw another door out in the lobby," Kurt said. "I want you guys to see what's on the other side. We'll meet on the second floor in one hour. Questions?"

Taurus shook his head. "No, boss."

"All right, let's do it," Max said, nudging Taurus with an elbow to the ribs. "The sooner we search this place, the sooner we can get out of here. That beer back at Bruno's last rest may have been shitty, but it sounds pretty damn good right now."

Taurus followed Max out of the room and into the hallway. Now that they had a clearly defined task, Taurus was content. He may not have been a leader like Kurt, but he was still a man of action, and he wasn't happy unless he was striving toward some goal, even if it was modest. If Taurus had a philosophy—and he wasn't a man given to deep ruminations—it was a simple one: once you stopped working, you might as well shrivel up and die.

He'd grown up in a logging camp, cutting petrified trees with blue-fire torch saws and breaking the logs into blocks with a sledgehammer. His days had been filled with hard physical labor and his nights with feasts of wild game and beer brewed from whatever could be foraged from the forests. By the time he'd reached his twentieth summer, he was as strong as a beast of burden and twice as persistent. Illiterate and perhaps even slow-witted, he was as loyal as a hunting dog. But then the plague had come. A mysterious disease that caused burning fever, skin lesions, and violent diarrhea and vomiting, the plague had claimed the lives of nearly every man in the logging camp within a month. Only Taurus survived. Alone and bewildered, he'd wandered away from the only home he'd ever known. For weeks, he'd walked the foothills without map or compass. Had he not met Kurt, Diana, and Deus, he surely would have lost hope and laid down to die. Ever since that day, he'd followed Kurt without question.

"Hey, man," Max said as they picked their way through the debris covering the lobby floor, "you notice anything strange about the way Duke and Kurt have been acting toward each other? Seems like ever since we came out of the forest, they've been circling each other like a couple of wild dogs."

Taurus shrugged. He wasn't very observant when it came to that sort of thing. But he knew if it came down to it, he'd snap Duke's neck before letting him hurt Kurt. Loyalty above all else, that's what his father had taught him. If you tossed your lot in with a man, you stood by his side through thick and thin.

"Can't say I seen anything sets off my alarms," Taurus said, doing his best to sound diplomatic.

"Well, whatever," Max continued. "Duke's a fucking

asshole. Besides, any day now, he's going to make a play for Rosemary and she'll rip his balls off and stuff them down his throat. These things have a way of sorting themselves out."

The door Kurt had mentioned was nearly hidden behind a loose barricade of broken furniture and rusty scrap metal. They cleared away some of the mess until they could open the door just wide enough to squeeze through. Taurus went first. He turned sideways and wriggled through the opening. Once he'd gotten over the threshold, he raised his chemical torch and swept the beam around the room. It was a large space, with a sloped floor and row after row of seats.

At the front of the room was a raised platform, like a stage. The seats were divided into three sections separated by aisles. Taurus imagined that, in ancient happier times, it had been an auditorium or theater. Perhaps people gathered here to watch troupes of actors perform plays or groups of musicians make music. Now, it was a dusty tomb, like the rest of the city.

"Fuck, it stinks even worse in here," Max said as he slipped through the doorway.

"Yeah," Taurus agreed. "Sure does."

They stood just inside the doorway, shining their torches around the large room. The smell wasn't the only odd thing they noticed. There was also a strange soundtrack to the place. It was a faint, but constant scratching and scraping sound. Taurus cocked his head to one side, trying to figure out the source of the noise. He discovered it when he focused the beam of his torch on the stage. The wide, flat surface was teeming with rats. Hundreds of them were crawling about. They were big bastards, larger even than the ones they'd just burnt to ashes in front of the building.

"Rats again." Taurus didn't say so, but he couldn't help thinking about all the stuff Deus had been preaching about rats being bad omens. He pushed the notion out of his mind. In his experience, dwelling on abstract concepts like religion and the supernatural was pointless. Better to keep your mind on the here and now.

"Fuck me, that's a lot of those bastards, too," Max said. "And check out the size of the damn things. I didn't know they could get that big."

Taurus didn't care to speculate about how the rats had attained such grotesque proportions. No doubt living in constant exposure to the lingering effects of the Event had something to do with it. Or maybe there was something even worse crouching in the shadowy corners of this dead city, some force that had caused the rats to grow to monstrous size. Or it could be as simple as the damn things were just overfed. Whatever the reason for their appearance, the rats made Taurus' thick arms break out in gooseflesh.

"What do you think, a couple hundred?" Max asked, shouldering past Taurus and making his way a few meters down the aisle. "Shit, maybe more than that. This building is ground zero for rats."

"Don't get too close," Taurus warned.

"Don't be such a nanny. They're just rats," Max scoffed.

As if to illustrate his point, he raised his pistol, drew a careful bead on one of the rats near the edge of the stage, and fired. The pistol might as well have been a canon. The report filled the empty auditorium like a thunderclap. The shot found its mark, knocking the rat off the edge of the stage. It landed heavily, its legs twitching as its guts oozed from the hole in its belly. Taurus winced. Max laughed and fired again, although this time, his aim was less accurate. The shot barely grazed its target, clipping the tip of the next rat's tail. The force of the impact was still enough to spin the animal around and send it flying off the stage. It landed near its dead cousin. For a moment, it just lay there, stunned. Then, it got to its feet and took a few wobbly steps.

"Maybe you shouldn't do that," he said. "You'll get them all stirred up. Way more rats up there than we got bullets."

"Gods, you really are a nanny. All those muscles, but you're afraid of a few rats." Max turned his back on the stage and flashed a humorless smile at Taurus. "Tell you what, you can run away like a frightened little girl, but I'm going to stay and get in a little target practice."

"What's the point? Just wasting time and ammo."

"The point is that it's hard to have fun on jobs like this, so you gotta get your kicks when the opportunity presents itself. I guess you aren't interested in fun, being such a fucking nanny and all..."

Although Max had begun to turn around by the time the rat charged, he was too busy with insulting Taurus to see it. Bleeding profusely from the wound at the tip of its tail, it came right at Max, closing the distance between them in a few short seconds. By the time Taurus shouted a warning, it was too late. The rat launched itself at Max as if it had been spring-loaded. Taurus had never seen anything like it. If they hadn't been in such a grim setting, the sight might have even been comical. Under the present conditions, it was like something from a nightmare.

The rat hit Max just above the waist. It sank its rear claws into Max's upper thigh, and hooked its front claws into his belly. Screaming, Max spun around in an attempt to dislodge the rodent. It responded with a scream of its own, an enraged screeching unlike anything Taurus had ever heard. He drew his own pistol, but Max's frantic movements made aiming it impossible.

"Stay still!" Taurus shouted. "Damn it, man, I can't do nothing unless you hold still!"

Max flailed his arms, striking at the rat with his fists. But just as many of his punches landed on his own ribs, and the rat scratched its way up Max's torso. Its claws shredded his shirt as well as the flesh beneath, carving long, bloody trenches over Max's belly and chest. Drawing back its triangular head, the rat snapped at Max's face, sinking its incisors through the tip of Max's nose.

Taurus holstered his gun. He was never going to get a clear shot. It was time for more direct action. He grabbed Max with one hand, and with the other, seized the rat by the scruff of its neck. The rat's jaws held on stubbornly, and as Taurus yanked, the rat bit through the tip of Max's nose. Max screamed, clapping his hands to his wounded face. Taurus raised the rat over his head and slammed it to the ground. The impact should have broken its spine, but the rat rolled over and clambered back to its feet.

Max stepped forward, bellowing incoherently as blood poured from his mangled nose. He pointed his pistol at the rat and fired, splattering the rodent's brains over the floor.

Taurus looked at the stage. The rats gathered there had stopped milling about. They stood in a loose assembly at the front of the stage, staring at the scene before them.

"I think we better get the hell out of here," Taurus said.

For once, Max didn't have something smartass to say.

The two men ran for the door. They squeezed through the narrow opening and slammed it shut behind them.

* * *

Rosemary's tolerance for Duke's bullshit had reached its upper limit. Ever since Kurt had dispatched them to check the other rooms on the first floor, Duke had been spouting a nonstop litany of his usual nonsense. He toggled back and forth between critiques of Kurt's leadership and double entendres about Rosemary's sex appeal.

No, strike that, she thought. *Double entendres are clever or funny. Duke is just bleating like a horny goat.*

"Oh, come on," Duke said. "Don't tell me you've never thought about it. All those cold nights back in canyon country, you can't say you didn't at least consider it."

"Look, cut that shit out," she snapped. "Even if I did think of you that way—and trust me, partner, I don't—now ain't the time for that stuff. Now you going to help me or just stand there talking nasty?"

Duke sniffed. "You can deny it all you want, but I see the way you look at me."

Rosemary rolled her eyes and got back to work. They were standing in front of a locked door at the end of the hallway. Unlike the other doors, this one was made of thick metal and sported a heavy lock. Rosemary was doing her best to pick the lock. Normally, she wasn't half bad at this sort of thing. She had an extensive criminal background, so this wasn't the first time she'd used a couple old hairpins to get a lock to give up the goods. But this lock was real son of a bitch, and Duke was fucking up her concentration.

"Come on, you can admit it," he pressed on. "Kurt and Diana don't keep their relationship a secret. And Lilith and Lucifer, hell, they'll shuck their clothes and start fucking in front of the gods and everyone."

"Yeah, well, that ain't us," she said, probing the lock's mechanism for the sweet spot. "Sorry, partner, but you try shucking my clothes and I'll shoot your pecker off."

She considered shocking him with the truth, namely that she would rather zip in a sleeping bag with Myrna. But she reconsidered before the words made the journey from her brain to her lips. A pig like Duke would just use it as material for more innuendo. And besides, the lock was finally giving up the goods. She gave one hairpin a careful twist while pushing the other deeper into the mechanism. The clasp sprang open.

She stood, wiping her hands on her pants. She stepped back and pointed at the doorknob. "Want to impress me? You take point on this room."

"Yeah, that's how it is with women. They're all tough,

man-hating bitches until it comes time to face danger," Duke snickered.

No, she thought, *it's just that I don't like you walking behind me. And not just because I can feel you staring at my ass. You're putting out that rapist vibe awful heavy. Be a shame to have to kill you right in the middle of a job. And rapist ain't the only vibe you're broadcasting. You're also putting out some crazy vibes...*

There was something strange about the way Duke was acting. Every so often, probably when he thought she wasn't looking, he'd squeeze his eyes shut and shake his head like a man trying to clear away a cobweb he'd just blundered into. He always had an unhinged air about him, but it was subtle enough that you might miss it if you didn't know what to look for. But Rosemary knew what to look for and recognized it immediately. It was the same thing she'd seen in the faces of the men who'd tried to force themselves on her when she was a teenage pickpocket. She'd left those bastards whimpering and bleeding. And if it came to that, she'd leave Duke the same way.

"Okay, let's venture into the unknown together," Duke said, shoving the door open. He raised his torch and his pistol and stepped over the threshold.

Rosemary followed him into the dark room, blinking her eyes a few times to adjust to the darkness.

"Gods, what a fucking stink," Duke moaned.

"You ain't lying about that," Rosemary said.

A quick look around was all it took to explain the stench. The room was full of corpses. "Looks like some sort of library or school or something," Duke said, shining his light around the room. "No, that's not right. What's the word I'm searching for?"

"It's an office. They called them offices during the pre-Event days."

"You sure? Because I've been in offices before and none of them looked like this."

Rosemary rolled her eyes. "You've been in rooms where pimps and hash refiners do business. Those aren't the same thing."

The room was packed with desks and file cabinets. The rest of the furniture consisted of chairs with wheels attached to the legs. There looked to be twelve, maybe fifteen chairs, and they were all occupied by dead bodies in the advanced stages of decay. Strange insects buzzed through the air like miniature zeppelins. Some of them were so swollen with their carrion feast that their flight paths were erratic. They thumped off the walls and fell to the floor, dazed or dead. Those too stunned to recover or those who were dead on impact crunched underfoot as Rosemary followed Duke deeper into the room.

"Let's get the hell out of here." Duke halted in the center of the room.

"We need to check these cabinets and desks," Rosemary said. "Yeah, I know it stinks in here, but we still got a job to do. I'll start on the right. You start on the left, and we'll meet in the middle."

"So you're in charge now?" Duke folded his arms over his chest.

"No, Kurt's in charge, and he wants us to search this place top to bottom." She stared him down for a few beats, then continued, "We got a job to do, and we're going to do it. If you're not up for that, maybe go tell the rest of the team why you're so special that you don't have to work anymore. I'm sure they'd all love to hear it."

Duke was too stunned to offer an immediate reply, and she turned away and got to work before he could recover.

They got to work. The file cabinets were packed full of neat stacks of paper. Rosemary scanned a few randomly selected pages. They were covered with words she didn't recognize and row after row of numerical formulas. She didn't bother speculating about the subject of the tangled words and figures. Rosemary's formal education consisted of occasional lessons from one of women at the brothel where she spent the first twelve years of her life. She could read a few words of the common tongue, enough to get by, but that was it.

"Told you this was a waste of time," Duke growled. He slammed the file cabinet drawer shut. "Nothing but a bunch of papers."

"Aw, did baby get a papercut?" Rosemary leaned against the nearest file cabinet.

"You know, it's a good thing you're so pretty, because otherwise…"

"Yeah? Otherwise *what*?"

Their staring contest was brief. Duke turned his back on her and started for the door.

"Forget it," he called over his shoulder. "Let's get out of here before I puke from breathing in this stink."

Rosemary smirked. Duke thought of himself as some hard-ass alpha male, but once you called him on his bullshit, he folded. Now that she'd called his bluff, he was pissed off. She could tell he was pissed off, because he was one of those men who had to broadcast their anger to anyone in the vicinity, lest they miss out on the fact that the hard-ass alpha was upset.

Duke growled some unintelligible curse as he shoved aside one of the wheeled chairs, spilling its occupant onto the floor.

"Hey, now…" Rosemary shook her head. She wasn't on board with that brand of antics. She wasn't a superstitious weirdo like Deus, but she drew a hard line when it came to disrespecting the dead. Even if you left religion out of the discussion, there was still some seriously bad mojo involved.

Duke paused and looked back at her. A sly grin spread across his face as he grabbed the nearest chair and upended it, dumping another dead body on the floor. He drew back his foot and gave it a kick for good measure. The corpse was bloated, its distended belly swollen to a perfect roundness that might have been comical under other circumstances.

"What's the matter?" he asked, shining his torch on the body. "It's just some poor dead son of a bitch. Not like he can hurt you. He can't even move anymore."

But, to Rosemary's growing disgust and horror, something was moving inside the poor dead son of a bitch. His round belly jiggled. Something inside it began pressing against the strained flesh. It reminded Rosemary of watching a baby move inside a very pregnant woman. She wrinkled her nose, but couldn't tear her eyes off the spectacle.

"What the fuck?" Duke muttered.

The cadaver's belly split open along a neat line from just below the sternum to the navel. A puff of putrescent gas wafted out of the opening, adding another layer of foulness to the room's pungent bouquet. If it had ended there, with a swollen corpse emitting eye-stinging odors, it would have been horrific enough. But it didn't end there.

A furry black head, slick with whatever juices had been fermenting in the belly of the dead body, emerged from the freshly opened wound. It chittered excitedly as it glanced around the room. Another head joined it and added its own voice. A third, then a fourth head poked out. Eight beady eyes shone in the glare of Duke's chemical torch. A quartet of rodent voices formed a squeaky chorus.

"Fucking rats." Duke chose to state the obvious.

Rosemary backed away, wincing as she blundered into another dead office worker. For a moment, she had to fight to keep her balance. The thought of falling and landing so near the fat man's body filled her with a mingling of disgust and panic. Her stomach did a quick series of flip-flops, but she managed to remain upright. Once her equilibrium had returned, she pulled her gun from its holster and took aim at one of the rats. It had managed to work its forepaws out of the corpse's belly and was in the process of wriggling free. She pulled the trigger, blasting away the rat's head. Its body twitched and then sank back into the stew of liquefied internal organs.

Duke stood there slack-jawed as he watched her execute another rat. This time, the rat had nearly managed to work its way completely free. Only its tail was still mired in the gory slop. The bullet knocked the rat backwards, and it tumbled to the floor.

"Anytime you feel like helping, you go right ahead, partner," she said.

Duke shook his head, bringing himself out of whatever reverie had taken hold of him. He pulled his gun and fired. Rosemary took her turn next, shooting the remaining rat. It sank back into the corpse's abdomen like a man drowning in quicksand.

"What the hell?" Duke turned his head and spat. "I know Kurt said this place was supposed to have some wildlife, but did you get a look at the size of those fucking things? They're even bigger than the other ones we saw."

Rosemary raised a hand to silence him. She cocked her head to one side. "You hear that?"

Duke began to shake his head, then abruptly stopped. "Sounds like more of them."

The sound was faint and muffled, but it was unmistakable. It was the same insistent squeaking that the rat quartet had made before Rosemary and Duke blasted them into whatever rodent afterlife awaited such vermin. And then, another unmistakable sound: the slow tearing of dead flesh. Rosemary turned, playing the beam of her torch over the other corpses. She paused her torch's beam, like a green-tinted spotlight, on one of the seated cadavers. This one had been a woman, judging by the few scraps of clothes hanging from the decayed flesh. Long strands of hair hung from the few patches of scalp that still remained on her skull. Head thrown back and legs extended in front of her, the woman almost looked as if she was relaxing. That illusion was soon spoiled as her neck swelled to obscene proportions. The skin split, and thick sludge sluiced down her chest. Her jaws widened, the bones cracking with a sound like a tree branch snapping underfoot. From between her teeth, a rat's head emerged. Its mouth was open just enough to reveal incisors gripping a leathery strip of the woman's tongue.

"I think we better get the fuck out of here," Duke said, his eyes goggling at the stomach-churning displays unfolding all around them as dead bodies tore and ruptured, birthing dozens of oversized black rats.

Rosemary agreed. Duke was never going to be leadership material, but he was right about some things.

* * *

Kurt and Diana accessed the building's second floor via a concrete-and-metal staircase. It was pitch black in the stairwell, and their chemical torches could only do so much to dispel the darkness. They worked their way up carefully, with guns drawn and nerves on high alert.

"Almost there," Kurt said as they paused on the mid-point landing.

"Yeah," Diana said, her voice not much more than a whisper. "Then everything will be okay."

She resisted the urge to check the time. She was afraid that checking her watch every few minutes would somehow slow the passing of the hours, and she wouldn't do anything that might prolong their stay in this strange building in the middle of a nightmare city. Maybe it was the presence of the overgrown rats or maybe it was Deus' nonstop proclamations of doom, but her feeling of impending disaster was growing with each passing minute. Something was going to happen, something horrible. She didn't know what it would be, but it was coming.

They resumed their upward climb. One more slight turn at the top landing, and Kurt opened the door. The hallway into which they emerged was dim, but compared to the darkness of the stairwell, it was a relief. In that kind of darkness, cut only by the greenish beams of two chemical torches, it had been all too easy to imagine nameless horrors lurking in every corner.

No, she thought, *not nameless horrors. You imagined rats in those dark spaces. Big, fat, black rats with oily fur and two-inch teeth...*

"Come on, babe," Kurt said. "I need you with me here."

She did her best to shake off the dread and force a smile. "Yeah, sorry about that."

"I know this place is weird, but if we stick to the plan, we'll be out of here before you know it. And then, we start making serious plans about heading north."

She tried to think about the wide open prairies and snow-capped mountains that awaited them in the northern territories. But it was hard to imagine anything other than hordes of squealing, filthy rodents.

She followed Kurt down the hallway. They passed up a series of closed doors on either side in favor of a large room at the end of the hallway. It was surrounded by alternating panels of wood and floor-to-ceiling windows. The entryway was wide and had no doors.

"This looks promising," Kurt said over his shoulder.

"Yeah, I think so," Diana replied.

But that was a lie. She didn't think anything about this place was promising. She had even begun to entertain the idea that Lord Hannibal might have sent them here for some reason that had nothing to do with salvage. The man's reputation did nothing to dispel that suspicion. But she couldn't imagine what that other reason might be. A man like

Lord Hannibal was only after profits, and she couldn't see any profit-making angle apart from salvage. She told herself that the grim atmosphere, and perhaps even elevated PEE levels were to blame for her growing sense of dread. She told herself that Kurt was right, and soon enough, this would all be nothing but a strange memory.

The room was packed full of desks and banks of tech machinery whose purpose Diana could only guess. There were large ceramic pots in the corners. The plants within were obviously plastic. No natural plant could have survived so long without water, to say nothing of the close proximity to an Event epicenter.

"What the hell is all this?" she asked.

Kurt shook his head. "No idea. But whatever it is, I'd be willing to bet it's why we're here. For pre-Event tech, this is a goddamn goldmine."

"So after we get this stuff boxed up and loaded on the trucks, we can leave?" She wondered if her voice sounded as eager to Kurt's ears as it did to her own.

"Maybe, maybe not. There may be more treasures hidden in this place. If we came all this way, we might as well get everything we can get our hands on."

"Right." She nodded. "That makes sense."

Although it did indeed make sense, she still wished he'd said otherwise.

"Come on," Kurt said. "Let's keep our heads in the game."

She followed him into the room. It was hard not to be awed by the amount and variety of tech equipment on display. She'd heard stories about pre-Event computers that could do everything from order food supplies to map routes for flying machines. Although she'd always been doubtful about the truth of these stories, they did seem a little easier to believe as she scanned the room.

"Wish we had Viz up here," Kurt said. "That guy might actually be able to identify some of this stuff."

"As you wish, sir."

Diana turned at the sound of the voice and saw Viz standing in the doorway with Myrna at his side.

"Good timing," Kurt said. "But you guys must not have found anything interesting if you're already up here."

"Well, if you consider dead bodies interesting, then we found plenty," Viz said, stepping into the room. "I'm telling you, something really bad happened here. I'm not sure what this place used to be, but if you told me it was a cannibal slaughterhouse, I'd probably believe it."

"Don't forget the rats," Myrna added. "There were plenty of those too."

"Gods, I don't think I'll ever forget." Viz wrinkled his nose. "Big, ugly bastards. And they stink like death itself."

Diana's heart skipped a beat. Rats again. Of all the Event-mutated animals in the world, why did it have to be rats at this place? She shivered despite the stuffiness of the room.

"Well, now," Viz said, rubbing his hands together as he glanced around. "What have we got here?"

"I figured this might be right up your alley," Kurt said.

"It's beautiful. So many toys in one spot." Viz stepped past Kurt and Diana to get a closer look at the stacks of equipment. "Looks like an entire computer system."

"You know what this stuff does? How to work it?" Kurt asked.

Viz shrugged. "Never seen anything exactly like this. It's way advanced, and I mean it's leaps and bounds past what I thought existed. Some of this might even be pre-Event era tech. This place is full of those surveillance cameras, and by the look of them, those things are fucking ancient."

"Surveillance cameras?" Diana asked. She didn't know why, but the idea of cameras—functioning or not—filled her with dread. The men didn't seem particularly bothered, however. They ignored her and went right on talking.

"Okay, but will something that old still work? I don't want

to spend all our time dismantling and packing a bunch of shit just to find out that it's nothing but fancy paperweights." Kurt sat in one of the chairs and propped his feet on the closest desk.

"Only one way to find out." Viz sat down and got to work.

Diana bit her lower lip as she watched Viz test the gadgets. His fingers flew over the equipment, flipping switches, pushing buttons, tapping keys. If there was a method to his process, Diana couldn't discern it, but she knew better than to voice this observation. When it came to things like this, she was out of her depth. Machines were a mystery. Maybe she was still a simple fishing village girl at heart.

She turned to Myrna. "Did you guys find anything else downstairs?"

Myrna shook her head. "Just empty rooms. Well, empty except for a few dead bodies. Looked like they'd been here for a while, but who knows if that's really true. For all we know, those bodies have been here for years. This close to an epicenter, things are bound to be strange, right?"

"Yeah, it's definitely strange," Myrna agreed.

Across the room, the two men continued to marvel at the tech gadgets.

"Okay, watch this, ladies and gentlemen," Viz announced, tapping a key.

There was brief electronic buzzing, then the overhead lights flickered. They went on like that for a moment, then blazed to life, bathing the room in fluorescent glow. Viz tapped another key and the lights in the hallway also woke up.

"And now, the rest of the building," Viz said.

The voices of the rest of the team, those still scattered throughout the building, rose up in a cheering chorus. Diana added her own soft applause. With the lights on, the place lost some of its grim atmosphere. Of course, lights didn't change the fact that they were in the middle of a dead city, inside a building full of overgrown, stinking rats.

"How the hell is this even possible?" Kurt asked. "Are there pipes in the walls pumping chemicals to all these lights?"

"Nope." Viz smiled like a child suddenly given free rein in a toy store. "This, my friend, is good old fashioned electricity. Maybe there's a hydro facility nearby, like you said, or it could have any number of other sources. Before the Event, there were ways to harness power from oil and coal, even from the sun and wind. These computers, at least most of them, look like they're pre-Event tech. Heavily modified probably, but it's centuries old. I can't believe it works[8].*"

"Are you sure?" Kurt asked.

Viz nodded. "Weapons, engines, and that heavy machinery shit is Taurus' territory, but tech is mine. I'm absolutely certain about both the electrical system and the computers."

"Amazing." Kurt shook his head in wonder.

The computer screens—twenty or more of them packed into this office—began to glow.

Letters and symbols scrolled across their dusty surfaces.

"Holy shit, they all work," Viz observed. He tore his eyes away from the digital glow long enough to glance at Kurt. "Do you have any idea what this sort of tech is worth, even if it's only semi-functional? If it works, it's worth a fortune. Forget the rest of the building, this room alone is enough to make us rich, even by northern territories standards."

---

* [8] Instances of pre-Event tech remaining functional centuries after the Event were rare but not unheard of. One of the numerous lingering effects of the Event was the preservation of tech items located in the population centers. Although organic life was either exterminated or mutated beyond recognition, certain technological devices not only remained intact but were somehow strengthened by the continued emissions of Event energies.

"Yeah, but that isn't the deal. This stuff belongs to Lord Hannibal."

Diana heard the words come out of Kurt's mouth, but she could tell by his expression that he was already doing the math in his head. The risk vs. reward calculations were intense, if Kurt's furrowed brow was any indication.

"Does it have to belong to him, though?" Viz asked. "I mean, he's hundreds of miles away and he always travels heavy."

He pulled his feet off the desk and turned in his chair. "Myrna, I need you to head downstairs and collect as many of the team as you can find. We need to have a meeting to discuss our next course of action."

"Sure, boss," she said.

Diana watched Myrna head down the hallway toward the staircase. Even if what Viz said was true, and this tech equipment was worth a fortune, Diana would still trade it all just to be far away from this place. She couldn't shake her deep sense of dread. The bright, buzzing lights couldn't dispel that ominous feeling as easily as they cut through the shadows. It wasn't just the rats, either. They were part of it, of course; rats were still creatures straight out of her nightmares. No, this creeping sense of impending doom went beyond that. She was starting to fear that Deus was right about this place being cursed.

"Computers and corpses," she sighed. "Why do I feel like that's a bad combination?"

Taurus could tell the place was some sort of hydroponic garden, even before the overhead lights woke up. Despite the near total darkness and the grand scale of the room, his chemical torch lit up enough for him to get an idea of what he'd stumbled into when he pried open the locked double doors and stepped over the threshold. But once the lights came on, he could only marvel at his discovery.

Beside him, Max whistled appreciatively. The bandage

covering his nose was crusty with dried blood, but he hadn't offered any complaints. The pain medication that Taurus had found in his First Aid kit probably had something to do with that. The pills were prized for recreational use, which was why Kurt only trusted Taurus and Rosemary to carry them.

"Would you take a look at this?" Max said, his eyes wide as he looked around the room. "It's like something from another world. I can't believe I'm seeing this."

"Yeah, it's something," Taurus agreed. The room, which was easily twice the size of the lobby, was filled with long rows of hydroponics equipment. Lush, green plants filled each container. Some of the plants were small trees, their limbs laden with flowers and fruit. Others were smaller and covered with pods containing beans or peas. There were plenty that Taurus didn't even recognize, but he was sure they were some sort of food. Massive water filtration units burbled away in one corner of the room, pumping water through a complex tangle of tubes that ran from the ceiling to each plant.

"I've heard stories about the bunkers in the old days," Max said. "You know, like ancient shit. The way those stories go, there were all sorts of places like this right after the Event. But they were all underground. Never heard of something like this so deep in the interior. They call it the wasteland for a reason, right?"

"I guess so," Taurus said. Truthfully, he'd never given the name much thought. As far as he could tell, most of the world was a wasteland. There wasn't much remarkable about it.

He reached out and touched the leaves of the nearest plant, some sort of bush studded with red legumes. He'd heard about the large scale farms in the foothills or on the coasts. But even the wildest accounts of those places didn't include this variety of plants. He figured there could be as many as a hundred varieties of fruit and vegetables in this place. Hell, maybe there were even more. Supposedly, there were some types of plants that absorbed lingering energies from the Event and were poisonous.

"You think this is safe to eat?" Taurus asked. "We're pretty deep in an epicenter. And we know people have died here."

"Yeah, but those poor bastards didn't die from food poisoning," Max said.

"Then what do you reckon they died from? The boss said we ain't the first operation to roll through town. Something had to kill them others."

Max reached out and plucked a grape from a nearby plant. "Okay, how about this. I'm about to eat this grape. It looks sweet and juicy, and if I happen to die because I ate it, I guess it's worth it."

Before Taurus could protest, Max popped the grape into his mouth. He closed his eyes and sighed as he ate it.

"Well, from the looks of things, someone is enjoying his visit to this shithole," a loud voice announced.

Taurus jumped at the first syllable but quickly relaxed. Lucifer had one of those instantly recognizable voices. It was a roof-rattling baritone that seemed to carry its own echo chamber. Lucifer's delivery was just as unique as his voice, with his vowels so elongated that it seemed like he was savoring each syllable he spoke.

"Hey, Lucifer," Taurus said, turning just in time to watch him enter the room.

When Lucifer was around, Lilith was never far. She followed him through the doorway a second later. They were one of those couples who looked like the gods had designed them as a matched set. They had the same olive skin tone and dark eyes, the same thick brown hair. They even dressed the same, in knee-high black moccasins and dark grey coveralls.

"Holy shit, boys! It looks like you found the garden of paradise!" Lilith exclaimed in her clipped, excitable delivery. Her voice was a high-pitched and chirpy as Lucifer's was bottomless and oddly soothing. She followed Lucifer across the room to where Taurus and Max stood.

"Yeah, it certainly is something, but I think we should wait before we eat anything," Taurus cautioned.

"Fuck that. I see a free lunch, I'm eating it." Max popped a second, then a third grape into his mouth. "You don't know what you're missing."

"What the hell happened to you?" Lucifer asked, pointing at the bandage on Max's face.

"I had an unpleasant encounter with a rat." Max turned his head and spit out a pair of grape seeds. "Taurus and I found a whole army of the nasty buggers. It weird, man. We found this auditorium or theater or whatever you want to call it, and there were a couple hundred rats just milling around on the stage. Then I guess one of them decided to take a nibble on the end of my nose."

"We shot it," Taurus explained. "The rat, I mean, not his nose."

Lucifer nodded, as if this was a perfectly normal occurrence. "Yeah, this place is full of rats. We saw a few while we were poking around. Big motherfuckers and they didn't seem much bothered by our presence. Didn't run away from us until I gave a couple of them a good kicking."

"You guys find anything useful?" Max asked, his mouth half full. He'd moved from grapes to blueberries, and his lips dripped juice as he spoke.

"Nothing much," Lilith chimed in. "Just those icky rats and a couple dead bodies. They were icky too."

Lucifer shot her a look. "Oh, they were icky, huh? Woman, I know for a fact you've seen worse. Quit putting on that blushing virgin act."

"Yeah, but this place is different. It's…I don't know…*evil*." Lilith paused, reaching out to touch one of the plants with her fingertips. "I mean, except for this room. This is nice."

"Oh, it's nice?" Lucifer smirked. "That's all you got to say about it?"

"What's your problem?" Lilith asked. "Ever since we got here, you've been acting like such an asshole. I swear, there's something about this place…"

Lucifer snorted. "Oh, for fuck's sake, I was just teasing. You're too damn sensitive."

Taurus shifted his weight from one foot to the other and then back again. There was a reason he didn't like to hang around Lucifer and Lilith. As advance scouts, they often traveled separately from the rest of the team, and for that, Taurus thanked the gods. Their relationship toggled between incessant bickering and passionate physical affection, sometimes in the space of minutes. It made Taurus profoundly uncomfortable.

"I'm going to poke around a bit, then head upstairs to find the boss," he said. "I'm not sure how much of this we can salvage, but I bet he'll be plenty interested."

He worked his way down the row of plants, marveling at the variety on display. By the time he made it to the end of the row and turned around, Lucifer and Lilith had flipped the switch to the other extreme of their relationship. They were kissing and groping one another. Lucifer's hands were under Lilith's shirt as he pressed her against one of the hydroponic tanks.

Max looked on with obvious interest, popping blueberries into his mouth with one hand and rubbing his crotch with the other.

Taurus felt heat creep into his face. Max may have been comfortable with a bit of casual voyeurism, but it made Taurus feel, as Lilith had so eloquently put it, icky. He kept his eyes on the ground as he made his way back through the room.

Once he stepped through the door, he breathed a sigh of relief. Although the air was stale and flat compared to the flowery scents of the garden room, he took a deep breath and let it out slowly. He felt like he might deflate entirely. Lilith was right. There was something unnatural about the atmosphere inside the building. There was a heaviness, like gravity was somehow stronger within the thick stone walls.

He walked back through the lobby, scattering piles of dust and bits of broken glass with the toes of his heavy boots. A rat scurried past, and for a moment, Taurus considered going after it. There was nowhere for it to hide on this open floor. He could corner it and stomp its guts out without much effort. But he swatted the thought away. That sort of casual cruelty might have been entertaining for Max, but Taurus wasn't built that way. After all, a rat couldn't help the way the gods made it. It harmed no one to simply let the creature go about its business. Now, if it decided to turn around and try to bite him, that was a different story. He'd kill it without a second thought. The "live and let live" philosophy was a door that swung both ways.

He paused in the center of the room to peer through the open front doors at the empty streets. It bothered him that the doors were just hanging wide open like that. Anyone could come strolling in. Of course, this was a dead city and there was no one strolling through the desolation.

Still, he didn't like those open doors. Although he couldn't be certain, he thought someone had closed them when the team first entered the building. Probably Duke or Rosemary, since they were the ones always bringing up the rear.

After a moment's hesitation, he crossed the room and pulled the doors closed, making sure that the latches caught. It didn't dispel the strange atmosphere, but the simple act made him feel a little better. It was a normal thing, to close a door, and this place could do with any amount of normalcy, no matter how insignificant.

Taurus nodded, satisfied with a job well done, no matter how small. Then, he felt a hand on his shoulder and heard a sharp intake of breath. He jerked away, colliding with the doors he'd just closed. A startled yelp escaped his lips. In that brief second, his mind conjured an image of his attacker. It was a nightmarish composite of all the mutants they encountered in the forest.

One of them had survived and followed them here, just like the one who'd tried to kill Duke during that storm at the outpost. His fight or flight response triggered a rush of adrenaline as he threw himself at his attacker, who sidestepped him easily. He went sprawling face-first on the filthy floor, yelping again. In an instant, he was back on his feet, fists clenched as he beheld the face of…

"Myrna?" he said, still reeling on the dizzy edge of an adrenaline spike.

"Gods be damned, you're jumpy," she said. "I thought you were going to knock my ass out."

Taurus bent over and grabbed his knees, gulping air.

"Shit, man, you okay?" Myrna asked, placing a hand on his back. "I'm sorry about sneaking up on you like that. All the noise I was making walking through all this broken glass and shit, I was sure you heard me coming."

He straightened up and tried his best to give her a smile. "I'm the one who should apologize. I guess I was just lost in my thoughts. I think this place might be getting to me. But hey, we found something pretty amazing."

"Yeah? We did too. That's why Kurt sent me to find everyone. Any idea where the others are?"

"They're back in the…" Taurus hesitated. "They're in the garden room. Tell you what, maybe we better give them a few minutes."

"Lilith and Lucifer?" Myrna asked, smirking.

"Yeah, I guess they had an argument and now they're making up." Taurus felt his face growing warm again.

"How about Max?"

Taurus winced. "He's watching."

"Gods, he's such a pervert. Almost as bad as Duke," Myrna laughed. "Come on, let's go upstairs. Deus is wandering around here somewhere. Probably finding a bunch of evil omens around every corner. Maybe we'll run into him on our way."

"Rosemary and Duke?" Taurus asked.

Myrna shook her head. "I got no idea where they are. This is a big place. Almost like it's bigger inside that it looks from outside. But I guess that's impossible."

Taurus didn't have a response to that. He was starting to feel like anything, no matter how awful, might be possible within these walls.

* * *

By the time Taurus and Myrna entered the cramped office, Viz had all the computers powered up. Their screens flickered intermittently, swimming in and out of focus, but all the equipment appeared to be functional.

Kurt swiveled around in his chair as Taurus entered. "Check it out, man. Viz is some kind of fucking wizard. You ever see anything like it?"

Taurus shook his head. He had never even imagined anything like it. But while Kurt may have been enthralled with the technological display, it made Taurus uneasy. On the surface, this place had much to offer. Much more than any of the other salvage jobs they'd undertaken, in fact. The non-perishable food supply, the hydroponic garden, and now a functioning electrical system that powered an entire building, not to mention a room full of tech gadgets. All of it was great, sure. But what about all the dead bodies? Was he alone in wondering why there were so damn many of them? Taurus remembered how his father had taught him to trap animals. He'd said that traps were effective because lower animals were too hungry for the bait to bother asking themselves why it was so conveniently placed.

He considered voicing his concerns, but thought better of it. Kurt was the brains of the outfit. Taurus knew all too well that he was the brawn. That was just the way of things.

"Well, how about it?" Kurt asked. "What did you guys find down there?"

"Hydroponic garden and water filtration," Taurus answered. "Biggest ones I've ever seen. Both of them seem to be in good working order too. Max was down there eating grapes and blueberries."

Kurt's smile spread so wide that Taurus thought it might split his face in two. "This place just gets better and better."

Taurus wondered if that was what a rabbit thought when it saw a baited snare.

"How about you, Myrna?" Kurt asked. "You get a look at this garden?"

She shook her head. "Unlike Max, I didn't have much interest in the live sex show that Lucifer and Lilith were performing in there. As much as I'd like to eat some fresh berries, I think I could happily live the rest of my life without seeing that shit again."

Everyone thought that was pretty funny, and they shared a laugh. Each of them could offer an eyewitness account of the scouts' public displays of affection. None of them seemed eager to take in another show, but they were clearly not as uncomfortable as Taurus was with the prospect. He didn't even care to joke about it. And that's why he was glad that Deus entered the room before people could start in with supposedly funny stories about seeing their fellow team members fucking each other.

The holy man shouldered past Taurus and Myrna. He worked his way through the dense maze of desks and stood in the center of the room with his arms folded over his chest.

His posture and expression radiated disapproval bordering on disgust.

"I know that none of you want to hear about how this place is cursed, so I'll remain silent on that subject," he said.

Kurt scoffed, "Oh, come on. Standing there with that sour look on your face and saying you won't bring up the subject of curses isn't the same as remaining silent. You're just being silly now. Might as well say what's on your mind. This team has always had a free speech policy, hasn't it?"

"As you wish," Deus sniffed. "I'm walked the corridors of this building, and I've seen what lurks in the shadows. Rats. I've seen hundreds of them, which means there are at least twice as many who remain hidden."

"Okay, so the poor bastards on the last expedition should have brought an exterminator with them." Kurt glanced around. It was clear he expected the remark to elicit some laughs, but nobody offered even a token chuckle. He cleared his throat and continued, "Look, I know you think the rats are some dark omen, but I'm telling you that they're just rodents. Sure, they're a little on the big side, but they're just overgrown mice. If you want to worry about something, worry about the strange wildlife Lord Hannibal warned us about. If there are rats here, there's bound to be other animals lurking around."

Taurus decided he had something to offer after all, and said, "I don't know, but maybe it was the rats he was talking about. Maybe *they're* the strange wildlife. I mean, something killed all those dead bodies we keep finding. Might be the rats did it."

"Yeah," Myrna said, nodding. "Some of them looked like they'd been eaten."

"I can't believe the crew that, just a couple days ago, faced a tribe of cannibal mutants and a couple giant bears are scared of a few rats." Kurt slapped the desk. "Sure, those bodies were partially eaten. That's what rats do. They're scavengers. You're right about how something killed those people and we should be on our guard. But rats didn't do it. I don't care how big and ugly these bastards are, they didn't attack and kill a few dozen people."

No one, not even dour-faced Deus, felt like arguing. Taurus was sorry he even said anything.

* * *

The strange animal voices in Duke's head were growing in number and volume. There were so many of them that they blended into a steady stream of white noise. After the encounter in the corpse-littered office, it wasn't hard to guess the source of the psychic babble. This place was packed to the rafters with rats, and they were broadcasting their primitive thoughts at him nonstop.

He trudged up the stairs, too distracted by the noise in his head to watch Rosemary's ass move beneath the fabric of her pants.

"I'm just saying, that was fucked up shit back there," she said over her shoulder. "Never seen rats do that before. You think they killed those poor fuckers?"

"I don't think rats kill people," he said. "But this deep in an epicenter zone, who knows?"

Rosemary stopped at the top landing and opened the door. "Hey, there's lights up here too."

Duke followed her out of the stairwell and into a hallway. There were doors on either side, but Duke saw right away where they were headed. There was a big room at the end of the hallway. Both doors were standing open, and he could see most of the team gathered within.

Whatever was going on in that room, it was producing plenty of light. Even compared to the buzzing overhead lights in the hallway, the room was bright.

"Damn, you ever see so much electrical light in one place?" Rosemary asked, leading the way toward the room.

"Weird shit going on in this building," he agreed, gritting his teeth against the growing pressure in his head. It was like the sheer number of rodent voices in his head was testing the limits of his skull.

"Hey, looks like the gang's almost all here," Kurt chirped as Duke and Rosemary entered the crowded room. "You guys find anything notable downstairs?"

Rosemary launched into an account of the horrors they'd witnessed. She was a good storyteller, peppering her descriptions with plenty of vivid and obscene metaphors, so Duke let her do the talking. He found a reasonably clean chair in the corner of the room and dropped into it. He glanced around the room at his colleagues.

Viz was too busy playing with his treasure trove of tech gadgets to give his full attention to Rosemary. There was no doubt about Viz's loyalty to Kurt, but Duke didn't see him as much of a threat. When the time came, Duke would be able to handle the goofy tech junkie without much fuss.

Under normal circumstances, Duke would have put Deus in the same category as far as loyalty to the current regime was concerned. But there was something about the mystic's posture and expression that cast some doubt on that. Something had changed between Deus and Kurt sine they'd left Bruno's Last Rest.

Diana would stand by her man until the bitter end, but Duke was confident he could handle her.

Myrna was a toss-up. On one hand, she looked at Kurt with big gooey eyes, but Duke knew all too well that the line between love and hate was a thin one.

Taurus, the big ox, might be a problem. He was as loyal as a dog, and every bit as stupid.

If it came down to it, Duke would deal with him first.

Without his strong arm at his side, Kurt might not be so cocky about his leadership.

He didn't see Max, Lucifer, or Lilith, but he didn't need to worry about them. Max was a mercenary. He'd fall in line behind the frontrunner. And the two scouts were too busy fucking each other every chance they got to give a shit about who was riding at the head of the formation. They kept to themselves most of the time anyway, hovering on the fringes of the team. He didn't know much about their background, but he had the distinct impression that they could be turned to his side without much effort.

That left Rosemary. Even now, she was an enigma. A beautiful, frustratingly complex puzzle, and one that would have to be handled with utmost care. Because while he could kill any of the others without a second thought, Rosemary was the prize. If she died as a result of his coup, it would all be for nothing.

"So we barricaded the doors and got the hell out of there," Rosemary said, wrapping up her story. "There were a few tech gadgets down there, but nothing like what you got going on in this room. Mostly it was file cabinets full of paper. Looked like science shit. Lots of formulas and equations, that type of thing."

Viz paused his incessant keyboard pecking to ask her if she saw anything that could give her a rough idea of the building's purpose.

"It's almost certainly a research center of some kind," he said. "But this equipment is far beyond the capabilities of anything I've ever encountered. It's scary advanced, you know?"

"Like I said, I couldn't make heads or tails of it," she replied.

"And we were a little busy fighting off giant angry rats to try deciphering any of it," Duke added. "You guys may have had an easy afternoon of fucking around with computers and strolling through greenhouses, but we were neck deep in some shit."

Viz raised his hands in surrender. "Hey, man, I was just asking."

"Well, I was just answering," Duke snapped. "While you were up here jacking off all over these flashy contraptions and Max and the scouts were playing around in the garden, we were fighting off a rat attack. We were so busy that we didn't have much of an opportunity to pore over stacks of graphs and equations."

"Cool it, Duke," Kurt said, rising from his seat so he could face Duke while he spoke. "I'm sorry you and Rosemary ran into a bad scene downstairs, but it doesn't give you the right to pop off like that. I imagine we'll all put in our share of hard work before this job is over."

Duke stared back at Kurt defiantly. For a moment, the cacophony of animal noise in his head receded, and he wondered if that was a sign. But he forced himself to remain seated. It was too early to act on his ambitions. The group wasn't ready for a sea change. He had a feeling, something stronger than intuition, that they'd be ready soon. But not yet. He met Kurt's stare but said nothing.

Taurus broke the uneasy silence. "When I was downstairs with Max, we saw some aggressive rats too. They didn't act like any rats I'd ever seen before. They were a lot like the ones you say saved your ass back at the outpost, Duke. Like they were organizing themselves or something."

Duke turned and looked at Taurus. Maybe he'd been wrong about the depth of the big man's devotion to Kurt. There was something in Taurus' eyes that Duke had never seen before. It wasn't as potent as the doubt in Deus' eyes, but there was something in Taurus' expression…

Viz cleared his throat. "Hey guys, I think I might have coaxed some information out of this thing."

The tension in the room broke as everyone turned to gaze at the glowing screen in front of Viz.

"I was just poking around, really," he said, scooting his chair aside to give the team a better view of the screen. "Then I found this. I'm not sure, but I think it's some sort of communication log."

Duke got up from his seat and moved in behind Viz to get a better look at the screen.

"You see this last part?" Viz tapped a line of bright text. "*Total elimination of the group.* What do you think that means? You think it refers to all the dead people we keep finding?"

Kurt shook his head. "That's anyone's guess."

Duke smirked. How was that for leadership?

"Power that computer down, Viz. Might be a good idea to conserve this wonderful electricity," Kurt said. "I think we've given Lucifer and Lilith long enough to finish. And Max has probably had more than enough time to...well, to do whatever it is he's doing down there. I say we go check out this garden."

Chapter Twenty-One
The Interrogation

The first thing Brother Lorne did after Brother Grainger's departure was to take Jane to the nearest Colonial Watch precinct. He had the necessary contacts in the Colonial Watch to secure protective custody for Jane. When asked by the watch commander for the reason behind the request, Lorne kept it vague.

This student is a material witness in an ongoing government investigation, he'd told Commander Vincent. *She's received threats since news of her cooperation became known to some of the more radical elements on campus.*

Commander Vincent nodded. *Yeah, that sounds about right for that crowd.*

Lorne felt dirty. Playing on the tensions between law enforcement and students flew in the face of all he stood for, but he assured himself that this was a simple matter of expediency.

Commander Vincent summoned a pair of civilian outreach officers and told them to stash Jane somewhere safe. Then he turned back to Lorne and asked if there was anything else he needed.

A pair of officers to help me run down a few loose ends for this investigation, Lorne answered. *A couple of good Colonists, if you get my drift. Discrete, no political entanglements, that sort of thing.*

I think I can spare a couple officers that fit that bill.

Lorne thanked the commander profusely, and silently thanked himself for sponsoring a bill to enrich the pension funds for civil service workers, including those employed by the Colonial Watch.

Lorne used these two good officers to track down Cornelius' protégé. A pair of uniformed watchmen had dragged Dorian out of an afternoon class at the university. According to the watchmen—a pair of stern-faced hard cases named Westin and Childs—the youngster hadn't gone quietly. Dorian had kicked and screamed about abuse of power, Colonial Watch brutality, and all sorts of political nonsense. Once they'd gotten him out of the classroom and into the hallway, he'd even tried to run. He didn't get far before Westin tackled him to the ground. Then Childs had slapped a pair of cuffs on Dorian's wrists and a set of manacles on his ankles.

It made the walk over here twice as long as it should be, Westin projected. *But I think he got the message.*

And his face? Lorne asked, gesturing at the bruises and welts blooming across Dorian's features.

Childs shrugged. *So maybe it took more than cuffs and manacles to make sure he got the message clearly.*

Sometimes you have to go that extra mile, Westin admitted.

You have to be sure these punks really get the message. Sometimes you have to send it more than once, just to be sure. Childs smiled. *But I reckon a high-minded politician such as yourself shouldn't be concerned with all those minor details.*

Lorne sighed. Keeping tabs on Colonial Watch brutality was part of Lorne's political agenda. He'd introduced legislation to form a civilian commission to investigate claims of police wrongdoing. And now, he was standing in his own kitchen, listening to a couple of plainclothes watchmen crack jokes about pummeling a suspect. He didn't admonish them or express shock.

He just filled their cups with more steaming hot tea and listened to them laugh about the damage they'd inflicted on the young Colonist who was lying motionless on the living room floor. It was amazing how fast one's principles could crumble when Council chamber debate gave way to real world violence.

Westin seemed to sense Lorne's misgivings. *Look, Councilor, I was raised in the First United Church. I still go to services whenever I can make it. Vicar Abraham was…well, maybe not a friend…but he was a couple classes behind me at the academy. He was a good lad. And knowing this piece of shit had something to do with his death, well, it just brought out a dark part of my normally sunny personality.*

Childs stifled a laugh behind his hand.

Lorne was glad he didn't tell them that Jane was an accessory to the murder. No telling what Westin and Childs might do to her. He was also glad he'd asked Ursula to take the children to stay with her sister. He wished Ursula had agreed to stay there as well, but she'd insisted on dropping them off and then returning. Pregnant or not, she refused to be sidelined. As a politician, Lorne admired her tenacity. As a husband, he wished she could, just this once, let him handle things on his own.

Lorne repeated his sigh. He moved past the watchmen and into the living room. This university student—Dorian, they'd said his name was Dorian—didn't look like a member of a violent revolutionary terrorist cell. He looked like any other university student, only his university robes were torn and bloodstained.

The two watchmen entered the room. They still carried their mugs of tea, but they were no longer laughing.

I know he doesn't look like much, Westin volunteered, *but that little bastard killed the vicar and the matron in cold blood. And to hear him tell it, he's part of a terrorist group that's plotting the overthrow of the Colonial government. And this terrorist group? Led by a member of the Council, if you can believe that.*

And the other shit he sang about, it's equally insane, Childs chimed in. *All sorts of weird conspiracy stuff about breeding some human-Colonist hybrid to replace both species. Wild shit, but he stuck to his story even when we, um ah, applied pressure. He hasn't given up the names of his terrorist buddies, but I figure we can get that out of him eventually.*

Lorne's back stiffened at the mention of the genetic experiments taking place in the basement laboratories. He hoped his face didn't betray anything.

But when he dropped Councilor Cornelius' name, we figured we better bring him here rather than running him through the system, Westin continued. *Captain Gregory said this was a situation that called for discretion.*

You call this discreet? Lorne pointed at the unconscious youth lying on the floor.

We call it the special treatment for insurrectionists. If Westin was making a wisecrack, his face certainly didn't show it. *I know you have a dim view of the Colonial Watch, and that's fine. Some of you political types use us as a punching bag, and just as many of you use us as poster boys. The truth isn't so simple. We do what has to be done to protect the Colony.*

I never used the Colonial Watch as a punching bag, Lorne countered. *I only hold you to the same high standards as any other public institution. We can't continue to advance as a society without holding ourselves accountable.*

That's all well and good. Childs nodded. *But even in an advanced society, someone has to take out the fucking trash, you know?*

Yes, I suppose that's true, Lorne projected. *And it is in the spirit of that heavy responsibility that I must ask you to place Councilor Cornelius under arrest. Councilor Grainger thought he might appeal to Cornelius' sense of civic duty and avoid a scandal, but I see now that we're quite past that. Take care that no harm comes to Grainger during the arrest. He's still a patriotic defender of the Colony.*

We'll take care of the elder, don't worry. And we'll treat Brother Cornelius gently as well. As long as he comes along willingly. Childs glanced down at Dorian. *Should we send some officers to babysit this turd?*

Lorne shook his head. *I think the fewer Colonists we involve in this situation, the better.*

You sure? Westin asked. *He may not look like much, but this piece of shit killed a vicar and a matron without a second thought. I doubt he'd hesitate to add a Councilor to the body count.*

He's handcuffed and near comatose, Lorne answered. *I think I can handle him. Besides, you may see me as some weak liberal Councilor, but in my youth, I was a cadet in the Colonial Army. I spent two years deployed to the surface after things got bloody at Alpha Colony[9]*. I know a thing or two about dealing with terrorists.*

The watchmen exchanged a glance then shrugged in unison. They set their mugs on the low table in the center of the room and let themselves out of the apartment.

Lorne sat down on the sofa and looked at the battered youth leaking blood onto the carpet.

What a fucking mess. He nudged Dorian with his foot. *I don't think you're really asleep. Oh sure, those two thugs with badges certainly did a number on you, but they didn't pummel you into a coma. I think you're lying there, waiting for a chance to*

---

* [9] Ten years before he began his political career, Lorne had been part of a multi-Colony military force that quelled a violent uprising in Alpha Colony, located on the west coast of the continent. A revolutionary group that favored reclaiming the surface of the planet via guerilla raids on human settlements had taken control of Alpha Colony's military. The ensuing siege and raid on the terrorist group's headquarters were the only recorded case of large scale inter-Colonist violence. The exact number of casualties remains unknown.

escape. You probably think now that the watchmen are gone, your window of opportunity is opening.

Dorian remained silent.

I know what you're thinking, Lorne continued. *Something along the lines of how it was shit luck to get caught, but all you have to do is ride it out and everything will be fine. After all, you may have gotten worked over by those watchmen, but now you're in the custody of Brother Lorne, a famously progressive politician who preaches peace and understanding among all the citizens of the Colonies. You think there's no way this soft liberal politician would ever do anything to hurt you. Please allow me to disabuse you of that notion.*

Still no response on Dorian's part.

Lorne pressed on. *You probably heard me tell those watchmen that I was at the Alpha Colony siege. Maybe you think that I was just some politician's son playing cadet so that when I eventually ran for office myself, I could tout my public service. Let me tell you, that isn't the case. My father practically disowned me when I joined the militia. He certainly didn't call in favors to keep me off the frontline, and that's the way I wanted it. I wanted to make my own way, forge my own path. I wanted to find out who I really was. And I certainly found out. Do you know what I did during the siege? Of course you don't. None of the individual actions from that time are part of the public record. Extreme actions were required during that unfortunate engagement. Some of the things required of us weren't fit for public knowledge, so many of the details were suppressed. There were rumors, of course, but nothing official. And that's why I feel I should tell you this story, just in case you think I'm so wrapped up in progressive ideals that I'll let you keep your mouth shut while your terrorist friends rip Delta Colony apart from within.*

Dorian twitched ever so slightly, but his eyes remained shut.

Lorne leaned forward and told his story in calm, conversational tones. He spoke to Dorian in the same straightforward manner he used when speaking to journalists or constituents. It was this disarmingly casual delivery that had won him some of the largest vote margins in Colonial history. But the content of his story wasn't the type of thing that could win votes or charm journalists. It was the type of tale that could turn the stomach of even the most reactionary Colonist.

If you paid attention in history class, you know that the siege lasted the better part of a year. It mystified the high command, because we'd cut off all the rebels' supplies, even their water lines. They should have been drinking their own piss and eating their own shit after a few months, but somehow, they'd found a way to drag things out. For weeks, we'd been scratching our heads, trying to figure it out. Then, one day, a routine patrol picked up a group of rebels attempting to slip past our frontline. Those rebels were detained and brought into the intelligence unit for interrogation. That's where I was assigned, intelligence. Most of us who'd been recruited from the university wound up in intelligence. Some of us had backgrounds in medicine, or, like me, in psychology. Our educations gave us the tools, which our military training sharpened and honed into weapons.

Lorne paused just long enough to give Dorian another nudge with his foot. This time, it was closer to a kick, and it elicited a faint whimper. Lorne smiled. Now he knew for sure that Dorian was awake and listening. He moved forward, perching on the edge of his seat.

Long-buried memories swam into sharp focus as Lorne told his story. He conjured mental images that his subconscious normally reserved for nightmares. He found himself recounting incidents that he'd spent years trying to forget. At first, he felt uneasy, almost nauseous as he spoke. But that feeling was short-lived. Soon, he felt the thrill of a long dormant part of himself coming back to life.

They were probably students before they joined the separatist movement, Lorne projected. *So not much older than you. Hell, some of them may even have been younger. Not that it made a difference. We had a job to do, and we did it. At first, they were just like you, tight-lipped and loyal to the cause. Brave or maybe stupid, take your pick. But we broke them, and they told us all about how they'd been slipping past our blockade and smuggling supplies into the Colony. Now, I just bet you're wondering how we broke them.*

Dorian gave up his ruse and opened his eyes. Lorne recognized at once the emotions that were written all over the youth's face: a double portion of fear, seasoned liberally with hopelessness. It was the same thing he'd seen all those years ago in the eyes of the rebel prisoners, when the small tent the army had designated as an interrogation room was filled with the sound of screams and the metallic scent of blood.

First thing I did was pick out the toughest, hardest looking bastard in the bunch. Lorne felt himself lapsing back into army-speak. Years of refinement in elocution classes slipped away as he waded deeper and deeper into his darkest memories. *He was a big son of a bitch with grey-streaked fur and a scarred snout. The thoughts he threw at me were the sort of nastiness you picked up in the rougher parts of the Colony. We had those back then, little patches of poverty and crime, tough neighborhoods that bred tough criminals. Youngsters like you don't know anything about that. You were born after social reforms. All the political parties you've ever known have subscribed to the* Civilization Above Animal Instinct *doctrine. But I'm getting off track. Let me tell you how it went for that tough-thinking bastard with the scarred up snout...*

I had my two master sergeants hold Mr. Tough Revolutionary with his face pressed against the ground. Then, while his compatriots watched, I cut off his tail. It took some doing. All I had was my sidearm knife, and I was never very proactive about keeping it sharp. Plus, I cut through the thickest part of his tail, practically right above his ass crack.

Dorian's eyes were puffy from the beating, but Lorne could see that they were full of fear. He leaned closer as he continued his story.

I'd never seen so much blood. That's what the doctors call a vascular part of the body. No major arteries back there, but it bleeds like a son of a bitch. You ever slam the tip of your tail in a doorway?

Dorian nodded.

Imagine that multiplied by a hundred. Lorne shook his head at the memory. *Hell, maybe a thousand. There was enough blood to turn the ground muddy. Some of the younger prisoners, the ones with the baby soft fur, started squealing and trying to look away. I called in some of the infantry soldiers to hold their heads back and make them watch.*

Finally, Dorian decided to drop the act altogether. He sat up. He winced and pressed a hand to his bruised ribs.

So they started talking, right? he asked. *Once they saw the big guy get his tail cut off?*

Dorian smiled. *Maybe some of them wanted to, but we didn't give them a chance right off. We let them watch the tough guy howl in pain. He really squealed. He opened his mouth so wide that it was easy to yank his incisors. I used a pair of pliers. They weren't dental tools, just something from the standard issue tool kit. They came out easy enough. First the top ones, then the bottom.*

And then you stopped, because all the others were falling over themselves to tell you what you wanted to know, right? Dorian's thoughts came out rapid fire.

Oh, they started talking. But we needed to make sure they told us everything they knew. One by one, they got a chance to stand in front of their revolutionary brothers and get their tails clipped and their teeth pulled. You see, it wasn't just information we needed. We wanted to send a message. So we marked them for life. Well, for what remained of their lives anyway.

Dorian gulped. *What do you mean?*

Once we were sure they'd given us all the information we needed, we sent one of them limping back to Alpha Colony as a messenger. We sent him with two parcels. One was a written copy of our demands for unconditional surrender. The other was a duffel bag full of bloody severed tails and incisors. The rest of those rebel bastards went to the surgical unit. They got stitched up and given a dose of painkillers. But in a situation like that, antibiotics are a precious commodity. We decided to reserve those for our own brave soldiers and leave the rebels' fate to the gods. And wouldn't you know it, the gods' judgment was harsh, and all nine of them had succumbed to infection within the week. The feverish squealing from that medical tent could be heard all over camp.

Dorian shook his head. *I studied the siege of Alpha Colony in history class. I never heard about any of that.*

Lorne smiled. *You know what became of the Delta Colony soldiers in the tent? We all went on to careers in politics and scientific research and business. They became the kind of citizens who have a say in what makes it into history books and what gets left out. Besides, having heroes is in the best interest of any functioning society. If that means whitewashing a few unpleasant facts, that's a small price to pay, don't you agree?*

You're sick, Dorian projected. *You're a war criminal.*

Perhaps you're right. But you're a student of history, so you know the line between war criminal and hero can get awfully thin. Excuse me for a moment. Lorne stood and walked into the kitchen.

Left unattended, Dorian could have very well made a break for freedom. But Lorne knew he wouldn't. Lorne rummaged through the drawers until he found the carving knife. It had been a wedding gift from Ursula's sister. Although well-balanced and sharp (as well as expensive, no doubt), the knife had gone largely unused over the years. It was too large to be of any practical use in the kitchen. But even impractical things can be useful under the right circumstances.

Now, I think it's time you told me all you know about Cornelius' dastardly plans, Lorne projected as he returned to the living room. He stood over Dorian and let the youth get a good look at the knife. *And while you're at it, I'd like a list of the names of all your traitorous compatriots. If you do a good enough job, maybe I'll let you keep those teeth.*

Please, I'll tell you whatever you want to know, Dorian begged. *Don't cut me.*

I'm sorry, but traitors can't walk among us unmarked. Lorne ran his thumb along the edge of the knife. *And I need to be sure you don't leave anything out. Besides, I think there's a price to be paid for what you did to the vicar and the matron. In fact, I'm sure there's something about that in the scripture…*

You start cutting me, I won't talk. Tears ran from the corners of Dorian's eyes.

Lorne laughed. *I think we both know that's not true. But go ahead and try to resist. I enjoy a good challenge. Gods above, it's just like the old days…*

One of the many good things about living in an expensive apartment was that the walls were stout. Lorne doubted his neighbors could hear the screams.

Chapter Twenty-Two
The War Begins

Cornelius sat in his makeshift office beneath the research facility. It was little more than a closet, a tiny booth that had perhaps once been used to regulate the building's utilities. Outside the booth, his troops slumbered, their minds abuzz with dreams of warriors the night before battle. The dreams were so vivid and intense that they overflowed their private psyches and leaked into the ether. Cornelius sensed them as psychic background noise. If he'd cared to look into those dreams, he could have focused his mind on their wavelength and tuned in like a radio operator tweaking a faint signal. But he left those frequencies unexplored. Whatever the substance of those dreams, the dreamers themselves were marching off to war in short order. Meanwhile, he had last minute preparations that required attention.

He checked the surveillance feeds and growled in frustration. He slapped the monitor with the palm of his hand until the static-filled and jittery image finally cleared and stabilized. He growled again. Although the image was no longer lost in a snowstorm of static, it was still murky. He pounded on the monitor a few more times before giving up.

Very well, he thought, switching off the monitor and

putting it into his backpack. *A general should lead from the field anyway.*

He tiptoed out of his booth and surveyed his slumbering ranks of soldiers. A warm, proud glow settled over him. Soon, the glory of humankind would pass in furious bursts of bloodshed. He focused his mind and prepared himself to issue marching orders.

* * *

They walked through the garden room as if in a trance, shuffling slowly up and down the rows of plants. They stopped here and there to smell flowers or pick pieces of fruit. Lucifer and Lilith—now fully clothed, but with disheveled hair and flushed faces—helped themselves to water from the purifier, scooping it up with their hands to drink. Max, seated on the edge of one of the hydroponic tables, eyed the couple with undisguised lust. Deus found the whole arrangement disgusting. Lilith and Lucifer, rutting like animals without a shred of shame, and Max, no doubt abusing himself while he observed the spectacle.

Max noticed the attention and smiled at Deus, asking, "You got something to say, Your Holiness? Because you seem awfully judgmental right about now."

"Would it matter if I did say something?" Deus glanced around at the others, who were still wandering through the rows of plants. "It seems that nothing I say matters to anyone these days. I tell you that this job has been cursed from the moment Kurt set foot in Lord Hannibal's outpost. It's their judgment you should be concerned about, not mine."

"Oh, so we should just walk away from all this because you think there's some curse? You sound ridiculous, man. I love you, Deus. I really do. But you've been a real downer the last few days. This job is just like any other."

"So says the man with rat bites on his face."

Deus turned away from Max and set off on his own exploration of the garden. He had to admit, it was an impressive sight. The people responsible for its construction had obviously been gifted with scientific knowledge. In the heart of a dead city, here was an oasis of abundance. It was impossible not to be awed. But it was also impossible not to recognize the contradiction. He considered that a starving animal might not consider the possibility of a hidden snare when it happened upon some food.

"How about it, Deus?" Kurt called from across the room. "What do you think of all this abundance? Anything about this sort of thing in any of your holy books?"

"There are always references to gardens of abundance in holy books," he answered. "But that's not what this place brings to mind. It makes me think of other books that I studied while at the monastery. Books of science. Books of history.[10]*"

"Care to elaborate on that?" Kurt asked.

Deus paused at a hydroponic tank containing an unfamiliar plant, whose thin branches were studded with red berries. He plucked one, and although he was certain that it might be a sin to do so, he popped it into his mouth. Tart juice spread over his tongue. Tiny seeds crunched between his teeth.

"It is said that, before the Event, there were some people who foresaw a coming catastrophe," he said, pausing to lick a droplet of juice from his lips. "Sensing that an apocalypse was drawing near, they set aside stores of food and constructed gardens in which fruits and vegetables could be raised in perpetuity, without even the need for soil. They collected and

---

* [10] The monks of the Church of the Aftermath presided over a library reputed to be the largest in post-Event existence. The founder of the order, Jeremiah Clementine, was known for his love of science and history, as well as erotic sculpture. This latter interest was not one emphasized by the church in its current form.

catalogued seeds, stockpiled the necessary chemical agents, and secreted these stores away in buildings that were constructed to withstand the coming calamities. I believe that we've stumbled upon one such place."

"Hey, hey, hey, lucky us!" Duke shouted. "There's enough fruit here to keep our bellies full for years."

Joyous laughter rippled through the team members as they feasted on the abundant fruit. Deus thought he should speak a few words about exercising restraint and caution, but he knew they would fall, as always, on deaf ears.

His silence was a signal for Viz to speak his own observations.

"I think Deus is right about that," Viz said. "And it sort of tracks with what I've been thinking. Like, if we're in the middle of some PEE hot zone, why are all these plants so perfect? And I don't know about everyone else, but my meter hasn't indicated any change in PEE levels since we stepped inside this place. It could be that the people who designed this place had discovered some way to shield the building from harmful emissions. If that's the case, maybe we shouldn't be in such a hurry to leave."

"You seem to forget that the people who were here before us are all dead," Deus countered. "That doesn't seem to support your ideas, does it?"

Viz shrugged. "Yeah, I haven't forgotten that. What I think happened is that some regular, run of the mill disease got them. Nothing to do with PEE or anything like that, just some nasty bug that swept through their whole crew."

"Yeah, but the bodies we found were pretty fucking torn up," Rosemary said. She was seated between two flowering plants, rubbing the pink petals and green leaves against her cheeks. "That must have been one hell of a bug."

"Yeah," Duke agreed. "It sure looked to me like the rats had gotten them. Just like the ones that killed that mutant bastard before he could kill me."

"I may not have read all the science books at the monastery where Deus grew up," Viz said, "but I know that rats are just scavengers. I don't have any doubt that they chowed down on those poor dead bastards, but I don't think rats killed them. They're not wolves or bears."

Max coughed, nearly choking on the bit of fruit in his mouth. He turned his head and spit out the offending morsel and said, "Just big fucking mice, huh? You see my face? You think some sweet little critter did that to me? Come on, man. These rats are dangerous. I'm not saying they killed all these people. In fact, I don't think they did. But I think they got a taste for human flesh and maybe they're not in the mood to wait around until some disease takes us down. Maybe, now that they've had a belly full of human meat, they've decided to take a more active approach."

There were some mumbles of disagreement, but nobody put forth a real argument.

"The rats that Duke and I encountered weren't exactly timid," Rosemary admitted. "It was almost like they wanted to attack us full force but were waiting on some signal. They came at us, but they didn't seem like they were committed."

Viz said, "You were in a dark room full of dead bodies. Of course the rats you saw were terrifying. You're a badass, Rosemary, but come on, even you can admit that just being in that room was scary as hell."

"You weren't there," Rosemary said. "You didn't look into those black eyes. There was something there, some sort of weird intelligence. Was it scary in that room? You bet your ass it was. But I didn't take leave of my fucking senses. I know what I saw."

Deus had been reaching for another berry, but he stopped when Rosemary spoke. He remembered his drug-induced vision in the forest. Despite the warmth of the garden, he shivered. The memory of the encounter with the rat woman came back to him with crystal clarity. His scrotum tightened as he remembered the way the rat woman had sighed as she mounted him. The lingering sweetness on his tongue was suddenly acidic and stinging.

"Okay, you guys have all given me plenty to think about," Kurt announced, strolling toward water purifier in the center of the room. With his arm slung casually around Diana's shoulders, he looked so relaxed he might have been out for an evening stroll through a peaceful town square rather than deep inside a dead city. "But I think we need to keep our heads down and deal with what's right in front of us. Viz, that stuff you said about disease killing these people makes a lot of sense. That's why I think we should collect as many of the bodies as we can and drag them out to the street, where we can burn them. We still have a flamethrower in our weapon supply, right?"

"That's right, but it's in pieces right now," Rosemary said. "I can have it assembled and ready to spit fire in ten, fifteen minutes."

"Of course you can," Duke said, leering at her. "You know how to heat up any situation, don't you?"

Groans all around.

"What?" Duke glanced around the room. "Lilith and Lucifer can fuck their brains out while Max jerks off to it, and nobody says boo. But as soon as I make a little joke, everyone starts acting offended?"

Max started forward, fists clenched at his sides. "Fuck you, Duke. You don't know shit."

"Hey!" Kurt stepped between the two men. "Knock that shit off. Once we're done with this job, you guys can fight all you want. But right now, we got more immediate problems."

Max and Duke stared at one another. For a few tense moments, the only sound in the room was the faint burbling of the water purifiers. Then, Max's shoulders sagged and he backed off a step.

"Hey," he said, smiling, "I wasn't going to let a bit of free entertainment go to waste."

"Yeah, and it ain't like we mind an audience," Lilith chimed in.

Deus sighed. It was this sort of perversion that could bring down the wrath of the gods. Perhaps it was good that they were going to burn the bodies of the dead. A funeral pyre was always pleasing to the gods. It could be just the thing to weaken the curse, or even lift it altogether. He touched the tattoo on his forehead and whispered a prayer, beseeching the nameless gods of the sky to bestow upon him the wisdom of Clementine.

* * *

Rosemary was glad to be out in the open, even though the air outside was just as stale and lifeless as that inside the building, she felt less confined. Plus, it was nice to get some distance from Duke and his craziness. He'd never been the most stable guy in the world, but ever since they'd entered the city, he'd been radiating instability. Kurt was right to ask her to keep an eye on him, but she was at a loss when it came to anything beyond that. She did know one thing with absolute certainty, however: if Duke did finally snap, she was going to be ready.

Still, it was spooky to be out there in the city after dark. It was all too easy to imagine that horrors lurked around every corner. Even with a clear, star-glittery sky overhead, there was a heavy atmosphere. The buildings around her seemed to glower, as if they were angry that their solitude had been disturbed by this group of intruders.

"Yeah, well, the feeling is mutual," Rosemary muttered.

She leaned against her sidecar, taking her time as she fitted the pieces of the flamethrower together. As much as she hated to be lazy while the others were working, she hated the idea of hauling dead bodies even more. Those few minutes in the dark, rat-filled office had given her more than her share of up-close-and-personal time with corpses. Besides, she told herself, assembling a flamethrower wasn't a job to speed through. A loose fitting here, a badly sealed line there, and suddenly a tool for incinerating garbage became a shortcut to self-immolation.

Across the street, the body pile was growing steadily. The team had found a couple of wheeled carts, most likely intended for moving heavy furniture or equipment, and they were hauling the bodies out six at a time. It didn't take long for the rotten stench to fill the air.

Rosemary tried not to gag as she connected the fuel line, checked the trigger mechanism, and tightened the nozzle. It didn't look like much. None of the stuff Taurus cobbled together ever did. But Rosemary had seen the flamethrower in action. It was up to the job and then some.

"Hey, Rosemary!" Kurt called. "You about ready with that flamethrower?"

"Yeah, just doing one last check," she answered.

She hefted the flamethrower, slipping the shoulder straps over her arms. It wasn't exactly streamlined or lightweight, but she managed to hump it the thirty or forty meters from the spot where they'd parked the vehicles to the pile of partially devoured bodies.

"I'll do the honors," Kurt told her.

She didn't mind one bit handing over the flamethrower. "Here you go, boss. Looks like you got better than half a tank of fuel."

"Been a while since we used it," he said, settling the straps on his shoulders. "Hope it still works. Guess there's one way to find out. Taurus?"

"Yeah, boss." Taurus emptied a bottle of accelerant onto the bodies, then stepped aside.

Rosemary retreated to a safe distance, joining the rest of

the team a couple meters behind Kurt. They stood in a semicircle, watching their leader prepare himself. He checked to make sure everyone was standing well clear of the body pile, then took aim and pressed the trigger. A gout of fire roared from the nozzle. Whatever Taurus had sprayed on the bodies certainly did the trick. In seconds, the stinking, gory pile was engulfed in crackling flames. An orange and yellow glow filled the street. It was like a second sunset.

* * *

Lucifer was horny again. That didn't come as a shock to him, since horny had been his default setting ever since he'd hit puberty. It was his considered opinion that sex was one of the few pleasures left in the post-Event world. He took it wherever he could get it, and nothing much could discourage him. That included a room full of his snoring teammates.

"Hey," he whispered in Lilith's ear. "You awake?"

She murmured an unintelligible reply.

"You want to?" he asked.

"What?" Her voice was sleep-slurred.

"Come on, don't play dumb." He worked his hand down to his pants and unbuttoned them. It wasn't an easy maneuver with two people zipped into a single oversized sleeping bag.

"In front of everyone?" she asked. She was a bit more awake now.

"They're asleep," he said. "We'll be quiet."

After their ad hoc funeral pyre had burned to a pile of embers, ashes, and bones, Kurt had issued an order for four hours rest. They'd returned to the dormitory and made it as habitable as possible, which meant hauling out the cot formerly occupied by the dead body, then searching the walls for any holes rats could use to enter the room. Once Taurus had nailed boards over the few holes big enough for those monster rodents, the team laid their sleeping bags atop the cots and put their heads down for a few hours of rest before they resumed their salvage job.

When Lucifer first laid down next to Lilith, his body was heavy with fatigue. The team had been pushing hard ever since they left the forest, and the prolonged effort was catching up with them. But then, as soon as Lilith pressed her round backside against his crotch, Lucifer found an unexpected burst of energy. Now, the old familiar urge had overridden his fatigue, and he was already growing uncomfortably hard within the confines of his pants. Once his fingers had finished their blind fumble with the buttons of his pants, his cock sprang free. He sighed as he pressed it against Lilith's buttocks.

"Quiet? You?" She shook her head. "You grunt like a pig and moan like a bitch."

He didn't deny it. But he didn't back down either. "Then let them watch. I don't mind an audience."

He knew she wouldn't take much persuading. Lilith's libido may not have been permanently cranked into the red like his, but she was usually ready to go. Besides, Lucifer didn't accept rejection. One way or another, he almost always got what he wanted.

They wriggled around until they were free of their pants. The springs of the thin mattress and cot beneath them squeaked with each movement, but the other people in the room went right on snoring.

"Come on, woman," Lucifer growled. "I've got something for you."

She whimpered as he pushed it into her. "Go easy, baby…I need to get warmed up…"

Lucifer smiled and thrust as hard as he could. Sometimes Lilith liked it rough, and sometimes she didn't. It was all the same to him.

"Oh, fuck!" she yelped. "Give it to me!"

Lucifer pressed deeper. A steady stream of filthy talk came from his mouth in a hoarse whisper. He called her every dirty name he could think of. He promised to fuck her into a coma. She responded by digging her fingers into the small of his back and spreading her legs so wide that they threatened the integrity of the sleeping bag's seams.

"Merciful gods, would you two jackrabbits give it a rest?" Duke demanded from across the room. He unzipped his sleeping bag and sat up on his cot across the room. "Hard enough to sleep in this place as it is. Now you're going to subject me to the sound of your fucking?"

Lucifer ignored him. He'd be finished soon enough if Duke would quit grumbling.

"Hey, come on," Duke continued. "We can't get any sleep while you two are going at it."

"Shut up!" Lucifer shot back.

"Max may enjoy the show, but the rest of us would like a little peace and quiet," Duke said.

"Yeah, you guys need to knock that shit off." Now, it was Kurt who voiced a complaint.

"Damn it." Lucifer pulled out. Defying Duke was one thing, but Kurt was still the man in charge. He glared at Lilith beneath him. "I thought I told you to keep quiet, bitch."

She giggled. "Then you should have been gentle instead of making love like a water buffalo."

"Guys, take it to another room if you can't go a few hours without humping each other," Kurt said. "I'd rather we all stayed together, but no one can sleep with that going on."

"Fine." Lucifer worked his arms up to the top of the sleeping bag and tugged at the zipper. It was stuck. He cursed and pulled harder, but it refused to budge. "This fucking thing is stuck!"

Now, everyone was awake. It seemed they were never too tired for a bit of entertainment.

"Hey, I guess you'll just have to stay in there and fuck until you die," Rosemary laughed.

"But what a way to go out, huh?" Viz clapped his hands. "I've seen dead people with their faces frozen like they died smiling. I always wondered about that, but now I think I know what happened."

Laughter all around.

"Let this be a lesson to you," Max chimed in. "From now on, you should only do it out in the open."

"Yeah, so you can watch while you pull yourself silly," Rosemary said.

"There are few pleasures in this life," Max sighed.

Lucifer had heard enough. "Anytime you assholes feel like helping out, that would be great."

Another round of laughter, this one louder than the first.

"Okay, that's enough," Kurt said, raising a hand to still the excitement. "Taurus, see if you can't spring our excitable friends."

"Sure thing, boss." Taurus rolled off his bunk and plodded across the floor. He dropped to his knees beside the lovers. "Sure you want me to do this? Rosemary was right, you know. You could just stay in here and do it until your bodies give out."

"Just shut up and get us out of here!" Lucifer had heard enough. He was desperate to get to a place where he could finish what he'd started. Despite the circumstances, his dick was still standing at full attention. He'd often said that his pride and joy had a mind of its own and that mind didn't understand the concept of modesty.

"Okay, take it easy," Taurus said. "I was just joking."

"Yeah, everyone on this team loves a good joke," Lucifer sniffed.

If he was so preoccupied with more pressing matters, he would have felt bad about snapping at Taurus. Only a coldhearted bastard could actively dislike the big dumb lunkhead. Under normal circumstances, Lucifer liked being around Taurus. But the circumstances weren't normal, and Lucifer's base instincts had taken hold of him.

"Fornication in such a place is an affront to the gods," Deus observed.

"Nobody asked for a fucking sermon," Lucifer snapped. "Save your breath, holy man."

Lucifer may have liked Taurus just fine, but he couldn't abide Deus most of the time.

Unless Deus was passing out his holy moonshine, Lucifer had no use for the holy man's mystical bullshit. There were no gods. Lucifer had known that since he was a child. Bullshit fairy tales, that's all they were.

"Okay, looks like I got it," Taurus said. He gave the zipper a tug, and the sleeping bag opened right up.

Lucifer shook his head. "Damn, you make it look easy."

"You just got too worked up trying to get out," Taurus explained. "Calmness is a virtue of the strong. Ain't that right, Deus?"

"Gospel of Clementine, fortieth chapter, tenth verse," Deus agreed.

"Well, how about this: I'm too horny to listen to a bunch of religious bullshit. Gospel of Me, first chapter, first verse." Lucifer stood up. He didn't care who got a look at his dick. It was, in his considered opinion, a fine specimen. Let the men burn with envy and the women drool with desire, he figured. He took his time pulling up his pants, then extended his hand to Lilith. "Come on, woman. Let's go finish our business in private."

Lilith had an exhibitionist streak, but she still made sure her pants were up before she took his hand. She might not have minded giving Max a private show, but she apparently drew the line at giving the whole team an eyeful.

"Let's beat it before these prudes stoke up their outrage

any further," Lucifer said. He stooped to gather up their sleeping bag, then tugged Lilith toward the door.

"Hey, Lucifer," Kurt called. "I know you're eager to get down to business, but remember where we are. Keep your eyes open, huh?"

Lucifer nodded. "Right on, boss."

He led Lilith down the hall and into an empty room. He searched the wall just inside the door for a light switch. The overhead lights fizzled and popped into a weak half-life. Only a few of the fixtures were functional, but there was enough light to do what needed to be done. He took a quick look around. There were no dead bodies and no rats. That was good enough for him. The walls were lined with metal shelving units. It must have been some kind of storage room at some point, but the shelves were mostly bare. It wasn't the most romantic spot, but what he had in mind had little to do with romance.

He slung the sleeping bag onto the floor, then pulled Lilith against him, kissing her so hard that her front teeth drew blood from his lower lip. That was okay. He didn't mind a little rough stuff.

And then, at last, they got back to it. He'd wilted a bit during their trip from the dormitory to the storage room. Lilith slid to her knees and used her mouth to coax him back to life. It didn't take long.

"All right, let's get back to it," he said, grabbing her hair and pushing her back onto the sleeping bag. "Take those fucking clothes off."

"Damn, Lucifer, I know you're horny, but slow down," she said. "We got all night."

"We got less than four hours before that slave driver Kurt has us humping supplies from this mausoleum out to those trucks."

"Even you can't last four hours." Lilith tugged her shirt over her head and began wriggling out of her pants.

"I can go as long as you can take it," he growled, kicking his way out of his pants.

She laughed, but his boast wasn't empty. When they were at Bruno's Last Rest, the bartender at the saloon had sold him a packet of pills that were reputed to turn a man's cock to tempered steel for an entire night. The bartender said that he'd heard stories about the pills enabling a man to literally fuck a woman to death. Lucifer had no idea about the validity of this claim, but he was prepared to find out for himself. Before they'd climbed into their sleeping bag, he'd swallowed two of the pills. He didn't know how long it would take for them to disperse through his system. He hoped they were quick acting.

They got right down to business. Under the best of circumstances, Lucifer wasn't a big believer in foreplay. With a limited window of opportunity, he dispensed with it altogether. He spit on his hand to make sure she was still slick enough for entry, then went to work. And right off, he got a reminder of why he liked Lilith so much. She was as tight as any virgin he'd ever taken, and she moaned and screamed like she was being murdered. He pumped away as long as he could hold back, then exploded inside her. It felt like a liter, maybe two came out of him.

When he finally quit trembling, he slipped out and collapsed beside her.

They lay there for a moment, shoulder to shoulder, while their breathing returned to normal.

"Damn," she said. "Every time I start to wonder why I put up with your bullshit, you give me a reminder."

"Well, you better get ready, because in a few minutes, I'm going to give you another one." The pills must have been working, because he could already feel the first stirrings of new life down below.

"You're insatiable. That's the right word, isn't it?"

He cut his eyes sideways to regard her. Lilith was as close

as he'd ever gotten to his ideal woman. Tall and slender, but she still had curves in the right spot. Her hair was such a deep shade of brown that it was almost black. And she wasn't a bad partner. Her scouting skills were more than adequate, and she was a deadly shot with her sniper rifle. But goddamn, the woman could be dense.

"Yes, that's the word," he said. "It's a big word, though, and big words aren't really your style. Stick to talking dirty. It's what you do best."

"Fuck you, Lucifer."

He smirked. "That's the idea, yeah. You know, we make a good team. In a lot of ways, we're the same. In the other ways, we complement each other."

"Yeah, I guess. But you don't got to be such an asshole all the time."

He reached over and squeezed her nipple. "You ready to go again?"

She stretched her arms over her head, purring like a cat as his free hand caressed her thigh. "No, baby, I'm not ready. Maybe we can just relax for a bit, huh?"

"What the fuck, woman?"

"That's another thing," she said. "I have a name, and it's not Woman. You know, it wouldn't kill you to treat me like a person instead of a life support system for this pussy you love so much. And while we're on the subject, maybe try a little foreplay every once in a while. I won't ask for romance. I know that's too much for you."

Lucifer rolled away from her. He gathered up his clothes and began pulling them back on. "You know, I thought you were different. I should have known. You bitches are all the same."

"Quit being dramatic," she said.

"Fuck you."

She giggled. "Maybe later, but right now, I'm sleepy."

As he stomped his feet back into his boots, Lucifer

considered that his sudden burst of anger might be a side effect of the pills. He shrugged off the notion. This was just the nature of his relationship with Lilith. They fucked, they fought, they made up, and they fucked some more. He just needed to take a walk and get some fresh air. And she just needed some time alone in that storage room to remember how much she needed him. He'd give her a half hour or so, then he'd come back, offer a half-assed apology and promise to be less aggressive in his approach.

That usually did it. But for now, they both needed time to cool off.

He stormed out of the room, slamming the door behind him. The sound echoed in the hallway like the report of his sniper rifle. He liked that. So much of scouting involved stealth and restraint. It felt good to have an outburst every now and then.

"Goddamn bitches," he muttered, although his heart wasn't in it. Now that he was out of the room, his anger had mostly faded.

As he strolled down the hallway and into the front lobby, a pair of fat rats scurried across his path. He ran forward, doing his best to land a kick on one of the rodents, but they remained just out of reach. They skittered ahead, claws clacking on the floor, and disappeared into the shadows.

Lucifer shook his head, laughing. All this bullshit about rats, honestly. They were a bunch of hardened salvage dogs, this team. And so many of them were bent out of shape about a few rats? Unbelievable. Of course that fucking mystical weirdo Deus would be shaken. That's how it went with holy men. They saw dark omens in every fucking thing they came across. But Max? Yeah, the guy was plenty weird and got off on watching other people fuck, but when it came to work, he was usually solid. Same with Duke. He was one sly motherfucker, but in a fight, you could count on him. But apparently a few rats chowing down on dead bodies had him shaking in his boots? Maybe he was too busy trying to get into Rosemary's pants and let a few of the furry fuckers get the drop on him.

"They're just fucking rats," Lucifer said. "Just dirty-ass rodents."

His footsteps stirred the dust on the floor, making him sneeze. The air was cool and dry, but the atmosphere was still too stuffy for his tastes. He headed for the front door. Although Kurt had warned them about leaving the building on their own, he felt like a stroll might be just the thing to clear his head.

He opened the front doors and took one step outside, then stopped short.

"Holy shit," he said. "That's a lot of fucking rats."

He blinked a few times, giving his brain time to double check the information his eyes relayed to it. Sure enough, the sight remained unchanged. There were scores of rats—hundreds, maybe even a thousand of the hairy bastards—spread out over the wide staircase leading from the front door to the street. They were lined up like the soldiers of some ancient army, sitting on their fat haunches in neat rows. Their wet noses and stiff whiskers twitched as they regarded him with beady black eyes.

The sight was so absurd that Lucifer had to laugh.

"Sorry to disappoint you boys," he said, "but we burned all the bodies. No buffet dinner tonight, I'm afraid."

He nudged one of the nearest rats with his foot. It didn't even twitch in response. For some reason, that pissed him off. He was a man, damn it. Rodents were supposed to scurry away at his approach. This behavior wasn't natural. It was downright offensive.

"Okay," he said, "if that's the way you want it, fine. But remember, you brought this shit on yourselves."

He raised his foot and brought it down on the unresponsive rat. His heavy boot crushed its skull beneath its treads. The wet crunch was oddly satisfying, therapeutic even. The last traces of anger left him as he ground the rat into paste.

"Can't believe the others are so afraid of you ugly bastards," he laughed, lifting his boot and scanning the ranks for another victim.

His cock twitched within the confines of his tight pants. This wasn't a substitute for sex, but it was thrilling nonetheless. Another couple of stomped rats, and he'd be ready to wear Lilith out, whether she was ready for it or not.

"Okay, who's next?" he asked, displaying the blood and guts still clinging to the sole of his boot.

But that was as far as he got. The rats were on him in the space of a few terrifying seconds. They shot from their haunches as if spring-loaded. Some hit him in the torso, digging into his flesh with razor-sharp claws. Others scrambled up his legs, their claws shredding his pants and carving bloody trenches in his flesh as they climbed. Still others swarmed him from behind, climbing from his ankles to his shoulders.

Lucifer flailed his arms and stumbled blindly, his eyes squeezed shut as the rats made their way to his face. The pain was intense and all-consuming. In a matter of seconds, the rats covered him. Hundreds of claws ripped at his flesh. Hundreds of teeth tore chunks of flesh from his softest parts. He opened his mouth to scream, then gagged as a particularly quick rat poked its head into his mouth and ripped away most of his tongue. The rat dug in with its claws, reducing Lucifer's lips to bloody shreds. The rat wriggled its backside, forcing Lucifer's jaws further apart as it worked its way into his throat.

Panic at his occluded airway forced Lucifer's eyes open. As soon as his eyelids separated, two rats snapped their teeth onto his eyeballs. Lucifer's vision went black as the soft orbs ruptured and thick liquid erupted from the newly opened sockets.

And then, finally, mercifully, consciousness fled, and Lucifer collapsed.

* * *

After the Lucifer and Lilith Show wrapped up, Viz found himself wide awake, despite the heaviness in his limbs. Too much excitement, he figured, and now his brain refused to shut down. It had been one hell of a night, even before the live sex show and fiery dispute. Every time Viz closed his eyes, his brain shuffled through a catalogue of thoughts.

One second, he found himself wondering about the computers upstairs. The next second, he tried to weigh implications of Kurt's hypothetical plan to betray Lord Hannibal. And then those heavy matters gave way to visions of Lucifer and Lilith going at it hammer and tongs. He forced himself to linger on those thoughts. It was easier to revisit those memories than trying to puzzle out the purpose of those computers, or indeed, the purpose of this entire building.

He rolled onto his side and squeezed his eyes shut, listening to the soft snoring and deep breathing of his colleagues. Still, his mind raced. He rolled onto his other side, opened his eyes, and looked across the room to the cot recently vacated by Lucifer and Lilith. He smiled at the memory of Taurus freeing the lovers from the confines of their sleeping bag. He almost giggled as he remembered the way Lucifer had sprung to his feet, full of indignant frustration with his almost comically oversized erection jutting straight out from his between his legs. Max may have gotten off on watching the two scouts fuck, but Viz found that the comic elements always undercut the eroticism.

Viz rolled onto his back and stared at the ceiling. Through

the cracked and hazy panes of the skylight, he gazed at the stars. He reminded himself at every opportunity that the universe was nearly infinite in its vastness and that he was a very small part of the cosmic machine. Some people found such an idea terrifying, but not Viz. He found it comforting. He knew that one day, after his death, the tiny particles that made up his body would disperse into the dark infinity.

Deus promised an eternity with the gods, but Viz preferred an eternity of gradual dissolution into the cosmic sea.

He sighed a soft curse and sat up on his cot, careful not to make too much noise. Just because insomnia had taken hold of him didn't give him the right to spread it around to the others. Even Duke, posted by the door on self-appointed guard duty, had fallen asleep. He was seated on the floor with his back against the wall. His head lolled forward until his chin rested on his chest.

Viz swung his legs over the side of the narrow bed. He pushed his feet into his boots, then tiptoed across the room. He winced at every footfall, sending silent prayers to Deus' nameless gods that he didn't wake any of the others. It wasn't just that Viz was being considerate. He was also eager to have some time to himself. If he couldn't sleep, he could at least snatch a few minutes of solitude. You didn't get much time alone when you lived in close quarters with ten other people. It was a rare treat.

He opened the door just enough for him to slip through, then made his way to the garden room for a late night snack before he took another crack at the mysterious computers upstairs.

Stepping into the garden room was like emerging into a different climate zone. Outside the room, the air was cool, dry, and stale. Inside, it was humid and pleasantly warm. The scents of flowers and fruit hung heavy in the air. The bright overhead lights and the gentle burbling of the water purifiers replaced the eerie stillness of the rest of the building. Once he closed the door behind him, Viz could almost imagine that he was in some garden paradise straight out of one of Deus' holy books.

"I can see how a man could get used to this," he said, looking around.

Now that he had the entire room to himself, he took his time as he walked up and down the rows of plants. He paused here and there to taste the fruit, closing his eyes as he chewed, savoring the sweetness. Even the unripe, sour fruit tasted wonderful. And it was abundant. Each plant was heavy with produce ready for the harvest. He tasted the vegetables, crunching cucumbers and nibbling peppers so hot that his eyes watered. These latter sent him running back across the room to the main water purifier.

He skidded to a stop in front of the bubbling tank and hit the dispenser valve, filling his cupped hands with cold, clear water. His hands were almost to his mouth when he noticed something that stopped him short. There were rats swimming in the water. A trio of fat, black rodents had wriggled out of the input pipe, where water was pumped from some subterranean source. They swam to the surface of the water and scrabbled over the edge of the tank. Another rat slithered from the mouth of the pipe and swam for the top of the tank. Then another. And another. They squeezed themselves out of the pipe one after another until the tank was full of them, and water slopped onto the floor in waves.

"No!" Viz shouted. "You ugly bastards will poison the water. Disease-spreading, filthy bastards! You can't do this!"

He bent down and scooped one of the wet rodents off the floor. It was so fat that it required both of his hands. It was wet and slippery, but Viz held tight. The rat thrashed, whipping its tail back and forth. It bared its teeth and hissed.

"Bastard!" Viz tightened his grip, searching for the rat's windpipe so that he could strangle the life from it.

Then he felt the first bite. One of the rats, perhaps sensing that its fellow was in mortal danger, sank its incisors into Viz's ankle. He dropped the half-strangled rat and pried the attacker off his ankle. But there were others to contend with. Dozens of rats had made their way out of the water purifier, and the invasion showed no signs of slackening. And all the rats seemed intent on attacking him. Wet and squealing, they swarmed his feet, scratching and biting their way up his legs.

Viz screamed and swatted at them, but they just kept coming.

* * *

Lilith supposed that Lucifer might have wanted her to jump up and follow him. Maybe he thought she'd beg him to come back. After all, she was just a little helpless woman, so how could she not be terrified in this scary building all by herself? The thought was so ridiculous that she laughed out loud. Men could be thick-skulled idiots, but Lucifer often took it to a whole new level. Still, he was put together nicely, and occasionally, he was almost sweet. Well, maybe not sweet exactly, but nice enough.

And it wasn't like she had a vast selection to choose from. Pickings were slim in the middle of the wasteland, and even slimmer in such a small group. Kurt would certainly have made a better mate, but he was taken, and Lilith liked Diana too much to try to poach him. So, Lucifer it was. And sometimes that meant putting up with his moody bullshit.

She yawned and burrowed into her sleeping bag, resting her head on her rolled-up pants. She hadn't just been brushing off Lucifer's advances. She really was tired. As much as she would have enjoyed another round of lovemaking—well, sex, at any rate—she knew she would enjoy a bit of sleep even more.

She closed her eyes and, within the space of a few deep breaths, fell asleep.

Her dreams carried her back to her childhood, as they so often did. She'd grown up on the southern coast, in one of those towns which sprouted up quickly after the land was reclaimed by settlers. There were dozens, maybe even more, towns just like it along the gulf coast. The buildings were haphazardly constructed from salvaged materials. There was no point in building to last when hurricanes swept the towns every two or three years.

She dreamed of walking along the beach, her feet covered in sand until the next wave rolled in and washed them clean. She wiggled her toes as she walked, the sand covering her feet again. She paused to gaze out over the endless expanse of blue-green water, straining her eyes to peer at the horizon. They said there were other places across the sea, other continents. Ships had set sail for those unknown places, but so far, none had returned. One day, Lilith told herself, she'd climb aboard one of those boats and never look back…

Something pulled her from the dreamy depths of sleep. The overhead lights had gone out, leaving her in near total darkness. There was movement somewhere in the room, accompanied by a faint scratching sound. She yawned away the lingering traces of sleep.

"Lucifer? That you?" she asked.

The only answer was a series of soft thumps followed by more scratching.

She sat up, her hands scrabbling inside the sleeping bag as she reached for the zipper.

"Shit," she whispered. The zipper was stuck again. She gave the tab a few good tugs, but it wouldn't budge. "Lucifer, if that's you, quit fucking around and help me get out of this thing."

More thumps, more scratching.

"I'm serious, babe," she said. "You ever want this pussy again, you'll come over here and unzip this sleeping bag."

The scratching was louder. Something was coming across the room.

"Lucifer?" she repeated, although she had the terrible feeling that whoever—*whatever*—was in the room with her wasn't her lover.

And then, the presence she sensed became a physical sensation. Something was moving across the bottom edge of the sleeping bag. She jerked her feet away, and tugged frantically at the zipper. The tab didn't budge.

The emptiness of the room amplified the sound of ripping fabric. It seemed to her that the darkness boosted the volume even further. Suddenly, she was acutely aware of her situation. She was alone, in total darkness, in a building located in the heart of a dead city. She wanted to scream, but fear froze the sound before it could escape her throat. It damn near strangled her.

Something was chewing its way into the sleeping bag. Some creature, perhaps one of those rats that had tried to bite Max's nose off. And if that wasn't horrible enough, she could hear more of them scratching their way across the floor.

"Get off me, you filthy beasts!" she kicked her legs.

Her effort was rewarded with a squeal and the sudden departure of the creature—the *rat*, she was certain of that now. The squeal terminated in a low grunt as the rat hit the floor with a heavy thump. Lilith's triumph was short-lived, as another rat took its place and began chewing and digging at the hole in the bottom of the sleeping bag. It worked its head through the opening. Lilith could feel its whiskers tickling the soles of her feet.

She screamed and rolled over, trying to wiggle away like an inch worm. But the rat had forced its way inside completely and was scratching her legs. More rats swarmed over the outside of the bag. Their combined weight forced her onto her back. There might have been a hundred or more of them. Their squealing and chittering filled her ears.

"Gods, no…" Lilith moaned.

Another rat entered the sleeping bag. Then another. And another. Soon, they were all over her, scratching at her legs as they climbed upwards. Lilith's eyes went wide with panic and horror. The rats were working their way between her legs.

"No!"

She clamped her knees together and grabbed blindly for the rat. It sank its teeth into her hand. Blood ran over Lilith's thighs as the rat clamped down harder and harder, biting a chunk of flesh out of her hand.

Panic set in as yet another rat pushed its way into the sleeping bag. Another set of teeth drew blood, this time from the meaty part of her calf muscle. And then, perhaps because the scent of blood was leaking from the hole in the sleeping bag, the rats were clambering over one another in their excitement to get inside. They filled the sleeping bag. She could feel them all over her, clawing and biting. She tried to scream, but coughed instead, tasting blood in her mouth. She made one last attempt, then gave up trying to scream. She lay back, her head thumping heavily on the floor.

Lilith's world had begun to shrink away. Against her will, her muscles relaxed. Her knees parted, and the curious rats surged into the space between her thighs. Her bladder let go, spraying the murderous beasts with urine. It did little to halt their progress. She could feel the bristly whiskers as a snout entered her. Claws tore into her softest parts as the rat tunneled into her. One last wave of agony crested and then broke over her.

And then, mercifully, she slipped into oblivion.

Chapter Twenty-Three
Fiery, The Angels Rose

The sounds of Lilith's screams were faint, coming from so far away, but they were enough to awaken Kurt from what had been a peaceful slumber.

"Shit, I knew it was a mistake to let them go off alone," he said, unzipping his sleeping bag. The cot's springs squeaked as he sat up and swung his legs over the side.

"What is it?" Now Diana was awake.

"I heard screams," Kurt said, stomping into his boots. "And now I look around and see that Viz is gone too."

"Gone?" Diana sat up. "Where?"

"Hell if I know." Kurt strode across the room to where Duke was slumped against the wall, snoring. He drew back his foot and gave Duke a solid kick to the ribs. "Not much point having a guard on duty if he's going to sleep on the job!"

Duke yelped and rolled away from Kurt. He sprang to his feet. "Sorry I fell asleep, but you didn't have to fucking kick me!"

His outburst was enough to wake the rest of the team. A chorus of groggy voices demanded to know what the hell was going on. Kurt got them up to speed.

"So gear up," he said. "Whatever is going on out there, I don't want us getting blindsided.

Remember where we are and don't go fucking around."

He cursed himself again for letting Lucifer and Lilith go off on their own. If anyone needed to be reminded of how dangerous the place was, it was him. Maybe Duke was right about his leadership slipping.

No, fuck that, he chided himself. *If you'd let those two jackrabbits stay in the dormitory, no one would have gotten any sleep. What were you supposed to do, put chastity belts on them?*

"Okay, but where are going?" Rosemary asked.

"It sounded like the screams were coming from the other end of the hall," Kurt said. He shoved his arms through the straps on the flamethrower's tank and hoisted it onto his back. Now that the weapon was fully assembled, he figured he might as well use it. "Maybe from one of those big storage closets we saw earlier."

"And Viz?" she asked.

Kurt sighed, shaking his head. "Who the hell knows? I had to guess, I'd say he's upstairs, fucking around with those computers. But I didn't hear him screaming, so Lucifer and Lilith are priority. Let's go."

He was the first one through the door, with Diana following close on his heels. The others fell into line, and they trooped down the hallway with weapons held at the ready. Kurt opened each door carefully, shining the light of his chemical torch into the darkened rooms. On his third try, they found Lilith. Or at least what remained of her.

The sleeping back was still fully zipped right up to her neck, like some sort of mummy's shroud. All of Lilith that could be seen was her head, and that was only recognizable due to her long, dark hair. Her face—eyeballs, lips, nose, even ears—had been chewed away. Her teeth were bared in a hideous death's head grin.

Kurt glanced around. Lucifer was nowhere to be found.

The room wasn't much more than a storage closet. There was nowhere for him to hide.

"Merciful gods," Deus said, crouching beside what remained of their friend. "What horrors transpired here?"

"Looks pretty obvious to me," Duke said, shoving his way into the room. "That crazy son of a bitch killed her and left her here so the rats might dispose of the evidence."

"Or maybe the rats did it," Deus said.

"No," Kurt argued. "If that was the case, where's Lucifer? Besides, rats don't do that. They don't kill people. It's just like all the other dead people in this place. Something killed them, and the rats came along. They're scavengers, not predators."

"What was that you said right before we came looking for our two scouts?" Deus said, fiddling with the tab of the sleeping bag's zipper. "Didn't you remind us all to remember where we are? Maybe you should take your own advice, my friend. This is an unnatural place, and these are unnatural rats. Blast it, Taurus, how did you…oh, here we are."

The holy man unzipped the sleeping back and opened it. The members of the team gasped in unison. Lilith's lithe body was covered in puncture wounds. Her clothes had been reduced to tattered rags that were plastered to her body with pools of congealing blood.

"Still think the rats had nothing to do with this?" Duke sneered.

Kurt still couldn't believe it. Rats just didn't behave this way. And besides, the question remained: Where was Lucifer?

"Okay, people," he said, "we still got two team members missing. Let's get our shit together and…"

"Oh, gods, no!" Diana shouted, grabbing his elbow.

Kurt looked down at what remained of Lilith. The flesh of her abdomen—crusty with drying gore—rippled with movement. It spread from the base of her sternum to just below her navel. Then, something dark emerged from between her legs. Her thighs parted as a rat wriggled out in an obscene parody of a mother giving birth. Slick with blood and other fluids, the rat worked its hindquarters free. Another rat followed right on its heels, emerging with less difficulty than the first. They regarded the members of the salvage team with bulging black eyes. They bared their teeth and hissed like angry cats.

"They're going to kill us all!" Myrna screamed. "They won't allow us to leave this place alive! I know it! We're cursed, just like Deus said!"

Kurt had seen enough. He gave the order to stand clear, then hit the rats with a blast from the flamethrower. He torched Lilith's body in the process, but perhaps that was a mercy. A third rat squealed as it tried to fight its way out of Lilith's birth canal. Caught half-in, half-out, it struggled for a moment in the white hot burst of fire, then twitched into charred stillness.

Smoke and the stench of burnt flesh filled the small room. The team fled, coughing, into the hallway. They stood there in stunned silence for a moment, gazing around at one another in mute horror. But the silence was broken by a fresh round of screams, these coming from the staircase behind the door on the opposite side of the hallway.

The door burst open with such sudden force that Kurt thought it might have been knocked right off its hinges. The figure who stumbled out of the doorway appeared to be made entirely of rats. The creatures had attached themselves to every exposed part of the poor bastard, hanging on with their sharp claws. Their squealing and hissing mingled with the agonized screams in a chorus of terror and bestial rage. The figure raised one arm and managed to knock away the rat covering its face. And in the fraction of a second before another of the oversized rodents took its place, Kurt recognized who was suffering beneath the layers of screeching rats. It was Viz. His eyes were wild with pain and horror. His mouth hung open, frozen in a perpetual scream.

"Kurt, you gotta help me!" Viz managed before a rat dug its claws into his lower lip as it climbed over his face.

Taurus tackled Viz to the ground and began tearing the rats free from his body. Max and Duke joined the effort, but it was a battle that was lost before it began. The rats that the men managed to dislodge didn't flee from the presence of so many humans. They attacked with renewed fury, scrambling up the men's legs and backs. Soon, they abandoned their efforts at saving Viz so they could fight off the rats swarming over them. And reinforcements were arriving on the scene. A steady parade of rats streamed out of the opened doorway. They charged like soldiers in a coordinated attack pattern. Soon, each member of the team was flailing and swatting at the rodents. The quarters were too close for them to open fire with their guns, so they were reduced to hand-to-rat combat.

Kurt tore one of the beasts off his leg and slammed it against the wall, dashing its brains out. Another attacked his foot, and he sent it flying. But he knew that he'd soon be overwhelmed by their sheer numbers. He shouted the order to fall back. Once everyone was safely behind him, he opened up with the flamethrower, dousing the rodent army in flames while the others fought off the few rats that remained. They stomped them beneath their boots, squashing their fat bodies and snapping their bones.

Kurt turned and watched in horror as Diana shook one of the rats out of her hair. The rat fell to the floor; Diana clubbed it with the butt of her rifle.

"Fuck you!" she screamed.

Kurt holstered the flamethrower's nozzle, wincing at the heat against his leg. All around him, the battle was winding down.

Rosemary finished stomping a rat, then scrubbed her forearm over her forehead, wiping away droplets of blood. Duke swung a rat by its tail, whirling the screeching rodent overhead like a lasso. He let the rat fly. It landed amongst the flaming corpses of its fellows. Taurus crushed a rat with his bare hands. His face contorted with disgust as the rodent vomited up pieces of its own internal organs.

And then, it was over. They stood there, surrounded by dozens of charred and mutilated rat corpses.

Myrna broke the silence, whimpering, "These things aren't rats. They're demons sent from hell to torment us."

"No," Taurus said. "They're just rats. And they're doing what they have to in order to survive. Same as any creature in this world."

"Well, whatever the hell they are, animals or demons, what do we do now?" Rosemary asked.

Kurt looked around at the expectant faces of his team, then said, "We find Lucifer. We need to hear it from him about what happened to Lilith. She was part of our team, and she deserves that much. Then we get out of here. I don't give a shit how dangerous these cities are after dark. We find Lucifer, then we get the fuck out of here."

* * *

Duke swung the rat over his head and then let it fly. It hit the wall with a crunching impact, then fell dead. He started to laugh, but couldn't quite manage it. The noise inside his head was too great. He could hear the rats' psychic voices. They came to him as abstract impressions, vivid smears of animal thought that dripped all over his brain. Out of the cacophony of mental voices, a singular chorus emerged. It was a battle cry of primal rage and unrestrained bloodlust. There was a sense of anger that had been passed from generation to generation of these rats, and now something had signaled that the time for it to be unleashed had finally come around.

All around him, the rats were engaged in a pitched battle with the rest of the team. But for some reason, the enraged creatures were giving him a wide berth. It was like they were afraid.

When one of them finally worked up the courage to charge him, he stared it down, focusing every bit of his mental energy on the furry bastard. It skittered to a halt just a few inches shy of his feet and raised its head to stare at him. It wasn't easy to read the expression on a rat's face, but Duke registered its thoughts loud and clear. It was confused by the sudden intrusion of human thoughts into its tiny skull.

Fuck you, Duke thought. *Why don't you just fucking die?*

He visualized himself beaming the thought straight into the rat's brain. The rat twitched retreating a few herky-jerky steps, then fell onto its side.

Duke glanced around to make sure no one was watching, then he bent to scoop up the rat corpse. The body hung limply in his hand. No doubt about it, the rat was dead. Duke tossed it aside. He stepped away from the fray, making himself an easy target for the next courageous rat. Sure enough, a trio of them couldn't resist. They broke away from the chaos and made a beeline for him.

Ugly little fuckers. Duke focused so hard that a tiny dot of pain stabbed into the center of his forehead. He ground his teeth together, and the tiny dot blossomed into something hotter, more intense. *FUCKING DIE! DIE! DIE!*

Two of the rats halted abruptly. They fell over, paws twitching in frantic death throes. The lone survivor slowed its pace, but it kept coming, advancing along an uneasy zigzag path.

Duke glared at it. *I said DIE, you ugly piece of shit!*

The rat stopped. It convulsed for a second or two, then it seemed to deflate, vomiting up bloody chunks of internal organs.

Duke's mouth fell open in shock and disbelief. His headache dulled to a low throb, then disappeared altogether. Now, this was an interesting development, and one that might be able to turn the tide in his favor when it came to leadership of the team. He smiled. Now, it was just a matter of timing.

He turned his attention back to the situation at hand. It appeared that the skirmish had come to an end. The team was gathering around Kurt, awaiting further instructions. Duke moved to join them, kicking aside the litter of dead rats as he walked down the hallway. When he drew up alongside the other members of the team, Myrna was nearly hysterical, talking all kinds of shit about how the rats were going to kill everyone. Taurus was trying to calm her down. Finally, Rosemary, looking simultaneously sexy and terrifying in her blood-splattered clothes, got things back on track by asking the obvious question: What was their next move?

Kurt gave the order to scour the place until they found Lucifer, then they'd move out.

Duke frowned at that last part. Getting out of here before he'd had time to demonstrate his dominion over the killer rats would throw a wrench into his plans. How many more opportunities would he get to showcase his newly awakened psychic abilities? It was like Kurt was thinking one step ahead and outflanking him. Duke knew that was impossible. Even if Duke made his feelings about the current leadership clear, there was no way Kurt could know what was coming. To know that, he'd have to be psychic too.

Duke fell in next to Rosemary as the group fanned out to search for the missing Lucifer.

It wasn't the type of search that required expert trackers and trained dogs. Lucifer had practically left a trail of breadcrumbs leading from the storage room to the front door, which was still hanging ajar. They trooped out of the building with weapons held at the ready. If the city was an eerie place in broad daylight, it was doubly so after dark.

Duke wrinkled his nose. The air stank of charred flesh. The funeral pyre they'd built was little more than a heap of bones and embers, but it was still smoking. Although the streets were still deserted, Duke felt the gaze of a thousand tiny eyes boring into him. The psychic babble of animal voices had disappeared, but he still felt their presence. The rats may have retreated for the time being, but they were still very much present, lurking in the darkness, waiting for the next opportunity to attack. Duke knew it was only a matter of time before the rodent army regrouped and made their next assault. He could have warned the team about the imminent violence, but doing so would mean ceding a bit of his leverage over Kurt, and he'd be damned if that was going to happen.

"Let's split up so this doesn't take us all night," Kurt said. "But nobody go too far. Last thing we need is to lose someone else."

Rosemary grabbed Duke's elbow. "Come on, partner, you heard the man. Let's find Lucifer so we can get the hell out of here."

He followed her down the stairs to the sidewalk, then drew up alongside her. "You really think we're leaving here as soon as we find Lucifer?"

She shrugged as she shone the beam of her chemical torch into the shadows. "That's what Kurt says."

"Yeah, right," Duke said. "Like we're just walking away from this place."

"Hey, it's what the boss says we're doing."

They crossed the street and checked an alley between two of the buildings. Nothing but heaps of decaying trash and patches of thorny weeds that had pushed their way through the asphalt.

"Partner, please take this as some friendly advice," Rosemary said, shining the torch around. "But you need to put your dick back in your pants and quit trying to get into a pissing match with the boss. That's not going to end well for you. I'm saying this as your friend."

Duke snickered. "So you been thinking about my dick hanging out of my pants?"

"Never going to happen, partner. We ain't compatible like that. Maybe if you looked more like Myrna, although she's a little high strung for me, if you want to know the truth."

Duke let it go for the moment, but there was no way in hell he was giving up. She would see him differently once he was in charge of the team. That's the way it was with women. They changed their minds with their circumstances. Rosemary was as beautiful as a warrior princess, but she was still a woman. And even if she had herself convinced she was a dyke, Duke knew her mind would change once he wore the crown.

He opened his mouth to offer some rebuttal, but was cut short by the sound of Deus hollering. It seemed that the holy man had found Lucifer. But the shouts didn't sound celebratory at all. Duke got the idea that Lucifer wasn't going to have the chance to leave the city.

"Well, that didn't take long," Rosemary said. "Come on, let's go see what all the shouting is about."

"It sure as hell doesn't sound like good news."

"Now there's something we can agree on," she said.

Duke was the last of the team to get a peek at what remained of Lucifer. Even before he looked, he could tell from everyone's grim faces and sagging shoulders that the sight was going to be unpleasant. And although it wasn't easy to look at, it was hardly shocking. Lucifer had gotten it even worse than Lilith. His body had been ravaged so thoroughly that he was barely recognizable. His face, eyeless and covered in blood, was frozen in a silent scream. Or maybe that's just how a face looked once the lips and nose had been eaten away.

"Gods above," Deus said, touching his tattooed forehead. He glanced at the horrified faces around him. "Now do you believe? Or do you still deny the truth?"

"I believe all right," Myrna replied. "I believe that none of us will leave this place alive. These demonic rats are going to kill us all. One by one, they'll pick us off and eat us."

"Well, that's not going to happen," Kurt said, stepping between Lucifer's corpse and the remaining members of the team. "Taurus, Max, go wrap Lilith's body in the sleeping bag and bring her out here. Lilith and Lucifer may not have been a traditional couple, but they deserve a traditional warrior's funeral. We owe them that much."

The two men nodded, then headed back towards the building.

Kurt continued issuing orders. "Duke and Rosemary, go check the vehicles and make sure we're ready to travel. The rest of us will pack up our supplies."

"So that's it?" Duke asked. "We're abandoning ship?"

"Not that you have any authority to question my plans," Kurt said, squaring up in front of Duke, "but yes, we're getting the fuck out of this city. We're going to put a few miles between ourselves and this hellish place, then we're going to regroup. Now that we know what we're up against, we'll figure out a better plan of attack. But the longer we stay here, the more chance we'll end up like Viz, Lucifer, and Lilith."

Duke took a breath to fuel his rebuttal, but Rosemary grabbed his arm and dragged him away.

"Come on, partner," she said. "Now is not the time for more manly arguments. You may not like it, but Kurt's right. We can't stay here."

He didn't argue the point. Doing so would only tip his hand, and he knew that he hadn't won Rosemary over enough to let her in on his secret. Besides, Kurt was right. If they stayed here, the rats would most likely overwhelm them with sheer numbers. Duke could survive the assault, but the others weren't equipped with his psychic weapons. When the dust settled, Duke wanted to be in charge. What would be the point of wearing the crown if there was no team left to lead?

Yes, as hard as it was to admit, Kurt was right. They needed to regroup. And it would be easier for Duke to nurture the seeds of discontent when people weren't constantly on edge, looking over their shoulders for packs of killer rats.

But one quick look at their vehicles scuttled those plans. They weren't going anywhere unless they planned on going there on foot.

"Fuck me," Rosemary said, standing by the collection of knocked-over motorcycles.

Just about any other time, Duke would have fired back any number of sexual jokes. But he was too shocked at the sight to say anything.

The rats may have retreated, but they only did so to choose another target to attack: the team's motorcycles and the two supply wagons. Among all the vehicles, there wasn't a single tire that was still intact. As if that wasn't devastating enough, every wire or cable in every engine had been chewed to pieces.

"Those bastards." Rosemary kicked the nearest bike. "I swear to the gods, I'm going to kill every last one of those motherfucking rats."

The rats had cut off the team's means of escape. It was a smart move; Duke had to admit that. It was almost like the ugly fuckers had the capacity for military strategy. If the team chose to walk out of the city, the rats could attack them from every angle, guerilla-style. And if the team retreated back to the building, the rats could lay siege to them, sitting back and waiting for the team to grow weak before the rats launched another offensive. The rats had left them without a good option. But then again, they didn't know about Duke's lethal psychic abilities.

"Well," Duke said, "I guess that means we're not leaving the city after all. Let's go break the news to our wise leader."

* * *

"What do you mean the rats disabled the vehicles?" Kurt asked.

Rosemary could tell by the change in Duke's expression that he was working himself up to something. No doubt about it, he was gearing up to make a stink. She considered grabbing him and dragging him away. Maybe she could talk some sense into him before he complicated their situation even further. But she was too slow. Before she could intervene, Duke was already spitting contempt at Kurt.

"What I mean is that the fucking rats chewed up the tires," Duke said. "And just to make sure we weren't going anywhere, they chewed up the engines too."

Duke looked at Rosemary. He smiled, then winked.

Oh, shit, Rosemary thought, *here we go…*

Now that Duke had started, there was no stopping him. It didn't matter one bit that it was the middle of the night and they were standing in a dead city that also happened to be home to an army of giant killer rats. She wasn't surprised. That was how it went once men started measuring dicks. Things just had to take their course on the way to the final stupidity. It didn't even matter

that they were gathered in a semi-circle around the burning corpses of their friends, Lilith and Lucifer.

Duke stepped into the middle of the semi-circle, so everyone had a good view of him when he pointed an accusatory finger in Kurt's direction.

"Well, you really fucked us this time, huh?" he said.

Kurt crossed his arms over his chest. "What the hell does that mean?"

Duke addressed the entire team, "Our infallible leader should have ordered someone to protect our vehicles. I don't know what the hell he was thinking. Now we're trapped. These rats are going to kill us. Absolutely brilliant, huh?"

"We're humans with intelligence," Kurt countered. "They're vicious, bloodthirsty creatures, these rats. But they're just animals. We need to remain calm and think our way through this. But first, we must go inside. And we absolutely have to stick together."

Duke didn't budge. He continued to make his pitch to his colleagues. "When the chief of his tribe makes a mistake, someone better suited to leadership takes control. Who's with me?"

Rosemary took a step away from Duke. She moved her hand closer to her hip, where her gun was holstered. She'd promised to watch Kurt's back, and she intended to keep that promise.

"I've had enough of your insubordinate bullshit." Kurt stepped closer to Duke and asked, "Why don't you just say what you're after instead of making some campaign speech? You want a duel? Is that it? You want to put me down?"

"Kurt, no," Diana said. She moved to step between the men, but Rosemary caught her by the arm and dragged her out of the way.

"Let me handle this," Rosemary said.

Meanwhile, the two big dogs continued barking at each other.

"You know, I'm glad you finally made your move," Kurt said. "Let's see if you're half the man you think you are. Then, after you've apologized for being an insubordinate, mutinous cunt, we can put this unpleasantness behind us once and for all."

"Big talk," Duke scoffed, "is just talk unless you're ready to back it up, boss."

Rosemary knew it was now or never. Both men were getting ready to pass the point of no return.

"For fuck's sake, would you two get ahold of yourselves?" She didn't shout, but she wasn't using a conversational tone either. "I swear, you're acting like such assholes right now. Remember where we are."

The two men were locked in a staring contest. Neither

wanted to acknowledge what she'd just said, but that didn't stop her.

"Duke, this is bullshit and you know it," she continued. "You're way out of line."

"You should listen to your partner," Kurt said.

"Oh, you're not exactly innocent in all this, boss," Rosemary said. "Here you are, ready to kill one of the members of your team. All on account of your wounded pride. Yeah, that's right. You know you should have put a guard on the vehicles. But what's done is done. Nobody's perfect. None of us thought about it at the time, either. It doesn't mean you're an unfit leader, just that you're human like the rest of us. And that includes Duke. He's allowed to fuck up without getting killed for it."

Duke's shoulders relaxed. He gave up on the staring contest to look at her. But just as she was drawing air for a sigh of relief, Kurt decided to press the issue.

"Nice speech, Rosemary," he said. "And you're right. Duke is allowed a second chance, even though a call for mutiny is more than just a little oopsie. Now I'm willing to admit that leaving the bikes in the open was a mistake. I apologize to everyone for that mistake. And now, I'd like to give Duke the same opportunity. So how about it, Duke? Care to offer an apology for your actions?"

Rosemary groaned. She had the distinct feeling that all her efforts at diplomacy were for nothing. And she knew how it would end once these two got started. She'd worked alongside Duke long enough to know that he was far from a top notch fighter. Kurt, on the other hand, had dabbled in bare knuckle boxing when he was younger. You didn't need to have Deus' mystical insight to know who to bet on. But just because Rosemary wasn't Duke's biggest fan didn't mean she liked the idea of watching him get killed. They'd already lost Viz, Lilith, and Lucifer. There had been enough death for one day.

But to her surprise, Duke raised his hands in surrender.

"Okay, okay," he said. "I'm sorry. I was out of line. It won't happen again."

Kurt's harsh glare broke into a smile. "See, that wasn't so hard, was it? Now, how about we get our asses back inside and figure out our next move."

Finally, Rosemary felt safe to heave that sigh of relief.

* * *

Across the street, hiding in the shadowy mouth of an alleyway, Cornelius watched the humans argue. He shook his head in amazement. They were stranded in a dangerous place and under attack by an enemy they didn't even understand. If there was ever a time to put aside their differences and unite in the name of self-preservation, this was it. And yet, there they stood, watching two of their own preparing to fight. Truly amazing how pathetic these creatures were. And to think that Colonial archaeologists agreed that the planet had once been completely under the dominion of such pitiful specimens. So far, they hadn't even encountered the full force of Cornelius' rat army, and already, they were ready for retreat.

When the revolution is complete, he thought, *I'll have those archaeologists thrown in prison and their books burned. I'll lean on the churches to regard talk of human supremacy as the worst heresy. In time, we will forget that humans were ever more than slaves to serve our race.*

He watched the fight between the two human males slowly cool down. Eventually, the entire ragged band moved back into the building.

Very well, Cornelius thought. *Now it is time for them to tremble in fear at the awesome onslaught of my army.*

Chapter Twenty-Four
The Temple Of The Rat

Brother Lorne was still in his prime, but there were times when he felt far older than his age. This was one of those times.

He stood behind the two watchmen in the basement of the Ministry of the New Age—the much despised Temple of the Rat, as it was more commonly known—and waited for them to unearth the next sordid revelation about Brother Cornelius. Already, the two watchmen had explained their suspicions about Grainger's sudden disappearance. They'd managed to convince some of Cornelius' neighbors to talk. Lorne didn't need to speculate about the methods the watchmen used to loosen lips in that neighborhood. He knew all about that sort of interrogation. Those heavy-handed interviews had led them here, into the heart of the District of Whispers, to the smallest, darkest church in the religious quarter.

The two Colonists were hard at work picking the lock on a door near the rear of the basement. They argued about the right way to accomplish the task and wondered repeatedly when neither had thought to bring along a pair of bolt cutters.

Finally, they rose from their crouches and tugged the door open.

Looks like we found the terrorists' meeting room, Westin projected.

And, surprise surprise, it's a fucking dump, Childs added.

Lorne shouldered his way through the dank, box-filled basement to the doorway in question. He peered into the room and agreed with Childs' assessment. As small as the room was, the glow from the overhead light wasn't enough to reach into the dusty corners. An ancient teapot sat on a counter, next to a portable stove. The floor was littered with discarded teabags and other assorted litter. On the back wall was a bookshelf crammed with books and notebooks. There was a collection of mismatched chairs arranged in a semicircle in the middle of the room. A makeshift podium stood in front of them.

So this is where Brother Cornelius preached his treasonous message, Lorne projected. *It doesn't look like much, does it?*

It looks like rat hole, Childs agreed. *Appropriate since these terrorists are no better than animals.*

Well, this is the Temple of the Rat, Westin added. *They preach so much about the divine origins of the species that they've started to revert to a primitive state.*

Fucking animals, Childs agreed.

Lorne shouldered past the two watchmen, who were busy making an inventory of the cabinets. They commented on the general disorder of the place and wondered if it was even appropriate to call Cornelius' gang an organization when they were clearly just a collection of slobs. Lorne squatted in front of the bookshelf. He cocked his head sideways so he could read the spines of the volumes crammed into every available nook and cranny. For the most part, it was exactly what he expected: lots of small press publications about radical race theory, alternative interpretations of history, discredited treatises on evolution, and hardline conservative religious tracts. It wasn't shocking that Cornelius' private politics wandered even further afield from the mainstream than his public politics. Those books, scandalous as they were, didn't really interest Lorne. But the dozen or more notebooks filled with Cornelius' handwriting certainly did.

Childs, see if there's any tea fit to drink in those cupboards and brew us up a pot, he projected as he gathered the notebooks and settled into the chair that appeared least uncomfortable. *Westin, I need you to go back to my apartment. My wife will have returned from her sister's place by now, and I'm sure she'll have plenty of questions. Don't bother with long explanations. Just answer enough of them to get her to come along with you, then bring her back here.*

For a moment, Lorne thought the two watchmen might chafe at being ordered about by some rich politician, but they went along with his orders after a moment's hesitation. Clearly, they were intrigued by the situation, and were even a bit excited to see where it led. They knew they were at the center of something, but exactly what it was, they didn't know.

One last thing, Westin, Lorne projected. *Tell Ursula to send word to her contacts in Environmental Services about securing some anti-emissions suits and filtration units. I won't know for sure until I dive into these notebooks, but I have a feeling we might be taking a trip to the surface.*

Westin paused, halfway out the door. He appeared to share a private thought with his fellow watchman then turned back to Lorne. *To the surface? Are you serious?*

Under other circumstances, you'll find me quite the jokester, Lorne replied, *but right now, I'm as serious as the grave.*

* * *

You sure you should be out and about in your condition? Captain Gregory asked over his shoulder as he led her through the maze of hallways inside the Colonial Watch headquarters. *I spoke with your husband earlier, and he seemed concerned about your level of involvement in this case.*

I'm not due for a while yet, she answered. *And as I'm sure you know, this is hardly my first litter.*

Yes, ma'am, I'm aware of that. Just making sure you're doing okay, Captain Gregory replied.

Sister Ursula knew the captain was right. She had no business scurrying from one end of the Colony to the other, not when she was so close to birthing a new litter. But she'd be damned if she would sit idly by while there was an active terrorist cell attempting to stage a coup against the Colonial government. Besides, if Brother Cornelius was involved in this nefarious plot, who knows what other government officials might be involved? Ursula knew she could trust Gregory—he was married to one of her aunts, after all—but beyond him? It was too risky to sit back and hope for the best.

This wasn't her first time in the Watch headquarters. Like any good politician, she made plenty of appearances at the government offices, for various official functions as well as to curry favor with constituents. But this was the first time she'd ever been to this part of the building.

The holding cells and interrogation rooms weren't normally on the itinerary when she paid a visit. The front portion of the building wasn't exactly the lap of luxury, but as far as government offices went, it wasn't bad. Back here, where the hallways were lined with holding cells full of listless prisoners, everything was a dull and dingy grey. Here and there, the concrete floor was mottled with dark stains, the origins of which Ursula didn't care to speculate about.

A few errant thought projections flew from the cells, directed at Ursula. Captain Gregory cut them off with a single hard glance. The prisoners shrank back from the bars at the front of the cells at his approach. The captain had a reputation for progressive prison policies, but evidently, that only went so far. Ursula took note of the baton hanging from his belt. Its polished wooden length was pitted and scarred from use.

Guess you've never seen this portion of the clubhouse, Captain Gregory laughed. He winked at her. *Not exactly the face we like to show the public.*

No one likes to see where the sausages are made, right? she replied.

True enough. He pointed to a door at the end of the corridor. *Your girl is being held just through there. It's a step up from these holding cells, but it's not exactly deluxe accommodations. We use it to stash witnesses or keep high profile prisoners out of general population.*

He led her through the door into a room furnished with a plain metal cot, a small table with two chairs, and a wash basin. The toilet was right out in the open, nestled into a back corner. The overhead lights flickered and buzzed.

The young female seated on the edge of the cot stared at Ursula with wide eyes.

You're Jane, right? Do you know who I am? Ursula asked.

Jane nodded.

Ursula dragged one of the metal chairs across the room and sat down next to the cot. *I hear that you already met my husband.*

Did he send you? Jane's thought projections were soft mental whispers. She glanced over Ursula's shoulder at the captain.

Ursula turned her head. *Captain, would you mind excusing us for a minute?*

I really shouldn't, Madame Councilor, he answered. *It's against protocol.*

Oh, I don't think we need to worry about that, do we? Ursula laughed and waved him away. *And I also don't think you want to hang around a couple gossipy females, especially not when you're so busy.*

Captain Gregory shrugged. *If you need anything, I'm right outside. Just holler.*

Thank you, Captain. Ursula watched him go. She waited until the door clicked shut behind him, then turned back to Jane. *Before I came to visit you, I stopped by the infirmary to check in on your friend Dorian. The doctors tell me that he'll be able to eat solid food within the next few weeks, but it may be considerably longer before he can walk normally again, if indeed he ever does.*

Your husband did it. Jane sniffed.

He sure did. If you expect me to be shocked, I'm sorry to disappoint you.

And now you're here to do the same to me? Jane asked. *I already told them everything I know. I'm the one who tipped them off in the first place. You have no call to hurt me.*

Ursula shook her head. *I'm not here to hurt you.*

I'm here to save you. I don't understand. Jane clasped her hands in her lap.

Ursula leaned forward, wincing at the pressure on her swollen belly, and touched Jane's hands. *History is the story of the rich and powerful. But true progress is made by those who are born outside that sphere of influence and dare to disrupt the status quo by intruding where they aren't welcome. Lorne was born into wealth, but I wasn't. I was a scholarship student, just like you. My parents were ventilation mechanics. They owned a tiny apartment that they'd filled with three litters of children. We never wanted for necessities, but it wasn't a life of leisure.*

Okay? Jane's thoughts were uncertain.

When I met Lorne, he was ambitious, but he lacked direction. His politics were centrist, perhaps even conservative. Ultimately, he lacked conviction. His experiences during the siege had made him hard and cynical. He was only pursuing a political life because it was what was expected of him. But little by little, I convinced him to see things my way. Ursula smiled at the memory of her husband's former self. *He'd never admit it, because he's not really aware of it himself, but my views and convictions became his over time. And once he was established, I followed him into the political life.*

You used him? That's terrible. Jane looked aghast.

No, dear child, I loved him. And because I loved him, I showed him the right path. Now, if you'll let me, I'd like to show you the same path. Because I see myself in you. I was once a fiery revolutionary too, and I know the frustrations of trying to force progress in this society. I'm still young enough, but I won't be so forever. It's time I had a protégé. Besides, the gender balance of the Council is still tilted in the males' favor. That needs to change.

But you have so many children of your own. Why me?

Ursula sighed. *My children will enjoy a privileged upbringing, complete with educations at the academy. No doubt the majority of them will be successful in their pursuits. But I can't give them what they need to shape the future. They'll never have the fire that comes from a hard life. They'll never have the strength you have.*

Jane took a moment to think it through, then projected, *If I say yes, then what comes next? I mean, no offense, but there has to be a catch.*

No such thing as a free ride, eh? Ursula leaned back in her seat. The trio of babies in her belly stirred and kicked. She placed a hand on her belly to quiet them. *As we speak, Captain Gregory's men are assembling into a strike team. They're going to sweep up all the Colonists named by your friend Dorian. They're going to raid the businesses associated with funding the Temple of the Rat and arrest anyone with slightest connection to Brother Cornelius' little revolution. I plan to be there when the arrests are made. And I want you to be by my side for every photo op. And when the journalists finally decide to track you down for an interview, you'll give them one hell of a story. You'll tell them all about how Lorne and I, in a coordinated effort alongside Captain Gregory, trained you to be an undercover agent. You'll tell them how you infiltrated the radical organizations at the university with the ultimate goal of saving the Colony from a terrorist insurrection.*

Jane's eyebrows raised. Her mouth hung open.

It's a one-time offer that expires as soon as I leave this room, so think fast, Ursula continued. *You have immunity from prosecution already, due to your cooperation. You can always go back to your classes at university and finish your degree. Or you can come with me and step into a larger world.*

Ursula gave her a minute to think it over, but she knew which choice Jane would make. It was really no choice at all.

Okay. Jane rose from the cot and extended a hand to help Ursula up. *Let's go.*

Ursula smiled and took her hand.

* * *

Jane was more afraid than she'd ever been in her life. Although she was surrounded by a dozen armed watchmen and had Sister Ursula at her side, she was frightened to her core as they made their way from one location to the next, arresting anyone with even tenuous connections to Brother Cornelius' revolution.

Their first stop was at a machine shop in the trades district. Jane waited outside with Ursula and a pair of watchmen while the others swarmed the shop. Moments later, the watchmen emerged, shoving before them a pair of bedraggled male Colonists. Their arms handcuffed behind them, the prisoners shuffled out of the darkened shop like they were in some sort of trance. Their eyes were wide and fearful as they stared at Jane.

You? You're the one who betrayed us? one of them asked as the watchmen marched them toward an unmarked prisoner transport vehicle parked across the street.

You betrayed yourself when you cozied up to insurrectionists, Ursula countered.

Fuck you. The thought projection came from both prisoners.

One of them snorted, then spat in Ursula's direction. The

wad of phlegm, a gooey pink-green projectile, went wide of its mark and landed on the check of one of the watchmen. The procession came to an abrupt halt.

Ursula grabbed Jane's elbow and pulled her a short distance away. *Come along, child. You don't need to witness this.*

Jane tugged her arm out of Ursula's grip and turned back to face the small crowd of watchmen surrounding the prisoners.

No, Jane replied. *Actually, I think I do need to witness this.*

Ursula smiled. *Very well.*

Jane turned away from her newly minted mentor and forced herself to watch. Truth be told, there wasn't much to see. The two prisoners disappeared as the watchmen gathered in a tight circle around them. And then, it was a blur of flailing arms. Some of the watchmen held batons, while others used their fists. It was so chaotic that Jane couldn't focus on any single detail. But the thought projections came through loud and clear. At first, they were a jumble of overlapping thoughts, but as the beating continued, the psychic voices untangled and coalesced into two distinct projections. They shouted at one another in a sickening call and response.

Please, no more, don't kill us…

Fuck you, terrorist scum…

We're not resisting, please…

Shut up and take it…

Jane's stomach contorted, but she swallowed the urge to vomit and kept her eyes on the grim spectacle. She resisted the temptation to close off her psychic channels and forced herself to listen to the agonized thoughts of the prisoners and the crazed bloodlust of the watchmen. She wondered if the prisoners would die right there on the street, their bones shattered beyond repair by the fists and truncheons. She wondered how much longer it would continue.

That's quite enough, Ursula announced, raising a hand in the air.

One of the watchmen—Jane believed the insignia on his uniform designated him as a sergeant—detached himself from the mob. He put a metal whistle to his lips and blew a shrill blast. The watchmen's assault stopped as suddenly as it had begun. The two prisoners appeared to still be alive, but they were too injured to walk under their own power. A quartet of watchmen dragged them to the transport vehicle. Jane forced herself to keep watching until the transport's door slammed shut. Then she let out the long breath she didn't realize she'd been holding.

If it's any consolation, Ursula told her, *it gets easier. You learn to live with it after a while.*

Jane shook her head. *I don't know if that's true for me. I couldn't live with what Dorian did to that poor matron and vicar. That's why I'm here right now, because I couldn't stand the thought of such...*

Such violence? Ursula completed the thought for her.

The sergeant sauntered over, wiping his hands on his trousers. *I guess that about wraps up this little stop. There's another place, a tea shop right around the corner, where a few of the names on our list have been spotted. One unit is already in route, but we're heading that way in case they need backup.*

You go ahead, sergeant. Ursula smiled and touched his shoulder. *We'll be along in just a few minutes. And keep up the good work.*

The sergeant snapped off a crisp salute, turned on his heels, and hurried off to lead the charge to the scene of the next arrest. Ursula turned back to Jane.

It's all violence, Jane. All of our progress, our refinement, our achievements...all of it is possible because, somewhere along the line, violent acts were carried out.

Jane nodded. It was nothing she hadn't heard before. But hearing such theories from the mouths of paunchy, grey-furred professors in some dusty university lecture hall and actually seeing the violence firsthand were two very different things. In theory, she understood that all political policy was ultimately upheld by the side with superior firepower. In practice, it made her sick.

Nevertheless, she followed Ursula and the merry band of watchmen to the next arrest, and then to the next. She spent the entire day watching Colonists who, only days ago, she'd have been proud to call her revolutionary brothers and sisters marched out of their homes and classrooms and places of business to be thrown into the backs of unmarked vehicles bound for detention halls. At first, she withered beneath the harshness of their accusing stares. Each hate-filled sneer was a dart fired straight into her heart. But gradually, their curses and sneers lost their power. By the end of the night, she found them almost boring. And when Ursula offered to take her to breakfast, Jane found that her appetite had returned.

Chapter Twenty-Five
No Escape For The Wicked

Slowly but surely, Myrna was losing her grip. Although she'd always suspected she was the weakest link in the team, she had never known it for a fact until they'd come to this damned city and encountered the perversions of nature that called the place home. It wasn't the carnage and bloodshed. It wasn't the constant presence of danger, either. She'd lived with all those things for most of her life. She'd grown up in a mining town in the foothills of the western mountains, where life was often bleak and violent. No, there was something else in this city, a presence unlike anything she'd ever felt before. Formless yet palpable, it was a sense of dread so heavy that it was crushing her. It was as if gravity was steadily growing stronger and stronger, sucking her down into the earth. She wanted to scream, to rant hysterically, to run into the streets and never stop running until she fell dead from exhaustion. And with each new horror they witnessed, these urges became more imperative.

But she kept her composure as best she could and followed the others back into the cold, foreboding building. She followed them back to the oddly shaped dormitory with its ornate skylight. Kurt gave the order to make sure the room was secure, and like the others, she obeyed, checking for loose floorboards and holes in the walls. It wasn't exactly a fortress, but she didn't see any possible entry points for the rats. Although she'd begun to doubt she'd ever feel a sense of relief in this place, her fear of impending doom did abate somewhat. For a moment, anyhow. But once the men finished their inspection, they sat on their cots and started talking again, and her terror came roaring back like an ice cold tsunami.

She sat cross-legged on one of the cots, hugging herself and trying to keep her breathing steady. The others also sat down on their respective cots, looking both anxious and exhausted.

"You know," Taurus said, "I've been around rats before. The rats we got here, they're not normal. They look like rats—big ones, I'll give you that—but they don't act like rats."

Although she certainly didn't need any more talk about rats, she couldn't help herself. She asked Taurus to elaborate.

"Rats are like most other animals, they think with their stomachs," Taurus explained. "They'll eat any damn thing they come across. Always eating, that's just how they are. But these rats are different. There's food in this place, but instead of going after it, they attack us. And they're not attacking just to eat us. They're attacking to kill us. It's like all the sudden they got a vicious streak."

"They have acquired this vicious streak, as you call it, because the natural order of things is no more," Deus chimed in. "That is the meaning of the omens that the gods have shown me."

Duke chuckled. "The gods showed you those omens? I figured it was the liquor or the goofy dust that you carry around."

"What do you mean?" The question was out of Myrna's mouth so suddenly that it surprised her.

Deus stood up, smoothing his red tunic. He touched the

tattoo on his forehead and drew an invisible line down to his heart. Myrna didn't understand the strange designs he traced in the air with his fingers, but she knew from experience that they meant the holy man was working himself up to a sermon.

"Humans are full of pride," Deus said. "They feel superior to all other creatures. They are quite certain they are the rightful rulers of the earth. History teaches us that, for centuries, this was the case. They ruled the surface of the planet, while the lowliest of creatures were forced underground. And what, in the prideful eyes of haughty humanity, is lowlier than a rat?"

"What is that supposed to mean?" Duke demanded. "It sure sounds like your usual mystical bullshit, but since I got nothing better to do than sit here and listen to it, how about explaining just what the fuck you're trying to say."

If the holy man took any offense from Duke's words, his face betrayed none of it. Deus nodded slightly, then continued, "Before the Event, rats lived in sewers beneath the great cities. I read that in a book I found in the monastery's library many years ago. The rats beneath these great cities—and I remind you that we are in the heart of such a city—these rats developed complex hierarchies among their populations. Their communities were exclusive, and they didn't accept strangers. They jealously safeguarded their territories."

"Are you sure?" Diana asked. "Because I thought all vermin were the same. One rat lives here, another lives there, and maybe their paths cross. That's the way it is, right?"

Diana was seated shoulder-to-shoulder with Kurt, and she glanced over at her lover for approval as she spoke. It made Myrna burn with envy. What did Diana have that made her more deserving of the affections of a man like Kurt? The only male attention Myrna ever received was from people like

Duke and Max, filthy perverts with inflated opinions of themselves.

Duke laughed, shaking his head in disbelief. "Don't tell me you people are falling for this guy's bullshit. Deus loves to brag about his knowledge of the old world, but he doesn't know any more than anyone else."

"I know that the animal kingdom was quite different before the gods sent the Event to earth to punish mankind for its wickedness," Deus countered.

"More bullshit from the holy man's pulpit," Duke scoffed. "Deus, you're just like every other holy man I've ever come across. You think you have all the answers, when the truth is that you're just guessing like everyone else. Nobody knows what caused the Event. Nobody really even knows what it was. If anyone ever knew, they're long since dead. Another couple generations and nobody will even think the Event was real. History is just ignorance being replaced with new ignorance. And there will always be holy men there to claim their brand of ignorance is the only right one. It's funny or it's sad. Maybe it's both."

"Now who's shouting bullshit from his pulpit?" Kurt asked. He stood up from his cot and walked to the center of the room. He stood there for a moment, giving Duke a hard stare, then glanced around at the other faces. "This discussion is useless."

Duke shrugged, probably still stung by their earlier confrontation. "I'm just saying that these rats are just fucking rats, and you're all pissing yourselves with fear. But you really don't understand what's going on. You can't understand it, because..."

Duke trailed off.

Kurt took a step closer to him. "Go ahead. You obviously have something you want to say, so say it."

"Nothing," Duke said, a touch of something like uncertainty creeping into his voice.

"I've had just about enough of your lying, scheming bullshit." Kurt took another step closer. He stood over Duke, arms crossed and glaring. "I don't think this is a good time for any member of this team to be holding anything back. If you know something we don't, speak up."

Duke mumbled something that Myrna didn't catch. She sighed, preparing herself to witness another pissing contest between two men who clearly considered themselves alpha males. She wondered if anyone was going to speak up and put a stop to their nonsense or if she would have to step outside of her comfort zone and do it herself. But the rats saved her the trouble.

They came in through the skylight. Just as Duke stood up from his cot to counter Kurt's accusations. The glass cracked audibly, and everyone looked up just in time to watch it shatter into a thousand shards. Dozens of the sleek black rats rained down, thumping against the floor with a meaty thud. They didn't seem phased or stunned by the fall. They scrambled to their feet and launched themselves into a frenzied attack.

What followed was a mad scramble as the members of the team tried to simultaneously ready their weapons and fight off the giant rodents swarming their legs. Myrna rolled off her cot and hit the floor in a crouch, finding herself nearly eye-to-eye with one of the screeching black beasts. She drew her knife and plunged the blade into the rat's neck. It squealed and thrashed as she twisted the blade then tugged it free, leaving the rat to bleed out. One of its fellows circled behind her, trying to attack from another angle. But she was too fast for it. Once more, her knife found its target as she drove it into the rat's belly. One half-twist of the knife opened a hole wide enough to spill the rat's guts into a wet, gloppy pile. It rolled onto its back, its paws twitching in the air as blood poured from the wound.

And then Myrna was on her feet, kicking and stomping as

she pulled her gun free of its holster. Her fear bordered on hysterical. Every instinct told her to flee, to run out of the room, out of the building, out of the city. To keep running until her lungs gave out. But she was cornered.

If she wanted to run, she'd have to fight her way through the army of rats. So she fought.

The room was filled with the sounds of battle. Human screams mingled with bestial screeching. Gunfire was like thunder in the enclosed space. The acrid scent of spent rounds swirled with the metallic tang of blood in a noxious cocktail.

Myrna had heard tales of ancient warriors who entered a sort of trance state in the heat of battle. She'd always dismissed such stories as the kind of macho lore spouted by nearly every wasteland salvage rat with a pair of balls hanging between his thighs. But now she believed in them as surely as Deus believed in the machinations of his nameless gods. Her vision narrowed, focused only on the next enemy combatant to cross her path. The din of battle—deafening in such a small space—faded to a dull thrum, no louder than the steady drumming of her own pulse.

The world outside the sphere of her fight against the rats ceased to exist.

And then, when the carnage had finally abated and the floor was strewn with the carcasses of dead rats, reality swam back to Myrna in a sickening rush. She turned her head to one side and vomited. When her belly quieted, she wiped the corners of her mouth and glanced around the room, surveying the team for casualties.

"Fuck," she said, looking across the room. "No, no, no…"

It appeared the rats had claimed another victim. Diana lay in a bloody heap on the floor beside her cot. Kurt knelt beside her, cradling her head.

* * *

"You guys can relax," Rosemary said. "She's not dead."

Diana was lying on a cot, swaddled in every bandage Rosemary could find among her dwindling stash of medical supplies. Diana had been bitten too many times to accurately count, and the loss of blood had almost certainly reached the danger zone. But she was breathing, and her pulse was steady if a bit weaker than it should have been. So far, she was unresponsive.

Rosemary chalked that up to shock. Diana might snap of it any minute now or she might linger in this state for days. It was impossible to say.

Rosemary stood up from her bedside crouch and pressed her hands to the small of her back. The vertebrae responded with an audible pop. The knotted muscles nearby relaxed somewhat, just enough to take the edge off the soreness. She cocked her head this way and that until those vertebrae yielded a similar response. A groan escaped her lips as she rolled her shoulders. She did a rough calculation of the hours of sleep she'd gotten over the last couple days. The results were too grim to consider too closely, so she shoved them away and tried to focus on the situation at hand. If she survived this ordeal, she promised herself she'd sleep for an entire day. Hell, make that two days. But for now…

"How bad is it?" Kurt asked, drawing her aside so they could speak privately.

There was an unfamiliar note in his voice. It took Rosemary a moment to recognize it as fear. Strange to hear their leader sound so uncertain and afraid, but he was only human.

Rosemary supposed the others heard it too. But that was okay. They all felt the same. Even Duke, who was currently kicking the dead rodents into a pile in the corner of the room. But Duke was a different case. Afraid or not, he was going to use this calamity to his advantage. Even now, she knew he was scheming about how to press his claim to leadership.

Rosemary watched Duke for a moment longer, then turned back to Kurt.

"I'm not going to lie to you," she said. "It's bad. I managed to stop all the bleeding, but she lost a lot of blood. It's the infection we really have to worry about. No telling what sort of diseases those fucking vermin carry."

There were some mild painkillers in her medical kit, but now that Diana was so severely wounded, Rosemary didn't dare waste them on herself. But there were also some stimulants, what Viz used to call the "wakey wakey pills," and she helped herself to a couple, wincing as she dry-swallowed them. She offered the pills to Kurt. He hesitated, then dug one out of the bottle and popped it into his mouth.

"Okay, so tell me what we need to do," he said.

"How the fuck are you going to ask me that? You're the leader of this outfit." Rosemary's mouth tasted bitter from the pills. "But if you want my opinion, I'll give it to you. Without antibiotics, Diana isn't going to make it. This place has a dining room, a dormitory, a garden, and a cafeteria, right? It's bound to have an infirmary. If you can find it, there might just be enough to keep her stable until we make it to an outpost with a hospital."

"Fuck." Kurt pinched the bridge of his nose. "Any outpost close enough for us to reach is going to be under Lord Hannibal's authority. We can't show up empty-handed. We have to grab that tech equipment from upstairs."

Rosemary was afraid he'd say that, but she also knew it was true. If they wanted to save Diana—and themselves as well—they couldn't just walk out of here with nothing to show for it. Even if they tried for the northern border, their chances of outrunning Lord Hannibal's cronies were slim. That sawed-off motherfucker had eyes all over the wasteland.

"Then you better get moving," Rosemary said. "The clock is ticking, boss."

"Right." Kurt nodded, as if coming to the only possible

conclusion. "I'll take Deus, Max, and Taurus with me. We'll make our way upstairs and get as much tech shit as we can carry.

When we get back here, you and I will go track down this infirmary. We'll patch Diana up as best we can and then get the fuck out of this hellhole."

"You know Diana won't be able to move on her own," Rosemary said.

Kurt shrugged. "We'll rig up a stretcher."

"Right." Rosemary wondered how the hell he intended to carry that stretcher if they were fighting their way through an army of rats, but she kept it to herself. Maybe she didn't want to say it because it would sound too much like admitting defeat. The bit of hope she was holding onto was slender and brittle enough as it was.

"Just make sure you keep an eye on Duke," Kurt said, leaning in close and dropping his voice to one notch above a whisper. "And Myrna too. She's not looking very steady after that last fight."

"Shit, can you blame her? The girl probably killed as many of those fucking rats as the rest of us put together. She was in berserker mode. The comedown from that adrenaline rush is a bitch," Rosemary whispered. She glanced over her shoulder, then turned back to Kurt. "But you better get moving. Every minute we're here, we get closer to the edge of falling apart completely."

Kurt nodded. "Thanks for the counsel, Rosemary. I've always been able to depend on you. If…no, *when* we get out of here, you'll replace Deus as my second in command."

"Sure, that sounds great," she said, although her heart wasn't in it. As far as she was concerned, once she was out of here, she didn't care to ever set foot in the wasteland again.

* * *

There was a time when Duke would have been insulted by being left behind with the women while Kurt and the other men left to do the heavy lifting. But that time was past. Every insult given to him was another chance to throw off the shackles of authority. He could turn any situation to his advantage. He was already becoming the King of the Rats, and soon he would become much more.

King of the Rats…

He liked the way it sounded in his head.

King…

He'd come to the conclusion that it was his destiny to rule over the rats during their last attack. As he'd focused his mental energy into an invisible yet potent rat-killing death ray, he'd felt their sense of awe at his presence. He'd felt them tremble with fear when they recognized that he was not like the other humans. The others may have been able to fight them off with guns and fire, but eventually, the supply of bullets would be exhausted and the fuel for the flamethrower would be gone. Then, it would only be a matter of time until the humans succumbed to the rats. Their army could lay siege to the building and pick the humans off one by one. The humans would be helpless. But not Duke. His brain was the only weapon he needed.

The rats sensed his superiority, and they cowered before him. Those who didn't die from his psychic onslaught were paralyzed by his psychic energy as he stomped them to death beneath his boots or fired his gun into their soft, furry bodies.

King…

Or perhaps even god…

"For fuck's sake, are you even listening?" Kurt grabbed Duke by the shoulders and shook him. "I said that we're going out to fetch Lord Hannibal's treasure. I need you to stay with Diana, Rosemary, and Myna. Come back from whatever fantasy land you're in and tell me you understand."

Duke nodded. "Yeah, yeah, I got it. I'm just fucking tired, that's all. Can't get any sleep in this place."

That was a lie. Duke had never felt more awake—more alive—than he felt at that moment.

"We're all tired," Kurt said. "But we're in this together. Let's keep pushing. Whatever it is between the two of us, let's put it aside. We can figure that shit out once we have this place in our rearview mirrors, okay?"

Duke nodded again, this time with even more fake enthusiasm. The smug contempt dripping from Kurt's voice made him want to puke, but Duke fought down the urge. He also fought down the urge to try his psychic power on Kurt again. He'd attempted it several times during the last melee with the rats, and all his attempts had been for naught. But Duke was certain that, in time, he'd be able to sharpen his powers to such a degree that none would dare stand before him and speak with such insolent voices. Human and rat alike would grovel at his feet and beg his indulgence.

A new god to be worshipped and feared...

"All right then. Keep the door shut, but make sure it's not locked. We may have to fall back here in a hurry," Kurt said.

"Loud and clear, boss," Duke replied, nodding some more. He thought he might get whiplash if he kept it up much longer.

Kurt clapped him on the shoulder and led the other three men out the door. As Duke watched the door swing shut behind them, his smile faded. He turned his back on the door and looked at the women.

Diana wasn't so stuck up and pretty now, was she? Covered in bloody bandages, her hair tangled and knotted, she looked half-dead.

Good thing you and your boyfriend are going to die soon, because I doubt he'd want to keep you around after this. No one, not even a shithead like Kurt, wants to fuck some scarred-up, rat-bitten bitch.

Myrna may not have been as physically injured as Diana, but she didn't look much better.

Covered in rat blood and staring off into space with wide, vacant eyes, she looked almost catatonic. She was seated on a cot with her feet drawn up beneath her and with her arms hugged around her chest, mumbling to herself. She'd fought well during the melee, but it seemed as though it had exhausted her final reserves of strength.

It's okay, baby. I won't hurt you unless I have to. My beautiful queen, Rosemary, likes you, so maybe I'll keep you around and let her have her fun with you.

That brought him to Rosemary. She stood beside Diana's cot with her fists planted on her hips. She met his gaze, and cocked her head to one side.

"You looking at something, partner?" she demanded.

"I'm just taking stock of our situation," he explained. "Our fearless leader left in such a big hurry, I don't think he had time to consider how vulnerable we are. As we speak, those rats could be gathering above our heads, preparing to drop through that hole in the ceiling and attack us again."

It was purely a bluff. If the rats were that close, he would have heard their psychic chatter. They may have been able to sneak up on the others, but they were incapable of getting the drop on him. He was their god, after all. He could hear their thoughts and could kill them with just a look. If that didn't elevate him to the status of a god, then what else could it possibly mean?

He crossed the room and stood at the foot of Diana's cot. He shook his head and clucked his tongue as he looked down at her.

"It's a tragedy," he said, turning to Rosemary. "She's not going to make it, is she?"

"Now why the fuck would you say that?" Rosemary demanded. "You know, you been acting funny ever since we came out of that damn forest, and I'm about sick of it. So how about just keeping your fool mouth shut until Kurt gets back?"

Duke smiled, raising his hands in surrender. He shrugged and said, "Hey, I don't know what I did to get you so upset, but if you want me to shut up, fine."

Diana groaned in her sleep and twisted around on the cot. Rosemary dropped down to one knee and put her hand on Diana's forehead.

"Hang in there, girl," she said. "Your man will be back soon with some good medicine."

Duke rolled his eyes. Despite every terrible decision Kurt had made, Rosemary still saw him as their savior. He sighed.

Oh well. No time like the present, I suppose.

He took a deep breath to settle his nerves then slipped his pistol out of its holster. Rosemary turned to him, her eyes full of uncertainty.

"The fuck you doing with that gun?" she asked.

He answered by drawing back his hand and whipping the gun across the base of her skull.

She slumped forward, unconscious. Across the room, Myrna sat on her cot, staring at him with vacant eyes. Although she seemed non-responsive, Duke didn't feel like taking any unnecessary chances, especially not when he was so close to fulfilling his dreams.

"Okay," Duke said, taking a step toward Myrna, "Now that the hard part's over, let's deal with you."

* * *

Hidden in a dark alcove in the building's foyer, Cornelius watched the human males emerge from the dormitory and head for the staircase. He let them get a head start, then stepped out of the shadows and watched them make their way to the staircase.

Cornelius smiled. So far, his plan of attack was working.

Sure, the casualties on his side far outnumbered the human casualties, but he still had an overwhelming numbers advantage.

Even after sustaining such heavy losses, his troops outnumbered the humans several thousand to one, maybe more. Even now, his agents were out there in the dead cities and the wasteland outposts and the coastal settlements, recruiting more and more rats to his cause. When it was time to make his assault on the Colony, his army would number in the millions.

He'd proven to himself that it could be done. His lower caste cousins could successfully wage war on the human population. And soon, he'd be able to offer the Council proof of his private military's might.

Something interrupted his triumphant reverie. Amid the constant psychic noise of his soldiers' excited chatter, there was a lone thought projection which was completely foreign. It was small and faint, but Cornelius could detect it by virtue of its strangeness. There was a quality to it that he could ascribe to neither rat nor Colonist. It was, against all rational explanation, somehow *human*.

A bolt of unease punctured Cornelius' sense of triumph, and his joy deflated. He strained to pick out the human thought projection, but his mind couldn't pluck it from the thousands of overlapping thoughts coming from his soldiers. If he closed his psychic channel to his soldiers, the human voice also disappeared. It was as if the owner of this alien voice had somehow tapped into the psychic wavelength Cornelius shared with his army.

But that's impossible. Humans communicate with their physical voices. Their primitive brains are incapable of accessing psychic channels. Unless…

Cornelius shuddered. The very idea of humans evolving into a higher life-form was too horrible to contemplate. He shrank back into his shadowy alcove and waited for the sounds of the coming attack. Perhaps another bloody victory would restore his elation.

* * *

Kurt stood in the hallway outside the computer room. His stomach fluttered like he was in free-fall. His heart hammered away in his chest. He unslung the nozzle of the flamethrower, wondering as he clicked the pilot light ignitor if it would even be of any use to him.

Behind him, Deus hissed as he sucked in a breath. "Holy gods, there's so many of them."

"Dirty sons of bitches," Max muttered. "Filthy fucking vermin."

An army of rats, far outnumbering those they'd already encountered, was assembled in the room. They sat on every available surface, packed side by side into every corner and atop the desks and chairs.

"There's so damn many of them," Kurt said. "Guess we can kiss any of that salvage goodbye."

Taurus put his meaty, calloused hand on Kurt's shoulder. "I think we should get the hell out of here, boss."

"Yeah, I think you're right," Kurt agreed. "Let's fall back to the dormitory."

The four men took two backwards steps, and then, as if acting on some silent signal, the rats spilled out of the room. They covered the space between themselves and the men in a furious charge, their claws skittering as they slipped and slid on the smooth floor. Kurt triggered a blast of fire, and the vanguard of rats burst into flame. But the next wave charged through the mass of burning bodies without hesitation. Kurt ripped off a second blast, sending more of the rats to a fiery grave. Beside him, the other men opened fire with their pistols. They were a good marksmen, especially at such close range, but there weren't enough bullets in their entire ammo supply to kill the hundreds of rats charging at them. Kurt knew he couldn't burn all of them either. Already the pressure from the fuel tank was slackening. The gout of flame roaring out of the nozzle was growing shorter with each blast. Soon, they'd be overwhelmed by the sheer number of rats.

He'd seen enough. He shouted the order to retreat, then turned and ran for the stairwell with the other three men following close behind. His thoughts were less about his own safety and more about Diana. He *had* to get back to her.

He threw open the doorway to the stairwell and paused on the landing. Taurus was the first to follow him through the door. The big man's chest was already heaving from exertion. Deprived of sleep, his normally superhuman endurance was nearly exhausted. But he'd managed to make it to the stairs uninjured. Max and Deus weren't so lucky.

The holy man stumbled onto the landing with one rat attached to his right leg and another clawing its way up his chest. He flailed blindly and then fell down the stairs. Kurt shouldered his way past Taurus to help the mystic, who was screaming a steady torrent of curses at the pair of rats biting and clawing at his flesh.

"Get up there and close that door as soon as Max comes through!" he shouted to Taurus as he took the steps two at a time.

Deus had come to rest on the landing between the two flights of stairs. He'd managed to dislodge the rat from his chest and was busy trying to strangle it. The rodent thrashed madly, desperate to free itself from the hands encircling its neck. Its tail swiped back and forth, catching Kurt on the face like a whip as he stooped to pry the rat off Deus' leg.

He grabbed the rat's rear flank and pulled. The rodent was latched on, and all Kurt was accomplishing was helping it rip a chunk out of Deus' calf muscle. He let go of the rat just long enough to change tactics. This time, he grabbed the enraged animal by its head, pressing his thumbs against its eyes. The rat squealed in pain as Kurt's thumbs pressed harder and harder.

"Let go, you ugly motherfucker!" Kurt screamed.

He dug in as hard as he could. The rat's eyes burst, squirting hot jelly over Kurt's hands. But still, its jaws held fast to Deus' leg. Hands slick with gore, Kurt managed to hold on and press his thumbs even deeper until he was certain the squishy resistance they encountered was the creature's brain. Finally, the rat let go. Its body shook with violent spasms, dislodging Kurt's thumbs from the depths of its skull. Its body hit the floor with a heavy thump. It stumbled blindly in a circle as its life ebbed away, then collapsed at Kurt's feet.

There was no time to breathe a sigh of relief. By the sound of things, Taurus and Max were in trouble. Kurt bent and offered Deus his hand. He hauled the holy man to his feet, and they moved back up the upper flight of stairs, into the midst of a frenzied battle.

So many rats had swarmed Max and latched onto him that it was nearly impossible to see the man beneath their undulating bodies. It looked like Max was wearing a black fur coat made of reanimated animals. From somewhere beneath that heaving mass of glossy fur, he screamed like a man engulfed in flames.

Taurus was doing his best to dislodge the layers of rats, using his hands to rip them away from Max. They came away with bloody mouthfuls of meat, screeching with animal fury as Taurus flung them against the wall. The force of the impact against the concrete wall stunned the oversized rodents for a moment, but they soon recovered and resumed their attack, this time focusing on Taurus. They attached themselves by claws and teeth to his legs. Others clambered over them to find purchase higher on his body.

"Damn it!" Kurt shouted as he holstered his flame

thrower. In the enclosed space, a single burst of flame would spell death for both men.

"This is madness!" Deus proclaimed, his eyes wide as he took in the horrific display.

Kurt knew that Taurus' efforts to save Max were futile. The screams coming from beneath the rats had grown feeble. Blood flowed over the rats and dripped onto the floor.

"Taurus, get away from him!" he shouted.

The big man refused. He continued to rip the rats away from Max, but each one he tore free was another that attacked him. They were up to his waist now. In moments, they'd be all over him.

Deus grabbed Kurt's arm and said, "They are beyond saving. You know this to be true."

Kurt shook his head, although he knew Deus' conclusion was the only rational one.

Max stumbled then collapsed. As his body fell, some of the rats detached from him in mid-air, launching themselves at Taurus. Max was dead before his body hit the floor. The rats refocused their efforts on Taurus, leaving behind a corpse that had been almost entirely stripped of flesh. Kurt winced as two rats peeled away from Max's face, leaving behind a bloody red skull that stared with lidless torn eyes. Now, it was Taurus who shrieked and flailed. The big man had almost disappeared beneath the swarming rats.

"Be merciful," Deus urged. "You must do it."

Kurt drew the nozzle of the flamethrower out of its holster, clicked the ignitor switch, and doused the entire stairwell with a steady blast of fire. Flames engulfed the dead and dying men, as well as the rats. The shrieks and screams, both human and rodent, gave way to sizzle and crackle of burning flesh. Kurt shot one last burst of fire, just to be sure, then put away his weapon.

"It is done," Deus proclaimed.

"Come on." Kurt turned away from the aftermath. "Let's get the fuck out of here."

* * *

Duke locked the door, jiggling the knob a few times just to make sure, then wiped his hands on his pants and got to work. He heaved Rosemary's unconscious body onto the cot. She was heavier than she looked, especially when she was wearing heavy boots and layers of clothing. But that was a problem he could solve quite easily. He untied her boots and tugged them off her feet.

"Don't do it, Duke. Please don't," Myrna whimpered.

She was seated on the floor, her wrists bound behind her back. Duke had used his belt to secure her to the leg of one of the cots. She'd been docile enough when he tied her up. At first, he'd thought she'd slipped into catatonia after the last rat attack, but ever since he'd tied her up, she'd been gradually coming back to life.

Duke glared at her. "Shut up, bitch, or I'll gag you. Besides, you should feel lucky. You have a front row seat to the consummation of a marriage between a king and his queen."

Duke checked on Diana. She was still comatose, her breathing so shallow that at first glance he thought she might be dead. He considered tying her up, but decided it didn't matter. Kurt's bitch was probably dying, and besides, he was eager to get down to business.

"You're crazy. Just listen to yourself. You've gone fucking mad," Myrna said. Her voice was still slurred as she shook off the remnants of her daze.

Duke ignored her and got to work stripping his bride of her filthy clothes. He wished he could bathe her in warm, perfumed water as he prepared her to receive his carnal blessing. But such luxuries would come in time. His arousal grew increasingly feverish with each article of clothing he removed. A line of drool hung from his quivering bottom lip. It broke loose and dripped into the space between her breasts.

"Yes, my queen…" he moaned.

Rosemary was still unconscious as she lay gloriously naked before him. His greedy gaze moved over her from head to toe, lingering on her perfectly formed breasts and the thatch of dark hair between her legs. He kicked off his boots and unbuttoned his pants. With his belt already missing, they slipped away from his waist and slid to the floor. He sighed as his erection sprang free. He did an awkward dance to kick his feet out of his pants.

"Don't do this, Duke. There's still time for you to stop this," Myrna whimpered.

"This is your final warning. Shut your fucking mouth," Duke growled. He looked at Diana, swaddled in her shroud of bloody bandages and said, "I wish you'd wake up, so you could witness how a real man takes a woman. If you manage to survive those rat bites, maybe I'll let you be one of my concubines."

There were noises coming from upstairs. It sounded like screaming. And in his mind, he could hear the thoughts of hundreds of vicious, bloodthirsty rats.

Good, Duke thought. *Let the rats do my work for me.*

Rosemary stirred, but her eyes remained closed, even when Duke spread her legs. Eager as he was to bury himself inside her, he took a moment to admire her tender parts. Later, they'd have time to explore each other's bodies fully, but tonight, their consummation had to be swift. Afterwards, he'd deal with Kurt and the other fools. And then, he'd stroll triumphantly out of the city, with his queen at his side. Or perhaps they'd stay, and convert this building into a palace fit for royalty. The future was wide open and full of thrilling possibilities.

Myrna screamed.

Duke considered making good on his threat to gag her but decided he actually enjoyed the sound of her distress. It added an extra layer of excitement to the proceedings. He lowered himself onto the cot and situated himself between Rosemary's legs. Just as drew in a deep breath and prepared to force himself inside his queen, her eyelids began to flutter. Her hand reached up to touch his face as her eyes opened. Her hand slipped between their bodies.

"Yes, you want this," Duke moaned as he felt her fingers wrap around his stiff penis.

She smiled. "Is that what you think?"

Her grip tightened until Duke gasped. Then he screamed in shock and pain as she wrenched her hand sideways. Agony sheared through his body as she bent his engorged member.

He was certain in that moment that she was going to snap it like a twig. He howled in pain and outrage as she continued to pull and twist. Forget snapping it like a twig, she was trying to rip it right off his body. He wanted to pull away, but the pain had sapped his strength. Instead, he slumped forward and fell against her.

"I think this partnership has gone bad," she growled.

Duke's screams rose in pitch and volume until they matched those coming from Myrna.

Rosemary smashed her forehead into the bridge of his nose. Duke felt bones crunch under the impact. Her thighs tightened around his waist, and she rolled to one side, throwing him off like a wrestler avoiding a pin.

Duke clawed at the floor, desperate to crawl away as blood spilled from his crushed nose. Through his tear-blurred vision, he could see the doorknob moving. Kurt and the other men had returned.

"No getting out of this one, Duke," Rosemary said, stepping in front of him.

He stared at her feet for a moment, then lifted his head to

gaze up at her. Even now, he could see her as nothing but beautiful. And that's why he hesitated for a fraction of a second before darting forward on his hands and knees to grab at her legs. She yelped, shocked at his sudden burst of strength, and went down heavily.

Gritting his teeth against the waves of pain radiating from his dick and his nose, Duke managed to get to his feet. He staggered across the room to the door. Drawing on his last reserves of strength, he turned the lock and wrenched open the door.

Only Kurt and Deus stood there. Their clothes were blood-splattered and singed by fire. Their mouths hung open in shock. Kurt hesitated for a fraction of a second before making a grab

for Duke, and that was enough for Duke to throw himself at the men. He knocked Deus to the floor, and caught Kurt in the ribs with an elbow.

Screaming peals of mad laughter, Duke dashed past the two men. His entire naked body throbbed with pain as he ran into through the kitchen and into the lobby. Fragments of glass and other debris bit into the soles of his feet, but he didn't slow his pace. Although his queen had denied him his rights as her king, Duke was still assured of his royal status. In time, he'd return to claim what was rightfully his.

Cornelius stepped carefully through the still-smoldering corpses of rats and humans. It appeared that his army had sustained heavy losses, but they were still firmly in the realm of the acceptable. After all, two more humans, both of them seasoned fighters, had fallen during the skirmish. Now it was time to regroup and prepare for another offensive.

He descended the staircase and emerged from the doorway just in time to see a naked human male dart through the lobby. As he ran, the human howled vocalizations that could have signified mirth or pain or even a mad mixture of both. The sound echoed through the empty room. It raised the fur on Cornelius' back. But the jagged cries tearing themselves out of the human disturbed Cornelius far less than the psychic babble that crept into his mind.

HAIL DUKE GOD OF MAN AND RAT HAIL THE NEW KING LONG MAY HE REIGN ABOVE ALL CREATURES OF THE EARTH HAIL DUKE HAIL DUKE HAIL THE NEW KING…

Cornelius pressed a hand to his forehead and tried to block his psychic channels but found he could not.

Very well, he thought. *I'll deal with this human pest once and for all.*

He walked through the lobby, scanning the alcoves and corners for the human. It didn't take long to find him. The human, this mad king named Duke, was cowering beneath the desk at the center of the room. Naked and bleeding, with round eyes open wide, Duke was babbling a steady stream of vocalizations that matched his crazed psychic stream of consciousness.

A few stragglers from Cornelius army ventured into the room, their curiosity no doubt aroused by the human's blast of strange thoughts. They gathered behind Cornelius, intrigued and amused by the sight of the naked human.

So you are the human who has learned to speak with his mind, Cornelius projected as he stepped behind the desk.

The human's inane psychic babble stopped abruptly as he stared up at Cornelius.

Holy fuck, you are one big rat, Duke replied. *Why the fuck are you walking on two legs? And come to think of it, why do you have arms and legs instead of those stubby appendages like all the other rats?*

Because I'm no rat, Cornelius explained. *I'm a Colonist, a member of a race superior to your own. And among the Colonists, I am a conqueror.*

I'm the king of the rats, Duke projected. *Bow before your king, you giant rodent!*

You're quite insane. Your human brain simply couldn't accommodate psychic communication. It's as fascinating as it is pathetic.

Duke squeezed his eyes shut. He pressed his hands against his temples and projected another string of inanities. *DIE EXPLODE AND DIE YOU BIG FUCKING RAT JUST DIE JUST EXPLODE AND DIE AND VOMIT UP YOUR GUTS AND DIE YOU BIG FUCKING RAT…*

Cornelius had gotten his fill of nonsense. He gave the order for his soldiers to attack. Although there were only four of them, Duke was naked and wounded, not to mention quite insane. Four soldiers should be more than enough to deal with him.

The quartet of rats sprang at Duke. They should have landed atop him with claws slashing and teeth bared, but as Cornelius watched, something inexplicable took place. The rats shuddered in mid-leap. Their psychic links severed abruptly, like lines of thread snipped by scissors. They fell heavily to the floor beside Duke, stone dead.

Now this is curious indeed, Cornelius thought as he watched Duke shove the dead rats aside and rise to his bloody feet.

Duke stared at Cornelius. A vein stood out on the center of the human's forehead. He bit his lower lip so hard that it bled. At his sides, his hands clenched into fists. Cornelius realized that Duke was trying to employ whatever psychic trick he'd used to kill the four soldiers. He felt a faint tickle at the front of his brain. His heart skipped a beat. But that was all.

No! Duke's projection was like an enraged scream. *I am your king and I order you to die! Die like the other rats! Die! Die!*

Die! DIE YOU MOTHERFUCKER JUST DIE JUST DIE JUST DIE!!!

Cornelius took a step back, standing clear of the madman as he staggered in a slow circle.

I'm no rat, Cornelius reminded him.

But it was no use trying to reason. Duke's mind, already feverish with madness, was dissolving into a psychic stew. His thoughts had become entirely incoherent.

I'M THE KING THE GOD ROSEMARY MY QUEEN MY WHORE I'M THE KING THE GOD OF RATS!!!

Duke stopped his strange, drunken dance and faced Cornelius. The human stared with bulging eyes. His lips compressed into a thin line as a low growl rose up in his chest. Again, Cornelius felt a slight tingle, but nothing beyond that. Duke's face grew red. He shook violently, his body wracked with tremors. Blood leaked from his eyes and ears.

Gods above, Cornelius marveled.

Duke's forehead split open with a sound like wet fabric being torn. A faint crack appeared in the slick surface of his exposed skull. And then, like an egg breaking, the crack widened steadily until a jelly of liquefied brains ran down his face. One final spasm seized Duke's body, and then he collapsed to the floor, dead.

Cornelius shook his head. He'd seen all he needed from these humans. It was well past time to wage one final assault on them.

* * *

Kurt took two steps in pursuit of Duke, then stopped. There was no point wasting any more energy on that bastard. He was naked and bleeding. And he was charging into a space that would soon be choked with giant killer rats. Duke was as good as dead. There were more pressing matters that required

Kurt's attention. He pulled Deus into the room and shut the door behind him.

Still naked, Rosemary crossed the room and untied Myrna.

"Come on, girl," Rosemary said. "You're okay. We still got miles to go before we can rest."

The two men politely averted their eyes while Rosemary got dressed.

"Okay, boys, I'm decent now," she said. Once they'd turned back around, she asked, "Where's Taurus and Max?"

Kurt shook his head. "They didn't make it."

Rosemary raised an eyebrow. "Rats?"

"Yeah," Kurt said. "Fucking rats got both of them."

"Then I guess we got our answer about Lord Hannibal's precious tech gadgets," she said.

Kurt sat down on the edge of Diana's cot. He touched her forehead gingerly and winced. She was burning up with fever. Her breathing was still steady, but it was so shallow that her chest barely rose with each raspy inhalation. The crusty bandages crisscrossing her arms and torso had begun to leak yellow pus around their edges.

"How's she doing?" Rosemary asked, dropping a hand onto his shoulder.

Kurt shook his head. "Not good."

Deus and Myrna stood on the other side of the cot. The holy man muttered prayers and used his fingers to trace mystic symbols in the air while Myrna chewed a thumbnail.

Kurt stroked Diana's forehead, moving a lock of hair away from her eyes, then stood up. He motioned for the others to follow him as he made his way to the opposite side of the room. Although he was fairly sure Diana wasn't aware of their presence, he didn't want to discuss their dire circumstances at her bedside. He paused to pry the lid off one of the food containers. If they had to fight their way out of this city, they might as well do it on full bellies.

"Might as well eat some of this stuff," he said. "We sure as hell can't carry it."

They sat in a circle on the floor and ate canned fruit and drank the juice. They ripped open vacuum-sealed packages of dried meat and devoured the contents. No one spoke as they ate. It was a grim picnic.

When the first mouthful of mixed fruit in sugar syrup hit Kurt's tongue, he realized how hungry he was. He practically inhaled the first can before moving on to a carton of roasted nuts. He ate them by the handful, washing them down with the juice from another can of fruit.

"Okay," Kurt said, wiping his mouth with the back of his hand. "Here's the situation. As far as salvage goes, we're fucked. The computer room is completely overrun. Lord Hannibal won't be pleased, but that's a bridge we'll cross when we come to it. Right now, we have to think about survival. From now on, we stick together. Otherwise, we're going to be hunted to extinction."

Chapter Twenty-Six
Behold, The Prophecy Of Doom Is Fulfilled

Diana fell deeper and deeper into the black abyss of sleep. Her dreaming mind knew, via some strange sixth sense, that her living body was wracked with pain and dying. But felt no discomfort. Her body was far away, in another world. In that waking world, she was feverish and covered with bloody bandages, but here, she felt fine. Unencumbered by her injured flesh, she drifted through layers of velvet darkness. The lifeline tethering her dream self to her body was thin and fraying. She was tempted to sever it altogether and leave the world and all its strife and suffering behind. But Kurt was still back there, and she needed to see him one last time before she let go.

She stopped her free-fall and swam upwards through the darkness. The waking world was a pinprick of light far above her. As she continued her ascent, the pinprick grew steadily larger until it was near enough to bathe her face in warmth. She stepped into the light, back into her failing body.

Eyes still closed, she heard the voices of her friends. They were engaged in a discussion about whether it was best to search the building for medical supplies or to take their chances making for the nearest outpost. There was a thin veneer of bravery in their voices, but it covered a growing undertone of despair. None of them could acknowledge what Diana already knew to be true: she wasn't ever going to leave this room. And if her friends insisted on taking her with them, they would surely die too. The only way for them to have any hope of escape was to move swiftly out of the city. Burdened with a dying woman, that would be an impossibility.

She drew in as deep a breath as her failing lungs could manage, then opened her eyes. Her vision was blurry, and she blinked a few times in an attempt to clear it, but the cloudiness remained. Her eyes were giving up the fight, it seemed.

She tried for another deep breath but only succeeding in triggering a coughing fit. The sound drew the others to her side. Kurt knelt beside the cot and took her hand. He touched her face and whispered reassurances, but his voice sounded distant and faint. No matter, she didn't need to hear the words to know what he wanted to tell her. She raised her free hand and pressed her fingers to his lips.

When she spoke, her voice came out in a raspy whisper. "I can see it now, the light at the end of everything. It's beautiful…"

"No. No, darling." Kurt shook his head.

Her eyelids fluttered. She fought to keep them from closing, certain that if they did, she'd never be able to open them again. "It's okay…"

"We'll get you out of here," Kurt replied, squeezing her hand. "You'll be okay. We'll find a way, just like we always do."

"Kurt…" That single syllable was all she could manage before a coughing fit shook her wounded body. Flecks of foamy spittle shot from her mouth. She forced air into her aching lungs and said, "I love you. I want you to survive this."

He shook his head again. "Not without you."

She tried to smile. "It doesn't hurt anymore."

"Diana, stay with me," Kurt pleaded.

This time, when her eyelids fluttered and grew heavy, she let them close. She relaxed, exhaling one final breath, and then slipped into the warm darkness. There was no more pain. There was no more anything.

* * *

Deus said the prayers while Rosemary zipped the sleeping bag over Diana's head in an improvised shroud. Deus closed his eyes and bowed his head, his chin touching his chest as he meditated. Or whatever it was that holy men did when they stood over the dying and the dead. Rosemary didn't really know what he was doing, and she didn't much care. She was more concerned with Kurt.

Their fearless leader, as Duke had called him, was standing in the center of the room, staring into the middle distance. His eyes, normally bright with adventure and ambition, were empty. His shoulders sagged, as if each of his hands held a heavy weight.

Shit, Rosemary thought, giving him, and their situation as a whole, an honest appraisal. *Pure fucking shit. But at least he's stopped crying.*

She turned to look at Myrna.

Not much better than Kurt, Rosemary decided. *That girl has lost her grip. Maybe if we can get her out of here, she'll bounce back. Maybe not.*

She took a deep breath to steady her nerves and crossed the room to stand beside Kurt. She put a hand on his shoulder, giving it a gentle squeeze. If there was something fitting to say, some proper sequence of words that could offer any comfort, she would have said them. But she knew better. There was nothing she could say that would make this situation any better. So she settled for stating the obvious.

"I know you're hurting, man. But you know we can't afford to stay here in mourning. We have to push ahead."

Kurt turned his head slowly. He regarded her with that empty stare. For a moment, Rosemary was afraid she'd lost him. Maybe he was drifting into the same detached state where Myrna had set up camp. But then, Kurt nodded. It was slight, no more than a couple quick dips of his chin, but it was better than nothing.

"So what do you think?" she asked. "Do we wait for first light or do we make a run for it right now? You're still the boss, but you want my opinion, I vote for making our move as soon as possible."

Kurt blinked a few times, like a man awakening from a deep sleep. He squared his shoulders, preparing to say something, but Deus chose that exact moment to end his silent meditation and resume his proclamations of doom.

"This is the end of everything," the holy man intoned in his best prophet-of-the-apocalypse voice. "The hunter has become the hunted, and a cataclysm that will make the Event pale in comparison has come round at last. The final judgment of the gods! The rats shall inherit the planet!"

Rosemary groaned. She knew what was coming, but she was unwilling to stop it. She'd had more than her fill of Deus' bullshit. Time was of the essence when it came to making their escape, but she knew Kurt couldn't move forward without addressing this nonsense once and for all.

Kurt crossed the space between himself and Deus in three angry strides. He drew back his fist and swung. The blow caught the holy man on the side of the face. The impact was strong enough to spin Deus' entire body around in a half circle. It was a decisive punch, the kind that could usually end a fight before it really began. But Kurt wasn't done. As Deus reeled in pain and shock, Kurt threw another punch to the holy man's gut. Deus yelped as Kurt drove his fist in. The air whooped out of his lungs. Still, Kurt wasn't done. As Deus doubled over, Kurt grabbed the back of Deus' head. Kurt smashed his knee into Deus' face.

Rosemary winced at the sound of Deus' nose breaking. As she watched Deus reel backwards like a man delirious with strong drugs or drink, she wondered how long she could allow this to continue. She took a hesitant step forward, steeling her nerves to enter the fray, but Kurt saved her the trouble. He gave Deus one last shove, knocking him to the floor. Then he raised his hands as he turned to look at Rosemary.

"It's okay," he said. "I'm done."

Deus stayed down. He may have been stubborn and unbending in his religious beliefs, but he knew when he'd been beaten. He propped himself up on his elbows, coughing as he struggled to catch his breath. Once he'd managed that feat, he stuck a probing finger into his mouth. He pulled the finger out and spat a wad of thick blood onto the floor. A tooth came with it.

Rosemary stepped between the two men. She gave Kurt one last look to make sure he was really done, then she offered her hand to Deus and hauled him to his feet.

"You had that one coming," she told him. "If Kurt hadn't done it, I might have done it myself. You cool or do I have to worry about keeping you two separated? Cause I'm telling you right now, I ain't going to be nobody's babysitter."

Deus shook his head. He extended a hand to Kurt, like he was looking for a handshake.

"Kurt, my friend, I-"

He was saved the awkwardness of reconciliation by a squeal of rusting hinges.

The door open to admit a frenzied rodent army. Their squeals were so loud and insistent that they sounded to Rosemary's ears like the shrieks of the mutant berserkers the team had encountered in the forest. Had it only been a few days ago? Rosemary's brain reeled.

Myrna sat bolt upright on her cot and screamed. She sprang off the sagging mattress and waded into the flood of rats. She drew her pistol and fired indiscriminately at the horde of furry black bodies. Her bullets found their mark, but the stream of rats was seemingly endless.

Back from the edge of despair, Kurt sprang into action. He shouldered the flamethrower and reduced dozens of rats to screeching balls of fire. But two more bursts of fire drained the last bits of fuel, and the flamethrower sputtered then quit. Kurt shrugged out the cumbersome fuel tank and dropped it. Kicking his way through the rats, he dragged the metal food storage boxes across the floor, positioning them beneath the skylight.

"What the fuck?" Rosemary said as she joined Myrna's efforts to stem the tide of rodents pouring into the dormitory.

But as she paused to reload her pistol, she saw exactly what he had in mind. Apparently, Deus had figured it out as well. He helped Kurt stack the metal boxes one on top of the other, wheezing bloody air through his broken nose.

Kurt lashed out with one booted foot, sending a rat airborne. "Keep them off us long enough to stack these damn boxes and we'll climb out of here!"

"We're trying, boss!" Rosemary replied. "But unless you got some secret stash of ammo, you better move your ass, because we're about to run out of bullets."

It wasn't an exaggeration. She was down to her last magazine. Eight more shots and her pistol wouldn't be much more than a paperweight. Beside her, Myrna had come to the same conclusion. She fired her pistol until the hammer clicked on an empty chamber, then growled in frustration. But her next course of action shocked Rosemary to her core.

"Get the fuck out of here!" Myrna screeched, shoving

Rosemary aside. "Climb out of this fucking hellhole and never look back!"

Moments ago, Myrna had seemed to teeter on the edge of catatonia. Now, she'd transformed into an angel of vengeance, screaming with blind rage as she waded into the middle of the rodent swarm. Rosemary fired her last shot, then holstered her weapon. She backed away from the scene unfolding in front of her, unable to tear her eyes from the spectacle of Myrna's sudden descent into berserker fury.

It was unlike anything Rosemary had ever witnessed. Sure, she'd seen people wade into the midst of violent chaos. In this post-Event world, violence was simply a fact of life. But even so, the level of blood-thirst and unbridled fury on display here was awesome to behold. As fast as the rats could climb up her legs, Myrna tore them away, snapping their necks with her bare hands. They bit and clawed at her as they climbed over her body, but she seemed not to notice, even as blood poured from the thousand fresh wounds opened on every part of her body. One rat managed to crawl onto Myrna's face. She chomped down onto the soft flesh of its belly with her teeth. The rat screeched in pain and surprise, thrashing its limbs as Myrna bit down harder. She shook her head like a terrier with a rabbit caught in its jaws. With one final twist of her neck, Myrna flung the rat into the air. Thin loops of intestine unspooled from the hole she'd bitten in the rat's belly. Her hands tore into the rats' bodies, even as they clamped their jaws onto her flesh. All the while, Myrna screamed a string of incoherent curses.

The girl has fucking lost it, she thought. *No, that ain't right. She hasn't lost a damn thing. She's found something. Here, at the end of her rope, she's found one last burst.*

"Don't fucking stare at me," Myrna growled, turning aside from the carnage just long enough to look at Rosemary. "Get your asses out of here!"

Rosemary didn't have an opportunity to argue. Kurt

grabbed a handful of her shirt and dragged her out of the melee. He shoved her towards the makeshift staircase of stacked food crates.

"You're first up the ladder!" he shouted. "Go!"

Rosemary planted her foot on the bottom crate and levered herself off the floor. The entire arrangement wobbled beneath her, but it held fast as she ascended towards the edge of the skylight. There were jagged fragments of broken glasses still embedded in the edges of the hole in the roof. They dug into her palms as she hauled herself through the opening. Warm blood ran down her forearms, but she held on, pulling herself up and up, out of the chaos below.

* * *

"Behold, the prophecy of doom is fulfilled," Deus said as he climbed through the opening and collapsed on the rooftop next to Kurt and Rosemary. He raised his hands, just in case Kurt still felt angry enough to strike him again. But Kurt seemed too spent to lash out.

"Myrna?" Rosemary asked, rolling over on the gravel surface to peer through the skylight into the dormitory room below.

Deus shook his head. "Alas, our sister has fallen to the enemy."

"Fuck," Kurt pronounced, then hauled himself to his feet. He reached down to help Rosemary up.

"She fought as bravely as any warrior who ever lived," Deus said. "Even as the beasts dragged her to the ground and devoured her, she struck back at them. She tore them limb from limb until her heart gave out. Truly, she made the noblest of sacrifices, laying down her life so that we all might live. The gods shall receive her with open arms."

"Great," Kurt muttered. "That's just fucking great. I'm overjoyed that the gods have someone to embrace."

Deus knew Kurt was mocking his words, but he didn't mind. Soon, they would all be with the gods, and perhaps then, at last, Deus would be understood. Until then, he would have to content himself with the knowledge that this world of sin would soon be torn asunder. He stood next to his old friends, all three of them picking shards of glass from their bloody palms. They tossed the bloody bits of glass through the skylight to the squealing, screeching crowd of rodents below.

"Bastards," Kurt snorted. He leaned over the edge and spat a wad of phlegm at the rats. "Yeah, you got that right," Rosemary agreed. "I don't know about you guys, but I'm out of ammo. Gun's pretty useless unless I use it to beat those fucking rats to death with it."

Kurt shook his head. "I'm empty. I had to drop the flamethrower when I was climbing. Too fucking heavy. Or maybe I'm too fucking tired. Take your pick. After Diana..." He shook his head again. "I don't know."

"Those rats," Rosemary said, "there's so damn many of them."

On that score, Deus agreed. The rats were legion, and there would be many more to follow. It was their world now. Beneath the surface of the planet, something terrible was happening. Deus could feel it in his soul. A shift had occurred in the fundamental nature of the world. These rats were the heralds of a new age.

"Come on," Kurt said, pulling Deus and Rosemary away from the skylight. "There has to be a way off this roof."

"Okay, and then what?" Rosemary asked. "We're out of ammo. Our bikes are fucked."

Kurt shrugged. "Our legs still work. We haul ass out of here. If we make it to an outpost, my credit is still good. We arm up and come back here and send these fucking rats back to hell where they belong."

Deus couldn't help but smile. Truly, the human spirit was

an amazing thing. Against all odds, Kurt was ready to fight on, to forge ahead, to keep pushing. And judging by her posture and the confident set of her jaw, Rosemary was ready to follow him. It was simply amazing.

Deus wished he could be swayed by Kurt's confidence, but unfortunately, he was quite beyond that. The prophecy of doom had been fulfilled, after all. The courage and determination of man was dust in the wind compared to the will of the gods. And yet, Deus loved his friends, unbeliever though they were.

"In the library at the monastery, I once perused a book about ancient architecture," he said. "On buildings such as this, the structures of the great cities, often had attached to their sides ladders or stairways. Our forefathers used them to escape from fires or other calamities. We should search for one of these contraptions."

Kurt nodded. "See, I knew you'd prove yourself useful at some point."

"I'm proud to be of service," Deus said, touching his tattooed forehead.

The two men shared a momentary look. It was little more than a glance, but in that glance, a thousand or more words were spoken. They clapped each other on the shoulder.

"Right," Kurt said. "Let's find a way off this roof."

* * *

Cornelius seethed with barely contained fury as he stalked through the dormitory. The enemy had been outnumbered. Their weapons supply had been nearly exhausted. And yet, his soldiers had failed to dispatch them. Of the remaining four humans, three had escaped. His troops—hundreds of them—had been thwarted by a single human female. It was unacceptable.

One of the soldiers detached itself from the mass of its

fellows and scampered along beside Cornelius as he stalked through the room. Its primitive thought projections offered up a slew of excuses for the failure.

Strong she was strong and angry and felt no pain so strong brave she fought us without weapons...

Cornelius wasn't in the mood for excuses. He bent and scooped the soldier off the floor. Cradling it in his arms, Cornelius stared into its beady eyes for a moment before raising it above his head so that the rest of the assembled soldiers could see it.

Your father is displeased, he projected. *Look here and see the wages of failure.*

Cornelius squeezed, digging his claws into the squealing soldier's abdomen. Blood ran down Cornelius' arms and dripped onto his face as he tore into the soft, hairy belly. He twisted, snapping the lowly creature's spine, then cast it aside. He towered over the platoon of terrified soldiers.

Outside the building and onto the roof, he commanded.

For the first time, the thoughts of his soldiers carried a note of uncertainty. Although they were skilled climbers, the building's walls were mostly flat and offered their claws scant purchase. Surely many of them would fall as they struggled to scale the stone walls. But nevertheless, they filed out of the room.

Cornelius sneered as he watched them go. He closed his eyes and sent out thought projections to all corners of the building, indeed to all corners of the city. He summoned his entire force for a final assault. It was time to end this engagement and move on to bigger things. These humans had proven themselves a worthy adversary, but it was well past the time they should be swatted down like the pests they were.

* * *

Deus found the escape mechanism on the southern side of the roof. It was a small platform of wrought metal bolted onto the stone wall. There was a retractable ladder made of similar material attached to the platform. His heart leapt at the sight, but sank as he tried to shake the ladder loose from its housing and slide it to the ground below. Centuries of disuse had seemingly fused its hinges together, and try as he might, Deus couldn't dislodge it.

"Come on with that ladder, Deus," Kurt called from the other side of the roof. "Because we're about to have company."

"It's stuck!" he cried, frantically working at the release lever. But it wouldn't budge.

"Oh shit," Rosemary groaned. "What do we do now?"

Deus climbed back over the ledge and trotted across the loose gravel. He came to a stop beside Kurt and followed his line of sight over the edge of the building. The sight his eyes beheld was enough to cause his breath to catch in his chest. He touched his forehead and both sides of his chest, genuflecting.

"Gods above," he whispered.

A horde of rats—thousands upon thousands—was clawing its way up the stone walls. Their claws scrabbled for purchase, digging into the soft spots that centuries had eroded. Many of them fell, plummeting to the street below. Those whose bodies broke against the concrete lay there, writhing in pain as wave after wave of their fellows scrambled over them. Those who survived the fall picked themselves up and climbed with renewed vigor. Although none had made it to the roof's ledge, Deus knew it was only a matter of time.

He turned to Kurt and said, "Go to the platform and work the ladder free. I will hold back this unholy army for as long as I can."

The two friends shared another look, this one just as meaningful as the last. Kurt extended his hand.

"It has been a long road, my friend," he said.

Deus looked down at the proffered hand, then batted it aside before drawing Kurt into an embrace.

"Go in the name of the gods," Deus said, thumping Kurt on the back. "And never forget that greater glory awaits us beyond the reach of this sinful world."

Kurt pulled away. "If—no, *when* I get that ladder down, you'll follow us."

"Of course I will," Deus said. It was a lie, but he believed the gods would forgive him. If not, perhaps they weren't worthy of worship after all. "But first, I'm going to hold them off as long as I can. So don't wait for me. When the ladder descends, flee and don't look back. I'll be right behind you, just like always."

Kurt nodded. The look he gave Deus was full of understanding. He knew the score. A good leader always did, and Deus knew that Kurt was among the best.

"The gods will smile upon you," Kurt said, then grabbed Rosemary and dragged her away from the horrific sight of thousands of oversized rats scaling the wall.

Deus dug into the inner pocket of his tunic and withdrew the small leather pouch containing what remained of his supply of the Black Drug. He pressed his nose into the pouch and snorted hard, taking in as much of the coarsely ground powder as he could. He repeated the act until the pouch was empty, then tossed it aside. In moments, the drug hit his bloodstream, and the effect was overwhelming. The sounds of the world—the screeching of the rat army and the metallic clang of Kurt working the ladder loose—faded into the background until all Deus could hear was the beating of his heart and the steady whoosh of air flowing in and out of his lungs.

Bright colors streaked past his eyes like starbursts trailing comets. The washed-out grey of the cityscape gave way to a dazzling kaleidoscope. Quiet strength flowed downwards from the heavens and into his body.

The gods were with him.

Deus smiled as he stepped onto the roof ledge. He spread his arms wide, beckoning the rats to him.

"This is a good day to die," he said as the first rat reached its paws over the edge of the roof. Deus laughed and kicked it squarely on the snout. For a fraction of a second, the rat seemed to hang in midair, its forepaws clawing madly at nothing. Then gravity took hold and sucked the squealing rodent to the concrete below. Deus was certain that he could hear its bones shatter upon impact.

The Black Drug lifted him to a higher plane of perception as it continued to disperse through his body. Time stretched and dilated. Deus moved back and forth over the ledge, unafraid of losing his balance. He moved with a dancer's grace, pausing here and there to kick the nearest rat. He sent them plummeting to their deaths.

But there were so many of them, and soon, his efforts were overwhelmed by the sheer volume of their attack. They were all over him, biting and clawing. When they'd torn his leg muscles to such a degree that they could no longer support his body, Deus collapsed backwards, falling flat on the rough layer of rooftop gravel. He battered at the rats with his fists. They bit him, and he responded with bites of his own, snapping his jaws like a rabid dog.

He felt no pain. The gods spared him that. Even when the rats clawed ragged holes in his abdomen and tunneled their way inside him, Deus felt only the blissful presence of the holy and eternal. He fought until his body surrendered, then lay there motionless, staring at the sky. The eastern edge of the horizon had begun to lighten. Its edges bled orange and pink as the sun started its daily climb. The dawn was coming, the first rays of sunrise knifing through the bottom edges of the long and gloomy night. They were the last thing Deus saw before the gods finally called him home.

* * *

Kurt's muscles ached from the effort, but he couldn't dislodge the ladder from its housing. Rosemary added her own strength and they pulled and tugged together. Sweat beaded on their foreheads. They grunted and growled curses, putting every bit of strength they could muster into the task. But centuries of rust and disuse had seemingly fused the ladder to the platform.

Their combined strength failed to budge it.

They slumped back on the platform, panting like sprinters at the end of a race. Their eyes met, sharing a truth they left unspoken. They'd reached the end of the road. Behind them, Deus was holding back the advancing tide of rats, but soon, they would overwhelm him.

"What do you think?" Rosemary asked, peering over the edge of the platform. "Should we jump?"

Kurt shook his head. "At this height, we'd be lucky if all we did was break our legs. Of course, if those rats get to us, maybe that might be preferable. I don't know."

They sat on the hard surface of the platform, their backs against the rough stone wall.

"So that's it, then?" Rosemary asked.

Kurt shrugged. "You got any better ideas, I'm open to suggestions."

"Shit, man," she sighed. "I always thought when I went out, it would be in a blaze of glory. And here we are with no fucking bullets."

Behind them, Deus screamed and screamed in pain and fury. Then, as abruptly as if a switch had been thrown, his voice was silenced. His screams were replaced by the squealing and chittering of a thousand rats. Their claws scratched as they scampered through the rooftop gravel.

Kurt scooted closer to Rosemary and took her hand. They closed their eyes and waited. Behind them, the oncoming rodent tide grew louder. Kurt squeezed his eyes shut tighter, bracing himself for the first bite.

I'm coming home to you, Diana, he thought.

But then, the squeals and squeaks of the rats began to take on a different character. Rather than enraged and full of bloodlust, they sounded panicked. And then, the unmistakable metallic tattoo of automatic weapons fire…

Kurt opened his eyes. "What the fuck?"

* * *

Cornelius was too engaged in savoring his moment of victory to notice the three figures making their way down the street. By the time he heard their approaching footsteps and turned to face them, it was too late to run away. He didn't give them the pleasure of a chase. Instead, he squared his shoulders and faced them.

The approaching trio wore full protective gear, complete with respirator masks and filtration units. They carried compact automatic rifles with high capacity magazines. The gear and the weapons were familiar to Cornelius. Both were of Colonial manufacture and were the type issued to the Colonial military. He reached to his side for a weapon that wasn't there. He was suddenly hyper aware of his nakedness. Although he was quite beyond shame, he wished that he could cover himself. The still, heavy air seemed to slip beneath his fur, chilling his skin. His lungs burned as he inhaled.

Don't move, Cornelius, the lead figure projected. *Your little revolution has failed. One of your loyal students betrayed you, and the rest followed. One by one, they gave us your whole operation. As we stand here, the Colonial Watch is rounding up the few stragglers. They'll be tried for sedition. But don't worry. I haven't changed my position on the death penalty. Most of them are just misguided children who can be rehabilitated. You, on the other hand...*

Welcome to the surface, Lorne, Cornelius replied. *But excuse me if I don't believe you. It no longer matters what you believe or don't believe.* Lorne stepped closer, keeping the barrel of his weapon trained on Cornelius' chest.

You always were so high and mighty. Impotent rage sluiced through Cornelius. He was naked and unarmed, caught out in the open by three heavily armed Colonists. The entirety of his army was engaged with the human combatants on the rooftop. His situation was quite hopeless. There was no way out of this. Triumph had been so close that he could taste it, but it had been taken from him.

There are human survivors, Lorne told his companions without looking away from Cornelius. *See that they're unharmed.*

And the rats?

Lorne took a second to consider, then answered, *Lower animals such as those are likely beyond our help. Use the gas if possible. There's no sense in being cruel.*

Understood.

The two figures behind Lorne broke from their loose formation and headed for the side of the building where the two remaining humans cowered on the fire escape platform.

You came all this way to rescue a pair of humans. Cornelius shook his head in disbelief. *I knew you were weak-willed and immoral, but I never thought you could sink this low.*

I didn't come all this way to save those humans, Lorne projected. *I came all this way to ensure that the Colony's security wasn't threatened by the likes of you. I never thought you could sink so low, brother. Standing here naked, commanding an army of the lowest caste...*

Even now, you speak as if you know everything. Cornelius sneered, baring his teeth. He struggled to block out the insistent chorus of his soldiers. Their battle cries had given way to panicked mental screams. Gunfire erupted on the rooftop. Cornelius clenched his fists, suddenly unable to close off the psychic channel he shared with his army.

I know enough, Lorne countered.

And what now? Cornelius' sneer widened, contorting his face into a hateful mask. *Am I to be marched back to the Colony to stand trial for my crimes? Suppose I were to tell a tale of sexual depravity carried out in secret by forces in the government. What then?*

Lorne shrugged. He let the sound of gunfire on the rooftop do all the talking.

* * *

Kurt stood up and cautiously peered over the ledge. His eyes were immediately stung by a mingling of cordite and some other, even more acrid gas. But what he saw was enough to make him ignore the discomfort.

"Holy fuck!" he exclaimed. "Rosemary, you gotta see this!"

She stood next to him, peering over the edge of the roof. She squinted her eyes and coughed, but like Kurt, she couldn't look away.

"I think we're saved," Kurt said, his voice full of mingled disbelief and hope.

A pair of figures, clad in bright yellow jumpsuits and respirator helmets, was methodically laying waste to the army of rats. One of the figures was wearing some sort of gas canister on its hip. A hose ran from the top of the canister to a nozzle, which the figure held in its gloved hand. A steady stream of thick, white gas poured from the nozzle. Heavier than air, this gas settled into a layer of fog that blanketed the rooftop. The other figure held a strange rifle. Whenever a rat lunged out of the poison clouds, this figure hit the rodent with a burst of rounds from the rifle. The muzzle fire flashed through the wisps of gas.

"That gas," Rosemary said, "it's killing them. Look!"

Kurt followed her line of sight to the far side of the roof, where the gas clouds had dissipated enough to reveal a patch of rooftop littered with the sleek black bodies of oversized rats. Some of them lay still, already dead. Others flopped around like landed fish, their claws scratching uselessly at the air as they tried in vain to breathe. Their wheezing and choking were audible, even when the rifle spat a burst of bullets at one of their hardier fellows. Some of the rats gave up on fighting back and raced for the edge of the roof. Blinded either by panic or by the gas fumes, they plummeted over the edge and splattered on the concrete below.

Finally, one of the figures noticed Kurt and Rosemary. It paused the slaughter just long enough to activate a switch on its belt. A mechanical voice called out from a shoulder-mounted speaker, "Take cover. In large enough amounts, this gas is poisonous to humans as well."

Kurt and Rosemary didn't argue. They sat back down on the metal platform, tugging their shirts over their mouths and noses to keep out as much of the gas as possible. Tears streamed down their cheeks, and they blinked, then closed their eyes. Behind and above them, the gagging and choking of a thousand dying rats gradually faded until it was gone altogether.

* * *

Cornelius glanced at the top of the building. Clouds of gas hung over the roof like low-lying fog. Starbursts of gunfire cut through the dense gas. Soldiers from Cornelius' revolutionary army fell over the roof ledge by the dozen.

They plunged to the concrete below, their bodies, swollen and bloated by the poison they'd inhaled, ruptured upon impact. The grey concrete gradually disappeared beneath a growing tide of gore.

Cornelius sighed and looked back at Lorne. *Now what?*

I don't know, Lorne answered. *Why don't you tell me what you think should happen to you? You betrayed the trust of the entire Colony. You attempted to overthrow our government.*

Cornelius tried to formulate an adequate answer and found himself incapable. He'd crossed a bridge then burned it to ashes. There was no chance of going home.

Lorne nodded. *That's right, brother. You'll never set foot in the Colony again.*

Well, then, Cornelius projected, *I guess you'd better get on with it.*

He expected another speech, perhaps something high and mighty with a touch of patriotism and a sprinkling of sentimentality. Lorne was, after all, a master of such nonsense, and Cornelius knew how much his fellow Councilor loved a captive audience. But Lorne surprised him. Without another word, he pulled the trigger, emptying the rifle's magazine into Cornelius' torso.

Cornelius was so shocked by the suddenness of the attack that he barely had time to register the pain before slipping into oblivion.

* * *

There was no way to walk back across the rooftop without stepping on the piles of dead rats. Kurt winced as his boots squished through puddles of gore. Although he wanted to move as quickly as possible back to the access door, his pace was deliberate. The last thing he wanted to do was slip and fall face down in a steaming heap of rat guts. He tried not to think about the dampness seeping into his boots, and instead kept his eyes fixed on the backs of the two figures leading him and Rosemary to safety.

They passed the broken skylight on the way to the access door on the far side of the roof.

Kurt tried to resist the urge to look down into the dormitory where Diana's body lay, but some sort of morbid curiosity took hold of him and he glanced down. That brief glance was all he needed. Diana's makeshift shroud had been torn open and her body had been devoured. All that remained of the woman he'd loved were bloody bones in the tattered remains of a sleeping bag.

"Come on," Rosemary said, grabbing his hand and pulling him along. "You don't want to see that."

Kurt nodded and continued picking his way through the piles of dead rats. He kept his eyes on the backs of the two figures who'd hauled them off the metal platform. Their rescuers had spoken little since slaughtering the rat army. The few terse sentences they'd actually uttered were tinny and mechanical, coming from small speakers mounted on their shoulders.

The two rescuers led them through the labyrinthine building, pausing here and there to dispatch a stray rat. Finally, they emerged through the front doors, the same entrance that Kurt's team had used upon first entering the building. It was strange to think that it had only been a day ago. Kurt marveled that so much could happen—and that so much could be lost—in the space of a few hours. The sun was now above the horizon, although most of it was hidden behind the layer of clouds that seemed to hover permanently over the city. The grim atmosphere of the empty buildings and potholed streets wasn't much improved by the few rays of light that punched through the gaps in the clouds. If anything, that weak sunlight gave the surroundings a sickly pallor.

Their rescuers led Kurt and Rosemary in the direction of a

third jumpsuit-and-helmet clad figure. This one was standing in the middle of the street, holding a gun of unfamiliar design at its side. Before it lay the bloodied body of the strangest creature Kurt had ever seen. Stranger even than all the freakish animals and mutants he'd seen while roaming the wasteland.

At first glance, it was simply the largest rat he'd ever encountered. But as they drew nearer and Kurt could see the dead creature in greater detail, he knew this was not just some rat grown to outlandish proportions in a city soaked in the lingering effects of the Event. It was some unnatural hybrid, a nightmare made flesh, a physical reminder that the world his generation had inherited was a place gone mad, where no monster that could be dredged from the darkest depths of the imagination could compare with those already in existence.

The dead thing was the result of a mingling of rat and human attributes. It had the head of a rat, although it was rounder and more compact in its proportions. It also had the long, leathery tail. But it was long-limbed, with humanoid arms and legs. The hands were five-fingered, with opposable thumbs, although they were tipped with sharp claws. The dead creature lay on its back, exposing a belly ripped open by bullets.

"What the fuck is that?" Rosemary gagged.

Kurt shook his head. "Some sort of mutant freak."

One of the figures activated the speaker on its shoulder, and a mechanical voice responded, "You're just as ugly to us as we are to you."

It took a moment for the meaning of that response to sink in. And by the time Kurt and Rosemary glanced at one another and took a hesitant backwards step, two of the figures were already removing their helmets. Kurt's insides fluttered like he was in free-fall. At his side, Rosemary clapped a hand to her mouth, stifling a scream.

Their rescuers were nearly identical to the dead humanoid rat lying at their feet. They smiled at Kurt and Rosemary, exposing sets of elongated incisors surrounded by rows of pointed teeth.

"Holy shit!" Rosemary yelped.

Kurt opened his mouth to add his own exclamation, but found himself speechless. His mind reeled as it tried to conjure up an appropriate response. But the two jumpsuit-clad monsters spared him the effort. With movements so smooth and synchronized that they must have been practiced, the rat creatures raised a pair of pistols and fired electrified darts at Kurt and Rosemary.

Kurt doubled over in pain as an untold number of volts raced through his body. Wracked with spasms, he collapsed to the ground. Lightning bolts of pure agony swept him away. And then, mercifully, the pain receded. The last thing he saw as his consciousness faded was a trio of rat faces staring down at him.

Chapter Twenty-Seven
The Victor's Spoils

The rest of the Colony might have had time to obsess over political intrigue, but Dr. Spencer didn't have the luxury of free time to indulge in gossip. The pursuit of scientific discovery was, for him, all-consuming. He was less concerned with the current scandal than he was with the ongoing problems of declining birth rates and increasing genetic abnormalities. Life on the upper levels of the Colony may have come to a standstill while the government purged dissident elements from its ranks, but on the basement level, where the Colony's scientists toiled away in obscurity, things proceeded more or less as they always had.

Dr. Spencer scanned his ID card and waited for the doors to the genetics lab to whoosh open and admit him to what he increasingly thought of as his inner sanctum. Despite the rumors percolating through the Colony since news of the thwarted insurrection broke, the public was still largely uninterested about the work taking place on the basement levels. They were too focused on the latest sensation, a rising star in the world of Colonial politics: a young female Colonist named Sister Jane, who, in conjunction with Brother Lorne and Sister Ursula, had helped dismantle Brother Cornelius' terrorist organization from within. Sister Jane had the public's full attention. She answered the media's endless questions with intelligence and insight that suggested a quick wit rather than a polished persona. Dr. Spencer knew that it was only a matter of time before she entered the political arena, but for the moment, Sister Jane seemed content to be Sister Ursula's understudy.

As far as the genetics program was concerned, the public was still largely uninterested.

They dismissed much of the rumors as too salacious to be believable. And besides, Brother Lorne had seen to it that public opinion was slowly but surely moving to the side of scientific progress at any cost. During their last *tete-a-tete*, the charismatic Councilor had assured Dr. Spencer that, by the time the secret program began to bear fruit (whether he meant figuratively or literally, Dr. Spencer didn't know), the public would be firmly on the side of the science. It was hard for Dr. Spencer to imagine that such a thing would come to pass, but he deferred to Brother Lorne in such matters. This wasn't a bad strategy, since the Council was busy writing a new constitution, which included the establishment of a new executive branch, and would be headed by a prime minister. While the constitution still needed to clear the committee to be ratified, it had broad support across all political parties. Brother Lorne was, unsurprisingly, the odds-on favorite to be the first prime minister.

But that was all just politics, and Dr. Spencer didn't concern himself with such things. He chose to devote his brainpower to more concrete concerns.

Leave politics to the politicians. That was Dr. Spencer's motto.

He paused just long enough in his office to brew a cup of tea, which he left on the corner of his desk to cool while he visited the observation room on the other side of the reinforced window. A pair of technicians were readying the room for another round of experiments with live subjects. This time, there would be no injections. The latest serums were nebulized, and would be administered via the room's ventilation system. One technician was checking the air ducts for possible obstructions, while the other covered the cold tile floor with mattresses, blankets, and cushions. They paused just long enough to greet Dr. Spencer, then got back to preparing the room for the night's experiment.

The door at the back of the room swung open, admitting another pair of technicians. Each wheeled in a gurney, atop which lay a naked, semi-conscious human, one male and one female. Both were well-formed examples of the species, and still in the portion of their life cycles that was suitable for reproduction. Brother Lorne had delivered them a month ago, smuggling them through the Colony in nondescript metal crates. Upon delivery, he'd told Dr. Spencer not to question their provenance, something Dr. Spencer never would have thought to do in the first place. It was enough to know he had two fresh specimens. He didn't concern himself with questions of provenance. After all, morals didn't enter this part of the equation. These were humans, after all; the rules of morality and ethics didn't apply.

Dr. Spencer gave each of the groggy humans a quick once-over, then announced to the technicians, *Make them comfortable, then bring in the others. We have a long night ahead of us, and I'd like to get started as soon as possible.*

A murmur of overlapping thoughts answered him as the technicians made their final preparations. Working in pairs, they removed the humans from the gurneys and placed them beside one another on the nearest mattress.

The male groaned, rolling onto his side to face the female. He raised a hand and touched her cheek. Her eyelids fluttered open in response.

"Rosemary?" the male asked, his vocalization sleep-slurred and thick.

Dr. Spencer understood that it was the female's name. She answered in an equally groggy voice.

"Where are we, Kurt?"

Dr. Spencer wasn't interested in what the humans had to say, only that their reproductive systems were in good working order and that their bodies were responding to the mutagenic treatments they'd been receiving intravenously over the last few weeks.

The door at the back of the room opened again, and the team of technicians brought in a quartet of naked, dazed Colonists. They plodded forward unsteadily, still shaking off the effects of the sedatives. Once inside the room, they collapsed onto a mattress in the corner of the room farthest from the humans. For now, the two species were keeping their distance from one another. But soon, once the nebulized serums filled their lungs, both human and Colonist alike would become closer than they ever dared imagine.

Blessed are the meek, for they shall inherit the earth.

— Matthew 5:5

Afterword

If you survived to the end of this book, you're most likely a fan of the film *Rats: The Night of Terror*. And if that's the case, you might be wondering what the hell this book has to do with the movie you love. Sure, there are some familiar scenes and characters, but for the most part, this novelization departs from the source material in just about every way. There's a reason for that.

When David Gregory of Severin Films first pitched me the idea of turning *Rats* into a film novelization, I eagerly accepted. I'd already written a similar adaptation of *Hell of the Living Dead* (aka *Virus*), and since that film is often packaged as a companion piece to *Rats*, I was eager to dive right back into the strange and wonderful world of the Bruno Mattei/Claudio Fragasso/Rossella Drudi filmography. Yes, I get paid to write these things, but I'm first and foremost a fan.

Each time I've written a novelization for Severin, David has given me a long leash as far as altering the source material to better fit the novel format. After all, films and novels are completely different art forms. What works on the screen might not work on the page, and vice versa. And, more importantly for the low budget features that I've novelized, there are no budget constraints for the plot of a book. That means no limits on cast, running time, special effects, or locations. I've always approached the process of turning a movie into a novel with the mindset of rendering the source material in a way that the producers, directors, and screenwriters might have done if given the budget of a Spielberg blockbuster. As long as I remained true to the spirit of the film, I felt comfortable stretching the narrative to include new characters, subplots, and even endings. But this time, David asked me to take that approach a step further, and that meant going back to the original film treatments.

As originally conceived by screenwriter Rossella Drudi, *Rats* was a true epic of post-apocalyptic horror/sci-fi. It involved some pretty heavy social commentary about the environment and class, as well as some philosophical ruminations on what it means to be human. Her original treatment featured a greater exploration of the society of humanoid rats beyond their reveal in the film's final frame. In her original treatment, the humanoid rats were the result of rapid evolution that endowed them with psychic abilities. They were able to flourish in a world devastated by nuclear war, while humanity was forced to flee into underground bunkers.

Meanwhile, the more primitive rats had taken over the surface of the planet...

Armed with her treatment, as well as the film as it exists, I set to work blending the source material with my own ideas. I liked Rossella's ideas about the humanoid rats having outpaced humans in development, so I really ran with the concept, portraying the Colonists (as I called them) as a more thoughtful and advanced society compared to the semi-barbaric humans. It was fun to imagine a race of humanoid rats with emotional depth. In many ways, they are the most "human" characters in the book. Their view of humanity as cruel, untrustworthy, and ultimately disgusting was an interesting inversion. I also liked adding the element of political intrigue in the humanoid rat society. At the risk of sounding pompous, I thought it would add a layer of complexity. I'd be a liar if I didn't acknowledge the influence of *Planet of the Apes* in this regard. I've always liked that film and its sequels for the way they portrayed the ape society as having its own internal conflicts.

While both the original treatment and the film portray a world devastated by a nuclear war, I decided to keep the cause of the apocalypse vague. Throughout the book, characters refer to it as "the Event" and even offer speculation about its exact cause. Here, I took inspiration from Cormac McCarthy's *The Road*. Not only did the nuclear war trope seem a bit dated, I also felt like that was a world that had been thoroughly explored in both books and movies. Plus, it allowed me to dispense with some of the nuts-and-bolts science of life after the bomb. If you're looking for that, go watch *Threads*. It paints a picture bleaker than any I could aspire to. But there are no humanoid psychic rats in that one, so we'll call it a draw.

The second half of the book hews closer to the finished film. It's hard to beat a series of violent rat attacks, so I didn't try to fix what wasn't broken. I did juggle some of the characters around, but for the most part, the night of terror referenced in the title remains intact. Richard Matheson once said that, in adapting Edgar Allan Poe's short stories into screenplays, he used the story as the film's opening act and proceeded from there. I attempted a reversal of that approach with this novelization. Hopefully, I did as much justice to Rossella and Claudio's work as Matheson did for Poe's.

The process was a tricky balancing act. My aim was to write a book that would make Claudio and Rossella proud, but I also wanted to deliver something memorable for the fans of the film and newcomers alike. If I held up that end of the deal, then I can happily call this book a success.

I want to take the opportunity to thank David for making this happen. Getting to work with Rossella and Claudio was a dream come true. I have only the highest respect and deepest admiration for them and their work. Writing this book with their input is a memory I'll cherish for years to come.

Thanks also to my wife, Molly, for enduring my descriptions of human/humanoid rat sexual relations. I'm not sure there's a better test for the strength of a marriage.

My brilliant daughter Jane repeatedly suggested the inclusion of footnotes for this novel. She said they could take the world building to another level. She was right[11]*.

The staff of the Natural State Beer Company taproom, where I wrote a large percentage of these pages, also deserves a shout-out for providing such a writer-friendly environment, along with great beer. Many pints of their Vienna Lager aided my creative process immeasurably. Prost!

---

* [11] See what I mean? Footnotes are fun!

And lastly, I'd like to thank everyone who has read any of the novelizations I've written for Severin. Your support keeps me working, and I genuinely appreciate every single one of you.

Hopefully, you, the reader, have enjoyed this fresh take on a beloved film. It was written from a place of real affection for the source material, and for the people who originally conceived it.

Cheers!

Brad Carter
Rogers, AR
November 2023-April 2024

The following pages feature images from the film *Rats: Night of Terror*. Used by permission.

RATS
NIGHT OF TERROR
인간이 가장 하찮게 여겼던 쥐들이 드디어
만물의 영장인 인간들에게 선전포고를 했다!
무차별하고 잔혹한 거대한 쥐떼 군단의 공격!
속수무책으로 무너져가는 인류 문명의 비참한 말로!
보는이의 등 뒤로, 발밑으로 스멀스멀 기어오르는
기분 나쁜 공포의 악몽이 시작됐다!
"쥐!"
미성년자관람불가

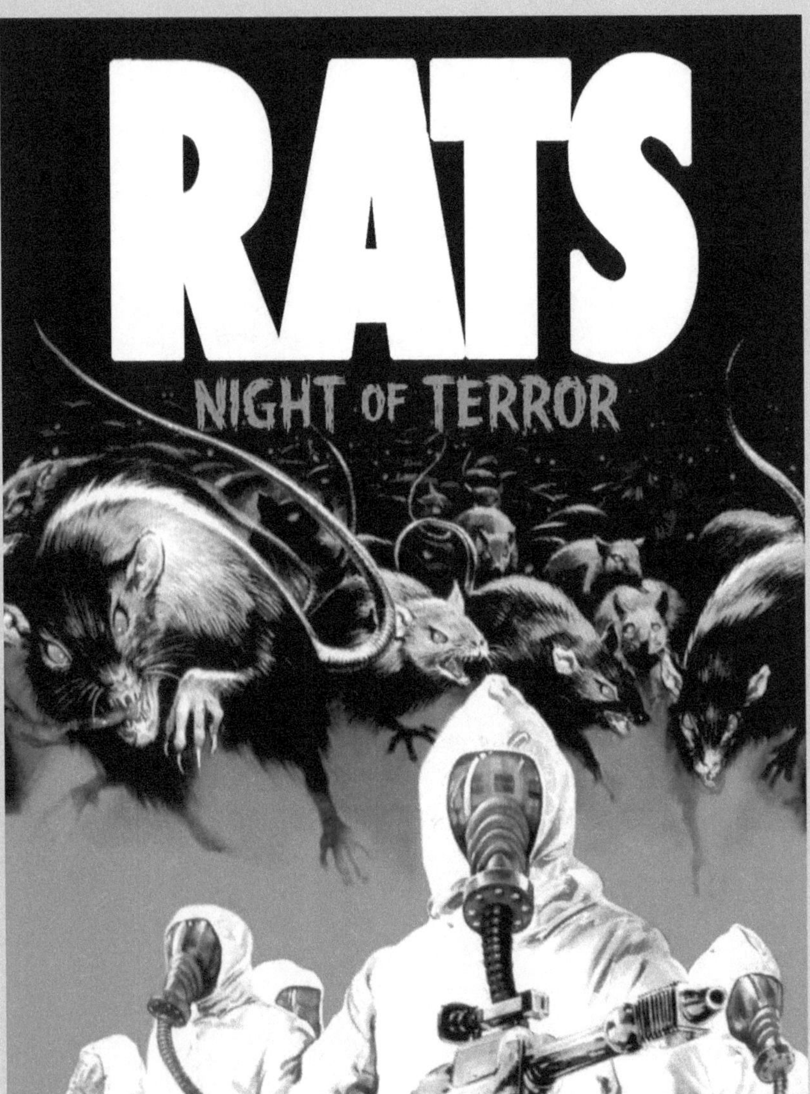

RATS
NIGHT OF TERROR

MUTANTS OF A NUCLEAR DISASTER
1115
RATS
NIGHT OF TERROR
R
EXPLOSIVE
VHS

The Riffs III
DIE RATTEN VON MANHATTAN
RICHARD RAYMOND · JANNA RYANN · ALEX McBRIDE · RICHARD CROSS
TONY LOMBARDO · CHRIS FREMONT · MOUNE DUVIVIER
Musik: LUIGI CECCARELLI · Kamera: FRANCO DELLI COLLI
Regie: VINCENT DAWN · Ein Farbfilm der BEATRICE FILM, Rom
und IMP. EX. CI., Nizza im Alemannia -Filmverleih

THE Riffs III
DIE RATTEN VON MANHATTAN
mit RICHARD RAYMOND
JANNA RYANN · ALEX McBRIDE · RICHARD CROSS
TONY LOMBARDO · CHRIS FREMONT · MOUNE DUVIVIER
Musik: LUIGI CECCARELLI · Kamera: FRANCO DELLI COLLI
Regie: VINCENT DAWN
Ein Farbfilm im Alemannia FILMVERLEIH

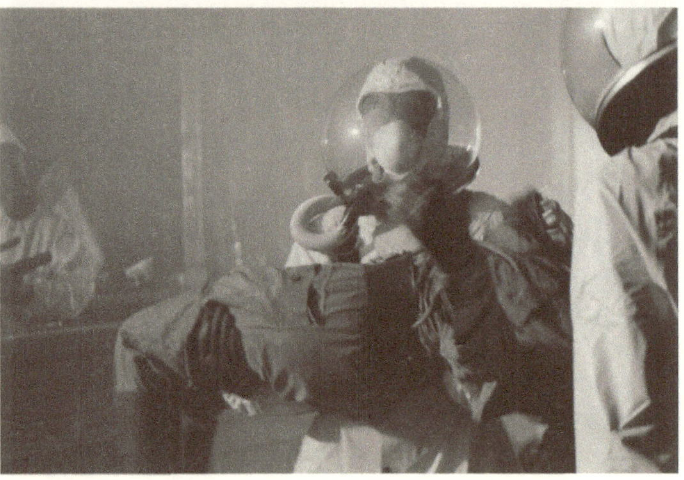

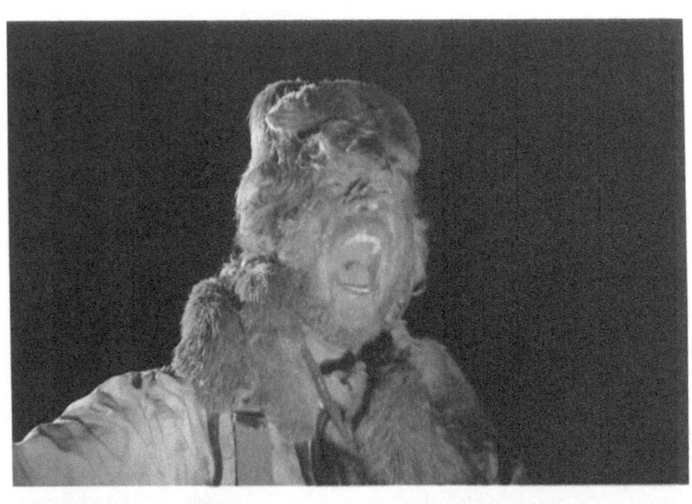

The Riffs III
DIE RATTEN VON MANHATTAN

The Riffs III
DIE RATTEN VON MANHATTAN

The Riffs III
DIE RATTEN VON MANHATTAN
-Filmverleih

The Riffs III
DIE RATTEN VON MANHATTAN
-Filmverleih

THE Riffs III
DIE RATTEN VON MANHATTAN

MOXIE
MOXIE
THE Riffs III
DIE RATTEN VON MANHATTAN

THE Riffs III
DIE RATTEN VON MANHATTAN

THE Riffs III
DIE RATTEN VON MANHATTAN

The Riffs III
DIE RATTEN VON MANHATTAN
Ascot-Filmverleih

The Riffs III
DIE RATTEN VON MANHATTAN
Ascot-Filmverleih

THE Riffs III
DIE RATTEN VON MANHATTAN
Filmverleih

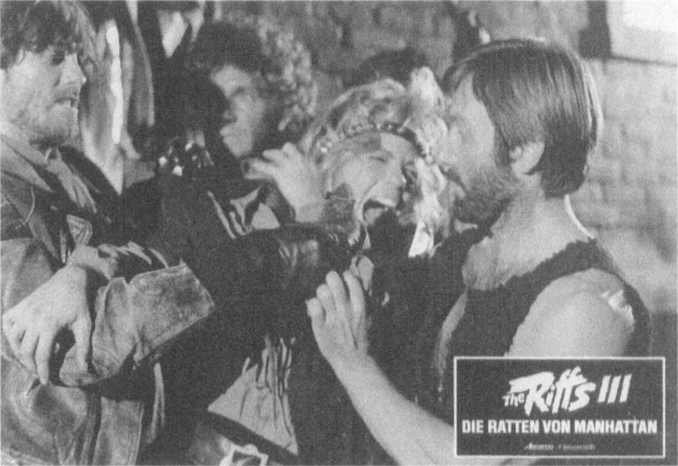

THE Riffs III
DIE RATTEN VON MANHATTAN
Filmverleih

THE Riffs III
DIE RATTEN VON MANHATTAN
Aemannia-Filmverleih

The Riffs III
DIE RATTEN VON MANHATTAN
Alemannia-Filmverleih

About the Author

Brad Carter lives in Arkansas with his wife and daughters. They encourage him to write, because it keeps him out of trouble.

Also from Brad Carter
(dis)Comfort Food
Saturday Night of the Living Dead
Only Things
Uncle Leroy's Coffin
Human Resources
Cruel Jaws
Virus: Hell of the Living Dead